Not Until Then

A Hope Springs Novel

Valerie M. Bodden

Not Until Then © 2022 by Valerie M. Bodden.

Scriptures taken from the Holy Bible, New International Version®, NIV®. Copyright © 1973, 1978, 1984, 2011 by Biblica, Inc.™ Used by permission of Zondervan. All rights reserved worldwide. www.zondervan.com The "NIV" and "New International Version" are trademarks registered in the United States Patent and Trademark Office by Biblica, Inc.™

All rights reserved. No portion of this book may be reproduced in any form without permission from the publisher, except as permitted by U.S. copyright law.

This is a work of fiction. Names, characters, places, and incidents either are products of the author's imagination or used in a fictitious manner. Any resemblance to any person, living or dead, is coincidental.

Valerie M. Bodden

Visit me at www.valeriembodden.com

Hope Springs Series

Not Until Forever
Not Until This Moment
Not Until You
Not Until Us
Not Until Christmas Morning
Not Until This Day
Not Until Someday
Not Until Now
Not Until Then
Not Until The End

River Falls Series

Pieces of Forever
Songs of Home
Memories of the Heart
Whispers of Truth
Promises of Mercy

River Falls Christmas Romances

Christmas of Joy

A Hope Springs Gift for You

Members of my Reader's Club get a FREE book, available exclusively to my subscribers. When you sign up, you'll also be the first to know about new releases, book deals, and giveaways. Visit www.valeriembodden.com/gift to join!

Need a refresher of who's who in the Hope Springs series?

If you love the whole gang in Hope Springs but need a refresher of who's who and how everyone is connected, check out the handy character map at https://www.valeriembodden.com/hscharacters

For now we see only a reflection as in a mirror; then we shall see face to face. Now I know in part; then I shall know fully, even as I am fully known.

            1 Corinthians 13:12

Chapter 1

This wasn't happening.

Bethany scanned the checkout counter around her, as if her purse would magically appear on it.

All she wanted was one day of the year where she had it together. It didn't feel like too much to ask that it be today.

But apparently she was bound to make a mess even of her daughter's birthday.

"That will be $21.99." The cashier—an older woman with kind eyes—repeated.

"I . . . Uh . . ." She felt at her shoulder again—the spot where her purse should have been. In the rush to get everything ready for Ruby's party, she must have forgotten it.

She rubbed at her temple. She couldn't show up to her own daughter's tenth birthday party without a gift. Not when everyone else would have one—probably one they'd purchased weeks ago. It was bad enough she was buying it at the grocery store, but she didn't have much choice; it was on the way to Ruby's school and it was almost time to pick her up.

She blinked at the necklace—a figure of a horse and a girl face-to-face within a heart. She had two choices: grab it off the counter and run out the door—or put it back on the shelf. There was a time in her life when the first would have seemed viable. But not anymore. Not even for Ruby.

"I'm sorry. I forgot my wallet. I guess I'll have to put it back." The words weighed her whole body down.

"Do you want me to set it aside for you?" The cashier slid the necklace into her hand and set it next to the register, sympathy in her voice.

"That would be nice, thank you." Bethany knew the woman's name, she was sure of it, but she didn't have the energy to search her mind for it right now. "I probably won't be able to get it until tomorrow. I have to get to my daughter's birthday party. Maybe I can give her an 'I owe you.'" She tried for a weak smile. At least she didn't have to worry about crying. The aneurysm had stolen that ability from her right along with a good chunk of her short-term memory.

"Here." A man's voice spoke from behind her, and someone reached past her to hand the cashier a credit card. "I'll get it."

"I . . . Um . . ."

Before Bethany could stop her, the cashier had already taken the card and run it through the register.

"That's very kind of you," the older woman said, beaming into the space behind Bethany. "Oh, doesn't this feel like the beginning of a romance movie? You make sure to get his name, dear." The woman winked at Bethany.

Bethany opened her mouth as she turned to look at the man. His left arm was in a sling, and he wore a gray flannel shirt, but the thing that struck Bethany the most was his face—all hard lines and angles, not a trace of a smile.

Say something, Bethany's brain screamed. But the words wouldn't arrange themselves in a straight line in her head.

"Here you are, dear." The cashier passed Bethany a small bag and handed the card back to the man.

Bethany was halfway to the door before she finally managed to turn and blurt, "Thank you," the words sticking together like paste as they came off her lips.

She didn't wait to see whether the man would acknowledge her gratitude.

Outside, the wind grabbed at her hair, and she pulled the zipper on her sweatshirt up higher against the early April chill as she scanned the parking lot. Usually she took a picture of where she'd parked, but she'd been in too much of a hurry today.

There. She let herself breathe out as she spotted the boxy maroon four-door only two rows away. Finally, something was going her way. Maybe that meant Ruby's birthday wouldn't be a disaster after all. She should have just enough time to stop home and wrap the gift before she had to pick her daughter up from school and bring her over to the stables for the party.

As she strode toward the car, she reached into her pocket for her keys.

When her fingers didn't brush against metal in her jeans pocket, she checked her sweatshirt.

Then she checked all the pockets again.

Empty.

Which meant she'd left the keys in the car.

"Please tell me I forgot to lock it," she muttered to herself as she reached the vehicle. With a quick prayer, she tried the handle.

It lifted—but the door didn't budge.

She peered through the window, letting her head rest against the cold glass as she spotted the keys dangling from the ignition.

"Really? Today of all days?" She hadn't slept well last night; she was sure that was the explanation for her increased forgetfulness today. But knowing why it was happening didn't change the fact that she was going to ruin her daughter's birthday. Poor Ruby hadn't done anything to deserve a mother who could barely remember to make a meal, let alone plan a perfect birthday party.

Be grateful, she reminded herself. She was still here to celebrate Ruby's birthday. Two years ago, that hadn't been at all certain. The aneurysm may have made things more difficult, but it hadn't taken her life.

She closed her eyes and offered a quick prayer of thanks—as well as a plea for help out of yet another situation. Then she let out a long breath and opened her eyes. This wasn't the first time she'd locked her keys in her car. Which was why she'd given a spare set to her brother Cam and his wife Kayla. She hated the idea of calling them to come to her rescue—again. But for Ruby's sake, she'd do it.

She reached for her back pocket, just as she spotted her phone—in the car's cupholder.

She groaned and pounded her fist against the car window.

Something like this would never happen to any of the perfect moms of Ruby's classmates—whose names she would probably never manage to remember.

She shook her head. Feeling sorry for herself wasn't going to help.

Okay, what else could she do? She could go in the store and ask to use someone else's phone—except it wasn't like she could remember any phone numbers to call. She had to look up her own any time she needed it, for goodness' sake.

She had no choice but to call a locksmith. But first she'd better call the school to let them know she was going to be late getting Ruby—again.

She tried the car door handle one more time, jiggling it up and down. "Aargh." She smacked the window again.

"Everything okay?" A man with his left arm in a sling, his right draped in shopping bags, frowned at her from the middle of the aisle.

"Yeah. Fine."

He stared her down. "You're sure? Because it kind of looks like you locked your keys in your car."

"I did." She sighed so hard it hurt. "It's my daughter's birthday."

The man gave her a strange look.

Right. There was no reason for him to care.

"Anyway—" She gestured toward the store. "I have to go call a . . ." Ugh. The word had escaped as she'd been talking. "Someone to unlock it."

"That could take hours." The guy moved closer. "I can get it open for you." Tension radiated from the set of the guy's jaw, and Bethany was torn between an instinct to run away and the need to get into her car.

"You're not going to break the window, are you?" Although if that was the quickest way to get her to Ruby, maybe it would be worth it.

The man made a sound she thought might have been a laugh, though there was no trace of humor in it and his mouth remained flat. "Hang tight a second. I'll be right back." He unloaded his bags on the trunk of her car, then jogged back toward the store, his slinged arm jouncing awkwardly at his side.

Bethany squinted after him until he reached the door, the beginning of a headache twinging behind her eyes. She took a few deep, controlled breaths in an attempt to stave it off. Her head could pound as much as it wanted *after* Ruby's party. But she refused to spoil her daughter's birthday any more than she already had.

Minutes passed. Bethany squinted toward the store. Maybe she should call someone after all.

She was just eyeing the guy's bags, trying to figure out what to do with them so she could go inside and ask to use a phone, when he emerged from the store. He jogged across the parking lot, his stride powerful despite the long metal rod in his good hand.

"Sorry. Took some convincing to get the manager to let me borrow these." He held up the rod and a screwdriver.

"What are you going to do?" A vague uneasiness crept over her. She'd never seen this man before, as far as she remembered—which admittedly wasn't saying much. But what if he was a con artist or something?

"Trust me. I've done this a thousand times."

"You've broken into cars a thousand times?" She pressed a hand to her stomach. Now what kind of mess had she gotten herself into? They seemed to follow her around these days. Her doctor said it was because the aneurysm had affected the impulse control center in her brain. "Maybe I should—"

"It's okay. I'm a cop." The way he said it seemed sincere, but Bethany eyed him. She didn't see a badge or a gun.

"Off duty," he said as if detecting her suspicion. He wedged the screwdriver between the roof and the top of the car door. "From Milwaukee."

"Oh." But that would be easy enough to lie about, wouldn't it? It wasn't like there was a way for her to check. She peered around the parking lot. It wasn't exactly crowded, but there were a few people getting into and out of cars. She supposed if he tried anything, she could yell for help.

Besides, by now she had to be at least fifteen minutes late getting Ruby. She didn't have any choice but to trust this guy.

He grunted as he pulled down on the screwdriver, opening a small gap at the top of the door. Bethany winced. If he damaged her car . . .

"Pass me the rod." He pointed his chin toward the metal rod he'd leaned against the car. Bethany picked it up and held it out to him.

He glanced at it, then at the arm that hung in a sling. "That's not going to work. Here." He took half a step back, still pushing down on the screwdriver with his other arm. "Come over here and slide the rod through this opening."

"Me?" How was she supposed to know how to do this?

The man made an impatient sound, and she stepped closer, catching a whiff of something slightly warm and woodsy and spicy that made her think of curling up in front of the fire on a winter day. Angling her body in front of his, she slid the metal rod in through the opening he'd created.

"Good. Now, see the unlock button on the side of the door?"

Bethany shifted to get a better view, accidentally bumping against his chest. An odd sensation went through her at the contact, and she scooted out of the way. "I see it."

"Good. You want to press that with the end of the rod."

"I don't think I—"

"You can do it." The quiet assurance in his words tugged at her, even though he'd obviously only said it so she'd try. He didn't even know her.

She pressed her lips together and concentrated on guiding the end of the rod toward the button.

She missed twice, but on the third attempt, she landed right in the middle of it. She'd never heard a sound as beautiful as the click of the doors unlocking.

"Yes!" She let go of the metal rod and grabbed the door handle, pulling it open—barely acknowledging the clang of the rod against the ground as it tumbled out.

"Thank you so much!" She threw her arms around the man, who grunted and didn't return the gesture. It took her a moment to realize it was probably because the hug was completely inappropriate. Stupid impulse control.

"Sorry." She let go and stepped back, then bent to pick up the rod.

The man nodded tightly as he took it. "You're welcome." He gathered up his bags, then started toward the store.

"Do you want me to take that stuff back inside?" It was the least she could do, and he surely had places to go too.

"That's okay. You have your daughter's party."

Bethany gasped. How did he know about that? Had she told him? Probably.

She suddenly realized she'd never called the school to say she'd be late. She jumped into the car and started the engine. At the last second, she remembered to open her window and call out one more thank you.

The guy lifted a hand in acknowledgment and kept walking toward the store.

As she pulled out of the parking lot, Bethany gave him one last look in her rearview mirror.

"That's not the way I expected you to answer that prayer, Lord. But thank you."

Chapter 2

James plopped his purchases onto the table of his sister's farmhouse. That had been the most bizarre trip to the store of his life. The forgetful woman with the blonde hair and dark eyes had refused to leave his thoughts all the way home.

Only because it had felt good to be able to help someone again.

You always have to be the hero, don't you? His ex-wife Melissa's voice cut straight through the good feeling. At least this time helping hadn't cost him anything—if only because he didn't have anything left to lose.

"I see you bought out the entire supply of junk food in Hope Springs." His sister Emma eyed the bags as she bustled into the room.

"If you didn't insist on stocking your refrigerator with all rabbit food, I wouldn't have to." He pulled a bag of potato chips out and carried it to the pantry, wedging it into place on a shelf between a jar of homemade spaghetti sauce and a package that said chia seeds, whatever those were.

"You know it's not fair that you can eat like that and stay in shape, right?"

"Could have something to do with the ten miles I run a day." He'd started running after Sadie . . . and never stopped.

"Just you wait. By the time you leave, you're going to appreciate that health food can be just as delicious as junk food."

He snorted. By the time he left. If it was up to him, he wouldn't be here at all. Not that he didn't want to spend time with his sister—it must have been at least three years since he'd visited—but he'd only been here two days, and already he was going crazy. His job had been the only thing keeping him sane for the past five years. But when his captain had told him it was either take some of the years' worth of vacation he had accumulated or ride the desk for the next six weeks while his shoulder recovered, it hadn't really been a choice at all.

"How's the shoulder?" Emma plucked a package of beef jerky out of his bag and carried it across the room.

He rescued it just as she opened the lid of the trash can. "It's fine. I should be working. Give me something to do around here, at least."

"You know you're supposed to be recovering from a gunshot wound, right?"

"It was a graze. I'm fine."

Emma hit him with a hard stare worthy of their mother. He only supposed he should be grateful Mom didn't know anything about what had happened. Unless—

"You didn't tell Mom, did you?" There was no need to worry her, after everything she'd already been through.

Emma watched him the same way he watched a suspect during an interrogation. They'd both gotten that ability from Dad.

Finally, she relented and looked away. "No. But James, things can't go on like this."

"Like what?" He crossed his arms. He was just doing his job. Same as Dad had taught him.

"Captain said you didn't wait for backup."

"He called you?" Captain Burke may have been as close as a father to him, but that didn't give him the right to go interfering in James's life.

"He was Dad's best friend, James. He's worried about you."

"Whatever. He shouldn't have called you."

"It was either me or Mom," Emma said. "And anyway, he just wants to make sure you get the help you need. So do I."

"I knew I should have gone to Mexico," he muttered. Not that there was anything he wanted to do in Mexico. Or anywhere else. All he wanted to do was work. And the captain had made even that impossible.

Emma raised her hands. "Sorry. I'll back off. But it's been five years, James. You can't keep punishing yourself forever. Sadie wouldn't want—"

"Don't." They were not going there.

Emma pulled a package of chocolate candies out of his bags and slid some cans over in the cupboard to fit it. "I'm just saying, I'm here to talk, if you want. Or we have a great pastor at our church. I'm sure he—"

"Is that what you call backing off?" He wasn't going to talk about it. Ever.

Emma gave him a look but kept her lips shut.

"Just give me something to do before I go crazy."

"With one good arm?" But then Emma's face lit up. "I know. We're hosting a birthday party in—" She glanced at the clock on the oven. "About fifteen minutes. I could use some help with the pony rides."

James's stomach hardened. A birthday party meant kids. And kids meant remembering. "I'll pass, thanks."

"James, you can't avoid—"

"I'll muck out the horses tomorrow. And anything else you need done. Leave me a list. I'm going to go read." He grabbed the bag of chips out of the cupboard, then sprinted up the stairs to the guest room Emma had prepared for him. He was going to have to call and talk the captain into shortening his leave. Because there was no way he was going to survive here for six weeks.

James tossed his book onto the bed and stood. He'd been reading for an hour, and he wasn't sure he'd retained a word of the story.

His conversation with Emma had stirred up too many of the memories he worked so hard to forget every day. He'd tried thinking about other things: work, the new condo in Florida he'd helped Mom move into last year, even the woman from the store.

That thought was the only one that had provided a measure of distraction. He couldn't deny that she'd been beautiful, if a bit scatterbrained.

And affectionate.

That hug had been . . . warm and spontaneous and sweet.

And completely inappropriate.

But still, it had threatened to poke a pinhole into the Kevlar that he kept wrapped securely around his heart. Fortunately, she'd come to her senses and let go before that could happen.

He glanced out the window, wondering again if perhaps the party Emma was hosting was for the woman's daughter. After all, the woman had said she was on the way to her daughter's birthday party. And she'd purchased a horse necklace.

Or, well, he supposed he had purchased it.

He didn't know what had come over him. Only that the woman had looked so broken at the thought of disappointing her daughter. And the necklace she'd held—Sadie would have gone wild for it. Aunt Emma's house had always been her favorite place, and she'd thrown her arms around him and planted a big, wet kiss on his cheek when he'd said the next time they came here she could have her first horse ride.

James ripped his eyes away from the practice ring, where Emma was helping a young girl onto a pony.

His throat burned.

What he needed was some water.

He trundled downstairs to the kitchen, opening the fridge and pushing Emma's stash of vegetables aside to reach for a bottle of water. A movement caught his eye as he closed the fridge, and he was instantly on alert, spinning to face the intruder.

"Oh!" The woman from the store jumped backwards, bobbling the cake in her hands.

James lunged toward her just in time to steady the wobbling platter. He ignored the sear of pain that shot through his shoulder. "Sorry. I didn't mean to scare you."

The woman nodded. Well, that answered the question of whether this was her daughter's birthday party.

Slowly, he took his hands off hers, making sure she wasn't going to drop the cake before withdrawing all the way.

"Did your daughter like the necklace?"

"I . . . Yes." The woman looked startled. "Sorry. Who are you?"

Nice one, James. "I'm James. Emma's brother."

"I didn't know Emma had a brother."

"Oh." There wasn't much else to say to that. He didn't suppose Emma went around talking about her brother to random clients. "Anyway." He held up the bottle of water. "I was just getting this."

"Okay." The woman stared at him for a moment, then glided out of the house with the cake in front of her.

James watched her blonde hair ripple behind her, then let out a breath. There was something about her that raised a whole lot of questions in his head. Like why had she seemed surprised when he'd asked about the necklace? And why hadn't she acknowledged that he'd come to her rescue—twice—at the store? Not that he wanted to be thanked or anything. But she'd hugged him there and now acted like she'd never seen him before.

He ignored the tiny spikes of warmth that went through him at the memory of the hug. It didn't matter how much she intrigued him; she had a kid. And even if he had been willing to risk his heart on a woman again, he'd never risk it on another child.

Chapter 3

"Hurry up, Rubes." Bethany slathered peanut butter onto a piece of bread, then swiped at the alarm on her phone. She hated its incessant beeping. But it was the best way she'd found to make sure she didn't forget any part of her daily schedule.

Not that it meant she ever managed to get Ruby to school on time.

"I can't find any socks," Ruby shouted from her room.

"Check the dryer," Bethany called.

Ruby skidded into the room, their cat Mrs. Whiskers following close behind.

"Hurry," Bethany urged again, grabbing another piece of bread for the jelly.

But Ruby stopped in front of the counter and made a face at the sandwich Bethany was preparing.

"What?" Bethany glanced down to make sure she hadn't messed it up. But she was pretty confident she could handle making a PBJ.

"Do you think I could have a turkey sandwich tomorrow?" Ruby asked.

"Of course. Just—"

"Remind you," Ruby chimed in, continuing toward the basement laundry room.

"Right." Except something about the way Ruby said it bothered Bethany. "Wait. Ruby. Did you already ask me for a turkey sandwich before?"

"It's no big deal, Mom," Ruby called up the steps. "PBJ is great."

Bethany let out a long sigh and tucked the PBJ in the fridge. She could always have it for her own lunch. She shoved leftovers out of the way to find the turkey and cheese and rushed to make a new sandwich. If she hurried, Ruby would only be a few minutes late. And at least she'd have the lunch she wanted.

Ruby's feet pounded up the basement stairs. "There's nothing in the dryer."

Bethany closed her eyes. "I thought I did laundry yesterday."

She flipped her notebook open—the one she used to keep track of tasks she didn't do on a daily basis. "Laundry" was written on yesterday's page. But it wasn't checked off. She tried to remember what had stopped her from doing it, but like most recent events, all she could picture was a blank canvas.

"Can you wear a pair of mine? Or dig some out of your hamper?" She cringed. What kind of mom told her kid to wear dirty socks? Or forgot what she wanted for lunch? Or couldn't get her to school on time even once a week?

"Sure." Ruby offered her typical good-natured smile, and Bethany was reminded of her own mother's easygoing nature. Her gut clenched. It was her fault that Ruby would never know her grandparents.

She tried to stamp out the thought. Why was it that painful memories from her past were always too eager to push their way forward, when the moments in the present she wanted to hold onto refused to solidify into memories?

"Okay. I'm ready." Ruby reappeared from the hallway, wearing a pair of striped knee socks.

"You used to wear those all the time."

Ruby's eyes widened. "You remember that? Are you getting your memory back?"

"I—" Bethany's heart quickened. Could it be? She hadn't given her comment much thought—it had just come out. But the image in her mind was of a much younger Ruby wearing those socks. "I don't think so. Dr. Kellar would say it was a long-term memory. But I'm glad I have it." She offered Ruby what she hoped came across as a bright smile.

But Ruby's shoulders fell. "Oh."

Bethany held her smile firmly in place. "But I know how we can make a new memory." She pulled her phone out of her pocket. "Say memories."

"Can we just go, Mom? I'm going to be late." Ruby slung her backpack over her shoulder.

"First say memories," Bethany insisted. She wasn't going to let every moment of the rest of her life pass her by just because she couldn't remember them.

"Memories," Ruby obliged.

Bethany couldn't tell if her daughter's grimace was supposed to be an attempt at a smile. But she kept the picture and tucked her phone in her pocket. "All right. Let's get you to school." She swept her notebook off the counter and flipped the page. Today she had—

She gasped.

The PTO meeting. She'd completely forgotten about it. And it started in—she glanced at the clock again—ten minutes ago.

She opened the door, waving Ruby through. But before Ruby got a toe out the door, Mrs. Whiskers charged past her, diving into the flower bed.

"Mrs. Whiskers!" They didn't have time for this.

"I'll get her, Mom." Ruby stepped outside, but Bethany grabbed her arm to stop her.

"It's muddy. I'll do it. You get in the car."

Ruby shrugged but obeyed, and Bethany tiptoed into the mucky flower bed, careful to avoid the puddles between the bushes.

"Come here, kitty." But as she reached for Mrs. Whiskers, the cat sprang toward the rose bush. Bethany lunged for her, sending a spray of mud into her shoe and up her leg. A thorn from the rose bush caught at her hand, but she pulled free and snagged the cat.

Holding Mrs. Whiskers unceremoniously out in front of her to avoid getting dirtier, she marched to the house and tossed the cat in the door. She glanced down at her jeans. Spatters of mud traveled up one leg, and her sock was drenched. But Ruby was already so late. Bethany was just going to have to go through her day like this.

Shoving her hair out of her face, she dropped into the driver's seat.

"Is Mrs. Whiskers okay?" Ruby asked from the back seat.

"She's fine." Bethany gritted her teeth and forced herself to take a long, slow breath before backing out of the driveway.

Every time she got in the car, she worried all over again that she was going to have another aneurysm while driving. She didn't remember last time, but poor Ruby did. Bethany could only thank the Lord that he'd kept Ruby safe when their car had gone off the road. And pray that it didn't happen again.

Thankfully, Ruby's school wasn't far. And the route was one of the things her messed up memory allowed her to retain. But by the time she'd parked the car and taken Ruby to the office to get yet another tardy pass—the school secretary didn't even ask for an explanation anymore—she was a good 30 minutes late for the PTO meeting.

She bit her lip, debating whether to skip it. It wasn't like she contributed anything anyway. But she used to be super involved in it—before the aneurysm. And she was determined to remain just as involved in Ruby's life and school. Straightening her shoulders, she requested a visitor badge, then marched down the hallway to the library, where the meetings were held.

She tried to slip into the back unnoticed, but there weren't many people here today, and it felt like every head in the room swiveled in her direction. Bethany ducked her chin and slid into a seat, tucking her mud-splattered pant leg under the chair.

"Glad you could join us," the woman at the front of the room called. Though her voice was kind enough, Bethany still heard the judgment behind it. She tried to come up with the woman's name. She should know it, since their daughters were in the same dressage class, but it refused to come to her.

To the room at large, the woman said, "So Sabrina and Amy are going to take care of the bake sale, and Justine said she'd work on teacher appreciation gifts. Marybeth, you're in charge of the concession stand for baseball season. And I'll speak to local businesses about donating items for the silent auction."

Bethany's head spun just listening to all the responsibilities these women were taking on. She'd had a hard enough time just getting to the meeting—late.

"Tiffany?" One of the women asked, and Bethany nearly shouted out loud. Yes! Tiffany was the woman's name. Fortunately, her impulse control seemed to be functioning properly at the moment, and she remained silent.

"Yes?" Tiffany smiled at the other woman.

"Are we going to talk about the field day? I understand Tess isn't going to be able to run it this year."

"That was next on my agenda," Tiffany said. "And you're right. Tess has decided to step back this year to focus more on some of her other volunteer work. So if anyone else wants to step up and organize the field day . . ."

She scanned the room, skimming right over Bethany.

Something jerked Bethany's arm into the air. "I'll do it."

Tiffany's gaze swung back to her, and she made a small surprised sound. Her mouth was round, eyes wide. "Are you sure? I mean, you have time?"

Bethany resisted snorting. Some days it felt like all she had was time. Sure, she helped with Cam's landscaping business, but that was more busywork than anything. More to give her something to do than to help him. Other than that, the biggest thing on her schedule was helping to muck out the stalls at Emma's stables once a week to help pay for Ruby's dressage lessons. Not that her brother hadn't offered to pay for them, but she already felt bad enough taking a salary from him for the little help she provided.

"I have plenty of time," she assured Tiffany.

"Um. Okay." Tiffany sounded uncertain as her eyes traveled to the other women in the room. "Do you want someone else to help? It's a big job."

"No thanks. I've got it." If all these women could handle their responsibilities on their own, so could she.

"Okay. Great." Tiffany's smile looked like it had been smeared onto her face. "Then I guess if we don't have further business, we can adjourn."

Bethany pulled out her phone and started to tap a reminder note. A bubble of doubt worked its way through her. How on earth was she going to do this?

Before she'd finished typing, Tiffany swooped down on her. "This might be helpful." She held out a thick manila folder. "It's Tess's notes—about where to get the food and equipment, what to set up where, how to collect tickets, all that stuff."

"Thanks." Bethany swallowed and took the folder, the bubble of doubt growing to a full-out balloon. She took a breath. She just had to be organized, break it down into little tasks, that was all.

"If you have any questions or need anything—"

"I've got it. Thanks." Bethany didn't mean to sound curt, but Tiffany wasn't asking any of the others if they needed help.

"All right." Tiffany's smile skirted the edges of genuine. "Thanks again for inviting Kimberly to Ruby's birthday party."

"Of course." Bethany tried to recall what Kimberly had given Ruby as a gift, so she could thank Tiffany, but she drew a blank.

"I'm having a birthday party for Kimberly in a couple weeks. I hope Ruby can make it."

"I'm sure she'd love that." Bethany relaxed a little. She didn't know Tiffany well, but she seemed nice enough. It wasn't her fault that her perfect hair and perfect makeup and perfect parenting made Bethany feel like a failure.

"Great. I'm taking the girls to the indoor water park in Green Bay. I thought we'd stay two nights so they can really enjoy it."

Bethany blinked at Tiffany. Green Bay? Two nights? Ruby had never even been away from home for one night, aside from at Cam and Kayla's. "I'll have to—"

"Sorry. I have to catch Amy before she leaves. I'll text you the details." Tiffany was already scurrying away as she finished the sentence.

Bethany sighed, glancing at the thick folder in her hands.

Her impulse control had chosen a great time to disappear.

What did she know about organizing a field day? She'd be lucky if she remembered to buy a ticket for herself, let alone got everything set up for everyone else.

She chewed her lip, flipping through the folder. Maybe she should give it back to Tiffany, tell her she didn't have time after all.

She closed the folder and took a step toward Tiffany. But just then the alarm on her phone blared from her pocket. She snatched at it, heart thudding as the eyes of everyone in the room flew to her. She'd meant to silence her phone before the meeting, but in the rush she must have forgotten. Big surprise.

It took two attempts to silence the annoying beeps. Bethany peeked at the screen, then at Tiffany, who was watching her with a sympathetic smile.

She looked back at the screen.

Next up on her schedule was mucking out stalls at the stables.

So she could either go shovel manure or go tell Tiffany she couldn't do the field day.

With one more glance at the folder in her hand, she marched toward the door.

She'd take care of the manure now.

And figure out a way to handle the field day later.

Chapter 4

"James Henry Wood, put that pitchfork down right now. And get your arm back in the sling."

James rolled his eyes at his sister's command and stuffed the pitchfork into the next section of hay, bouncing it a few times to sift out the soiled portions. He ignored the sharp pull through his shoulder as he lifted the dirty bedding into the wheelbarrow that he'd positioned in the aisle outside the stall.

"I told you, I need to work."

"And I told you, my friend Bethany is coming to muck the stalls today."

James snorted. "If that's how you treat your friends, I'd hate to be your enemy."

Now Emma was the one rolling her eyes. "She does it to pay for her daughter's dressage lessons."

"Just credit my work to her then." What did it matter to him who got credit for the work?

"I would, but she won't accept that. She wants to earn it herself."

James could respect that. But what else was he going to do with his day?

Emma had encouraged him more than once to take the horses out. But every time he considered saddling one up, all he could think of was how badly Sadie had wanted to ride.

"When is she coming?" he asked Emma.

"Should be here any minute now."

"I'll save some stalls for her."

Emma sighed. "Will you at least put the sling back on?"

"Fine." He maneuvered the uncomfortable contraption into place. "Happy?"

"I'd be happier if you were happy. But this will have to do for now. I have to run up to the Ploughman's farm to pick up some hay. Just don't scare Bethany, okay?"

James made an impatient sound. He had no intention of talking to this Bethany, let alone scaring her.

Emma watched him for another minute, then strode out of the barn.

James pulled in a breath of the sweet-sharp scent of hay and animals and waited until the echo of her footsteps had faded before he pulled his arm out of the sling. Dull pain pulsed through his shoulder. But pain was good. It kept his mind on the here and now.

Outside, a horse nickered softly from the pasture. The sound had frightened Sadie the first time she'd heard it, and she'd climbed into James's arms, trusting him to keep her safe.

He bent and scraped his pitchfork harder against the ground. He needed to work, not remember. He threw himself into the rhythm of finishing the stall, then stepped into the alley to fetch a fresh bale of straw.

But he jerked to a stop as his eyes fell on the woman standing there. It was the woman from the store. And the birthday party.

"What are you doing here?" The question may have come out more like an interrogation, but the strange woman had popped into his head at the oddest times over the past few days, and he had been working hard to banish thoughts of her.

"That's my job." She gestured to the pitchfork, propped against the wall next to him.

"I guess that means you're Bethany." He didn't know why he liked having a name to go with her face. "Emma said you were coming. Don't worry. I left plenty of stalls for you. I just thought I'd help out. It's either that or go crazy with nothing to do. I hope you don't mind."

James closed his mouth at the look the woman was giving him. Was he babbling? The last time he'd strung that many words together had probably been when he'd argued with the captain not to make him take this time off.

"Who are you?" Bethany asked.

James blinked at her. He was sure he'd introduced himself the other night. "James. Emma's brother." When she showed no sign of recognition, he added, "From the store. With the necklace." He lifted a hand to the strap of his sling, as if it were a necklace. "And your daughter's birthday party. I almost made you drop the cake." *All right, stop.* It was starting to sound like he'd kept detailed records of all their interactions.

"Right." But the tone of her voice rang false.

She didn't remember him at all.

Ouch. But it wasn't like it mattered.

Bethany watched him a moment longer, then disappeared into the next stall, emerging with the water bucket and feed tub, which she placed to the side. Then, without sparing him a glance, she marched to the far end of the barn, returning with a pitchfork and shovel.

James ducked into his stall, spreading the straw as he heard the scraping of the shovel next door. When an even layer of bedding covered the floor, he stepped into the aisle, noting that Bethany had scooted the wheelbarrow to a spot between their stalls.

"I'm moving the wheelbarrow," he called, sliding it to the far side of the stall she was working in, so he could reach it from the other side. Bethany didn't reply but emerged into the alley to deposit a fresh load of soiled straw into the wheelbarrow. He supposed he'd take that as confirmation that she'd heard him.

He fell into the rhythm of the work: Bend. Scoop. Toss. Bend. Scoop. Toss.

From the stall next door, he heard Bethany's movements, matching his own. After twenty minutes or so, he finished the stall and emerged into the alley. Bethany came out of her stall at the same time.

They both eyed the over-heaping wheelbarrow. Bethany made the first move toward it, but James shook his head.

He had no doubt she was perfectly capable of moving it, but what kind of man made a woman push a pile of manure? "I'll get it."

"Aren't you supposed to be wearing that?" She pointed to his sling.

He frowned. He didn't need another sister. "No."

Bethany shrugged and ambled down the alley to the next stall that needed to be cleaned.

James grabbed the wheelbarrow handles, wincing at the pull on his wound. On his way past the stall Bethany had entered, he couldn't help peeking inside. Her hair fell over her face as she worked, but her movements were fluid and graceful.

The wheelbarrow hit something and lurched to the side. With a sharp tug, he attempted to right it, sending a bullet of pain through his shoulder—and a crash of metal to the floor. The soiled contents spilled across the concrete.

"Are you— Oh." Bethany emerged from the stall and looked from James to the pile of manure and dirty straw, her eyes widening and a hand shooting up to cover her mouth. But she wasn't quick enough to stifle the giggle. "Sorry." She giggled again and clapped a second hand to her mouth. After a moment, she pulled her hands away, revealing a stunningly big smile. "I didn't mean to laugh. It's just—" She shook her head. "I'm always afraid that will happen to me."

"And has it ever?" He righted the wheelbarrow, then walked over to the post where he'd propped his shovel.

She watched him as if she were deep in thought. "Not that I remember," she finally answered, before picking up her own shovel and helping him scoop the mess into the wheelbarrow.

"Trust me, I don't think it's the kind of thing you'd forget." He grunted as a fresh shot of pain stabbed at his shoulder. Bethany gave a pointed look at his sling but didn't say anything.

James kept scooping.

It only took a minute to fill the wheelbarrow again.

"Maybe I should take it this time." Bethany's smile hadn't diminished at all as they'd worked.

James snorted. His pride wasn't exactly wounded, but he wasn't going to admit defeat. "I've got it."

By the time he returned with the empty wheelbarrow, Bethany had pulled the food and water buckets out of all the remaining stalls and was standing at the ready with her pitchfork.

As the morning went on, they made their way down the stalls, working next to each other, pausing to empty the wheelbarrow when it got full. Neither of them spoke, and yet the silence wasn't oppressive. It was more like . . . Well, he didn't know what it was like. Only that it left him feeling less weighed down than he had in years.

"Thanks for the help," Bethany said after they'd cleaned up their shovels and pitchforks. "This usually takes me all morning."

He shrugged. "I needed something to do. If Emma had her way, I'd just sit around here all day 'recovering.'" He made air quotes around the last word. "I'm not so great at sitting still." That's what Melissa hadn't understood when he'd returned to work almost right away after Sadie. . . . She'd wanted him to stay home and just sit with her. But what purpose was there in that? The only thing sitting did was give him time to remember, to hurt. And that didn't benefit anyone.

Bethany gestured at his sling. "What happened to your arm?"

He hesitated. Emma had said not to scare her. "Got hurt at work."

"What do you do?"

"I'm a detective." And a good one. Who should be on the job. Not standing here talking to some strange woman.

I could think of worse ways to spend your time, his heart prompted. James ignored it, but for some reason he couldn't make himself turn away.

An alarm sounded on Bethany's phone, and she pulled it out of her pocket. "Sorry." She read the screen, then looked up, seeming embarrassed. "I have to go."

"Okay." He almost said, "See you later," but then realized it would probably be best if he didn't see her again. So he turned and walked away.

Chapter 5

Bethany groaned as her alarm woke her from a dream. She didn't remember it, exactly, only that it had left her with a pleasant, warm feeling. One that made her want to stay in bed and dream a little longer.

But the alarm was insistent—and annoying. She rolled over to turn it off, scrolling through the other notifications that had come up on her phone. There were a few emails, a reminder to take her medication, and a calendar alert that it was Easter Sunday. She blinked at the screen a few times. Was it really Easter?

A vague sense of unease settled over her, like there was something she was forgetting. The feeling had become her normal state, but she still hated it.

She reached for her notebook to double-check she hadn't missed anything.

There it was, at the bottom of yesterday's schedule: *Hide Easter eggs*.

Had she done that?

She tried to remember. Tried to picture stuffing the colorful plastic eggs and finding the perfect hiding spots for them.

But she knew she hadn't.

Ruby had had a dressage competition all day yesterday, and by the time Bethany had gotten home, made dinner, and gotten Ruby to bed, she'd had a terrible headache. So she'd showered and gone to bed herself.

Without checking her notebook one last time.

Nausea rolled over her.

What kind of mother forgot to hide Easter eggs?

Maybe Ruby was still asleep, and she could hide them right now. But it took only a moment of listening to pick up the sound of the TV.

There was no way she could sneak past her daughter to get the plastic eggs from the basement—not to mention that she had nothing to fill them with.

Ugh. She covered her face. Did she have to go out there and explain to her ten-year-old daughter why there would be no Easter this year?

Unless... Maybe there was an Easter egg hunt somewhere in town today. She picked up her phone and did a quick search. But it seemed everyone had done their egg hunts last weekend. She was about to turn off her phone when another calendar alert popped onto the screen: *Brunch. Emma's. 11:00.*

"Thank you," she whispered, then tapped out a quick text to her friend. *Any chance you're planning to do an Easter egg hunt? I completely forgot.*

The reply came quickly: *Happy Easter! I didn't have one planned, but I know I have some plastic eggs around here. I'll hide them before church.*

Bethany let out a long breath. *You're a lifesaver.*

She took her time getting dressed, not quite ready to face her daughter yet. She might have come up with a backup plan, but Ruby was a bright girl. She'd likely see right through it.

Finally, she couldn't put it off any longer. She had to get Ruby some breakfast and make sure she was ready for church.

"Happy Easter," she said brightly as she entered the living room and turned off the TV. "Time to get ready for church."

"Happy Easter." Ruby stood and stretched. "Are you making cinnamon rolls like you always do?"

Cinnamon rolls. That was the other thing she'd forgotten.

She focused on keeping her smile in place. "I didn't want to ruin our appetite for lunch at Miss Emma's. We're going to do our Easter egg hunt there too. I thought it'd be more fun on the farm. Don't you think?"

Ruby shrugged, looking away. "I'm ten, Mom. I don't need to hunt for Easter eggs."

"Of course you do." Bethany dropped a kiss on top of her daughter's head as she moved toward the kitchen. "How about some cereal before church?"

She could feel Ruby watching her, but she didn't turn around. "Sure, Mom. Cereal sounds good." She heard Ruby shuffle down the hallway and forced herself to take another deep breath as she pulled bowls and spoons from the cupboards.

Easter wasn't about the food or the eggs. She knew that. And Ruby knew it too.

Still, she tried to imagine any of her friends, any of the moms of Ruby's classmates, anyone, forgetting to make the day special for their child. But she couldn't come up with a single person who would—except herself.

"What are you doing?" James paused in the doorway after his morning run, watching his sister bustle around the kitchen. Though the day had dawned with frost on the grass, sweat sucked his t-shirt to his skin under his sweatshirt, and his shoulder throbbed. He subtly tucked his arm back into his sling before Emma looked up.

"Happy Easter!" Emma's smile reflected joy. "He is risen!"

James grunted. He knew the traditional response. But any reason he'd had to worship God had been stolen from him five years ago. "Those Easter eggs?"

Emma rolled her eyes. "No. They're Arbor Day eggs." She pointed at a pile of bright wrappers on the table. "Make yourself useful."

"Huh?"

"Stuff those in the eggs, would you? I think another twenty or so should be good."

"Hey." He stepped to the table. "Is that my candy?"

"Relax. It's for a good cause."

"What cause?" James tucked a chocolate into a yellow egg and snapped it shut.

"I'm having some friends over for brunch after church, and we're going to have an Easter egg hunt for the kids."

"And you decided to wait until the last minute so you'd have to steal my candy?" That didn't sound like his sister, the consummate over-planner.

"Would you let the candy go? I'll buy you some more next time I go to the store. Anyway, the egg hunt was a last minute addition." She hesitated. "You know my friend Bethany?"

Something in James pinged, but he ignored it. "The one who helps with the mucking?" Working in the barn on his own the last couple of days had felt oddly lonely—but he wasn't about to ask Emma when Bethany would be back. He stuffed a piece of candy into an egg and snapped it shut.

"Yeah." Emma slid a few more eggs his way. "She forgot to hide eggs for her daughter. So I said I could hide some here."

"Ah." *Look, Daddy, I found a blue one. That's your favorite color.* James shook off the memory and snapped the egg shut harder than he'd meant to. He stared at the crack that now splintered one side.

"Here." Emma took the egg from him and swept the candy out, tucking it into a new egg. "So what did you think of Bethany?" she asked with a sly grin.

He shrugged, keeping his face blank. It was obvious where this was going. But he wasn't interested in playing along. "She seems like a hard worker. Quiet. Maybe a little scatterbrained."

Emma chucked an egg at him. It bounced off his shoulder and fell to the floor.

"Hey. What was that for?"

"She's not scatterbrained," Emma said. "She had an aneurysm a couple years ago. She almost died."

James looked up sharply. That was not what he'd expected his sister to say. "Is she all right?" He pictured her mucking stalls and carrying around water pails. She'd seemed so capable. And yet a wave of protectiveness went through him. His ex-wife would have called it his hero complex.

"Physically, yes," Emma answered. "But she has some short-term memory issues. And some language difficulties. I think she gets frustrated sometimes. But she's come a long way." Emma closed the last egg, then swept them all into a big basket.

"Wow. I had no idea." He tried to digest the information. "What did she used to be like?"

Emma shrugged. "I didn't meet her until she was in a coma after the aneurysm."

James blinked at his sister. She'd always been friendly, but . . . "You befriended someone in a coma?"

"Of course not." Emma laughed. "My friend Kayla did. She was the first on the scene when Bethany's car went off the road. Anyway, one thing led to another and now she's married to Bethany's brother."

"Wow. That's crazy."

"Crazier things have happened." Emma studied him. "You know . . . Bethany's an amazing woman. You should really get to know her."

James shook his head. That was one crazy thing that was not going to happen. "So where are you going to hide those?" He nodded to the basket of eggs on her arm.

"Outside. I think." Her eyes went to the clock. "But I'll have to do it fast. Church starts in half an hour."

"Here." He held out a hand for the basket. "You go. I'll hide them."

Emma's face fell. "You're not coming to church?"

He didn't mean for his laugh to sound bitter. "No."

"James—" Emma reached for him, but he pulled away, grabbing the basket from her.

"I'm not going to change my mind, Emma." God had closed the doors of the church to him the day he'd buried his daughter. And as far as he was concerned they could remain closed forever.

"Maybe not today." Emma pecked him on the cheek. "But I pray that someday God will change your mind for you. And your heart."

James didn't bother answering. There was little to no chance of that happening. Ever.

He followed Emma out the door and watched her get into her truck. "Thanks, James," she called. "I know Bethany will appreciate it. And don't hide them anywhere too hard." With a wave, she closed her door and started down the long driveway.

James pulled the first egg out of the basket, surveying the expansive property for a good hiding spot—and trying not to think about Emma's parting statement that Bethany would appreciate this. He wasn't doing this for her. He was only doing it for . . . Well, he didn't have a good reason for doing it. But it wasn't for her.

As she sang along with the closing strains of "I Know that My Redeemer Lives," Bethany closed her eyes and let the words wash over her.

This. This was what mattered.

Not whether she'd hidden the Easter eggs. Not whether she'd made cinnamon rolls. Not even whether she ever regained her full abilities. What mattered was Jesus.

That was something she needed to do a better job of remembering. In fact . . . as the service ended, Bethany pulled out her phone and tapped out a quick reminder: *Jesus matters most*. She set it for every day at 6:00 a.m. There. Now she couldn't forget.

Tucking her phone into her pocket, she gave her daughter a hug, then wished her friends a Happy Easter as they all filed into the lobby.

"We're all set," Emma whispered as she sidled up to Bethany, careful not to let Ruby overhear.

Bethany offered her friend a smile she hoped conveyed the depth of her gratitude. She wondered again how God had managed to bless her with such an amazing group of friends. Her first years in Hope Springs, she'd been so careful to keep to herself so she wouldn't end up with the wrong sort of people again—people who would lead her right back into temptation. But then she'd had an aneurysm and been in a coma—and when she'd woken up, she'd been surrounded by not only the brother she'd thought she'd lost forever but a whole army of friends he—or rather, his now-wife—had managed to amass for her. She didn't know what she would have done over the past two years if it hadn't been for all of them. She wished sometimes that she didn't have to rely quite so heavily on others—but today wasn't one of those days. Today, she was simply grateful.

"I hope you're ready to hunt for eggs," Emma said to Ruby. "I had my brother hide them, and he's an expert."

Ruby offered Emma a polite smile. "I'm too old to hunt for Easter eggs."

"Ruby! Miss Emma went through a lot of work—"

"It's okay, Bethany," Emma said gently, then turned to Ruby. "I know *you're* too old to hunt for eggs, but what about Ella Lynn and Liliana and Matthias? They're going to need help from you and the rest of the big kids."

Ruby's smile turned genuine. "I can help them. Hey, Liliana," she cooed, moving toward the toddler in their friend Violet's arms. "You want me to help you find some Easter eggs?"

"You're a genius," Bethany whispered to Emma. "Thank you." She pushed down the feeling that she should have been the one who knew how to make the Easter egg hunt appealing to her daughter.

Emma squeezed her arm. "Come on. Let's go get this hunt started. I told my brother not to hide them anywhere too difficult, but if he's anything like my dad, it could take all day to find the eggs."

Bethany laughed. Her dad had always enjoyed searching out the hardest spots to hide eggs too. Like the year he'd hidden Cam's basket in the trunk of the car. Dad had chuckled for days over that one. Bethany's laugh dried as a wave of regret swept over her. That must have been the last year they'd celebrated Easter before her first trip to rehab. An ache opened in her chest as she wished she could get that time back—wished Mom and Dad could be here to celebrate Easter with the granddaughter they'd never gotten to meet.

"Happy Easter." An elbow nudged her, and she grinned at her brother, his greeting chasing away the sad thoughts. She'd see her parents again someday in heaven. And right now, she could be grateful that her relationship with Cam had been restored.

"Happy Easter. Where's Kayla?" But she spied her sister-in-law directing her wheelchair toward them. Cam stepped aside for her, and Bethany bent to hug Kayla, then set a hand on her sister-in-law's belly. "How much longer?"

She probably asked every time she saw them, but Kayla practically glowed as she answered, "Only two more weeks."

"You're going to be such a good mom." It didn't matter that Kayla used a wheelchair. She was good at absolutely everything she did.

Behind Kayla, Cam cleared his throat.

"And you're going to be a good dad." Bethany stood and slugged his arm.

"That's all I wanted to hear." Cam gave a satisfied nod and rested a hand on his wife's shoulder.

Bethany's eyes lingered on them for a moment. The kind of happiness they'd found together was . . . something she didn't need.

Besides, she was happy already. With her friends, her family, and her daughter. She didn't need anything else.

"Come on, Rubes." She moved toward her daughter. "Let's go find some eggs."

Chapter 6

James stepped out of the shower and scrubbed the towel over his face until his freshly shaved cheeks were raw. Hiding the Easter eggs had been easy enough, except that with every egg, a barrage of memories had slapped at him. The time they'd taken Sadie to the zoo to see the Easter bunny—who had scared her when he'd taken off his head. The first time she'd tried to eat a hard-boiled egg—with the shell on. The time she'd thrown a tantrum right in the middle of church on Easter Sunday—and the way the pastor had joked with them after the service and even given Sadie a jellybean.

He tossed the towel on the floor and pulled on his clothes. Should he have gone to church with Emma? After all, it *was* Easter.

But he shook his head against the thought.

He'd shown up for God every single Easter—nearly every single Sunday—his entire life. And the one time he'd asked God to show up for him, he'd been answered with a big fat *no*. And with that one no, God had destroyed James's life.

James pulled on a pair of jeans and a flannel shirt, picked up his dirty running clothes and his towel, and stepped into the hallway. A strange rattling came from the kitchen, and James tossed his dirty clothes into the guest room, then charged down the stairs to let his sister know he'd successfully completed his mission. "You can call me the master egg—" He spluttered to a stop. It wasn't Emma in the kitchen.

It was Bethany. His heart did a weird sort of patter against his ribs.

Because of what Emma had told him about Bethany's struggles. No other reason.

Bethany glanced over her shoulder at him, then turned back to the cupboard. "Sorry. I was looking for the . . ." Her hands stilled, and she dropped her head to stare at the counter.

James watched her. Was she going to finish that sentence?

"Band-aids," she burst out triumphantly, as if the word had just come to her. "My daughter has a bad habit of scratching at her scabs."

He should turn around and go back upstairs to hide in his room for the duration. But instead his feet led him toward her. He opened the cupboard next to her and pulled out the box of band-aids.

"Thanks." She blinked at him. "I'm Bethany."

"Yeah." He should have asked Emma what to do when face-to-face with Bethany's memory issues. "I'm James."

She studied him. "You've told me that before, haven't you?"

He shrugged. "It's no big deal." At least maybe this meant she also didn't remember him tipping over the wheelbarrow full of manure the other day.

The door behind Bethany burst open, and Emma flew through. Her eyes skipped quickly from James to Bethany, and she grinned. James took a step backwards.

"Good. You found them," Emma said to Bethany. Then to James, "Come on. The kids are about to start hunting for the eggs. We need you to make sure they don't miss any."

James shook his head. That hadn't been part of the deal. Emma knew the rule. No kids.

"You hid the eggs?" Bethany's smile was gentle and grateful, and it seemed to hold a strange power to make James speechless.

"Come on," Emma repeated. Bethany smiled at him again and turned toward the door. He felt his feet pulling him after her.

But the moment he stepped outside, he knew it had been a mistake. There were kids *everywhere*.

He tried to retreat, but Emma was there, blocking his escape. She took his elbow and led him forward.

"Everyone." Her voice carried across the yard. "This is my brother James."

The group of adults and kids that had been scattered near the porch all peered toward him. James raised an awkward hand, said "hi," then tried to wriggle away. But Emma didn't let go of him.

"You already know Bethany. And that's her daughter Ruby, one of my best dressage riders." Emma pointed to a young girl who embodied the phrase "spitting image of her mother."

James's throat tightened as he nodded in the girl's general direction. Everyone had said Sadie had his eyes, but the rest of her features she'd gotten from her mother.

"And this is Bethany's brother Cam and his wife Kayla," Emma continued, pointing to a tall man whose hands rested on the shoulders of a pregnant woman in a wheelchair. They both smiled at him.

He nodded back. He didn't need to know who all these people were. It wasn't like he was going to be spending any time with them.

"And then that's Kayla's brother Nate." Emma insisted on continuing the introductions. "And his wife Violet and their little Liliana."

The toddler waved a pudgy fist at James. He looked away, the slice of his swallow sharp against the memories of Sadie's pudgy arms around his neck.

He didn't know how much longer he could handle being out here.

But Emma pointed to another happy family. "And this is Sophie and Spencer and their twins Rylan and Aubrey. And Spencer's brother Tyler, his wife Isabel, and . . . Where are the kids?"

Tyler laughed, pointing toward the side of the house. "Playing with the kittens. Where else?"

James shifted on his feet. From the time she'd turned four, Sadie had asked almost every day if she could get a cat. He'd always answered that she could have one when she was older. Except, she'd never . . .

He forced his attention to Emma. He still didn't care who these people were. But it gave him something to focus on other than the jackhammer pulverizing his heart.

"That's Austin and Leah. And their son Jackson." Emma pointed to a tall young man. "He's in his second year of college." The adults all beamed at the kid, who ducked his head.

"Let's see. Who did I miss?" Emma glanced around the yard.

"It's fine, Emma. I'm sure everyone wants to get on with the party. Not stand around and wait to be introduced to me." He took a step toward the house, reaching subtly behind him for the doorknob.

"That's where you're wrong." A guy with a toddler propped in his arm stepped forward and held out his hand. "I'm Dan. This little guy is Matthias, and that's my wife Jade and our daughter Hope." He nodded toward a woman who offered James a warm smile. The girl's smile was equally as warm. James ducked his head but shook the guy's hand.

"What about Grace and Levi?" The woman Emma had introduced as Violet asked. "I thought Grace would have sung at church this morning, but I didn't see them."

"They went to Tennessee to celebrate Easter with her family. And Ethan and Ariana took Joy to Disney."

A car turned in at the end of the driveway. "There's Jared and Peyton and Ella Lynn," Emma said, letting go of James's arm as she stepped forward.

James let out a breath. Finally, he could escape.

He made a quick, stealthy turn and disappeared inside, easing the door closed behind him as he heard someone—it sounded like Bethany's voice, he thought—asking everyone to gather for a picture.

He thundered up the stairs, pretending he didn't hear his sister calling behind him.

He spent the next three hours reading and trying to ignore the joyous sounds—and delicious smells—drifting up the stairs. Part of him said he was being stupid not to go down there and fill a plate. But the smarter part of him said it wasn't worth the risk. He could eat later—whatever the loud rumblings from his stomach might say in protest.

It took forever, but the chatter downstairs at last grew quieter, and he heard the sounds of car doors closing and engines starting. He waited a good fifteen minutes after he heard the last car pull away to emerge from his room. Pausing to listen at the top of the stairs, he heard the sound of water running from the faucet but no voices.

If having to help Emma with the dishes was the price he had to pay for leftovers, he'd gladly do it. And he'd even put up with a lecture about how he shouldn't have disappeared earlier. As long as she'd saved him some mashed potatoes.

"It's about—" For the second time that day, he clamped his mouth shut as he reached the kitchen and found not Emma, but Bethany, her hands immersed in a sink full of dishwater.

He stopped and looked around. Who else was still here? "Sorry. I thought everyone had left."

"They did." Bethany looked up with a smile, not taking her hands out of the water. "It's just me."

"My sister left you to do the cleanup?"

"I volunteered. She took Ruby out to the barn to work on a new dressage movement."

"I was just going to grab some food. But I can help you with the dishes first." What else was he going to do? Sit here and eat while she worked?

"That's okay. I like the quiet." She turned back to the sink.

Was that a hint that she wanted him to leave? He supposed he could get some food later. It would be less awkward for both of them. He turned to head back up the stairs.

"Wait, um . . ." Her voice reached for him. "Emma's brother."

He paused on the bottom step, unable to keep the edges of his lips from tipping up. "James," he supplied.

"I knew that."

"Oh really?" He turned toward her with an eyebrow raised—a gentler version of the look he'd hit a suspect with if he knew they were lying.

"No." Bethany laughed self-consciously. "Sorry. I have—"

"Short-term memory loss," James filled in. "Emma mentioned it."

Bethany nodded and rinsed off the plate in her hand. "How many times have you told me your name?"

He shrugged. It was four. But it didn't matter. "It must be hard." Though some days he wanted nothing more than to lose his memory. It had to be better than recalling everything with near-photographic detail.

Bethany stilled, as if formulating an answer, but then turned to the sink without saying anything.

He was about to tromp up the stairs—foodless—when she said, "It's hard, yes. But it's taught me that God puts people into our lives for a reason."

James grunted. Yeah. To steal them away again.

"Were you going to get some food?" She glanced at him over her shoulder, her smile catching him in the chest. "Or did you forget?" She laughed lightly at her own joke.

"I . . ." He gestured toward the stairs, but her eyes didn't leave his. "Yeah. I was."

He dug the leftovers out of the fridge and loaded them onto a plate. He popped it into the microwave, unable to keep his gaze from sliding to Bethany as he waited for it to heat up.

A small smile played on her lips as she washed another plate, and he had the strangest desire to know what she was thinking.

He turned to the microwave, staring at his food as it rotated in a slow circle. When it was done, he debated carrying it upstairs to eat in his room. But that seemed rude. Not to mention he'd been trapped up there all day. And it was oddly peaceful here in the kitchen.

He set his plate on the table and pulled out a chair. Bethany peeked at him over her shoulder—that smile still hovering quietly—then went back to the dishes.

James wondered vaguely if he should attempt to make conversation. But Bethany looked completely content in the silence, and he relaxed into his seat. It was nice being with someone who didn't constantly urge him to "talk about it."

By the time he'd wolfed down his meal, Bethany was on the last few dishes.

He carried his plate to the sink. "I can finish up the rest."

"That's okay. I'm having fun."

He gave a short laugh. "You have a strange concept of fun." Not that he could talk—he wasn't sure he remembered what *fun* was anymore. "At least let me dry. Can't let you have all the fun yourself."

She gestured to the towel on the counter. He slipped his arm out of his sling, picked up the towel, and took the bowl she passed him. They fell into an easy rhythm, silent except for the splashing water and clanking dishes. Every once in a while, when he stepped closer to her, he caught a scent of peaches that made him think of summer and sunshine. He let his mind go pleasantly blank, the memories that had been hunting him down all day finally relenting. He'd never realized doing the dishes could be so therapeutic.

"Last one." Bethany passed him a china serving platter. James reached for it, but Bethany let go a second before his fingers could grasp it.

He lunged for it as it careened toward the ground, exhaling as his fingers closed around it. But something about the dish felt strange—too soft. He glanced down to find Bethany's fingers wrapped under his.

"That was close," she breathed.

"Yeah." He should let go of the dish.

"Guess what, Mom!"

James wrenched his hand away as the door flew open and Bethany's daughter burst through it, followed by Emma. Fortunately, Bethany managed to keep her hold on the platter. Unfortunately, the look on Emma's face said she thought there was something very different going on from what was really happening—which was nothing.

Bethany reached past him to set the wet platter on the counter, then turned to her daughter. "What?"

"Miss Emma says I'm ready for loops at the next competition." The enthusiasm in Ruby's voice punched straight at James's gut. Sadie had been so enthusiastic about everything too—from getting ice cream to spotting an ant on the ground.

"That's great." Bethany wrapped her daughter in a hug.

James dropped the towel on the counter, the heaviness of his own empty limbs weighing at his sides. He slid his left arm back into the sling.

"Don't think I didn't see that," Emma mock scolded. "But since you came out of your room, I won't yell at you about the sling."

"How good of you," he muttered.

"Do you have my eggs?" Ruby asked her mom.

"Um . . ." Bethany glanced around the room.

"Right here." Emma swept a small bag of plastic eggs off the counter. "I thought you had more than this."

Ruby shrugged. "Hope didn't find that many, so I gave her some of mine."

"That was nice of you." Bethany tucked her daughter's hair behind her ear, and James suddenly saw Sadie's wild curls that would never stay put.

"I thought I said not to hide the eggs in spots that were too hard." Emma directed a laughing frown at him.

"It wouldn't have been any fun if they were too easy to find. And anyway, they weren't *that* hard."

"In the downspout?" Emma lifted an eyebrow.

He chuckled. "All right. But that was the only really hard one."

"Not for me!" Ruby reached into her bag and pulled out a blue egg. "I found it!"

"Bummer." James didn't mean to talk to her, but the words came out before he could stop them. "I was hoping no one would find it, so I could have the candy myself."

Ruby stepped forward, holding out the egg. "Here. You can have it."

"No. That's—"

But she was already pressing it into his hand. Her fingers were warm and not nearly as sticky as Sadie's five-year-old fingers had been—but still the shock of the contact paralyzed him.

"Um. Thanks." He tucked the egg into his sweatshirt pocket, then retreated to the stairs. He was halfway up before he heard Emma apologizing for him. Vaguely, he wondered what she was telling them. But it didn't matter. From now on, he'd be staying as far away from Bethany and her daughter as possible.

Chapter 7

Bethany squinted at the man glowering on her doorstep. She should know his name, but . . .

"James," he said, as if he recognized her struggle. "Emma's brother."

"I know."

He made a face but didn't say anything.

"What are you doing here?" She supposed she could have asked that more politely, but it was too late to rephrase it.

"I was supposed to give you this the other day when you were at the stables. But I forgot, and I was coming into town anyway, so . . ." He passed her a book.

"Oh. Um. Thanks."

"Emma said it was for your women's Bible study tonight," he supplied.

"Right." She had completely forgotten she needed to buy a book for that.

"Okay. Well." He gestured toward his truck in the driveway.

"Hi, James." Ruby bounded to the door, sliding between James and Bethany. "Did you eat your candy?"

James took a step backwards, not looking at Ruby. "Not yet. I should—" He turned and jogged down the walkway, then jumped into his truck.

"I don't think he likes me," Ruby said matter-of-factly.

Instantly, Bethany's defensiveness sprang to life. "Of course he likes you. Who wouldn't?" Although she had to admit that the way he'd rushed away the moment Ruby appeared had been weird. "He's probably in a hurry."

"He seems sad." Ruby watched the truck as James pulled into the street. "We should do something to cheer him up."

Bethany laughed. That was what she loved about her daughter—she was always worried about other people's feelings. "For now, you have homework to do. And I have a chapter to read before I get you some dinner and then head to Bible study."

"Yay. Uncle Cam said he's bringing a movie tonight. And we're going to make popcorn."

Bethany ruffled her daughter's hair. "I'd say you got pretty lucky in the uncle department." And Bethany had gotten pretty lucky in the brother department. After the way she'd torn their family apart, he'd had no reason to come to her rescue by watching Ruby while she was in the hospital. More than once, she'd shuddered to think what might have happened to her daughter without Cam and Kayla.

More than once, she'd wondered if Ruby would be better off if they were still raising her. She pushed aside the thought. She had to trust that God had kept her in Ruby's life for a reason.

Two hours later, with her Bible study chapter read—and annotated to help her remember—Bethany greeted her brother, made him promise not to let Ruby stay up past her bedtime, then joined Kayla in the car.

"You look happy," Kayla said as she used her hand controls to back the car down the driveway.

"I do?" Bethany shrugged. She didn't have any reason not to be happy.

"Yes." Kayla grinned at her. "Any reason in particular?" The way she said it made it sound like she already knew the answer.

But Bethany had no idea what it could be. "Not that I can think of."

Kayla shook her head, still grinning. "So it has nothing to do with James?"

"James?" Bethany gave her a blank look. What *was* she talking about?

"Emma says you've been spending a lot of time with her brother. So . . ." Her voice went up with expectation.

Oh. James, Emma's brother. His face popped into her head. "We haven't been spending time together."

But she did need to come up with a way to remember his name. Her doctor had suggested linking people's names with their most prominent feature. The trick had helped her remember the names of the new friends she'd met after her aneurysm. Like, Kayla was the "Wheelchair Queen," complete with a crown in Bethany's head. And Emma was "Cowgirl Emma" in Bethany's mind for the riding boots she always wore.

So what was James's prominent feature? The sling on his arm? Or the lips that rarely smiled? Maybe the muscles that flexed under his flannel shirt as he scooped out the horse stalls? Muscle-man James?

A giggle made its way out before she could stop it.

"I knew it," Kayla crowed as she slowed for a stop sign. "You like him."

"No." Bethany refused to acknowledge the tiny jump of her stomach. "I was just trying to come up with a name association for him. Like how you're the Wheelchair Queen."

"And?" Kayla asked. "What'd you come up with?"

"Um . . ." Bethany had to stall. She certainly couldn't tell her sister-in-law about Muscle-Man James. "James the Gray."

"Gray?" Kayla glanced her way. "I didn't notice any gray hair."

Bethany laughed "No. Me either." Though, if she had to guess, he was probably around her own age of forty. "Gray because he never smiles."

"Ah." Kayla turned into the church parking lot, her eyes sliding slyly to Bethany. "Maybe you can change that."

Ruby's words from earlier about cheering James up suddenly came back to her.

But she had plenty of her own problems to worry about. She didn't have time to figure out why James was sad—or what she could do about it.

She opened her car door and waited for Kayla to assemble her wheelchair and transfer into it—she'd learned long ago that her sister-in-law didn't need help with this, or most tasks—then walked next to her toward Hope Church, her thoughts lingering on James.

But once inside, she pushed him out of her mind and turned her focus to Jade, who was leading the study.

"Last week, we wrapped up our study of the book of Esther," Jade said. "So, keeping with our theme of 'Being a Woman God Uses,' I thought we'd look at Ruth next."

Bethany nodded as she opened the book about Ruth that James had brought her earlier and reviewed the notes she'd made. She so wanted to be a woman God could use. But she didn't know how that was possible. Not anymore. Maybe when she'd first come to Hope Springs. When she'd gotten past her addiction and turned her life around. But now, with the limitations her aneurysm had left her with, she had a hard enough time getting through the day without making too many mistakes—without forgetting too many words or leaving her daughter at school because the alarm on her phone hadn't gone off. How was God supposed to use that?

Shaking off the thoughts—this Bible study wasn't about her, it was about Ruth—she returned her attention to Jade. How long had she been talking? What had Bethany missed?

"When Ruth left her homeland and everything she knew," Jade was saying, "she did it out of love for her mother-in-law. She had no idea that God had a larger purpose in mind for her. She had no idea that out of her family—a family she didn't even know she would have yet—would come the Savior."

Bethany let the words slip down to her soul. It had only been a few months before her aneurysm that she'd started coming to church. And every time she heard the Word now, it felt like the first time. Not because she didn't remember it. But because it had taken on such rich meaning in light of everything she'd been through. If God had a larger purpose for Ruth, maybe it meant he had a larger purpose for her too.

James the Gray popped into her head again. But she popped him right back out. She may not be certain of her purpose, but one thing she was certain of—he was not part of it.

Chapter 8

"Guess what day it is?" Emma sing-songed, bursting into the kitchen with her Bible in her hand, at least a dozen sticky notes poking out of it in various places.

James looked up from the protein bar he was eating. He'd never admit it to his sister, but some of her health food was okay. Not great, but edible. He used the sleeve of his flannel shirt to wipe at a wet spot on the table. It felt good to move his arm freely again, now that he'd decided to completely forgo the sling.

"Uh. Wednesday?"

"Uh huh." Emma's grin rivaled the Cheshire Cat's. "And you know what Wednesday means."

"Not really." All the days seemed pretty much the same here.

Emma gave him a look like she was disappointed. He finished his protein bar and threw away the wrapper. He needed to get out to the barn to take care of the stalls. Wait. Wednesday.

Bethany.

"You just remembered, didn't you?" Emma pointed at him, her grin growing into a laugh.

"Remembered what?"

"Don't try that on me." Emma filled a bottle with water. "I have a doctor appointment this morning. I was thinking maybe you and Bethany could take Ace and Fancy Lady out for a ride after you clean the stalls." He noticed how she very purposefully didn't look at him as she said it.

"You're about as subtle as a basket of snakes, you know that?"

"What?" She turned to him with an innocent look he would recognize as fake even if he weren't a detective. "Fancy Lady gets loopy if she doesn't get ridden. And Ace needs the exercise. He's starting to look more like a cow than a horse."

"Right." James headed for the door.

"So you'll do it?" Emma called after him.

"You know I never could say no to my sister," he said over his shoulder. He heard Emma's snort, followed by her thank you, before the door closed.

He strode toward the barn, telling himself that was *not* extra energy in his step. He wanted to get the work done, that was all.

But the sound of tires crunching on the gravel driveway drew him to a stop, and he couldn't seem to control the way his lips responded to spotting Bethany's car. He'd seen her in passing the other day when she'd brought Ruby to her dressage lesson. They hadn't even talked. But the way she'd smiled had stuck with him ever since.

She has a kid, he reminded himself.

But Ruby had stuck in his head too—the way she'd waved at him from atop her horse when she'd spotted him from across the arena, the way her grin was warm and open in spite of the fact that he'd been rude to her the other day. He owed her an apology. Maybe he could pass it on through Bethany.

The car door opened, and Bethany stepped out. She didn't seem to notice him, so he let himself watch her.

Her hair fluttered in the breeze as she tucked her keys into her pocket, then closed the car door and tilted her head back with her eyes closed. A smile played across her lips, and he found himself wanting to know what it was about. After a few seconds, she lowered her head and opened her eyes—which seemed to land right on him. Her smile grew as she waved and started toward him.

He considered fleeing into the barn ahead of her, but his feet didn't want to move.

"Hey, James," she called when she was almost to him.

"Hey—" He broke off, staring at her. "Did you just remember my name?"

Bethany's laugh knocked against his ribs. "I guess I did. I had to come up with a name association. That's all."

"A name association?" He held open the barn door for her.

"Yeah. Like linking your name to something familiar."

"Do I want to know what you associated me with?" He fell into step next to her as they walked toward the back of the barn.

Again her laugh swept over him. "Probably not." She threw a smile at him, then slipped into the equipment room.

James remained outside the door for a second—just long enough to remind his heart that it was not allowed to develop feelings for this woman, even if her smile and her laugh and the way she said his name were all trying to storm the hard spots in his heart.

Then he followed her into the room. They silently collected their equipment and silently walked to the stalls and silently started working. But it was the most comfortable silence James had ever experienced. No demands. No expectations. No one telling him he should talk.

But the more they worked and the more comfortable he grew, the more he realized he couldn't go riding with her. He'd just ride each of the horses in turn. Because if he spent more time with her, he was going to want to spend *yet more* time with her. And that was a problem.

He heard Bethany grunt, and he stepped out of the stall he was working on to find her lugging a straw bale nearly as big as she was.

"I would have gotten that." He rushed forward and took the bale from her, its sharply sweet scent mingling with her fresh summery one.

"Thanks." She was breathing heavily from the exertion. "Sometimes I forget how heavy those are."

"No problem." He carried the bale to a spot between their stalls and cut the twine. Bethany grabbed her pitchfork and started scooping new bedding into her stall. After a moment, she glanced at him, and he realized he was still watching her. With a jerk, he hustled back into his own stall.

Yes, he was definitely going to exercise the horses alone.

"I'll clean up," he said as they completed the stalls. "You can head out."

"That's okay." Bethany collected her shovels. "It'll go faster together."

"Really," he insisted. "I don't have anything else to do today, aside from exercising Ace and Fancy Lady."

"You're going to ride?" Her eyes lit up, and James realized his mistake. He couldn't *not* ask her, not now that he could see how much she would love it.

"Yeah. Do you ride?" *Say no. Say no. Say—*

"My dad used to take us out when we were kids. Those are some of my best memories. I haven't been in years though. Not since . . ." Her wistful expression faded to one of regret. "Anyway, have fun."

She turned, and he almost let her walk away.

"Wait." The word came out kind of strangled, but Bethany stopped and turned around, giving him a perplexed smile.

"You wouldn't want to help, would you?" he asked. "Ride Ace while I ride Fancy Lady?"

"For real?" Bethany looked like he'd offered her a million dollars.

He shrugged, but it was impossible not to smile at her unchecked enthusiasm. "I mean, if you want to."

"Yes." She shot forward, her arms wrapping around his shoulders. He winced as she pressed against his wound.

"Sorry." She let go and jumped backwards. Her cheeks were flushed, and she ducked her head. "I didn't mean to— Sometimes I struggle with . . ." She toed the ground and let out a frustrated sounding breath. He waited, having no idea what she was going to say. Finally, she looked up. "I can't remember what it's called. When you do something without thinking about it first?"

"Spontaneous?"

She shook her head, frowning in concentration.

"Impromptu?"

Another head shake. A deeper frown.

He sought for another word. "Impulsive?"

"Yes!" Her shout was exuberant. "Impulse control. I have impulse control issues. Since the aneurysm. I didn't mean to hug you."

"Oh." What was he supposed to say to that? "It's okay." Fortunately, he was able to keep a lid on his heart, which was saying it was more than okay.

Chapter 9

There were a lot of things Bethany had done in her life that she regretted.

This was not one of them.

As Ace carried her along the trail that led from the barn toward the wooded part at the back of Emma's property, Fancy Lady and James right in front of them, Bethany drew in a long breath. The late morning air smelled earthy and damp and sweet with the scent of lilacs that had just begun to bloom. Around them, grasses waved in the gentle breeze, and up ahead, leaves in new green unfurled on the trees. The sun warmed the top of her head, and peace warmed her insides.

Thank you for this day, Lord. Her contentment burst out of her in a silent prayer. There was a time when it had looked like she wasn't going to have any more days—and now here she was, riding a horse and marveling at the beauty of God's creation. There may be a lot of things her aneurysm had taken from her—but she wouldn't let it steal her joy in rediscovering God.

Ahead of her, James reined in his horse and pulled it to the side of the trail so that Bethany and Ace could stop next to him.

"How are you doing?" The way he watched her, as if he wanted to make sure she was all right—really all right—did something strange to Bethany's stomach.

She pressed a hand to it. "I'm good. Though Ace keeps trying to graze."

James laughed, and she wondered if it was the first time she'd ever heard it—because she was pretty sure she would have remembered how gloriously rich it sounded. "Emma said he was getting chunky. Should we keep going, or do you want to turn around?"

"Definitely keep going. But first—" She leaned to the side in her saddle so she could finagle her phone out of her pocket. She opened the camera app, then lined James and Fancy Lady up on the screen. "Say horses."

James gave her a perplexed look but said "horses," and Bethany snapped a picture.

"Helps me remember," she explained, taking one of Ace's head and neck in front of her.

"Here." James leaned toward her and held out a hand. "Let me get one of you."

The strange feeling in Bethany's middle grew. James wasn't making fun of her for taking pictures of everyday things—he was helping her.

He snapped a couple of pictures, then passed the phone back to her. She tucked it into her pocket, and they started on the trail again. It was wide enough here that they could ride side-by-side, and the horses fell into step next to each other, Bethany tugging on Ace's reins every few minutes to keep him from grazing.

"Where did you learn to ride?" The question slid from her mouth easily even though she hadn't taken the time to formulate it in her head first as she usually did.

"Emma was horse crazy even as a kid. She convinced my parents to let her take lessons. Which meant I, of course, insisted on taking lessons too. Had to do everything my big sister did."

Bethany smiled. "Cam was like that with me too." At least until she'd gotten involved with drugs. She could only thank God that he hadn't followed her down that path.

"I hope it didn't drive you as crazy as it drove Emma. She hated when I copied what she did. My parents always told her she should be flattered that I wanted to be like her."

Bethany laughed. "Sometimes I think it's sad that Ruby won't know what that's like since she's an only child."

James nodded, but his jaw tightened, and he fell silent.

They continued to ride side-by-side until they came to a spot where the trail narrowed and disappeared into the woods.

"After you." James reined in Fancy Lady to let Bethany and Ace take the lead on the single-file trail.

As the trees closed overhead, Bethany felt like she was being transported into another world.

A dappled kaleidoscope of sunlight circled across the ground. The shadows and light moved with the breeze, playing tricks on her eyes and making the whole world shift.

She grasped for Ace's mane and closed her eyes for a second. When she opened them, everything spun. The motion of the horse beneath her made her head swim. Which way was up and which was down?

She moaned, closing her eyes again in an attempt to get her bearings. She felt like her body was moving in the opposite direction of the horse.

"Bethany!" The voice from behind her sounded garbled and far away.

"I'm okay." She forced the words out past the waves of nausea rolling over her. "Just . . . dizzy."

"Rein him in," called the voice behind her. "And hold on."

Somehow, she managed to obey, giving the reins a gentle pull. She couldn't tell if the movement below her had come to a stop since the world was still spinning and bright pops of color filled her vision. She needed to get to the ground. Right now.

She gasped as she slid to the side, but a pair of firm arms wrapped around her and slid her off the saddle. Oh. That was so much better. Her feet touched the ground, but the arms didn't leave her. She opened her eyes, and her vision cleared enough to make out James standing in front of her. His hands were on her elbows, steadying her.

"Can you stand on your own?"

She nodded but pressed a hand to her head as the motion reignited the spinning. She closed her eyes, concentrating on taking deep breaths. James's hands were firm on her arms, and when she opened her eyes, concern cloaked his face.

"Sorry about that. Sometimes motion gives me . . ."

"Vertigo?" James supplied.

She nodded, causing a few bright pops of color to explode in her vision. "I'm better now."

But the look on James's face said he didn't buy it. "Let's sit for a minute."

"No, really. I'm fine." Embarrassment suddenly washed over her. What must he think of her, unable to keep her seat on the gentlest horse Emma owned? And now she couldn't even stand on her own? She wriggled out of his grasp, and he let her go, though he kept his hands poised in front of her, as if he expected her to tip over at any moment.

"Where are the horses?" She turned her head, but the motion blurred her vision and the world slipped sideways again.

Next thing she knew, James's arms were around her, and he was lowering her to the ground. "Put your head between your knees."

Too dizzy to protest, she obeyed. She heard him rustling around behind her.

"Here. Lie back." With a hand on her shoulder, he guided her to lie on something soft.

She moaned quietly and lifted her forearm to cover her eyes. When would the spinning stop?

She had no idea how much time had passed—or whether she'd fallen asleep or remained awake—before she lowered her arm and tentatively opened her eyes.

Thankfully, the world seemed to have righted itself, and the gentle swaying of the leaves above her didn't make her nauseous.

She turned her head to the side to find James sitting next to her, staring into the distance.

"Sorry about that," she murmured.

He startled, as if his thoughts had been far off, but smiled as he turned to her. "Nothing to be sorry about. Feeling better?"

"I think so." She positioned her arms to push herself into a sitting position. But before she'd started to exert herself, James had scooted to her side and placed a hand behind her back, easing her up.

"Thanks." She gave him a brief smile but looked away at his intense expression.

"Any more dizziness?"

She waited a moment before answering to be sure this time. "Nope. I don't think so."

"Let's wait a little longer, just to be safe." James took his hand off her back, and she shivered.

"Cold?"

"No. Just damp from lying on the ground."

"I'd give you my flannel, but . . ." He reached behind her and then held it up. Deep streaks of mud covered the blue and white fabric.

"Oh no. I'm sorry."

He balled the shirt up. "Don't be. It served its purpose."

"Uh oh." Bethany spotted Ace, contentedly grazing at the side of the trail. "I think Ace may have *gained* weight from this walk."

James chuckled, the sound warming through her.

"You should laugh more." The words plopped off her lips. Oops. That would have been a good time to practice some impulse control. "I mean—"

But James gave her a thoughtful look. "It's been a while since I've had much to laugh about."

Bethany watched, waiting for him to elaborate. When he looked away, she considered asking, but she knew better than most that some things were too hard to give words to.

They sat in silence for a few more minutes, the sounds of the calling birds and scurrying squirrels supplying a soothing backdrop.

Bethany's phone rang, and she reached for it, surprised to find it still tucked into her pocket. She was reluctant to break the peace. But it could be Ruby's school.

Her eyes fell on the screen. Not Ruby's school. Cam.

He probably needed her to run an errand. She considered not answering—she could always take care of it later—but dismissed the thought. It was her job.

She lifted the phone to her ear. "Hey, Cam."

"Hey." He seemed breathless, and she heard what sounded like drawers opening and closing in the background. "Where are they?"

"Where are what? What are you doing?"

"Sorry. I wasn't talking to you." Cam's usually calm voice was frenetic, and Bethany sat up straighter. "Cam. What's wrong?"

Out of the corner of her eye, she saw James turn toward her, looking alert.

"Nothing. Sorry." Cam's laugh bordered on wild. "Kayla's water broke."

"Wow. Cam." Bethany covered her mouth. She was about to become an aunt.

"What is it?" James whispered, moving closer. "Is everything okay?"

Bethany nodded. "My sister-in-law's water broke."

"Ah." James's gaze shifted to the trees, but not before Bethany detected the trace of brokenness in his eyes.

"I think that's everything, right?" she heard Cam say on the other end of the phone.

"Yes." Kayla's laughing answer sounded much calmer than Cam.

"You take care of Kayla, Cam. I'll meet you guys at the hospital." She wasn't going to miss this for anything.

"Actually, that's why I called." A door closed as Cam muttered, "Oh man, I dropped that."

Bethany rolled her eyes. Anyone who met Cam right now would have a hard time believing he was an extremely capable businessman—who used to be a high-powered attorney. She supposed that was what happened when your wife was about to have a baby. Not that she would know—Ruby's father had been long out of the picture by the time Ruby was born. Bethany's drive to the hospital had been alone. As had every step of her parenting journey. Though she sometimes wondered what it would have been like to raise Ruby with a partner at her side, Ruby's father never could have been that man.

Her eyes strayed to James, who was again gazing into the distance.

"Anyway." Cam finally spoke into the phone again, and Bethany heard a door close and then an engine turn over. "Bill Jespersen called. There's some sort of problem with the stone we ordered. I was about to tell him I'd come check it out when Kayla's water broke. I think I might have hung up on him."

Bethany laughed.

"Glad it's so amusing to you," Cam said dryly. "But you know what a big client he is. We can't afford to lose him."

"Okay, Cam." She didn't remember who Bill Jespersen was, although for some reason she had a picture of a trout in her head. "I'll go deal with Bill Jespersen. You and Kayla go have that baby. And call me the minute you have news."

"You're sure? If it's too much, I can always call him and say I'll take care of it tomorrow."

Bethany tried to ignore the sting left by his question about whether she could handle it. "You're not going to take care of it tomorrow. You're going to be too busy being a dad."

Next to her, James seemed to twitch, and his shoulders visibly tightened. But her attention was pulled back to the phone as she heard Kayla tell Cam he'd missed the turn.

"Go," she said to her brother. "Take care of your family. I've got this." She hung up the phone, then started to push to her feet.

James scrambled up next to her, locking his hand around her elbow as she straightened. Even after she was upright, he held on, watching her.

An unexpected tingle went up her arm. "Thanks. I think I'm good now."

James let go slowly. "We should probably lead the horses, rather than riding."

As much as she wanted to protest so she could take care of things for Cam faster, Bethany nodded. A faint unsteadiness still clung to her, and if she had problems again, it would only delay her more.

James collected the horses, taking the reins of each in his hands, and Bethany fell into step on the far side of Ace. Though they couldn't talk with the horses between them, Bethany caught the way James checked on her every few minutes, and a new kind of warmth went through her.

By the time they got to the barn, her legs seemed to weigh an extra three hundred pounds, and she was bracing a hand against Ace's side to keep from stumbling.

James brought the horses to a stop, then came around to her side. Silently, he took her arm and led her to the decorative metal bench next to the barn door. "Sit."

"I have to—" But her legs ignored her protest and honored James's order.

"I know. Just sit for a minute. I'll be right back."

All Bethany could do was close her eyes and lean her head back against the barn wall. Just once, she wanted to be there when someone needed her. She was tired of letting everyone down. But she wasn't sure how she was going to walk to her car, let alone take care of things for Cam.

"Here." James emerged from the barn with a water bottle that he must have gotten out of the mini fridge in the back. He unscrewed the cap, then refastened it lightly and passed the bottle to Bethany.

"Thanks." How had he known she always struggled with those stupid caps? She downed a long swallow.

James's eyes didn't leave her the whole time.

As she lowered the bottle, the heaviness and nausea seemed to lift. "Thank you. I feel much better now." She pulled her keys out of her pocket.

"That's what you said before." James stood in front of her, blocking her way to her car.

"I know." She stood, which put her closer to him than she'd expected. He still smelled good. "I really am better. I have to go—"

"I can't let you drive in this condition." He held out a hand, as if he expected her to drop her keys into it.

"Cam needs me to—"

"I know." James plucked the keys from her fingers. "I'll drive."

"I— Really?" She felt like she was gaping at him, but she couldn't help it. He would do that for her?

"Come on." He waited for her to take a step, then fell in alongside her. "Where to?"

"To—" Wait. The name had been on the tip of her tongue. She'd repeated it to herself a thousand times on the walk back so she wouldn't forget. She could picture the trout in her head. But the name had escaped. "To, uh—" She shot him a look. "I forgot who it was." She couldn't call Cam back—not when he and Kayla were having a baby.

"You said Bill Jespersen on the phone." James's tone was calm and matter-of-fact, as if he hadn't just saved her life. Bethany turned to stare at him, but he simply shrugged. "I have a near-photographic memory."

"Wow." What she wouldn't do to simply have a regular memory, much less a photographic one. "That must be nice."

James's lips formed a grimace for a second before flattening. "Not always."

Chapter 10

Silently, James made the turn his phone told him to make. Bethany had found Bill Jespersen's address in the customer file on her phone. He glanced over at her, relieved to see that the life had returned to her cheeks. He hadn't seen anyone that pale since—

His knuckles tightened as he fought off the memory.

"This is my favorite view," Bethany murmured as they turned onto Hope Street, which ran parallel to the Lake Michigan shoreline. To their left, a steep hill dotted with flowers and a gazebo led down to the marina, where colorful yachts and sailboats rocked on the gentle waves. Beyond them, sunlight glinted off the water, making James squint. As they continued down the street, they passed quaint stores—a fudge shop, bakery, antique store—with a few people lingering outside.

"That fudge shop was how I knew I was going to love Hope Springs," Bethany said.

James glanced at her. "How long ago did you move here?"

"Eleven years ago," Bethany answered instantly.

"You remember that?" He didn't mean to sound surprised, but he'd expected her to at least have to think about it.

She shrugged, still looking out the window. "I can remember almost everything from my past." She turned to him with a rueful smile. "It's just new memories my brain doesn't like to make."

"Will it get better?" Maybe he shouldn't ask, but she fascinated him. Or, her condition did. Not her.

Keep telling yourself that.

"They don't know," she answered. "I see a— Um. A— Brain doctor." She rolled her eyes.

"Neurologist," he supplied, offering her a smile to let her know there was nothing to be embarrassed about.

"Thank you. She says it's improved since right after I woke up from the coma, but I can't remember that so . . ." She fell silent, then said, "I'm just grateful I remembered Ruby when I woke up. Can you imagine if I had forgotten her?"

James's hands dug into the steering wheel. There had been times over the past five years when he'd wished he couldn't remember Sadie—because if the memories of her disappeared, so would the pain—but he'd always taken the wish back instantly. It wouldn't be worth forgetting the pain if it meant forgetting the joy she'd brought him.

"Is something wrong?" Bethany peered at him.

He shook his head without looking her way. "Just checking the map. Looks like we need to turn . . ." He slowed. "Here."

He eased into the driveway, which was flanked by two stone lions, and pulled to a stop in front of a grand house right on the lakeshore. He whistled. "Cam sure knows how to pick his clients."

Bethany's eyes were huge as she looked up at the house. "Hopefully I won't screw this up."

"Why would you think that?" In spite of her memory issues, she seemed to be an incredibly capable woman.

But Bethany opened her car door and stepped out. James debated getting out too, just to get a better view of the house and the lake, but decided to stay put. This was Bethany's thing. He was only the chauffeur.

Bethany was halfway to the front door when a big guy in a golf shirt emerged. Bill Jespersen, presumably. Bethany held out a hand to the guy, but he ignored it, the boom of his angry voice reaching the car.

Instinct kicked in, and James shoved the car door open, quickly covering the ground between himself and Bethany. "Everything all right?"

Bethany looked over her shoulder, surprise—and possibly annoyance—scribbled across her features. Well, so what? He had a job to do, and it wasn't always making people happy—it was keeping them safe.

"No, it's not." Bill turned to him. "You work for Moore Landscaping too?"

"No." James shuffled closer to Bethany.

"Why would you?" The man threw up his hands in exasperation.

"What seems to be the problem?" James asked patiently. He'd learned in his years on the force that the key to diffusing a temper was remaining calm.

"What's the problem?" Bill shoved past Bethany and strode toward the backyard. James nearly grabbed the guy to remind him to use his manners but instead turned to Bethany to make sure she was all right. But she brushed past him, following Bill around the house. James waited a beat, then stepped in behind her. There was no way he was going to leave her on her own with this dude.

The backyard offered a stunning view of the lake, but Bill was gesturing to a large pallet of stone slabs. "Does this look like what I ordered?"

Bethany's nose crinkled as she examined the stone, and James realized she probably had no recollection of what the guy had ordered.

But James had already admitted that he didn't work for Moore Landscaping. So it wouldn't do any harm for him to ask. "Sorry, what did you order?"

"Slate," Bill spat at him.

"And this is . . ."

"Travertine," Bethany filled in, shooting James a look he decided was gratitude. She pulled out her phone and tapped it a few times, then scrolled for a moment. Finally, she looked up. "Are you sure you decided on the slate? Because our order form shows travertine."

"Your form is wrong." Bill crossed his arms. "And now my project is going to be weeks behind. My daughter is supposed to get married out here in two months, and my wife—"

"Miranda?" Bethany interrupted.

"Yes, my wife Miranda is freaking out about all the details."

"There's a note here that Miranda called to change the order to travertine." Bethany angled her phone so Bill could see it. He yanked it out of her hands, and James took a step closer to Bethany. She gave him a quelling look.

"Just a minute." Bill turned abruptly toward the house, Bethany's phone still clutched in his hand. "Miranda!" he bellowed, making both James and Bethany wince. He yelled the name three more times before he stormed toward the house and yanked open the French doors that looked out over the existing wood patio.

James eyed Bethany. "This guy's a piece of work."

"Why don't you go wait in the car? I've got this." Her tone was pleasant enough, but the stiff way she held her head spoke much more loudly than the words.

"Bethany, this guy is trying to intimidate you." James had seen the way the guy had sized him up when he'd gotten out of the car. He wouldn't do anything as long as James was standing here. But if he wasn't . . .

"I'm perfectly capable of handling this myself." Again the stiffness.

James opened his mouth to argue again, then changed his mind. "I'll be in the car if you need me." He turned back toward the driveway as Bill marched toward Bethany with a woman at his side. The woman, at least, was smiling, which set James a little more at ease.

He rounded the house and got into the car, staring out over the lake and trying not to think about why he felt so protective of Bethany.

It was his job to be a protector. That was all.

You always have to be the hero. His ex-wife's words slapped through his head to the rhythm of the waves hitting the shore.

Still, he remained on alert, listening for any signs of discord from the backyard. It was a good forty-five minutes before Bethany emerged around the side of the house and hurried toward the car. Some of the color that had returned to her face earlier had faded, and she rubbed at her temples.

She gave him a weak smile as she got into the car and fell back against the seat.

"Everything settled?"

"I think so." Bethany sounded exhausted. "Although I think those two may have some issues to work through."

James started the car. "Speaking of issues, I'm sorry if I overstepped. I just didn't like the way that guy was talking to you."

"That's okay." Bethany rubbed her head again. "I've dealt with much worse. I had it under control."

"I'm sure you did. My ex-wife always accused me of having an excessive need to protect people. Called it my hero complex."

Bethany looked at him in surprise. "I didn't know you were married."

Because he never talked about it. So how had she made him let his guard down enough to bring it up? "Yeah." Hopefully his short answer would clue her in that he wasn't interested in talking about it. Because talking about it would lead to talking about why they weren't together anymore. And that would lead to talking about Sadie.

And that he couldn't do.

Thankfully, before they could continue the conversation, Bethany's phone beeped. She pulled it out and read the screen, then squealed. "Cam and Kayla had the baby. It's a girl! Evelyn Rose."

Every muscle in James's neck clenched. *It's a girl.* She'd been so perfect. Ten fingers. Ten toes. Barely a strand of hair. But the sweetest smile, which the nurses said technically wasn't really a smile, but he'd seen it, right from that first moment.

Bethany's fingers flew across her phone, and she practically bounced in her seat. "Ruby is going to be so excited to meet her new cousin." She stopped typing and looked up. "Is that what time it is? Three twenty?"

James's eyes flicked to the dashboard. "I guess so."

"Oh no." Bethany's groan was pained.

"What's wrong?" Immediately his eyes went to her, but she was covering her face with her hands. "Bethany?"

She dropped her hands and scrolled through screens on her phone. "Ruby gets done with school at three. My alarm should have . . ." She made a sound of disgust. "I must have turned it off when I was talking to—uh—what's his name."

"Bill?"

Bethany nodded. "I don't remember turning it off, but that doesn't mean much." She tapped her screen again, then lifted the phone to her ear.

James listened silently as she explained to the person on the other end that she'd be late picking Ruby up, his shoulders tensing unexpectedly as the cutting tone of the woman on the other end came through the phone: "Again?"

Bethany closed her eyes but politely said "yes" and "thank you."

When she hung up, she let out a loud sigh.

"I'm sure she'll be fine," he tried to reassure her.

She frowned. "I know she will be. It's just, none of the other moms need an alarm to remind them to get their kid from school."

"None of the other moms have had to deal with the things you've dealt with."

Bethany's tight smile said she appreciated the words—but didn't believe them. "Do you mind if we swing past the school to get her before we go back to the stables to drop you off?"

James's muscles locked tighter. There was a reason he always declined the captain's requests for volunteers to visit schools. Seeing all those smiling, laughing kids—kids Sadie should be among—gouged him from the inside out.

He shook his head. He couldn't go there right now.

"Otherwise I can just . . ." Bethany said, and James realized he hadn't answered her.

"Yeah," he rasped, against his better judgment. "We can go pick her up."

Bethany directed him to the school, and too soon he was turning into the parking lot. His chest squeezed as if someone had cinched his bullet-proof vest way too tight. There was no room for his lungs to expand.

I had a great day, Daddy. But I missed you.

He pressed his foot to the brake and pulled in a shaky breath. *Compartmentalize.*

At least they were late enough that there were only a couple of kids lingering outside as their moms chatted. He pulled up along the curb and put the car in park.

"I'll be back in a minute." Bethany opened her door and jumped out.

Leaving him to fight the memories on his own.

Chapter 11

Bethany strode toward the school, working hard not to look over her shoulder at James. Was he that annoyed that she'd asked him to pick Ruby up, or was she mistaken about the tension that had rippled through him the moment she'd asked? She sped up. She didn't have time to worry about him right now.

There was only one small cluster of parents out here, their kids running around on the front lawn. Bethany should probably recognize the group of moms—but she wasn't about to stare at them long enough to figure it out. Which didn't keep her from feeling the judgmental looks stabbing into her back. She pressed the buzzer on the school door and announced that she was there to pick up Ruby.

"I'll send her out," the voice on the other end replied.

As Bethany waited, she sneaked a glance over her shoulder to make sure James hadn't left. The car was still at the curb, but James faced the other direction. Even though she couldn't see his face, the tension was clear in the rigid way he sat, his shoulders straining forward as if he could move the car by sheer force of will.

Hurry up, Ruby, she silently urged her daughter. She'd already been enough of a burden to James for one day.

"Bethany," a cheerful, airy voice called out.

Bethany cringed. She'd been so busy watching James that she hadn't noticed one of the women break away from the group and approach her.

The woman's daughter stood next to her in a skirt and matching top that could have come straight out of the pages of one of those designer catalogs. Even her socks and shoes were perfectly coordinated.

"Hey, Kimberly." Fortunately, the daughter's name came easily to Bethany, since she associated her with the riding lessons she and Ruby took together. And that meant the mom was . . .

She searched through the files in her memory as inconspicuously as possible. "Tiffany." She gave herself an internal high-five.

"I'm sorry you weren't able to make it to 'bring your mom to school day' today," Tiffany said. "I hope you don't mind that I let Ruby do the activities with me and Kimberly."

"Bring your mom to school day?" So much for that high-five. She pulled out her phone and scrolled, but it wasn't on her calendar. She'd have to check her notebook when she got home—but she didn't remember ever hearing about it. But then, she supposed chances were high that she wouldn't remember. "I— Um. Thank you." A hole the size of Lake Michigan opened in her stomach. As much as she couldn't remember all the instances she'd let Ruby down, she knew this wasn't the first.

The school door opened, and Ruby burst through, looking cheerful enough as she bounded over to them.

"Hey, Rubes. I'm so sorry I didn't make it to bring your mom to school day. I must not have put it on my calendar. I feel terrible."

"It's fine, Mom."

Bethany studied her daughter. There was something about her expression that made Bethany believe it wasn't as fine as Ruby said. But maybe she didn't want to talk about it in front of her friend. Bethany would be sure to apologize later—as long as she remembered.

"Let's go. James is waiting in the car."

"Really?" Ruby's eyes lit up. "How come?"

But it was too long of a story to get into right now.

"I was just going to check—" Tiffany fell into step next to Bethany, and Kimberly walked next to Ruby, the two girls bending their heads together and giggling. Bethany had a sudden flash of what it had been like to have such uncomplicated relationships as a kid.

Her eyes went to Tiffany, who was still talking. "How are things coming for the field day? Do you need any help?"

Bethany's foot hit the ground wrong, and she stumbled but caught herself before she ended up on her face. The field day. She had started to go through the folder of notes but had gotten overwhelmed and set it aside with the plan to return to it later. Only she'd forgotten all about it—until now.

"It's coming great." If her years as an addict had taught her anything, it was how to tell a convincing lie. Not that she was proud of it. But what other choice did she have? She didn't need to give everyone one more reason to doubt her competence. Besides, she'd start on it when she got home and work on it all week and all weekend, and by Monday it really would be coming along great.

"Oh. Good." Tiffany looked surprised—and skeptical. "Because if you need any help, I can—"

"Thanks. I've got it." They reached the car, and Bethany opened the back door, gesturing Ruby in.

"See you Friday for the trip to the water park," Tiffany said to Ruby. Then she turned to Bethany. "You got all the details I texted you, right?"

"Um. Yes?" At least if Tiffany had sent them, there was no reason Bethany shouldn't have gotten them.

"Great. We'll leave right from school, so remember to bring your bag," she said to Ruby, as if the ten-year-old was the responsible one here. "We'll probably be back early Sunday afternoon."

"Oh, but—" Two days was a long time. What if Ruby got homesick or something? But watching her daughter wave excitedly from the back seat as Tiffany and Kimberly walked away, Bethany knew it wasn't her daughter who would be homesick. It was her.

"And they have three pools and ten water slides. They sound scary, but Kimberly says they're so, so, so fun."

James could barely keep up with Ruby's chatter—which hadn't stopped since they'd left the school. But Bethany seemed lost in thought, which had left James to respond to the girl.

"Oh," he grunted now.

"Have you ever been to a water park?" In the rearview mirror, he could see Ruby wriggling in her seat, and he glanced to make sure her seatbelt was still in position.

"Once." The tension in his shoulders cranked tighter. Sadie had been too young to do much more than wade in the kiddie pool, but she'd loved it. James had told her she'd be a dolphin when she grew up, which had made her giggle. His jaw locked, and his throat convulsed. *When* she grew up—it had never seemed like it should be a question of *if*.

"Did you like it?" Ruby pressed.

"Yes." James barely got the word past his gritted teeth.

He looked to Bethany. Perhaps she wanted to take over the conversation? Since it was her daughter, not his?

Apparently sensing his eyes on her, Bethany sat up. "Hey, Rubes? I'm really sorry again that I didn't come to bring your mom to school day. I don't know how I missed it."

"I told you, it's fine, Mom."

"No it's not. It should have been in my calendar, but . . . I don't know what happened. When did you give me the sheet about it?"

"Uhhh . . . a couple weeks ago?"

James had been a detective long enough to spot a lie when he heard one. A quick glance in the mirror showed Ruby was toying with a thread on her shirt, not looking at her mom.

"It's so weird," Bethany muttered again. "But I promise I'll make it up to you. Maybe some ice cream for dessert tonight?"

"It's okay, Mom. You don't have to make it up to me. It was a lame day."

Another lie. And that was definitely guilt in her eyes. But why?

James glanced at Bethany, who still looked troubled.

"So what did you two do today?" Ruby asked, as if she didn't find it the least bit unusual that he was driving her mom's car and had come along to pick her up from school.

"We went riding," Bethany said. "And then we had to go to see a client for Uncle Cam because—" She gasped. "I can't believe I forgot to tell you. You have a baby cousin!"

"What?"

James hadn't realized little girls' voices could go that high.

"Is it a girl like I thought? What's her name?"

"Um . . . I think it's a girl." Bethany picked up her phone.

"Evelyn Rose." The answer came out before James could think it through.

What should we name her?

It doesn't matter. As long as we get to keep her.

"James?" Bethany's voice cut through the memory.

"Sorry. What?"

"I was just asking if you were going to turn, because you passed the driveway."

"Oops. Sorry. I'll turn around." He pulled into the driveway of Hidden Blossom Farms, the cherry orchard down the road, owned by some of Emma's friends. Already, tiny buds of green and white dotted the branches. James glanced away from the signs of life and accelerated faster than was probably necessary back toward the driveway to the stables. He had to get out of this car—away from this reminder of what it had felt like to have a family.

The instant he pulled up in front of the house, he slammed the car into park and opened his door. Bethany got out too, crossing in front of the car, toward the driver's side.

She stopped directly in front of him. "Thank you for driving."

"Don't mention it. You're good now?" He let himself study her face, relieved that she looked fine.

"Much better, thank you. I don't know what I would have done if—"

"No problem." He gave a curt nod, waiting for her to move out of the way.

"Is everything okay?" She peered at him closely, as if searching for something. "You seem . . ."

"Nope. Everything's good." He pushed past her and sprinted up the porch steps and into the house.

Inside, he grabbed a glass and filled it to the top with water, then downed it in one gulp.

"Thirsty?" Emma popped into the room, chuckling.

He set the glass down. But the water had done nothing to wash away the mixed up jumble of Melissa and Sadie and Bethany and Ruby in his head.

"So . . ." Emma raised her eyebrows at him. "It looks like you and Bethany made a day of it. Aren't you glad I suggested you go riding?"

"Ah, let's see. She got vertigo and almost passed out."

"What?" Emma gasped. "Is she okay?"

"She is now, but it took a while. I had to drive her to take care of a client because Cam and Kayla were having their baby."

"I saw that! I'm so excited for them." Emma's eyes were bright, and James could tell she meant what she said, even though she had often wished for children of her own. That just made her a better person than him—but that was no surprise. "Anyway, the client was a total jerk." He wished he'd clocked the guy for the way he'd spoken to Bethany. "And that took forever, so then we had to go pick Ruby up from school. And Ruby talked all the way home."

Emma laughed. "That sounds like Ruby. She's always reminded me of—"

"Don't," James cut in sharply. He knew exactly who Ruby reminded her of because she reminded him of the same person. But Ruby would never be Sadie.

"You can't just never talk about her, James. It's not healthy."

He grunted.

"You like Bethany," Emma pressed. "I can tell."

James shook his head. He was not getting into this with his sister. It didn't matter *what* he felt about Bethany. She had a kid. And that was a deal breaker.

"Seriously, James. What are you going to do? Spend the rest of your life alone?"

"You're alone," he pointed out.

"Thanks for the reminder," Emma said dryly, and he sighed. That had been unfair. He knew how much Emma had always wanted a big family of her own.

"I'm sorry." He crossed his arms and leaned against the counter. "I'm just saying, I'm perfectly happy on my own."

Emma's gaze held his. "You're not happy, James. And sometimes I think you want to stay that way."

He shrugged. It didn't make much of a difference whether he was happy or miserable.

"It's okay to move on, you know," Emma said gently. "Melissa called me the other day. She's remarried and—"

He held up a hand. He already knew his ex-wife had moved on. Ironic, since she'd been the one who'd complained that he'd gone back to work too soon after Sadie.

He didn't begrudge her for wanting a new family. But that didn't mean he wanted the same thing. Losing everything once was more than enough.

Emma's hands went to her hips. "Is this how you think Sadie would want to see her dad? Afraid to smile or laugh or be happy for a single minute because she's not here? Your misery can't bring her back, you know. So don't you think it's time to start living this life God has given you? Before it's too late?" She tried to stare him down, but James turned away.

Because he knew she was wrong. If God wanted him to live this life, then he shouldn't have asked him to live it without Sadie.

Chapter 12

"So are you going to see James today?"

Ruby's question caught Bethany off guard, and she accidentally pressed the accelerator harder than she meant to, making the car lurch forward.

"I don't know. Why?" But she couldn't pretend she hadn't felt the lurch in her stomach as well as the car.

"He's nice. You should ask him on a date."

"What? Ruby!" Now she braked faster than she meant to. Good grief. She was going to crash yet if Ruby kept talking such nonsense. "We're just friends." If that. Sometimes she couldn't tell. "Do you have your toothbrush?" It was high time to change the subject.

"Yep. And my swimming suit. And a towel. And pajamas. And clothes. And socks and underwear."

Bethany tried to recall what else had been on the list she'd made for Ruby. She still wasn't one hundred percent comfortable with being away from her daughter all weekend, but she couldn't very well withdraw her permission now. She knew Ruby would be in good hands—Tiffany was surely a more competent mom than Bethany would ever be—but she couldn't help feeling like it was a big step toward Ruby's independence. One Ruby might be ready for but Bethany definitely was not.

"And Kimberly's present," Ruby added.

Right. A present. At least Ruby was on top of things.

Bethany pulled into the school parking lot, glancing at the clock. They had five minutes to spare today, which might be a new record.

Tiffany waved to them from behind a car parked near the school, and Bethany pulled into the spot next to her.

"Oh good, you made it." Tiffany pounced on them the moment they got out of the car. "Kimberly already went inside. Ruby, why don't you go ahead too so you're not late. I'll get your stuff from your mom."

Bethany bristled. They were early today, thank you very much.

Ruby popped her arm through the strap of her backpack and turned toward the school.

"Ruby." Bethany didn't mean for her voice to come out harsh like that, but was her daughter really going to leave without saying goodbye?

Ruby turned around and Bethany held out her arms for a hug. With a not-so-subtle check of the parking lot, Ruby gave Bethany the briefest hug in the history of hugs. Then, with a cheerful "bye," she bounded toward the school.

"Have fun," Bethany called after her. "And be careful. Listen to Ms. . . ."

"Stemple," Tiffany filled in.

"I know. Listen to Ms. Stemple."

"I will. Bye, Mom. Have fun with James."

"I— Ruby—"

But with one last giggle, Ruby disappeared into the crowd of students surging for the door. Bethany could only sigh and watch her.

"They grow up too fast, don't they?" Tiffany came up next to her. "You're lucky. Kimberly stopped letting me hug her in public a year ago. No one ever tells you how hard it's going to be."

Bethany shook her head and opened the trunk of her car. Tiffany was clearly only saying that for Bethany's benefit. There was no way Miss Mom-of-the-Year had any concept of how hard it really was.

She pulled Ruby's bag and pillow out of the trunk and passed them to Tiffany, who loaded them into her SUV's already stuffed cargo area.

"That too?" Tiffany pointed into the trunk.

Duh. The present. Bethany reached for it. Ruby never would have forgiven her if she'd forgotten that.

Tiffany tucked the gift into the last remaining pocket of space in the SUV, then closed the hatch.

"So who's James?" Tiffany's voice pitched up, and she nudged Bethany. "The guy you were here with the other day? I've seen him around the stables."

"Oh. Um. Yeah. He's Emma Wood's brother."

"So you two are . . ."

Bethany stared at her. They were what?

"Together?" Tiffany concluded with a laugh.

"Oh." Bethany ignored the jump in her heartbeat. "Of course not. He was just— It's a long story."

Tiffany smiled, but Bethany wasn't sure she liked the way the other woman's eyes had lit up when she'd learned James and Bethany weren't together. "Well, I'd better get going. Enjoy your weekend to yourself."

"I will." But as she backed out of the parking spot, the word *yourself* hung heavily over Bethany. She knew she should probably be looking forward to some time alone, but the house was going to be so empty without Ruby. Maybe she'd invite her friends over for dinner tomorrow night. Cam and Kayla could bring baby Evelyn to meet everyone. A wave of nostalgia went through her as she directed her car toward home. She hadn't had anyone to introduce Ruby to when she was born. It was just the two of them against the world. She shook off the regret. They were surrounded by wonderful friends and family now. She cranked up the volume on the Christian radio station. Songs were one of the few things she could remember easily, and listening to them in the car usually meant that they'd stay with her for the rest of the day—a tangible reminder of God's love to carry inside her. It didn't take long before the music soothed her. Ruby would be fine. She would be fine. And in two days, they'd be together again. She blew out a breath. That wasn't so long.

The ringing of her phone cut through the music as Bethany pulled into her driveway. She glanced at the screen, smiling as baby Evelyn's picture came up. It hadn't taken Cam long to change his profile.

"Hey. I was just about to call and invite you all over for dinner tomorrow. Let baby Evelyn meet everyone."

"Sure. That would be great." Cam sounded exhausted but happy. "But listen, I was thinking, maybe you should show the mayor some options in limestone too. I know he doesn't . . ."

But Bethany missed the rest of Cam's sentence as she yanked the phone away from her ear to check her calendar.

Show samples to mayor, 9 a.m.

And now she remembered. When she'd gone to visit Cam and Kayla and baby Evelyn at the hospital the other day, Cam had asked if she could cover this meeting to show the mayor samples for the big marina job. And she'd said yes, of course she could.

Her gaze flicked to the time. 8:48. The pole shed Cam had recently built on the outskirts of town was only a ten-minute drive from here. She could make it.

She hit the speaker button on her phone and restarted the car.

" . . . think he'll wish he'd gone with something that matches the shoreline," Cam was saying.

"Absolutely." Bethany checked over her shoulder as she backed out of the driveway. "Match the shoreline. Got it."

"Thanks, Bethany. You're a lifesaver." A lusty baby cry cut through the phone. "Shh. It's okay," Cam cooed, and Bethany couldn't help grinning as she pushed her foot to the accelerator. That little baby already had her daddy's complete adoration.

But as soon as they hung up, her grin faded and the worry worked its way in. She'd forgotten the meeting. What made her think she wouldn't mess this whole thing up?

She shook her head. She wouldn't mess up. This was too important to Cam. She could do this.

But more questions wiggled into the cracks in her pep talk. What if she forgot to show the mayor the options Cam wanted? What if she forgot to take notes? Or took bad notes? Or— She forced herself to stop that line of thinking.

She was looking in the wrong place. She didn't need a pep talk. She needed a prayer.

Please give me the strength to do this, Lord. Please help me remember—

The prayer died on her lips as she spotted the brand-new wooden sign in front of Cam's building. Slashes of ugly red spray paint cut through the bright green letters that spelled out Moore Landscaping. She eased into the driveway, her hand going to her mouth. The same red spelled out a profane word against the bright white of the building's aluminum siding, and the window of her brother's office hung with jagged glass. In front of the building, Cam's work truck was also covered with spray paint and tilted at an odd angle, one tire completely flat.

Bethany's mind went blank, though she continued through the gravel parking lot toward the door. What was going on? What should she do?

Before she could decide, a black car tore around the far side of the building, spraying gravel as it gunned through the parking lot. Bethany slammed on the brake, freezing as the car ripped past her. She caught a glimpse of two young men before the car squealed out of the driveway.

Hands shaking, breath rasping, Bethany slid the car into park and pulled out her phone. Who should she call first: Cam or the police?

Dread hammered her ribs as she dialed Cam's number.

"Hey. So I guess—"

"Cam." Her voice froze up. She couldn't tell him.

"He didn't like the stone," Cam continued, and she wondered if maybe she hadn't said his name out loud after all. "Did you tell him—"

"Cam!" She said it loudly enough to make herself jump.

"What's wrong?" His voice became all seriousness, and she was suddenly reminded yet again of how much he had become like their dad.

"I don't know. There was this car. These people . . . They—" She halted, unable to get her thoughts straight. What was the word she needed?

"Wait. Bethany. Slow down. What people? Where?" Cam spoke slowly, and she knew he was trying to help her, but it only made her more frantic. Didn't he see how urgent this was?

"Here. Your building. The sign. The truck. They trashed it."

"Are you all right?" Urgency pulsed in Cam's voice.

"I'm fine. But, Cam—"

"I'll be right there. Just stay put. I'll call the police on my way."

Chapter 13

James patted Fancy Lady's side as he led her to the pasture. Maybe he'd take her out for a ride when he was done mucking. The thought made him lonely, and an image of Bethany slipped into his head. But she wasn't likely to be riding again anytime soon—not after almost falling off Ace the other day. His stomach turned every time he thought of it—followed immediately by the desire to find out how she was doing, make sure she'd seen her doctor about it. But he reminded himself that he wasn't supposed to care—that he *didn't* care. Caring was too dangerous.

He rubbed his hands over Fancy Lady's mane, then turned back to the barn. He'd just gotten started on the first stall when Emma rushed in.

"Morning, sleepyhead." Though she was usually the most chipper of morning birds, she'd still been sleeping when he'd gotten up. "I thought maybe you decided to take—" He caught a glimpse of Emma's face. "What's wrong?"

"Cam and Kayla's business was vandalized."

James let out a sharp breath. He'd been afraid it was something terrible, the way Emma looked. Though he supposed in Hope Springs vandalism was probably a relatively bigger deal than in Milwaukee—if only because it was rarer.

"The police are over there now," Emma said. "But I know they're really understaffed, and I thought maybe you could . . ."

But James was already shaking his head. Much as he hated to know someone was in trouble and not assist, this was way out of his jurisdiction.

"Bethany was there." Emma leveled her gaze at him. "The vandals almost crashed into her."

"What?" The shovel clanged as he shoved it against the wall. "Is she all right? Did you talk to her?"

"Kayla texted me, but I haven't been able to reach Bethany. She's probably talking to the police. But you—"

"What's the address?"

"701 Willowbrook. It's on the outskirts of town, over by the—"

"Got it." He'd already brought up a map on his phone. He jogged toward the door.

"James, wait."

He made an impatient sound but turned to see what his sister wanted.

"Tell them I'm praying for them."

He grunted, then jogged to his truck. His tires squealed as he pulled onto the road, and he pushed the truck faster than he should considering he wasn't in his squad car with the siren on. But if the department was understaffed, they probably didn't have anyone out patrolling.

The law's the law, son. No one is above it. His dad's voice jabbed against the inside of his skull. He eased his foot off the accelerator. But the need to see for himself that Bethany was okay pushed his foot back toward the floor.

"Sorry, Dad," he muttered.

The map had said it would take twenty minutes to get to the location, but James made it in thirteen. He slowed as he pulled into the driveway, anger hardening in his gut at the red paint covering the sign and building and truck.

A small cluster of people stood in front of the pole shed, and James searched them for—

A sharp stab of relief went through him as Bethany turned toward his truck. Her eyes widened, and she lifted a hand as he stopped the truck and jumped out.

He only barely resisted pulling her into a rough hug when he reached the group. Instead, he contented himself with a quick scan to verify she didn't have any injuries.

"James." Cam held out a hand, and James shook it. "Thanks for coming."

He couldn't take his eyes off Bethany. "You okay?"

She nodded, and he let himself breathe again.

"What are you doing here?" Her voice shook slightly—enough to make him resolve to catch whoever had done this.

"Emma told me what happened. I thought I'd see if there was anything I could do to help." He turned to the uniformed officer standing at Bethany's side and held out a hand. "Detective Wood, Milwaukee PD. I'm here on . . . vacation. But if you can put me to use, I'm happy to help out."

The officer eyed him before shaking his hand. "Captain Perry. We don't have much to go on. The vandals were here when Bethany got here this morning. She says she saw them, but she can't remember what kind of car they drove or what they looked like or how many there were." The captain's eyes slid to Bethany, and James recognized the look. Suspicion.

He stepped closer to Bethany.

Her body was rigid, hands clenched. "I'm sorry. I can't . . . remember. I'm trying." Her dark eyes swept to him, and he nearly took her hands in his. He moved toward the building instead, surveying the scene.

"At least it's not gang related." He peered at the artless bubble letters that formed the word.

"What makes you say that?" An older gentleman in khaki pants and a golf shirt stepped up beside him.

"Sorry." Cam stepped forward. "Mr. Mayor, this is James Wood, Emma Wood's brother. James, this is Mayor Harding."

James shook the mayor's hand, then pointed to the graffiti. "Gang graffiti is ugly. Plain paint, thin lines, gang tags and symbols. This isn't exactly the height of artistic ability, but you can tell they were trying. Probably some local kids. A prank or a dare. Have you crossed paths with any kids who might have had something against you?" he asked Cam.

Cam looked at him helplessly. "Not that I can think of. You think it was targeted?"

"Who would do that?" Bethany asked.

The captain peered at her again. "You're sure you don't remember anything?"

Bethany stared at the parking lot, as if trying to see a replay of the events, but after a moment, she shook her head. "It happened so fast," she whispered.

James moved toward the broken window. "Is anything missing?"

"A couple of leaf blowers from my truck, a hedge trimmer, and some solar lights." Cam scrubbed a hand over his face. "Thankfully, I had my laptop with me, and we don't keep any cash on site."

"Good. That's good." James glanced at Bethany, who was running her hands up and down her arms as if she was cold, despite the sunshine.

The captain's radio crackled and he stepped away from the group. James prowled the perimeter of the building. But aside from some scuffed up gravel with no clear shoe prints, the vandals had left no evidence.

The captain returned to them. "I've got an accident across town. I'll send you a copy of my report for insurance. We'll devote as many resources to this as we can, but we're down to two officers. Unless some evidence turns up . . ."

"I understand. Thanks." Cam shook the captain's hand. "We appreciate anything you can do."

"I'd better go get on the phone with the insurance company," Cam said as the captain drove away. "Mr. Mayor, I'm afraid we'll have to reschedule."

"Of course." The mayor clapped Cam on the shoulder. "I don't know what the world is coming to when things like this happen in Hope Springs." He turned to Bethany, who was still rubbing her arms. "I'm glad you're okay." And then to James, "Anything you can do to help is appreciated."

James nodded in surprise. He'd fully expected the same jurisdictional grandstanding he usually ran into.

The mayor got into his car and Cam went inside the building. And then it was only James and Bethany.

"Are you cold?" James moved closer, pulling off his flannel shirt and holding it out to her. A cool breeze cut through his t-shirt.

She looked at the flannel but didn't take it. "I can't . . . I know I saw them, but I can't remember. I keep trying, but . . ."

"It's okay." He settled the shirt over her shoulders, then planted himself directly in front of her. "Where were you when you saw them?"

Bethany's lips pressed into a line, and concentration creased her forehead. After a moment, she threw a hand in the air and pointed to the far side of the parking area. "Over there. I had just pulled in and I saw the graffiti and I didn't know what to do."

"Good. That's good." He took her hand and tugged her toward the spot she'd indicated. Reenacting a scene often helped to jog a witness's memory. Cold radiated from her fingers, and he was tempted to wrap his other hand around them too, to warm them. Instead, he let go as soon as they got to the spot. "You were here?"

"They came around that corner so fast. I was afraid they were going to crash into me." Her voice shook, and he pressed his hands into his pockets so he wouldn't take hers again.

"What kind of vehicle were they driving? What color was it?"

Bethany sighed. "I don't remember."

"That's okay." He kept his voice even. "Close your eyes." He waited for her to comply. "Here they come. They're tearing around that building. They're in a—"

Bethany's eyes popped open. "A car."

She grinned at him in triumph. "They were in a car. A small one. Sporty, I think."

"Good." A small car. That wasn't much to go on. But he needed to keep the momentum going. "What color is it?"

Bethany closed her eyes again, this time looking less tense. But it wasn't long before she opened them, frowning. "I can't remember. Dark, I think. Maybe blue? Or black?"

He didn't know how accurate he could expect her information to be—but it was better than nothing. Probably. "Does anything else stand out about it? A bumper sticker? License plate? Maybe a dent or something?"

Bethany shook her head but then closed her eyes, her brow furrowing. After a moment, she drew in a sharp breath and opened her eyes. "It made a funny sound. Like a whining noise."

"That's great. Good job." An identifying marker, something easy to spot, would have been better, but he wasn't about to tell her that. "Do you remember anything about the driver? How many people were in the car?"

Bethany shook her head but then stopped. "Wait. Yes. There were two of them, I think. Young."

"Boys?"

Bethany nodded. "Do you think you'll be able to find them?" Hope warmed her voice, and he wanted nothing so badly as to tell her yes.

But false hope could be worse than no hope at all. That much he knew for certain. So he gave her the only answer he could: "I'm going to try."

Chapter 14

She didn't want James to leave.

Bethany stood next to him, the warmth of his flannel shirt soft and comforting against her shoulders.

He made her feel safe. He helped her remember.

She tried to come up with another detail so he'd have a reason to stay, even after he'd finished searching the whole place, inside and out, and helping Cam board up the broken window.

"You're sure you're okay?" he asked.

Bethany smiled. Even *she* remembered that it wasn't the first time he'd asked since he'd gotten here. "I'm fine."

"And your vertigo from the other day?" he pressed. "Did you talk to your doctor about it?"

"I called. She said it was to be expected. She'll check me at my next appointment."

Worry still edged James's eyes, and Bethany laid a hand on his arm. "Thank you. For helping Cam and Kayla. It means a lot."

"Of course." James stared at the spot where her fingers rested on his skin, and she lowered her hand. Touching him had been unnecessary. But nice.

"I'm going to drive around town," he said. "See if I can spot anything. If it was a couple of kids, they're probably trying to figure out what to do with all the stuff they just scored."

"I'll come with you." The words popped impulsively out of her mouth. But she couldn't just sit here.

James frowned. "Absolutely not. No."

"I wasn't asking." She folded her arms in front of her and gave him her sternest look, which admittedly probably wasn't very intimidating to him, though it worked wonders when Ruby was misbehaving.

James shook his head. "It could be dangerous."

"You said it was a couple of kids. And anyway, maybe I'll recognize them if I see them."

James opened his mouth, then hesitated. But Bethany knew what he'd been about to say—how was she going to recognize them when she couldn't remember what they looked like?

"Plus," she added, "how are you going to know the sound I heard? I remember sounds better than anything else." She wasn't completely useless.

James sighed but nodded. "You have a point. But you do exactly what I say. No impulse control issues, okay?"

"I promise. Just let me go check on Cam quick." She was halfway to the door when she spun and pointed at him. "And don't even think of leaving without me."

"Wouldn't dream of it." The faintest hint of a smile found its way to his lips.

Bethany continued into the building, pausing to listen for Cam's voice. He'd been on the phone with the insurance company several times already this morning. But he must have finally gotten everything squared away because silence hung over the lawn mowers and gardening equipment that filled the garage space. She made her way to his small office.

But when she reached it, she stopped short. Her brother sat at his desk, head in his hands.

A memory slammed her—the same image, only instead of Cam it had been her father. *Why, Bethany? You know we would have given you anything you needed.*

Cam looked up, offering her a smile worn thin at the edges.

"Cam. I'm so sorry. I wish . . ."

"It's not your fault," he said firmly. He pushed back his chair and strode around the desk to pull her into a hug.

The movement was so unexpected that it took a second for Bethany to return the gesture. Though she knew he had forgiven her for the way she'd destroyed their family, he was rarely demonstrative like this. And she didn't blame him. This may not have been her fault, but she couldn't say the same for what had happened to their father's business.

"I'm just glad you're okay." He squeezed harder, then let go, looking her up and down. "You're sure you *are* okay, right?"

She nodded with an attempt at a laugh. "Scared the daylights out of me, but other than that I'm good. You?" She took a turn scrutinizing him. "You look exhausted."

"Someone could have warned me that babies don't believe in sleep."

Bethany laughed. "How are Kayla and Evelyn doing?"

"Good. I just called, and Kayla said Evelyn finally went down for a nap." He glanced toward the boarded up window. "I wish she wouldn't have to worry about this. She has enough . . ."

"Cam, your wife is the strongest woman I know. She can handle it."

"I know." He shook his head with a short laugh. "I called planning to tell her that everything would be all right, and instead, she was the one who ended up reassuring me."

"That's what partners are for." Or so she assumed. She'd certainly imagined more than once how nice that would be. She looked over her shoulder toward the door. Hopefully James had kept his promise not to leave without her. "There's nothing else you can do here. Why don't you go home and take care of your family. I'm going to go ride around town with James and see if I can recognize the guys who did this."

"Did you remember something?" Cam's eyes sparked with hope.

"Not much. But maybe if I see them again. Or hear their car . . ."

"I don't know, Bethany. That could be dangerous." Cam's voice took on that big-brother protective tone he'd adopted since her accident, even though she was the older sibling.

"I'll be with James. He's a cop. Nothing's going to happen to me."

Cam squeezed her arm. "All right. Be careful."

Bethany headed for the door. But as she stepped outside and spotted James, she had to slightly amend her promise to her brother. Nothing would happen to her physically, that she was sure of. But she couldn't be quite as certain about her heart.

Chapter 15

James massaged a kink in the back of his neck and glanced toward Bethany, who peered intently out her open window. They'd circled the entire town five times and driven out into the countryside on either end, but so far they'd come up empty.

How did he break it to her that this was pointless?

"What about that car?" Bethany gestured excitedly toward a black sedan down the block.

"It's pretty big." James failed to mask his frustration. She'd said it was a small car, and yet this was the seventh larger car she'd pointed out. Was she having doubts about the accuracy of her memories? Because he was.

"Let's just check." She leaned forward as James eased the truck closer to the car. "Are there two people in there?"

The car turned at the intersection in front of them, and James spotted an older lady—driving alone.

"I don't think it was her." He rubbed at his neck again.

"No." Bethany sank back into her seat. "Sorry. Again."

"It's okay." He almost reached to pat her arm but gripped the wheel tighter instead. "Driving around was always a long shot." He pulled into the driveway of the hardware store.

Bethany turned to him. "What are we doing?"

We.

James swallowed. He couldn't let himself enjoy the ring of that word. "If they bought the spray paint here, maybe someone will remember them."

"Smart." Bethany perked back up.

He shrugged. "We don't have a warrant, so . . ." Wait. Had he said *we* too? He opened his door. "But it's a small town. People like to talk. Maybe we'll get lucky."

He waited for Bethany to hop down from the truck, then kept an arm's length away from her as they strode toward the building. But he had to get closer to open the door for her, and her peach scent drifted past him, making him want to lean in. He waited until she was half a dozen steps into the store to follow.

"Where should we start?" She'd stopped to wait for him, and he couldn't avoid stepping close to her to keep from getting run over by a guy with a shopping cart.

He edged away as soon as shopping-cart-guy was gone. The smell of tire and grease drove out Bethany's sweet scent and made it possible to think again. "Over there." He pointed toward a man standing at the end of a row of checkout counters. Probably a manager of some sort.

"Excuse me," James called to the guy as they approached. "I'm Detective Wood. I was wondering if you remember anyone buying some red spray paint recently. Maybe two younger men?"

The manager eyed him, perhaps looking for a badge. There was a reason James hadn't specified his police department.

"Not that I remember," the guy said at last. "But I've been off for the past week. You can talk to Cheryl. She's always here." He pointed to a white-haired woman who was chatting with a young couple as she slowly rang up their purchases.

James and Bethany got in line behind them.

"Are you remodeling?" the cashier asked the couple.

"Sort of." The woman's smile was radiant as she looked to her husband and pressed a hand to her middle. "We're converting a room into a nursery."

"Congratulations!" The cashier stopped scanning their items to beam at them. "Is it your first?"

"Yep. Is it that obvious?" The man wrapped an arm around his wife's shoulders and dropped a kiss on top of her head.

James angled his face away, studying the packs of gum lining the end caps. Melissa had had terrible morning sickness throughout her entire pregnancy, so James had prepared the nursery himself—a sunny yellow that he later told Sadie was the reason she was such a cheerful baby.

"Really, Daddy?" she'd asked.

He'd laughed, tapped her nose, and told her no, it was actually because God had made her his little bundle of sunshine.

He still didn't understand why God had . . .

"James?" A hand on his shoulder made him jump. "Sorry." Bethany let go and gestured toward the cashier, who was waiting for them.

James blinked, relaxing his cramped fingers. With supreme effort, he summoned what he hoped would pass for a smile. "Cheryl?"

At the woman's nod, he moved forward. "Sorry to bother you." He glanced over his shoulder to make sure there was no one in line behind them. "I'm Detective Wood. I'm wondering if you might have seen a couple of young men buying red spray paint recently?"

Cheryl looked toward her manager, then down at her hands, which she had twisted together. "I'm sorry. I know I shouldn't have sold to them. They didn't have IDs, but they promised they were over 18. You're not going to arrest me, are you?"

"Of course not," Bethany cut in.

James glanced at her, then at Cheryl. "Do you happen to remember anything about them? What they looked like?"

"I . . ." Cheryl stared at her hands. "I don't think so."

"Please." Bethany slid closer to James and leaned toward the woman. "I know how hard it can be to remember, but this is really important. Maybe if you close your eyes." She glanced at James. "It helped me."

Cheryl looked from Bethany to James, who nodded. Slowly, she closed her eyes. Both James and Bethany leaned in, and Bethany's hair brushed James's arm. He didn't move.

"Wait!" Cheryl's shout made both of them jump. At least Bethany's hair was no longer silky against his skin.

"One had a scar right here." She drew a line above her eyebrow. "He seemed to be the leader. The other one was small and mousy. I felt sorry for him, to tell you the truth."

"Great. That's really great." Bethany reached across the counter and clasped the woman's hand. "Right?" She turned to James with a brilliant smile.

"It's good." James tried to temper her hope. They still had no idea where to look for these guys—if they even were the culprits. Buying spray paint didn't make them guilty of vandalism.

"Anything else?" James asked Cheryl. "Have you seen them before?"

This time, Cheryl closed her eyes without prompting. Bethany gave James a hopeful look, and he tried to put on an encouraging expression.

But after a minute, Cheryl opened her eyes. "I'm sorry. I don't think I've ever seen them around here before."

"And what day did they come in?"

Cheryl thought. "Sunday, I think. Or maybe Monday."

A guy with a cart full of plumbing parts approached the lane.

"Thank you. If you think of anything else, you can give me a call." James pulled out a card and passed it to her.

"Milwaukee?"

"Just helping out. You can reach me on my cell." The last thing he needed was for his captain to find out he was working a case way outside his jurisdiction—while on a forced vacation.

"And next time, make sure to get an ID," he warned.

Cheryl nodded. "I will."

On the way out of the store, he stopped to ask the manager about security footage, but the manager insisted they didn't have any. Which meant either the guy was holding out for a warrant—or he didn't feel it was necessary to have security cameras in a town as safe as Hope Springs.

"That was so great," Bethany bubbled as they exited the store. "Now we know what the guys look like."

"But not where to find them."

"True." Bethany frowned. "So what next?"

"There's not much else we can do." There he went with that *we* again. "I'll take you back to the shop so you can get your car."

"Wait. That's it? We're giving up?" Bethany crossed her arms as she waited for him to unlock the truck.

He pulled her door open. This was the part of police work he hated—hitting a dead end and knowing there was nothing he could do about it. "I'm sorry. I wish there was something else—"

"Let's at least drive around some more. Hope Springs isn't that big. They have to be here somewhere."

But that was just it. They could be anywhere. Including out of town. "The chances that we'll find them—"

"Please, James." Bethany reached for his arm. "Cam has done so much for me. I have to help him."

He had to say no. It was a fool's errand.

"All right." He puffed out his cheeks and expelled a breath. Apparently, he was willing to be a fool for her.

"Thank you." Bethany flung her arms around his neck and squeezed, then climbed into the truck before he could unfreeze.

"Sorry." But her smile didn't slip.

"That's okay," he croaked. Why could he still feel the imprint of her arms around him?

He closed the door and rounded the truck to the driver's side, getting himself composed on the short walk. Her hug had been nothing but a lack of impulse control, he reminded himself.

And his reaction had been . . . also a lack of impulse control.

He pulled his door open and climbed in, her grateful smile melting him the moment he looked in her direction.

"One condition." He started the truck and pulled out of the parking spot.

"What's that?"

"We get some food. I could eat a horse."

"Don't let your sister hear you say that."

He chuckled at her unexpectedly quick comeback.

"How about the Chocolate Chicken?" She opened her window as he pulled into the street, again peering intently at every passing car.

"Ice cream for lunch? Don't let Emma hear *you* say *that*."

Bethany's laugh filled the truck and seemed to seep in through his skin, filtering toward his heart.

"Wait! Did you hear that?" Bethany's face wore sharp concentration, and she swiveled her head back and forth.

"Hear what?"

"That whine. That's it!" She clutched his arm. "I'm sure of it."

James slowed the truck, listening. "I don't hear—"

"Shh." She pulled her hand off his arm to put a finger in front of her lips. "I heard it."

"Where?"

Her head swiveled more. "I don't know. Back there. Can you turn around?"

James bit back his doubts that she'd actually heard anything and turned the truck around, easing it slowly in the direction they'd come from.

"There." She pointed down a side street toward a small black car pulling into a driveway. "Hear that?"

But the car stopped, and James had to shake his head. Still, it might be worth getting a look at whoever had been in the car. He turned onto the street and sped toward the driveway. If whoever was in the car entered the house before James and Bethany got there, there'd be nothing he could do.

He pulled up along the curb as two guys got out of the car.

"There are two of them," Bethany breathed.

James put the truck in park. "Stay here." He strode casually toward the driveway. The guy who'd gotten out on the passenger side glanced toward him, then away.

"Excuse me," James called.

The kid looked his way again. James supposed he could be described as small and mousy. "Yeah?"

"I'm looking for Moore Landscaping. Can you tell me how to get there?"

Fear flickered in the kid's eyes, and his mouth tightened. "Moore Landscaping?" His voice squeaked an octave higher.

"Never heard of it." The bigger kid came down the driveway. "Sorry we can't help you." The scar above his eyebrow lifted as he directed a look at his friend. "We gotta get going." He raised a hand to scratch his nose, and James spotted the red rimming his fingernails.

Gotcha.

He allowed himself a slow, triumphant smile. "So you weren't over there earlier this morning?" he asked casually.

The small boy gulped loudly enough that Bethany probably heard it from the truck, but the bigger boy grabbed his friend's arm and pulled. "I said we gotta go."

The smaller boy tripped, catching himself at the last second.

"What's the rush?" James asked. He stepped closer to the car and peered into the back seat. "You two planning on doing some landscaping?" He pointed to the solar lights that covered the seat.

"That's my dad's stuff." The older boy smirked.

James smirked right back. "And I suppose the leaf blowers and trimmers are your dad's too?" He kept his eyes on the boys but raised his voice. "Bethany, could you call Captain Perry? These are our guys."

Both boys' eyes widened. The bigger one stepped toward the car, but James blocked him.

The smaller boy cowered. "Chris, maybe we should—"

"Shut up, Pete."

James smiled. Now he had names to put to the faces.

"You're not going to get far if you run. I'm pretty fast." He directed his comments to Pete. "Your best bet is to tell me what's going on."

"We were—"

"Shut up." Chris shoved his friend hard enough to knock him to the ground.

"Hey. That's enough." James sidled closer, getting a better read on the bigger boy. He was scared but afraid to show it—which made him act with a bravado James knew he didn't really possess. And which could make him do something stupid—especially if he was armed.

"Look. I get it." He kept an eye on Chris but spoke to Pete. "You were goofing around, right? You didn't think it was a big deal?"

"It was just a dare," Pete spluttered from the ground. "We wanted—"

"I said shut up!" Chris aimed a kick at Pete, but James was too quick for him, moving in to deflect the blow and pull the kid's arm behind his back in one smooth move.

"Hold still," he warned, loosening his grip but not letting go.

"You can't—"

A sharp siren split the air, and red and blue lights sped toward them. Chris stiffened and tried to twist away, but James had his arm locked in place.

"Good timing," James called as an officer he hadn't met before sprang from the car.

"Let go of him," the officer shouted as he worked his way toward them, hand on his hip.

"Whoa man. I called this in. I'm Detective Wood, Milwaukee PD. Captain Perry asked for my help this morning. These are the vandals from the Moore Landscaping case. This one was about to beat his friend to a pulp."

The officer didn't relax his posture, and James didn't blame him—he wouldn't have either.

"We did it," Pete whimpered. "Please don't arrest us. My mom will kill me if I go to jail."

Chris aimed another kick at the ground, but James yanked him back.

"You'll find the stolen items in the car." James tipped his head toward the vehicle. The officer looked in the car, then pulled out his cuffs. James adjusted his grip so the officer could fasten them on Chris.

"He didn't tell me we were going to steal anything." Pete's voice wavered as the officer cuffed him too. "I'm really sorry."

"Do they have all of Cam's stuff?" Bethany appeared at James's side.

"Looks like it." James grinned at her. "Nice detective work."

"Thanks." Her cheeks pinked.

"Let me finish up here. Then we can go get that lunch. I could eat *two* horses now."

Chapter 16

Bethany studied her checklist. She was relatively sure she had everything ready for tonight's dinner with her friends. She'd made a big slow cooker full of pulled pork, along with a pan of Snickerdoodles, and her friends would all bring food too. They always ended up with more than enough to eat at these gatherings.

But she still felt like something was missing.

She scanned the room, spotting Ruby's dress shoes in the corner. She picked them up and carried them to Ruby's room.

That was what was missing. Ruby. Or, more like she was missing Ruby.

Only a little longer, she reminded herself. Yesterday had flown by, with their search for the vandals. And today had been filled with cleaning up the house. Tomorrow, she'd go to church, and before she knew it, Ruby would be home.

"Hello," a voice called from the front door. "We're here."

Bethany hurried to the living room, her heart filling at the sound of her sister-in-law's voice. Kayla wheeled through the front door, followed by Cam, carrying a car seat with a sleeping baby Evelyn snuggled inside.

"Give me that little beauty." Bethany rushed for her niece.

"Okay, but if you wake her up, she's yours," Cam joked.

"Deal. You guys go relax. I've got her." Bethany crouched in front of the car seat and carefully extracted Evelyn from the straps. The sleeping baby curled against her shoulder. Bethany closed her eyes, soaking in the sweet, milky scent. Every once in a while, she let herself dream about what it would be like to have another baby. But with her issues—not to mention the fact that she was single—that wasn't likely to happen. So she'd just have to spoil her niece.

Somehow, Evelyn remained sleeping through the bustle of everyone else arriving and cooing over her. Bethany reluctantly relinquished her hold on the baby to give the others a turn. She helped Leah set out the appetizers she'd brought, then found a spot for Peyton's bread and Ariana's fudge and Sophie's spinach dip.

"Got room for this?" Emma waltzed into the kitchen, carrying a tray of deviled eggs. "I barely managed to pry them away from James."

"They can go right here." Bethany slid the pulled pork to the edge of the counter to make room. She peered past her friend toward the living room. But she didn't spot James among the crowd gathered there.

"I thought— I meant to invite him."

She didn't realize she'd spoken out loud until Emma said, "Don't worry, you did. I thought he was going to come, but then—" She shook her head. "He has a hard time with things like this."

Bethany glanced around the space. It was just a group of friends sharing a meal.

But before she could ask what Emma meant, Kayla rolled into the room, baby Evelyn looking cozy and sweet in her lap. "That's too bad. I wanted to thank him in person for getting Cam's stuff back."

Talk turned to the vandalism, but Bethany's thoughts drifted to James. Their lunch together yesterday had been fun and comfortable. She appreciated the way he didn't seem to expect her to fill every moment with small talk. And when she did talk, she felt like he really listened, waiting patiently when she had to pause to search for a word.

Easy. That was how being with him felt. Easier than anything in her life had felt since the aneurysm.

But maybe it didn't feel that way for him.

Maybe that was why he hadn't come tonight. When Emma said he had a hard time with "things like this," did that mean things like her?

"I'm so hungry, Mommy," a little voice cried plaintively. Matthias tugged at Jade, and she shushed him but looked to Bethany.

"I think everyone's here." Bethany smiled at Matthias. "Do you want to ask your daddy to lead the prayer?"

Matthias nodded and rushed toward Dan, who scooped him into his arms and nuzzled his hair. The pang of missing Ruby strengthened in Bethany's middle.

"All right, everyone," Dan called. "This little guy says it's time to eat."

"I'm a big guy," Matthias interrupted.

"Right. Sorry." Dan tickled his son's side. "This big guy is hungry. Let's join together in prayer." He waited a beat as quiet fell over the room. "Dear Lord, we come before you today with hearts overflowing with gratitude. Thank you for bringing baby Evelyn Moore safely into this world. Lord, we ask that you would help us all to support Cam and Kayla as they raise her in you. Lead us to encourage them and share your love with Evelyn. Thank you for bringing us together as a family of believers."

Bethany nodded. These people really were her family, and she was so grateful for them.

"Thank you for the delicious meal we are about to eat," Dan continued. "And for Bethany's hospitality in inviting us here this evening. May our little family here continue to grow. In Jesus' name we pray. Amen."

"Finally!" Matthias shouted, and everyone laughed, making the boy giggle.

"Why don't you go first," Bethany offered to Matthias. "And you're next." She turned to Kayla. "I'll hold Evelyn so you can eat." She stepped forward to take the baby before her sister-in-law could protest. Bethany urged the others to fall in line as well.

"I can take her," Cam offered, holding out his hands for his daughter.

But Bethany shook her head. "Get some food with your wife. It's my turn to take care of you guys for a change."

Cam's laugh was incredulous. "I'd say you already did. I still can't believe you identified the vandals."

"James was the one who caught them."

"That's not what he told me."

She looked up. "You talked to him?" Bethany had called Cam and Kayla on the way to lunch with James, then went right to their house afterward, but James had declined to go with her.

"I called him." Cam studied her. "He said you refused to give up the search even when he told you it was hopeless."

"You know me. I've always been stubborn."

"Seriously, Bethany." Cam refused to laugh off her deflection. "It means a lot to us."

"Yeah, well." She rubbed her fingers over Evelyn's wisps of hair. "You guys mean a lot to me. Now eat."

But the glow of Cam's appreciation stayed with her as she scooted past everyone to take a seat with Evelyn in the living room. She'd just settled in with the baby nestled against her shoulder when the doorbell rang. That was odd. Pretty much everyone she knew in the world was right here.

Except Ruby.

A bolt of fear went through her as she jumped to her feet, the movement disturbing the baby, who immediately broke into loud wails.

"Shh." Bethany rubbed the baby's back as she hurried to the door, fear making her knees spongy. If anything had happened to Ruby . . . "Please don't let it be a police officer, Lord," she whispered as she wrenched the door open.

"Oh." Her relief came out as a long exhale. At least she knew this police officer wasn't here to deliver bad news. "James. You came."

He nodded, Adam's apple bobbing as his eyes rested on the crying baby she held.

Bethany repositioned the baby, who calmed a little. "Meet Evelyn Moore. My niece."

James's jaw tightened, but he nodded again.

So he had come, but apparently he wasn't interested in talking.

"Come on in. Grab a plate. We just started eating." She stood back and gestured toward the kitchen.

"Thanks." His voice was quiet but warm, and a strange thrill went through Bethany at the sound, as if she'd gone too long without hearing it.

His warm spicy scent competed with Evelyn's baby smell as he stepped past her.

"James." Cam strode across the room, a full plate in one hand, the other outstretched.

Everyone else greeted James as well and thanked him for helping to catch the vandals. In spite of baby Evelyn's renewed cries, Bethany couldn't wipe the smile off her face. It felt like Dan's prayer that they bring more people into the family had already been answered.

He should leave.

It was the tenth time he'd told himself that.

Most of Bethany's friends had already headed home. Only he, Emma, and Cam and Kayla and their baby remained.

Seeing Bethany with the baby on her shoulder when she'd answered the door earlier had nearly sent him reeling back to his truck. It had been too reminiscent of seeing Melissa holding a newborn Sadie. But the way Bethany's eyes had rested on his, warm and welcoming, had drawn him into the house.

And now he'd been here nearly four hours and couldn't quite convince himself to leave. Not that he was wrapped up in the conversation between Cam and Kayla and Emma about some new ministry at their church. At the other end of the couch, Bethany appeared to be listening politely, but he could tell her attention had drifted, and she seemed to be struggling to stay awake. Another reason he should leave. So why didn't he want to?

Probably for the same reason he'd decided to come in the first place.

Because for the first time in five years, his insides didn't ache every minute of every day. And he had a strange feeling that the only way to keep them from aching so profoundly was to spend time with these people.

All of them, or one in particular?

Bethany rubbed at her temples, as if massaging a headache. All right. It was time to stop being so selfish and leave so she could go to bed. Maybe the others would follow suit.

He stood and stretched. "Thanks, Bethany. This was . . ." He honestly wasn't sure what word fit at the end of that sentence.

"Are you leaving?" Her eyes drooped with exhaustion, and he reminded himself that was likely tiredness in her voice—not disappointment.

"We should go too." Kayla wheeled toward the spot where Evelyn slept in her car seat. James averted his eyes from the peaceful expression on the baby's face.

"Me too." Emma got up as well.

James moved to the door and held it open for the others, then stepped into the cool spring night that carried a hint of flowers.

"I'm glad you came." Bethany followed him outside, covering a yawn as she spoke.

His swallow felt oddly strained. "So am—"

Her pocket burst into song, and he chuckled as she grabbed for her phone.

"What's that one for? Bedtime?" He was getting used to the numerous alarms she set each day.

But she shook her head, her eyes wide. "It's not an alarm. It's Tiffany. Ruby's at the . . . uh . . ." He could tell she was groping for the word. "With her." Her hands shook so that she couldn't hit the icon to answer.

James caught her hand to still it. "Hey. I'm sure Ruby's fine." He tapped the answer button for her, his stomach knotting and unknotting and reknotting in quick succession. This was why he couldn't get involved with someone who had a kid. He couldn't go through this again. In fact, he should be heading for his truck, pulling away from the house like the others were.

But he couldn't leave her alone, not with that fear etched on her face.

"Ruby?" Bethany gasped into the phone.

James watched her face impatiently, unable to hear the other end of the phone call. When the tightness in her mouth relaxed slightly, he let himself take a breath.

"I'll be there as soon as I can." Her voice was urgent but not panicked.

James studied her again as she listened to the person on the other end. A few times, she tried to interrupt, but the other person clearly wasn't giving her room to speak.

Finally, she shook her head, her mouth set. "I'm coming to get her. I'll call you when I get there." She hung up, then rubbed at her temples.

"Everything okay?"

"Ruby threw up and wants to come home. Tiffany said I should wait until she brings Ruby home tomorrow, but I'm not going to leave her there when she's sick."

James eyed her. "How far away is it?"

She was already tapping something into her phone. She turned the screen to show him the map. Ninety minutes.

She was in no shape to drive that far. "Maybe you should wait until tomorrow. She'll probably feel better if she sleeps."

Bethany stared at him. "She's my daughter. I'm not going to leave her there when she needs me. Trust me, if you had a kid, you'd be doing the same thing."

James stumbled back a step as she disappeared into the house, leaving the door open behind her.

His heart thudded against his ears. *If he had a kid* . . .

But he knew she was right. If that call had been about Sadie, he'd be jumping in his car right now, no matter the time or how tired he was.

He crossed his arms over his chest and waited for her to emerge, that *if* knocking against his nerves. *If* it hadn't been raining that day. *If* they'd have left five minutes earlier. *If* he hadn't stopped.

A white streak in the doorway caught his eye. Some kind of animal, making a dash for the side of the house. A ferret? He crept toward the spot where it had disappeared behind a bush. Not a ferret. A cat.

And one who didn't seem to know what to do now that it was out here.

"Hey, kitty." He held out a hand to the creature. "Are you supposed to be out here?"

The cat slunk forward and sniffed his fingers, then slid its fur against them. With his other hand, James swooped under the cat's belly and picked it up. Instead of fighting him as James had expected, the cat purred and curled into him.

"Don't get too comfy," he muttered, carrying it toward the front door. He stepped into the light spilling from the house as Bethany emerged.

She stopped short, staring at him. "You're still here."

"You had a runaway." He held up the cat, as if that was the reason he'd stayed.

"Mrs. Whiskers," Bethany scolded, holding out her arms. "Thank you. Ruby would be devastated if we lost her."

James passed her the cat, their hands getting momentarily tangled in the handoff.

Bethany tossed Mrs. Whiskers inside and closed the door, locking it behind her.

"Your car or my truck?" he asked.

"What?" Her brow wrinkled as if he'd spoken a foreign language.

"I'm driving either way. But which vehicle would you rather take?" He stepped into her path, ready for whatever argument she was going to put up.

But the long breath she released sounded more relieved than annoyed. "We can take mine." She passed him the keys and moved to the passenger door before he could even register that he'd won the fight.

Chapter 17

Bethany fought to keep her head upright, eyes open. It took a second to register that her head had bobbed forward again, and she snapped it back, suppressing yet another yawn.

"I don't know why you're fighting it." James's voice was soft, like a lullaby. "Just close your eyes. I'll wake you up when we get there."

With effort, Bethany pushed her lips open to form words. "I'm keeping you company so you don't get—" A giant yawn shook her. "Tired."

James snorted. "I've sat up all night on stakeouts. I'm good. Seriously, just sleep." She thought he turned to look at her, but she was too tired to move even her eyes.

"Maybe for a minute," she murmured, letting the drowsiness overtake her. A soft sigh escaped her lips, and she thought vaguely that she shouldn't feel this relaxed when Ruby was sick. But James was taking her to Ruby. James would take care of them . . .

She jolted awake as something changed. The car had slowed. She swiveled her head to James. "Why are we stopping?"

"We're here."

"Already?"

He chuckled. "Time flies when you're sleeping."

"I'm sorry. I didn't mean to—"

His hand fell on her arm. "It's okay. I told you to. Feel better now?"

Bethany paused. Her headache had completely disappeared, and she no longer felt like someone was trying to glue her eyelids shut. "Much. Thank you."

She opened her car door, moderately surprised when he did the same. She'd figured he'd wait out here. Not that she minded him coming with her. It was kind of nice, actually.

Inside the hotel, a desk clerk asked how he could help. "I need to pick up my daughter. She's in a room with . . . Uh . . ." She had known the woman's name an hour and a half ago. But her brain was still foggy with sleep. "Sorry." She pulled out her phone to find the name.

"Tiffany." Authority rang from James's voice. "Tiffany Stemple."

"Oh yes." The clerk shuffled through some papers. "She called down to let us know you were coming. Room 206."

She thanked the man, then headed for the elevator across the lobby, but James caught her arm and gestured toward the staircase in the middle of the room. "Stairs will be faster."

With a shrug, she followed him. Whatever got her to Ruby fastest was good with her. She practically ran up the stairs to keep up with James's long legs. At the top, he led them to the left. They stopped outside room 206, and James raised a fist to knock, but Bethany wrapped her hand around his knuckles. "I'll text Tiffany," she whispered. "In case they're sleeping." It was nearly midnight already.

"Good idea." James lowered his hand, bringing hers with it. She let go and pulled out her phone, tapping a quick message to Tiffany.

A moment later, the click of a lock echoed through the door, and it swung open.

"James!" Tiffany brought a hand to her hair, smoothing it, though it was already perfect, before her eyes went to Bethany. "I told you that you didn't have to come," she whispered, her eyes darting back and forth between them. "There was no need to interrupt whatever you were . . ."

"Where's Ruby?" James cut in.

"She's sleeping." Tiffany stood back to reveal a roomful of sleeping girls, most of them on the floor, though Ruby was by herself on one of the room's two beds. Her hair was matted to her face, and her cheeks shone as if feverish, but even so relief coursed through Bethany.

She hurried toward the bed, careful to tiptoe around the sprawled girls.

"Don't wake her." James's whisper was closer behind her than she'd expected. "I can carry her."

Bethany eyed him. He was certainly strong enough, but Ruby was also sick. Did he really want to get that close to her? Before she could ask, James had slid his arms under Ruby and hoisted her against his chest. His lips pressed shut, and he looked as if he was holding his breath. Hopefully Ruby didn't smell too much like vomit.

Tiffany passed Ruby's bag to Bethany.

"Thanks for having her," Bethany said dutifully.

"Of course." Tiffany stepped into the hallway with them. "I'll give you a call later in the week to touch base on how things are going for the field day."

Bethany swallowed roughly. "That sounds good."

She followed James, who strode right past the elevator.

"Wouldn't the elevator be easier?" She watched Ruby's head, which lolled on James's arm.

"Nope." He reached the stairs and started down.

"Don't drop her." She raced to stay at his side.

He glanced her way, his lips lifting a fraction. "Don't worry. I won't."

When they got to the car, Bethany helped him maneuver Ruby into her seat and fasten her seatbelt. The girl stirred, and Bethany pushed her hair off her cheeks. "Mom's here. Go back to sleep."

Ruby obeyed, and Bethany got into her own seat. James started the car and pulled onto the road.

"Thank you." The words felt inadequate, but she had no others.

"Anytime."

It didn't feel like the flippant *anytime* a regular person would give. It felt more like a promise.

Bethany scoffed at herself. Of course it wasn't a promise. He was just being nice. Doing his job.

"So what's this field day thing Tiffany mentioned?" James's low voice provided a welcome interruption to the crazy line of Bethany's thoughts.

"It's a big activity day and fundraiser on the last day of school. I accidentally volunteered to organize it."

"Accidentally?" Amusement warmed James's voice.

"Maybe not accidentally. More like—" Drat. Why could this word never come to her?

"Impulsively?" James asked

"Yes." And how did he always know exactly the word she was searching for? "But don't tell Tiffany that," she rushed to add. "I think she already doubts that I can do it."

"Why would she doubt you?" The genuine question in his voice filled Bethany, until he asked, "How's it going so far?"

"Uh. Well." Bethany concentrated on the view out the window, though she couldn't see much beyond the side of the road in the dark. "I haven't started yet. But—" She didn't want him to think she was a total flake. "I know what I'm going to do." That was maybe a stretch, but close enough.

She had some ideas. She only hoped she'd written them down, because none of them were coming to her right now.

"If you need any . . ." But he trailed off without finishing the sentence.

"Mom," Ruby's sleepy voice called from behind them.

"Hey, Rubes." Bethany twisted in her seat to check on her daughter. "How are you feeling?"

"Better, I think. Hi, James."

Bethany angled her head toward James.

"Hi." His knuckles stood out against the steering wheel, and he stared straight ahead. It wasn't the first time she'd wondered if he really did dislike her daughter.

If he did, then he was the one missing out. She turned to Ruby. "We're almost home. Why don't you get some more rest?"

"I had a dream about you."

"That's nice, sweetie. I'm here now."

"And you too, James," Ruby added. "You were walking down these big fancy stairs together. I think you were getting married."

A strangled cough came from the driver's seat, and Bethany wished this were a Flintstone car so she could slip right out the bottom.

She rubbed her eyes. "That was at the hotel, Ruby. James was carrying you down the steps, and I was walking next to him. We weren't getting married."

"Oh." Ruby fell silent, and Bethany turned slowly toward the front of the car, careful to avoid looking at James. She could only imagine what he was thinking.

"Do you mind if I turn on the radio?" She needed the distraction.

"It's your car." The words were clipped.

She turned on the radio and leaned back against her seat, letting herself lip sync to the lyrics.

"Mom?" Ruby trilled after a few minutes.

"What is it, Rubes?" She didn't turn around this time because she wasn't ready to look at James.

"Why don't you date?"

Oh, for heaven's sake! "I just— I don't—" She couldn't put together a sentence—not when she could feel James watching her. "I just don't." There. At least she'd put three words together.

She peered out the window, squinting desperately for landmarks. They had to be almost home by now.

There! The sign announcing that Hope Springs was five miles away. She only had to survive a few more minutes.

"I know!" The excitement in Ruby's voice sent a wave of nerves through Bethany. Heaven only knew what was going to come out of her daughter's mouth next.

"Oh look." Bethany pointed toward the marina, where the moon illuminated a sailboat painted in vibrant colors.

"You and James should date," Ruby said gleefully. "And then you really can get married and I can have a dad."

"Ruby!" Bethany's eyes went involuntarily to James.

He clutched the steering wheel so hard, she feared he might pull it right off. A muscle in his jaw worked, as if he were trying to crank it shut tighter.

"No one is dating or marrying anyone." She blew out a breath, making herself speak to James next. "Sorry. She clearly needs some sleep."

"No problem." His lips didn't move around the words, and he didn't say another thing the rest of the way. When they reached Bethany's house, he bolted silently out of the car and into his truck.

"Thank you again," Bethany called before he shut himself inside.

He nodded and pulled away.

At least she'd been right about one thing: no one was going to be dating or marrying anyone.

Chapter 18

James scanned the progress he'd made in cleaning the stalls, then checked the time. 7:30 a.m. Despite his early start today, there was no way he was going to finish before Bethany got here. Which meant he was going to have to see her. For the first time in a week. When she'd had to cancel helping at the stables on Wednesday because she'd come down with Ruby's stomach bug, he'd been relieved. Not that she was sick—but that he wouldn't have to face her after what Ruby had said.

He'd spent all week struggling not to think about the girl's blithe statement that he and Bethany should date and get married. *Then I could have a dad.*

As if he could so easily step back into that role. As if he'd want to, after the first time had shattered him.

He knew it wasn't fair to hold the words against Ruby; she had no idea that he'd ever been a dad.

But her words had been a wake-up call. He had to stop spending so much time with Bethany. Thankfully, his enforced vacation was almost over. Two more weeks and he'd be back to work. Or maybe he'd call the captain and convince him to take him back earlier. He jabbed his pitchfork into the soiled straw, ignoring the stab of protest from his shoulder. If he could muck a stall, he could take down a criminal. Hadn't he proved that when he'd caught those vandals last week?

With Bethany's help.

He shoved the pitchfork harder. Why did it seem everything he'd done since arriving in Hope Springs involved her? And why did the thought of going back to Milwaukee, where he would never see her, raise a grumpy protest in his chest?

His phone rang, and James wiped at the sweat on his brow before answering.

"Detective Wood?"

"Yes?" James set the pitchfork down, on alert. It hadn't been a number he recognized.

"This is Captain Perry. Of the Hope Springs police department. We met on the Moore vandalism case?"

"Of course, Captain. Did you get the report I sent over?" Not that it was required, since this wasn't his department and he'd given a statement to the officer on the scene, but he always felt better if he made a written record of everything.

"I did, thanks."

"Great." James tucked the phone between his ear and his good shoulder as he moved to the wheelbarrow. "If there's anything else I can do . . ."

"Actually, I hope there is."

"Yeah? What's that?" James hoisted the wheelbarrow and steered it toward the next stall.

"I was hoping I might be able to convince you to take a position here."

"What?" James picked up his head in shock, his phone sliding down his arm—straight toward the wheelbarrow full of dirty horse bedding. James swiped at it—but that meant letting go of the wheelbarrow with one hand. The whole thing tipped toward the right, and it was only his lightning reflexes that kept it from spilling all over the floor. A loud crack announced that the phone hadn't been so lucky. James lunged for it, inspecting it for signs it had gotten soiled before lifting it toward his ear. He held it a few inches away, just in case.

"Hello? Are you there?" The captain's voice sounded distant.

"Sorry about that. Dropped my phone."

"I'll take it as a good sign that you didn't hang up on me." The captain chuckled.

"Look, Captain, I appreciate—"

"I know I probably can't match your current salary," the captain interrupted.

"I don't care about the money." Being a cop had never been about earning a paycheck for him. It was about justice, about helping those who needed help, about honoring his father.

"Even better," Captain Perry joked. "Just give it some thought, would you? I spoke to your captain, and he thought the change of scenery might not be such a bad thing."

"What?" James's grip on his phone tightened to the point where he expected it to snap in half. Betrayal snapped harder. After everything he'd given the department, Captain Burke was ready to get rid of him?

"He told me what happened with your daughter." Captain Perry's voice took on that overly soft tone everyone used when they learned about Sadie. "I have a little girl, and I can't imagine—"

"Yeah." James couldn't have this conversation. "Thanks for the offer, but I have to run."

"Just think about—"

James hit the button to end the call and shoved his phone into his pocket.

Outside, a horse nickered, and in the barn, the scent of horse manure and hay closed in on him. He pressed a hand against the smooth wood of the nearest stall. He wasn't going to pretend there weren't things about

Hope Springs he'd miss. But that didn't mean he was going to stay here and take a job with the tiny department. He was needed in Milwaukee.

At least he had thought he was. Apparently, Captain Burke felt differently.

He considered pulling his phone out and calling the betrayer right now—but there was too big a risk he'd say something that would get him fired on the spot. He needed to wait until he calmed down. Which might take a while.

With a growl low in his throat, he seized the wheelbarrow handles and charged toward the door. By the time he'd emptied it and started back toward the barn, he'd constructed a rough outline of what he'd say to his captain if he could talk to him right now. Based on that, it was best he wait longer to make the call.

He stepped into the barn, his eyes taking a moment to adjust from the bright sunlight outside to the dimmer artificial light in here.

"Hi, James."

His gaze jumped toward her voice. She stood next to the stall he'd been in the middle of cleaning before Captain Perry's call. Her smile seemed nervous, her posture uncertain. He slowed as he approached her.

This was another reason he couldn't take a job in Hope Springs—he couldn't afford to get closer to her and Ruby.

"Hi." His greeting sounded stilted, and Bethany must have noticed too because her smile faltered. He felt bad. She probably didn't even remember what Ruby had said. "Are you feeling better?"

She nodded and picked up a shovel. James let out a breath as she turned toward a stall. If she did remember, at least she wasn't going to bring it up.

"Listen." She didn't face him. "I wanted to apologize for what Ruby said the other night. I hope you know she didn't get that idea from me. She's just . . ." She tilted her head toward the ceiling, as if she'd find the word she was looking for scrawled across the wooden beams.

James followed her gaze. His eyes landed on a bird's nest clinging to the corner of the rafters. "Precocious?" The word slipped from his lips before he remembered that the last time he'd used it was to describe Sadie.

"I was going to say ridiculous." Bethany's laugh still held a tinge of nervousness. "But that works too. What are you looking at?"

He smelled her soft, peachy scent first, before he felt her move closer to him.

"A bird's nest." He pointed toward the rafters.

"Where?" Bethany shifted, and her scent wrapped all the way around him.

"Right there." He shook his finger toward the nest, as if that would help.

"I don't see it." Her scent drifted away from him, and he dropped his arm.

"Here." He grasped her shoulders lightly—though not lightly enough to avoid the jolt the contact produced—and moved her into the spot where he'd been standing. He reached over her shoulder to point so that she could follow the line of his arm, right up to the rafters.

"Oh." A childlike awe filled her exclamation as a baby bird stuck its head up from the nest.

James dropped his gaze and took a step backwards. "I'd better get back to work."

"You got a lot done already."

"Yeah." He grabbed his pitchfork and returned to the half-cleaned stall.

After a few seconds, he heard the scrape of Bethany's pitchfork in the next stall. They worked in silence, James's brain whirring as he mentally revised what he planned to say to Captain Burke. He'd managed to come up with something almost civil by the time they were done.

When they'd put everything away, Bethany looked at her phone. "It's a good thing we got done quickly. They're supposed to clean up the graffiti today, and now I can go over there and supervise so Cam doesn't have to worry about it."

James tried to follow what she was saying, but he must have missed something. There was no reason anyone should have to supervise the cleaners. Unless— "Who's they?"

"The boys," Bethany answered, as if it were obvious. "The ones who did the damage. Cam talked to their parents and said he'd ask the prosecutor to drop the charges as long as they cleaned everything up and paid for the broken window and the truck repairs."

"That's—" The word *stupid* was on his tongue, but he held it back at the look on Bethany's face.

"Generous," she filled in for him, grinning as if she'd found a word he couldn't. "Cam's a big believer in second chances," she continued. "Fortunately for me."

He tipped his head. "How so?"

Bethany looked at him with the panicked expression he recognized as belonging to someone who had said something incriminating—but then she schooled her face into a smile. "Oh you know . . ."

James studied her—he *didn't* know, but he decided to let it pass. It was none of his business.

"Anyway, I'd better get going. Ruby's spending the day at Kimberly's to make up for missing part of the party." Bethany pulled out her phone and tapped the screen a few times, then lifted it to her ear as she strode toward the barn doors.

"Hey, Cam," he heard her say. "I'm on my way over to the shop. You stay with Kayla and Evelyn." She pulled her keys out of her pocket, then disappeared out the barn doors.

Uneasiness stirred in James's belly. *Leave it,* he commanded himself. Those boys had been pulling a stupid prank. They were unlikely to be a serious threat to Bethany. Not to mention that she wasn't his responsibility.

Serve and protect. That's the job, son.

Yeah, it was. But he wasn't on the job. Just like he hadn't been on the job the day he'd pulled over to help at that accident.

If he hadn't had such a hero complex, maybe Sadie . . .

Stop.

He couldn't let himself go down the *if only* road again.

Because no matter how much he wanted to change the past, he couldn't. All he could do was attempt to forget it. And the only way to forget it was to stay busy.

"Bethany. Wait." James shot through the stable, squinting in the sunlight as he burst out the door. But Bethany was already in her car. He called her name again as the engine turned over. But she must not have heard him. Her car rolled down the driveway.

He should go back into the barn. The last thing he needed was to spend more time with Bethany.

Her car pulled onto the road.

James stared after it a few seconds. Then instinct took over and he jumped into his truck and followed her.

Chapter 19

Bethany lifted her eyes to the rearview mirror again as she turned onto Willowbrook Street. The black pickup behind her turned too, and her heart accelerated faster than the vehicle. She wasn't sure how long the truck had been behind her—she hadn't noticed it at first because there had been a couple of vehicles between them—but the truck had steadily gained on her, and she was pretty sure it had been following her for the past few turns at least.

Lots of people drive this way, she reminded herself. She'd been watching too many cop shows lately. People didn't get followed in Hope Springs.

She slowed for the turn into Moore Landscaping, waiting for the pickup to tear around her. But it slowed too.

She was about to slam her foot onto the gas pedal and take off when the pickup got close enough for her to make out the driver.

James?

It sure looked like him.

Heart calming a little, she made the turn, the black truck following close behind.

She pulled up to the building and turned off her car, taking a moment to get her breathing under control before opening her door.

By the time she got out, James was already standing in front of her car.

A rush of unexpected anger hit Bethany as he stood there looking all calm and collected after nearly giving her a heart attack. She slammed her door and marched toward him. "You scared me half to death, following me like that."

James looked surprised—but not apologetic. "Sorry. I thought you'd recognize my truck."

She shook her head. Never mind that he should have realized she wouldn't. "What are you doing here?"

James shoved his hands in his pockets and looked away. "Didn't like the idea of you here alone with those punks."

"I— Oh." Well, that was sort of sweet. But unnecessary. "Trust me. I've dealt with worse. A lot worse." She wasn't proud of that time in her life, but she'd learned to take care of herself in some pretty awful situations.

James looked doubtful. "I don't have anything else going on. I might as well make myself useful."

Bethany peered at him. "You're not very good at relaxing, are you?"

"Ha. I don't really believe in just sitting around." His eyes jerked to the road as a car squealed into the driveway, sending gravel shooting behind it. The vehicle roared toward them, and James stepped in front of Bethany. She grabbed his arm with a gasp as the car skidded to a stop a foot in front of them.

"Second chances," James muttered, shaking his head.

Bethany stepped out from behind him, her pulse knocking against the side of her neck. The kid had only been showing off. She was sure he wouldn't really have hurt them—but suddenly she was grateful to have James at her side. It'd been a long time since she'd had to deal with anyone threatening.

The kid wore a sneer as he got out of the car. He looked Bethany up and down, his gaze lingering long enough that she crossed her arms in front of her.

James stepped toward the kid, whose eyes finally went to him.

"You don't have jurisdiction here." He smirked.

"Get to work, Chris." James's voice carried authority without threat.

"Who's going to make me?" Chris's smirk morphed into a sickening laugh. "You, old man?"

James pointed at the kid. "You want to throw away your second chance? Go ahead. If it were up to me, you'd be in jail."

"James." Bethany grabbed his arm, sending him a warning look. "Do you have cleaner?" she asked the boy.

Chris stared at James another minute, then looked away. "Yeah. I got it." He moved to the trunk. "I'm not starting until Pete gets here though."

"Of course. Make him do the dirty work, like always." James curled a lip. "How long did it take you to convince him to do this in the first place?" James gestured toward the spray painted building. "I suppose it makes you feel tough to know you can make a kid half your size do whatever you say."

"You don't know me, man." Chris glared at James, and Bethany put herself between them.

With an impatient grunt, James stepped around her. "Trust me. I know you. I see guys like you every day. And I know where they end up."

"James." Bethany's voice was sharper than even she expected. "Maybe you should go."

James threw his hands in the air and shook his head, striding to the far side of his truck but not getting in. Instead, he crossed his arms and leaned against the door, his back to them as he faced the road.

Bethany let out a long breath. What would she have done if he'd followed her impulsive order to leave?

"Your boyfriend needs to chill." Chris twisted his face with that sneer again.

"He's not my boyfriend."

"Oh, really?" The boy's eyes traveled her body again, and she barely resisted the urge to run away.

She pulled her arms tighter. "And he's right that you don't want to throw away your second chance. Trust me." How many chances had her parents given her? Five? Six? And she'd thrown away every single one. Until it was too late.

The crunch of tires on the driveway drew their attention to another vehicle approaching—this one moving much more slowly and driven by a woman who looked to be around Bethany's age.

Chris snorted. "He brought his mom." His face wore contempt, but Bethany heard the ache under the words. He scuffed his feet toward the building, the cleaner and a rag hanging limply from his hand.

Bethany moved around his car to the spot where the woman was parking the other vehicle. After a moment, the woman got out, as did the boy sitting in the passenger seat.

"Come over here before you get started, Pete," the woman called before turning to Bethany. "Carrie Smith. Pete's mom." She offered a tight smile. "I can't tell you how sorry I am about all of this. And Pete has something he wants to say too."

Pete reached his mother's side just as James appeared next to Bethany. To her surprise, the boy looked relieved to see James.

"Go ahead, Pete," his mother prompted.

"Thank you for the second chance," Pete murmured. Though Bethany had to strain to catch the words, she could tell they were sincere.

"That's my brother's doing," she replied. "Trust me, you're not the only one he's given a second chance. I hope you won't take it for granted."

The boy nodded.

"Go get to work, Pete. The cleaning supplies are in the back," Carrie said firmly.

Pete moved to the trunk and pulled out a large bucket filled with spray bottles, sponges, rags, and gloves. He eyed James again before making his way toward Chris, who stood leaning against the building, arms crossed, smirking toward them.

"I'm so sorry," the woman said again as Chris reached over to slug Pete's shoulder—hard, from the looks of it. Next to her, Bethany felt James tense. But Pete simply set down the bucket and started working. After a minute, Chris did too.

"I don't know what to do." The woman—her name had slipped out of Bethany's mind already—sniffed and rubbed under her eyes. "He was always such a good kid. But then my husband left and Pete started high school and met Chris." She gulped loudly. "Never mind. It's no excuse. I'll do better."

"I'm sure you're doing the best you can." Bethany moved closer and squeezed the woman's shoulder. "It's not your fault."

"My dad died when I was about Pete's age." It took Bethany a moment to realize the words had come from James, they were so soft-spoken. "I don't know how my mom made it through those years. I sure didn't make it easy. Got into all kinds of trouble."

Bethany blinked at James, trying to picture him making trouble of any sort. Impossible.

"What changed?" the woman asked.

"Spent a night in jail."

"Oh." The woman squeaked at the same time Bethany's jaw came unhinged. There was no way.

"Not like that," James clarified. "My dad was a cop and his partner arranged it. Said that was where I was going to end up if I kept going the way I was. And then the next day he took me fishing. Caught a bass this big." He held his hands out, and all Bethany could do was gape. Had he always been this talkative?

"So you think he needs a night in jail?" Pete's mom wilted against her car.

"Nah." James peered toward the building, where Pete was scrubbing against a slash of red. "I think this will be enough to set him straight. That other kid though . . ."

"Chris?" The woman sighed. "He has a sad story. His dad died during a robbery. I don't know much about his mom except that she seems to have checked out. Rarely leaves the house, except to go to the liquor store."

"Oh dear." Bethany pressed a hand to her heart. It was no wonder the boy acted out. She'd had the most wonderful family in the world, and still she'd gone down the wrong path. How was this boy—who had no one there for him—supposed to find his way? "Is there anything . . ."

She forgot what she was going to say as she realized James was striding away from them, toward the boys. Purpose clung to his steps. Pete kept working as James approached, but Chris stopped and crossed his arms, a quick flash of fear instantly replaced with a grating smirk. Bethany held her breath, praying James wasn't about to do something drastic.

But when he reached the boys, he simply bent and picked up a scrub brush and some cleaner and started working between them. Pete acknowledged him with a quick nod, and after a second, Chris started scrubbing again, harder this time.

"I should get back to work." Pete's mom clicked her phone on nervously. "Do you think it'd be okay if I come pick him up around three?"

"Oh don't worry about that. I can give him a ride home."

"You would do that?" The woman stared at her as if she'd grown a halo.

"Like I said, I know what it's like to need a second chance."

"Thank you." The woman squeezed her hand. "God bless you."

"Believe me, he has." As the woman drove away, Bethany went to help James and the boys with the cleanup. They worked mostly silently, aside from an occasional instruction from James. It took a good two hours of steady work before the building gleamed almost like new. Fortunately, the sign only took another hour.

By the time they'd finished, Bethany's shoulders ached and her stomach rumbled.

"Do you need a ride home, Pete?" James asked as they finished gathering up the cleaning supplies.

"I have a better idea," Bethany cut in. "Why don't you take Pete and Chris fishing?" She wasn't sure where the idea had come from so suddenly, but sometimes her lack of impulse control was brilliant.

"Fishing?" James stared at her—and she very much doubted he was seeing a halo. Maybe horns.

"You know, like your dad's partner—"

James shook his head. "*That* you remember?"

She shrugged. "It's not like I control it. And I also remember that you don't have anything else going on today and you don't like to just sit around, so . . . Do you guys like to fish?"

Pete was already nodding enthusiastically, looking at James as if he were a hero. Chris shrugged. "It's kinda lame, but whatever. It's not like I have anything else to do."

Bethany met James's eyes. Surely he could see how badly these boys needed this.

James rubbed a hand back and forth over the top of his head. "I don't have any fishing poles."

"Emma does." She wasn't sure how she knew that, but she did. "You run to the farm and pick them up. I'll pick Ruby up from her friend's house. We'll meet you at the marina. And I'll bring food."

Chapter 20

How in the world had he managed to get talked into this? James tried to loosen the tension in his neck as he turned onto the road that led down to the marina. His job was to put criminals in jail—not take them fishing.

He understood what Bethany was trying to do—admired it, even—but she had to realize that most people who were given a second chance blew it.

He glanced toward Chris, in the passenger seat. He couldn't ignore the fact that the kid's father had been killed in a robbery—same as James's dad. But whereas James's mother had taken on the role of both mother and father for him, this kid apparently had no one.

James pulled the truck into a parking spot. It wasn't likely that one fishing trip was going to change these kids' lives.

But he was here now, so . . .

"Hi, James." Ruby hopped out of the car that had pulled in next to them, sticking her hand in his open window.

He nodded to her, then quickly looked away. She had her hair in pigtails today, and suddenly all he could see was the lopsided pigtails he'd put in Sadie's hair. She'd never seemed to care that they were uneven.

James got out of the truck and scooted past Ruby to pull out the fishing rods and tackle box he'd picked up from Emma's house. His sister had quite the impressive collection of fishing gear.

He passed a rod to each of the teen boys, then one to Ruby and one to Bethany, who didn't look in the least concerned that she'd roped him into spending the afternoon in the last way he wanted to spend it.

"Can we go over there?" Ruby pointed to the end of the breakwater, where waves splashed against the large boulders that lined the sides of the wide concrete walkway.

"Sure." James shrugged. It wasn't like it mattered if they caught anything. All he had to do was survive for an hour or two and then he could be free.

"Thanks!" Ruby's smile poked its way right through James's heart.

"Come on." She turned to Pete and Chris with that same smile, already assuming a friendship with them. Both boys followed her, Pete looking enthusiastic, Chris giving her a begrudging nod.

James reached into the truck bed to grab the bucket he'd brought just in case they caught something. When he turned around, he was surprised to find Bethany waiting for him. He took the bag of snacks she held, hooking it over his arm.

They fell silently into step next to each other, following Ruby and the boys. Even from a few yards behind, James could make out her mile-a-minute chatter.

"Next time you could maybe consult with me first before volunteering me for something like this," he said in a low voice.

"Sorry." Her voice held no hint of remorse. "She's good at that, isn't she?"

James followed her gaze to Ruby, whose fishing pole swung wildly toward Pete as she kept up her enthusiastic chatter. Pete dodged but laughed.

"At what? Gouging people's eyes out?" James asked as her pole got dangerously close to Chris.

Bethany snorted. "No. That." She waved a hand toward the trio. "Talking to people."

James shrugged. They used to call Sadie Little Miss Talks-a-Lot, but Ruby might give her a run for her money.

"She thinks you don't like her."

"I— What? Who?" James swiveled his head in every direction as if he'd find some mysterious "she" Bethany was referring to.

"Ruby." Bethany said her daughter's name quietly, but a mama-bear protectiveness roared under the word.

"I— It's not—" How could he explain to Bethany that looking at her daughter was like looking through a mirror that showed everything he'd lost?

But she didn't give him a chance to try. "You're the one missing out. She's the best, sweetest little girl. And if you can't see that, it's your loss."

Before James could answer, Bethany had sped up, quickly closing in on Ruby and the boys. She said something to Ruby, who slipped her hand into her mother's. The girl smiled over her shoulder at James, making his heart contract so painfully that he wondered if he was having a heart attack. But then Ruby turned around again and his heart released. The pain in his chest lingered though, even as he caught up with the group and prepared their lines and showed them how to cast and how to set the hook if they felt a bite. It wasn't until he tossed his own line into the water that it eased a little. He'd chosen a spot several yards from Ruby and Bethany, which put him next to Chris. But right now he'd gladly take a juvenile delinquent over the chatterbox who reminded him so painfully of what he used to have. He was sorry if that made Ruby think he didn't like her—but it was the only way he was going to survive the afternoon.

He cast his line again and gazed across the waves to the horizon, letting his mind wander to Captain Perry's offer. Today was one more proof that Hope Springs wasn't for him. In Milwaukee, he never would have gotten roped into fishing with a couple of vandals, a crazy woman, and her daughter. In Milwaukee, he could do the job and then go home, day after day. In Milwaukee, nothing changed. Nothing brought him great joy, maybe. But nothing brought him sorrow either. He rubbed at his chest.

"Ah! Help!"

The cry startled James from his thoughts, and before he had consciously registered that it had come from Ruby, he was sprinting toward her.

"What's wrong?" he called, though he couldn't spot any immediate danger.

"Something is trying to steal my fishing pole." Ruby strained to pull it toward her.

James let out a breath as he reached her, chuckling. "That's a fish."

"It is?" Ruby's eyes went wide.

"Reel it in."

"I can't." Ruby appeared to be using all her strength to hold onto the pole.

"Here." James stepped behind the girl and reached around her to hold the pole. "I'll hold onto it. You reel. Slowly." The fish tugged on the other end of the line. "Feels like a big one."

"Really?" Delight sang from Ruby's tone. "This is fun."

"Keep cranking." He readjusted his grip so she could turn the reel more freely. "There it is." He pointed into the water a few feet from the boulders that jutted out from the breakwater. "Chris, climb down there and grab the line. You need to lift it over the rocks so we don't lose it."

Chris didn't reply, and the fish was getting closer. James gave an impatient sigh. "Pete, can you—"

"I got it." Chris climbed nimbly over the rocks and reached for the line.

"Easy," James cautioned.

"I said I got it." Chris shot him a look but pulled the line out of the water carefully. The fish dangled precariously on the end of the line.

"Grab it so it doesn't fall off," James called.

"You want me to touch it?"

"Yes. And hurry up before it ends up back in the water."

Chris made a face but wrapped a hand around the fish's middle.

"Watch the fins," James warned. "They're sharp." He let go of the fishing pole and moved to take the fish from Chris as he reached the top of the breakwater. "Nice job."

Chris shrugged, but James saw the way his expression softened. Maybe Bethany had been right that this was what the boys needed.

He held the fish out to Ruby. "It's a walleye."

She giggled. "That's a funny name. Can I touch it?"

"You can hold it if you want." Ruby nodded, and he placed it into her hands. "Hold it tight."

"Say 'fish.'" Bethany pointed her phone at Ruby.

"Fish." Ruby called, just as the fish wiggled. James lunged forward and helped her catch it.

"Get in there, boys," Bethany called. "This was a team effort." Both boys looked embarrassed but also pleased. James inched backwards, but Ruby smiled at him. "You too, James."

"No, that's okay. I don't—"

"You heard the girl. Get in there." Bethany lowered her phone, waiting for him. "If it weren't for you, that fish might have pulled Ruby right out to the middle of the lake."

James shook his head but stepped up next to Pete. It was easier than arguing.

After they'd taken the pictures, James helped Ruby put her fish in the bucket and reset her line. The rest of the afternoon, he was kept hopping from one person to the next, helping pull in fish and untangle lines. By the time they decided to call it a day, Pete and Bethany had caught one fish each, Chris two, and Ruby four. James hadn't had a spare moment to catch anything of his own, but he didn't mind.

"This was the best day ever, wasn't it?" Ruby bubbled as they hauled their catch and gear back to the parking lot.

Pete smiled at her. "It was fun."

Even Chris nodded. "You're a good fisherman."

"Fisher*girl*," Ruby corrected, making Chris laugh.

James set the bucket of fish down when they reached the vehicles. "I only have one bucket, so who's going to take the fish home?"

"I don't know how to clean fish," Bethany said. "So you boys can take them."

Pete shook his head. "My mom would kill me. She hates fish."

"All right. Chris, you take them." James passed the bucket to the teen. "Do you know what to do with them?"

The boy shrugged. "I'll figure it out."

"I can teach you." The words were out of his mouth before he could think. Maybe Bethany's impulse control issues were contagious.

He tried to figure out a way to take it back.

"That's a great idea." Of course Bethany had jumped right on that one. "You guys come on over to my house, and James can show you how to clean and cook the fish. I'll make some potatoes to go with it too."

"Bethany, I don't think—"

"Of course you do. Come on. Follow us." She jumped in her car before James could say anything else.

He eyed Pete and Chris, who were both laughing.

"Shut up," he growled.

But he gestured for them to get in the vehicle, then did the same and followed Bethany to her house.

"I'm sorry we didn't have any potatoes." Bethany carried the leftover fish to the counter and divided it into bags for Pete and Chris to take home. There wasn't much left—the boys had scarfed it down after helping James clean and cook it, and even Ruby had eaten seconds and then thirds.

"It's really fine." James's smile was overly patient.

"I've already said that, haven't I?" she asked sheepishly. Sometimes it was hard to keep track of what she'd said out loud and what she'd only spoken in her head.

James shrugged. "Don't beat yourself up over it. There was more than enough food."

A burst of laughter came from the living room, where Ruby had coerced Pete and Chris into a game of Pictionary.

"Do you think this will make a difference? For those boys?" She leaned against the counter.

James tucked the milk jug into the refrigerator. "Maybe." He turned to face her. "Maybe not."

"That's not very optimistic."

"After some of the things I've seen, that's as optimistic as I get."

"But you came," she pointed out.

"As I recall, I didn't have much of a choice."

Bethany laughed and loaded dishes into the dishwasher. "You're a funny guy. Did you know that?"

"Can't say I've ever been accused of that before." But his smile made him look almost cheerful. "What makes you say that?"

She studied him. "I don't know." Or maybe she did know, but she wasn't quite sure how to put it into words. "You seem so . . . all the time. But under it all, I think you're really . . ."

James's brow wrinkled. "I'm not sure if I should take that as a compliment or an insult."

She puffed in frustration. What was she trying to say? "You're . . . softer than you seem."

The sound James made in response said she had offended him.

"No, I mean that in a good way." Bethany scrambled for the right words. "I mean—you're nicer than you seem."

James's full laugh sounded genuine. "Maybe you should stop trying to fix it. I think you're only digging a deeper hole."

"Maybe." Bethany rubbed ruefully at her forehead. "It's been a long day." She loaded the last few dishes into the dishwasher and added soap, then started the machine. When she turned around, James was wiping the kitchen table.

The sight sent a sudden, sharp pain through her middle. It was so *normal*. So like the family she'd grown up in. So like the family she used to assume she'd have one day.

So far from how things had turned out.

She'd done the right thing, leaving Ruby's father—or the man who was most likely to be Ruby's father—the moment she'd found out she was pregnant. She never would have been able to leave that lifestyle and get clean if she hadn't. But sometimes she wished she didn't have to do it all alone.

"Bethany?" James's voice swam through her thoughts.

"Sorry. What?"

"Are you okay? You were staring."

"Was I?" She pulled her eyes away from him, pretending not to feel the heat climbing up her neck. "Sorry. Just tired."

"Yeah. I should get those guys home." He passed her on his way to set the rag by the sink, and his homey scent made her think of a protector. Made her want to move closer.

She moved toward the living room instead.

"Hey, Bethany?"

She paused.

"Thanks for making me do this."

She grinned at him. "Anytime."

In the living room, Chris was frantically tapping his drawing board with the marker while Pete and Ruby called out guesses.

Bethany studied the picture. "It's one of those— Uh— The things that— They grow underground and you eat them."

"Potato," Pete called.

But Bethany shook her head, frustration building. It was just a stupid game. But she was so tired of never being able to come up with the right word. "It's— Uh— It's red."

"Radish." James came up behind her, and she almost leaned back against him in relief. Yes. That was the word.

"Yep." Chris held up his board triumphantly, waving around the picture.

"Nice job," James murmured to her.

She pressed her lips together before she could say something about making a good team. It was nice to be able to exert some impulse control for a change.

"All right, guys." James gestured toward the door. "Time to go."

"No." Ruby pouted, but Bethany sent her a warning look.

"Can we do this again sometime?" Ruby asked as the boys made their way toward the door. "Do you guys want to play charades next time? I'm really good at that."

"Sure, Ruby. Thanks for having us," Pete said politely as he stepped outside.

Chris grunted his agreement.

"You're welcome anytime," Bethany replied.

"Wait," Ruby cried. She ran out the door to give first Pete and then Chris a hug. Then she eyed James, as if weighing how to say goodbye to him. Bethany saw the way his shoulders tensed and his mouth flattened.

"Come on, Ruby. Time to get ready for bed."

"Coming."

Bethany let out a breath. At least Ruby hadn't gone for a hug and been rejected.

"Thanks for helping me catch so many fish." Before Bethany could stop her, Ruby threw her arms around James's waist.

"Oof." James didn't return the hug, instead standing stock still, his eyes closed, jaw set as if he were in pain.

For heaven's sake. What could be so terrible about a hug from a little girl? Maybe Bethany had been wrong in thinking he was softer than he seemed.

"Come on, Ruby."

Ruby let go, and James's eyes opened. They landed on Bethany's, then shifted away. But not before she saw the same torment in them as she'd seen in the mirror for years. But for her, hugs from Ruby had helped to heal the pain.

So how had the girl's hug brought it to the surface for James?

Chapter 21

"You're serious?" James pulled the phone away from his ear to stare at Captain Burke's name on the screen.

"All I'm saying is, a change of pace might be good for you. Get away from the memories."

James massaged his neck. He'd called to beg the captain to let him come back early, and now the guy didn't want him back at all. Didn't he understand that the memories followed him wherever he went? The only thing that saved him from them was working.

And spending time with Bethany and Ruby certainly didn't help. That hug from Ruby the other day—she might as well have punched a hole right into his lungs. And the way Bethany had looked at him afterward—as if she'd seen right into his pain. No, he couldn't stay here.

"Look, the captain there says you've been a great asset and they could really use you."

James snorted. "It was a vandalism case, not a serial killer."

"And thank the Lord for that."

James shook his head. He'd stopped thanking the Lord for anything long ago.

"The point is," Captain continued. "It sounds like you're making a real difference there. Emma told me you seem happy."

Emma.

He should have known better than to tell his sister about the job offer. Of course she'd felt the need to butt in.

"Look, are you firing me?"

"Of course not." Captain's voice held the fatherly note that had always warmed James. But right now it made him want to punch someone. "I'm just suggesting that you consider what's best for you."

"I already have. I'll be back in a week." He hung up and tossed the phone onto the table.

"What's eating you?" Emma swept into the room, carrying a large box.

"You talked to Captain?"

Emma set the box on the table. "He wants what's best for you, James. I do too."

"I think I can be the judge of that."

"Can you?" Emma raised an eyebrow. "Because it seems like you're doing a good job of ignoring the great opportunities that are right here in front of you. Including this job offer. What'd you tell Captain Burke?"

"That I'd see him in a week." James pushed past her toward the door.

"Wait. Where are you going?"

"To the store. You need anything?"

"No. Well, actually, some protein bars, since you keep eating them all." Emma smirked at him. "But also, since you're going that way, would you mind dropping this off at Bethany's for me?" She gestured to the box, which appeared to hold random junk.

"You want me to bring her trash?"

Emma laughed. "Ruby needs it for a school project."

"Ah." James stepped forward, digging through the box to find a broken coffee maker, a stack of horse magazines, and a bag of fake snow, among other things. He squinted at his sister. "Why can't you do it?" He wasn't much in the mood to do her any favors right now. Not to mention that the thought of seeing Bethany and Ruby again unsettled him.

"I have a doctor appointment. I was going to do it after, but I have to get back in time for a private lesson."

James frowned. "Didn't you just have a doctor appointment?" If she was trying to set him up with Bethany, she could at least come up with a new excuse.

Emma shrugged, looking away. "It's a follow-up. So you'll do it?"

He studied her. There was something she wasn't telling him. About her "secret" matchmaking efforts? Or about her health? "Is everything okay?"

"Of course." She smiled brightly. "Tell Ruby I'm sure I can find more stuff if she needs it."

James nodded slowly. He wanted to press the issue, make her tell him if something was really wrong—but he didn't have the courage. Besides, his sister was the healthiest person he knew—and the most straightforward. If something were wrong, she would tell him.

He picked up the box of junk. As he carried it out to the truck, his eyes fell on a bottle of glitter.

Look, Daddy. I glittered your belt.

He dropped the box into the back and jumped into the vehicle. If this was another one of Emma's matchmaking tricks, she was going to be sorely disappointed. Because he was immune.

Where was it?

Bethany strained on her tiptoes on top of the kitchen chair, searching through the cupboards.

"Ruby?" she called.

"Yeah, Mom?" Ruby appeared in the kitchen a moment later.

"Do you know where the thing is?"

"What thing?"

"You know. The thing. For the . . ." She pulled her head out of the cupboard and waved her hands vaguely. She had known the word a minute ago.

"Kimberly's going to be here soon." Ruby glanced over her shoulder.

"I know," Bethany snapped. "That's why I'm looking for it."

"Looking for what?" Ruby raised her voice.

"Don't take that tone with me," Bethany warned. "Or you can forget about your sleepover."

"But I don't know what you're looking for," Ruby wailed.

"The thing!" Now Bethany was raising her voice too, and she hated it. But she hadn't slept well all week, and her frustration with her language issue had finally reached a boil. She never should have told Ruby she could have a sleepover. Why had she thought she could be a normal mom and handle keeping two girls entertained all night? Most days she could barely handle one.

The doorbell rang, and Bethany threw her hands in the air. Of course they were early. "Whatever. I guess you guys won't have cookies. Go get the door."

Ruby spun on her heel and marched toward the door, but Bethany was pretty sure she heard her mutter something about forgetting the sugar anyway under her breath.

She closed her eyes and counted slowly to five before climbing down from the chair. She supposed she could always go buy some cookies. Or take the girls to the Chocolate Chicken. Maybe that would go a little ways toward making up for yelling at Ruby.

She moved toward the front door, zipping on a smile. No need to make Tiffany question whether she was competent to watch her daughter for the night.

"Hi there. I'm so glad you—" She went mute as she spotted James in the door, passing a box to Ruby.

He lifted his head. "Everything okay? I thought I heard yelling . . ."

Ruby burst into tears and dropped the box, taking off for her room.

James shot Bethany an alarmed look. "I'm sorry. I didn't mean to—"

"It wasn't you. It was me. I was looking for something and I couldn't think of the word and I yelled at her." Her own eyes stung, but she knew no tears would fall. Though she wished sometimes they would. A good cry might be a relief. "Rolling pin." The word came to her suddenly. "I was looking for a rolling pin." She covered her face. "What kind of mother am I?"

James stepped into the house and touched a hand to her forearm. "Remember what you told Carrie the other day?"

"No." Bethany sniffed with a dry laugh. "I don't even remember who Carrie is."

"Sorry. Pete's mom. The boy who did the graffiti and—"

"I remember Pete," she interrupted.

"Okay, well, you told his mom that you were sure she's doing the best she can. And I'm sure you are too."

Bethany shook her head. "There's a big gap between my best and a normal person's best. I just— I don't know if I can do this anymore. And Ruby's friend is going to be here any minute and what's it going to look like if Ruby won't come out of her room and . . ." She ran out of words and took a shaky breath.

"Hey. It's okay. You just need a break." James's voice was calm and soothing. "Why don't you go take a walk?"

"I don't want to leave Ruby home alone."

"I'll stay here with her. She'll be fine."

"But what if Tiffany and Kimberly get here while I'm gone?"

"Then I'll tell them you'll be right back. It's going to be fine," he repeated. "Walk around the block or something." He nudged her toward the door. "Trust me, it will help."

"If you're sure you don't mind . . ."

"I'm sure." James gently pushed her the rest of the way out the door and closed it firmly behind her.

Bethany pulled in a deep breath of the lilac-scented air and started walking.

She hadn't been wrong in thinking that having someone to share parenting duties with would make life easier.

It's fifteen minutes, she reminded herself. *Not forever.*

Chapter 22

For crying out loud.

If Bethany's impulse control issues rubbed off on him one more time, James was seriously going to have to get his head examined.

What on earth had possessed him to offer to stay here with Ruby while Bethany took a walk?

But as much as he wanted to keep the question rhetorical, he already knew the answer.

It was the distress, the exhaustion, the *need* in Bethany's eyes. He couldn't bear to see it there and not do something—anything—to take it away. His hero complex at work again. Or maybe something else.

You're getting dangerously close to caring too much about this woman.

He plopped onto the couch with a sigh. Didn't he know it.

Fortunately, he only had another week to go, and then he'd never have to see her or Ruby again. He tipped his head back against the top of the couch and stared at the ceiling.

"Mom?" Ruby called from the hallway.

James closed his eyes for a second, then sat up. "She went for a walk," he called softly, not wanting to startle her.

"Oh." Ruby appeared in the living room as if she'd expected him to be there all along. "Why?"

Oh brother. What should he say to that? "She needed some fresh air."

"I didn't mean to make her upset," Ruby said quietly.

This might have been the first time James had seen the girl looking anything but cheerful, and he didn't like it. He considered telling a joke but instead said, "I know you didn't. And she knows too. She said it wasn't your fault."

Ruby frowned and slid onto the couch next to him. Every muscle in James's body tensed, ready to run away, but he was pinned between Ruby and the arm of the couch.

"Sometimes I wish she was like she used to be." Ruby played with a string on her sleeve.

"What did she used to be like?"

"I don't know. Different. Happy. Funny. We would do fun things together."

"Is that why you didn't tell her about bring your mom to school day?" James made sure not to allow any accusation to seep into his tone.

"I did tell—" Her face crumpled. "I didn't want all the other kids to say mean things and make her feel bad."

Oh man. The things this kid had to deal with. "That's fair. But don't you think she would have wanted to be there with you, even if it meant dealing with a few stupid kids?"

Ruby giggled. "Mom doesn't like the word stupid."

James laughed. "Sorry. But don't you think she'd put up with anything—even *silly* kids—to be with you?"

Ruby chewed her lip. "Probably."

"Trust me. I know she would."

"Are you going to tell her?" Ruby didn't sound scared. More like resigned.

"I'll leave that up to you. But believe me when I say you'll feel better if you do."

"You're just saying that because you're a grown-up. You're supposed to say it."

James laughed. "No, I'm saying that because I used to be a kid. One time I lied and told my dad I wasn't the one who threw a baseball through the window of his squad car. I felt sick for weeks until I finally told him."

Ruby seemed to consider that. "Was your dad mad when you told him?"

James thought about it. "He was disappointed that I'd lied. But he said he was proud of me for coming clean. He told me life would be full of hard choices between doing what's right and doing what's easy."

"Your dad sounds like a smart guy."

James chuckled. "He was. He's the reason I became a police officer. To be like him."

"Is he still a police officer? Or is he tired?"

"Tired?" James tried to make sense of the question. "Oh, retired? No. He's—" Was this an appropriate conversation to have with a ten-year-old? "He died in the line of duty."

"I'm sorry." Ruby patted his knee, as if she knew just what to do in such a situation.

"It's okay. It was a long time ago." He'd only been sixteen at the time. How had twenty-four years gone by since then?

"Is that why you're sad all the time?" The question was earnest and straightforward, and James looked at her in surprise.

"I'm not—"

The door opened, carrying Bethany in on a gust of fresh air. A healthy pink dotted her cheeks, and her hair had been tousled by the wind—but it was her smile that caught James off guard with the way it set his heart thumping.

Yep. It was time to go.

He tried to push to his feet, but Ruby used his leg as a springboard to vault toward her mom, shoving him back down into the cushions.

"Mom, I'm sorry." Ruby threw herself into Bethany's arms as they met in the middle of the room.

"Me too, Rubes. You didn't do anything wrong."

Ruby glanced toward James, who got to his feet. They didn't need him here for this. "I should go. Glad you're feeling better." He almost reached for Bethany's shoulder as he passed but diverted his hand at the last second and rubbed his neck.

"Thank you, James." Bethany's voice was soft and warm, and it sped his footsteps toward the door.

"Yeah. Thanks, James." Ruby's voice followed. "You know, you'd make a good dad."

"Ruby!" Bethany sounded mortified, but the word seared through James hotter and sharper than the bullet that had pierced his shoulder. He tore open the door but jerked to a stop just in time to avoid plowing over the woman and girl on the other side.

He gripped the door, trapped, trying to get his flight reaction under control.

The woman's eyes widened, and her lips curled into a smile. "James. I wasn't expecting to see you here." She glanced past him to Bethany. "Is now a bad time?"

"I was just leaving," James scraped out.

But before he could squeeze past her to get out the door, a furry streak bolted past him and into the bushes.

"Mrs. Whiskers," Ruby cried, running past them to follow the critter. "Come here, you silly cat."

But Mrs. Whiskers took one look at Ruby and darted for the nearest tree, scrambling up it in record time.

"Oh no. Mrs. Whiskers, come down," Ruby cried, running to the tree. The cat meowed but didn't move.

Ruby looked toward them. "We have to help her."

"She's too high," Bethany called back. "I don't have a ladder. She'll come down later."

Even from across the yard, James could see Ruby's lip tremble.

"I'll get her." He slipped past Tiffany and her daughter, working out the best route up the tree as he crossed the yard.

It took him a couple of attempts to get a grip—it'd been a long time since he'd climbed a tree—but once he did, the movements came back naturally enough.

"Be careful, James," Ruby called from below him.

He grunted. What on earth was he doing crawling around in a tree to rescue a cat that had nothing to do with him?

It shouldn't have mattered that Ruby had looked desolate at the thought of leaving her cat in the tree.

It shouldn't have.

But it did.

"Here kitty, kitty." James held out a hand. The cat eyed it but didn't move. He inched out farther on the branch. It seemed sturdy enough, but he listened for any cracks or pops.

So far so good.

"Come on, Mrs. Whiskers," Ruby called. "Go to James. He's nice." She stood right under the branch James and the cat were on.

"Ruby, do me a favor and move back, okay? Just in case."

"Just in case what?" Ruby blinked up at him.

"Just back up." He reached for Mrs. Whiskers, managing to snag her leg. The cat didn't resist as he pulled her closer to him. When he tucked her against his shoulder, she started purring. James rolled his eyes. "Stupid cat."

But then he remembered what Ruby had said about her mom's feelings about the word stupid. "Silly animal," he amended.

With the cat tucked securely against him, he contemplated how to get back to the ground. He snorted at himself. Maybe the cat wasn't the stupid animal here.

"Why aren't you coming down?" Ruby asked, still standing too close to the tree.

"I'm working on it," James shot back. "Move away from the tree."

It took longer than he would have liked, but he managed to lower himself enough that he could make the final jump. The instant he was on his feet, Ruby's arms were around him. It didn't feel as odd as it had the other day, and he found himself lifting one hand briefly to her back before he extracted the cat from his arms and passed her off to Ruby.

Now he could leave.

"That was heroic," Tiffany said as James tried to inconspicuously pass the little group gathered outside.

He shrugged, but Bethany's grateful smile slowed his footsteps. She opened her mouth as if to say something, but Tiffany beat her to it. "I have this huge bookshelf I've been wanting to move for months, but it's too heavy for me. If you're not busy, do you think I could borrow your muscles for a minute?"

"Uh . . ." How was he supposed to answer that?

"I'll sweeten the deal with cookies. I made them this morning."

"I guess. Sure." He didn't have much choice. It wasn't like he had anywhere else he needed to be. Although he suddenly had the oddest urge to stay right here.

"Great." Tiffany beamed at him, then turned to Bethany. "You're all good here then? You need anything?"

Bethany shook her head with a stiff smile. "I've got everything under control. I'll bring Kimberly home tomorrow morning."

"See you then." Tiffany sidled up to James, and Bethany's meager smile faded.

James waved to her. "See you later."

She nodded, then stepped inside and closed the door.

Tiffany hooked her hand around James's elbow, chatting animatedly about how she was redecorating her house. James tried to pay attention. But he found himself looking over his shoulder at Bethany's closed door, thinking of how cozy he'd felt inside.

***

Could she borrow his muscles? Bethany rolled her eyes as she stood to the side of the window, watching James's truck pull away and follow Tiffany's SUV. She wished she could forget that line. It was ridiculous. And also something she knew she could never come up with.

She had a hard enough time managing a normal conversation, let alone flirting.

Not that she wanted to flirt with James.

Besides, he and Tiffany had made quite the striking couple, strolling down her driveway, his jeans and flannel shirt a perfect contrast to her pencil skirt and dusty rose blouse.

Undoubtedly, it wouldn't be long before she heard the rumors around town.

She sighed. Ah well. It didn't matter.

She pulled out her phone and swiped to the list she'd made for tonight. *Make pizza.* Right.

But she had just turned on the oven when the sound of raised voices came from down the hall. She paused, listening.

The girls were probably just having fun—but why did it sound like they were shouting?

She slipped silently down the hallway. She wouldn't intrude unless there was a problem, but she had to get close enough to make sure everything was okay.

"That's not fair." It was Ruby's voice, and it was elevated. Bethany took a step closer to her daughter's bedroom door. There was enough stuff in that box of junk James had brought over that they shouldn't have to fight over it to complete their assignment.

"I met him first." Ruby was still shouting.

Bethany paused. This was about a boy? She rubbed at her temple. She definitely was not ready for that. But maybe it wasn't something she should get in the middle of. She could always talk to Ruby about it after Kimberly left tomorrow.

She turned toward the kitchen.

But Ruby's voice came again. "You already have a dad."

"Yeah, but he lives in Iowa."

"Well, I don't have any dad. Plus, he likes my mom better."

Bethany froze, bracing a hand on the wall. Were they fighting about . . . *James*?

She spun around and marched to Ruby's room. She had no idea what she was going to say—only that she had to put an end to this conversation. Immediately.

"Yeah right." For a ten-year-old, Kimberly carried sarcasm well. "*You* don't even like your mom better. Otherwise you would have told her about take your mom to school day."

Bethany pulled her hand back from the slightly ajar door, pressing it instead to her middle. Had Ruby intentionally not told her about the event? Because she didn't want Bethany there?

"You know what," Kimberly kept going, "I bet my mom and James will be dating by the time I get home tomorrow."

"Maybe you should go home right now!" Ruby shot back.

Bethany pushed the door open. "Hey, girls." She forced enough pep into her voice that she probably sounded like an over-the-top cheerleader. "Who wants some ice cream?"

Ruby toed the floor, not meeting Bethany's eyes. "We didn't have dinner yet."

Did she think Bethany had forgotten?

"I know that, silly." Bethany waved off her daughter's objection. "But if we eat dinner first, you'll be too full for ice cream. So I thought we'd go to the Chocolate Chicken now and then we can always have some pizza later if you guys are hungry. What do you think?"

"I think that's a great idea." Kimberly bounced off the bed, sending Bethany a syrupy smile. "You're the best, Ms. Moore." She flounced out of the room.

As Ruby slipped past, Bethany caught her arm. "We need to talk about this later."

Ruby nodded, not looking up. "I know."

"But for now," Bethany continued, "try to have fun with your friend. No more arguments, all right?"

Ruby lifted her head. "Yeah, Mom. All right."

"Good." Bethany gave herself a moment after Ruby had left the room to just breathe.

She may not be an expert at sleepovers—but she seemed to have salvaged this one.

Chapter 23

Two more days and James could return to Milwaukee. He'd have the weekend to get things in order at his house, and then he'd get back to work on Monday.

It was what he'd been waiting for all summer.

So why was he sort of dreading it? Not the work part—but the leaving Hope Springs part. Much as he hated to admit it, this little town had gotten under his skin. So much so that for a second the other day, when he'd been rescuing Ruby's cat, he'd wondered what it would be like if he took the job offer here. A few more cat rescue calls, a lot less homicides.

And a lot more Bethany . . .

He shook his head, shoving out the kitchen door and instinctively checking the driveway for her car. She wasn't here yet.

Probably for the best.

He made his way toward the barn, trying not to picture her frown when Tiffany had asked him to come over and help move her bookshelf. Bethany had looked . . . jealous wasn't the word. More like wistful, as if she wished . . . what?

He ran a hand over his head. It didn't matter what she wished. He was leaving.

Which was exactly what he'd told Tiffany after he'd moved her bookshelf and she'd insisted on plying him with cookies, then suggested that they get coffee or dinner sometime. In retrospect, the comment probably shouldn't have taken him by surprise, given the way she'd been acting, but it did.

At first, when he'd stammered out that he couldn't, she'd asked if it was because of Bethany. Even after he'd forcibly—perhaps too forcibly—denied it, she hadn't seemed to believe him.

Which was ridiculous. Since it was true.

Sure, it was also true that even if he weren't leaving town, he would have turned Tiffany down. But that had nothing to do with Bethany.

He slid in through the barn door and moved down the stalls, inhaling the sweet hay and horse scent. That was definitely one thing he was going to miss about Hope Springs.

But would he miss Bethany?

The door behind him opened, and his heart accelerated at the same time his mouth became a map of involuntary muscles, all pulling upward.

She was here.

He turned, trying to tone down his smile. "Hey, how— Oh, it's just you." He made a face at his sister.

Emma didn't offer the quick comeback he expected. She must be tired this morning—it wasn't like her to pass up an opportunity to joke with him. As she got closer, his heart kicked into fight or flight mode. Her expression—it was the same one Mom had worn when she'd told them Dad had been shot. The same expression the doctor had worn when Sadie . . .

He took a step backward, the pounding in his throat too strong to get any words past. It felt like there was a veil of water between them, keeping her from reaching him, making her form wobble. But when she finally stood in front of him, he grabbed her shoulder.

"Mom?" The word scraped its way out of his hoarse throat.

"Mom's fine."

A sharp breath pushed out of him, as if his lungs had been punctured. As long as Mom and Emma were okay. Two more names popped into his head, sending his heart rate back up. "Bethany? Ruby?"

Emma smiled faintly. "They're both okay. But now I know how you feel about them."

He shook his head. He wasn't going to play that game right now. "What then?"

"Let's go sit down." Her voice was way too gentle, and James dropped his hand to his side. "No. Tell me."

Emma sighed but met his eyes. And then he knew. "It's you." The whisper sliced across his vocal cords like a knife blade. She moved closer, but he held up his hands, as if they could shield him from the words.

"The reason I've been going to the doctor is that they're concerned about a mass on my ovaries."

"No." He shook his head. "You said it was a follow-up appointment."

"They think it might be cancer," Emma continued. "But—"

"No." He shook his head again, as if he could somehow dislodge the words. It couldn't be true. He wouldn't let it be true.

"James, listen." Emma used the same voice he'd heard her use to soothe spooked horses. "It's not as bad as it sounds." She took a tentative step toward him, holding out a hand. "They want me to have surgery. A—" She swallowed hard but then gave him a wavery smile. "A hysterectomy. They're hopeful that they caught it early enough that that's the only treatment I'll need."

"When?" He crossed his arms in front of him, as if he were interrogating a suspect.

"Monday." Emma took another step toward him. "It's going to be fine, James, okay?"

He nodded once. "I'll call Captain Burke. Let him know I'm going to need more time off. I imagine it'll be at least a few weeks before you're on your feet again."

"No. I called Mom, and she's going to come for the surgery and then stay for a while afterward."

"Good. Mom can take care of you. And I'll take care of all of this." He waved a hand around the barn.

"I do have a staff, you know. And my friends will help out." She patted his arm. "Everything is under control. You need to get back to your life. Unless..."

"Unless what?" He folded his arms in front of him. She had better not start talking about what would happen if she didn't make it. Because that was not an option.

"Unless you've decided your life is here with a certain someone..." She waggled her eyebrows at him, and he wanted to punch her and hug her all at once. How could she goof around at a time like this? But he knew she was doing it for his sake.

He shook his head. "I'm staying. Until you're on your feet. Don't get any other dumb ideas."

"You're a good brother. Have I ever told you that?" Emma's lip trembled, and she pulled him into a hug.

He squeezed her tight, closing his eyes, his arms shaking. *You can't have her too, God. I won't let you.*

Chapter 24

All the things she forgot on a daily basis, and yet Bethany couldn't get the image of James and Tiffany walking away from her house the other day out of her head.

"It doesn't matter," she told herself firmly before getting out of the car at Emma's stables. So what if this would be the first time she'd seen James since then—it wouldn't change anything between them, especially since there *was nothing* between them. Which was exactly what she'd told Ruby after she'd taken Kimberly home the other day. Fortunately, her daughter hadn't brought it up again, and the argument didn't seem to have affected the girls' friendship.

She sighed as she made her way toward the barn. The day was warm and sunny, and she tipped her head toward the blue sky and pulled in a deep breath. She had more than enough to be thankful for.

She opened the barn door and stepped inside. The sound of a shovel scraping against the floor carried down the length of the building, making her smile. James was already hard at work. As always.

She made her way to the stall, where he seemed to be attacking the bedding with unusual vigor.

"Wow. In a hurry today?" she joked.

But when he looked up, the sharp blade of his gaze stabbed right through her. He was broken—more broken than usual. But why?

"I— Is everything all right?"

James shook his head but resumed scooping. "You talk to Emma at all?"

"Not today, no. Why?"

James stopped shoveling and straightened but kept his back to her. "You should talk to her."

"Okay. But her car isn't here. What's going on?" Did he want his sister to break it to her that he and Tiffany were now seeing each other?

He turned toward her so slowly that she was surprised he didn't tip over, like Ruby the first time she'd ridden a two-wheeler. A deep frown creased his features. Today he really was James the Gray.

"She has to have surgery."

"Oh." Bethany let out a breath. That wasn't so bad. Lots of people had surgery every day. "I'm sure—"

"They think it's cancer, Bethany." Hardness coated his voice, but his face dissolved into soft lines of fear.

It took Bethany a moment to process the words. But as soon as she had, she couldn't keep her feet from carrying her across the stall or her arms from wrapping around him.

James stiffened and disentangled himself from her grasp. "Just. Don't." He looked away.

Bethany swallowed. She hadn't meant to upset him more. "I'm sorry. I just—"

"Impulse control. I get it. Can we get to work?" He resumed scooping before she could answer.

She watched him for a minute, then moved to her own stall across the way, sending up prayers for Emma and for James as she worked.

When they had finished, they cleaned up silently. Then James left the barn without a word. Bethany stood there, listening to the sounds of the nickering horses.

It seemed wrong how peaceful it was in here when turmoil swirled all around. But then, sometimes it seemed like that was the way life was. Peace and chaos. Beauty and pain. Joy and sorrow. A collision of opposites. *But God is here through it all,* she reminded herself.

Chapter 25

James blinked up at the ceiling, faint gray light finally illuminating the contours of the room. He didn't know how long he'd been lying here awake—only that he couldn't stand it for another minute. He hadn't slept well a single night since Emma had broken her news to him, and exhaustion was a constant companion.

He rolled himself out of bed and pulled on a pair of running shorts and a t-shirt. Exhausted or not, a run was the only thing that would clear his head—though he'd found that even those hadn't helped lately to banish the thoughts, the guilt, the anger, as everything he'd lost—everything he could still lose—collided in his head. He crammed his earbuds into his ears, cranking up the volume on his music in the hopes of drowning the thoughts out.

He made his way downstairs, tiptoeing past Emma's door to keep from waking her. He had no idea how she was holding up the way she was. He'd walked into the arena on Friday and found her teaching her dressage riders, her voice cheerful, same as always. Not even a hint that her body had turned on her.

On the one hand, he'd been proud of her. And on the other hand, he'd had to walk out of there, his eyes catching Bethany's for a moment before he'd let the door slam behind him. He'd thought that she might follow him, but he was grateful she hadn't. The compassion in her gaze, the understanding—it was too hard to take. He probably owed her an apology for the way he'd snapped at her for hugging him the other day. But it had been either snap or break down completely. And he couldn't afford to do that.

As he slipped out the front door now, James sucked in a couple of deep breaths of the damp morning air before taking off down the long lane that led into the trees where he and Bethany had ridden together. He pushed himself hard, letting the music drive him forward, relishing the pounding in his heart that came from running, as it pushed out everything else.

He followed the trail until it branched into two paths, one slightly overgrown. James frowned at it before taking it. He didn't recall ever going this way, but if he got lost, at least his outside circumstances would finally match his insides.

Only half a mile down the trail, it became so overgrown that he had to slow to a walk so he wouldn't trip. Still he kept pushing forward, ripping his feet through the tangle of underbrush and holding his hands up to shield himself from the wispy branches of low-growing trees that overhung the path.

"Ouch!" He lifted a hand to his face as a spiny branch snagged his cheek. His hand came away with a small streak of blood, and he growled at it.

He should turn around and go back. But a strange compulsion pulled him forward. Now that he'd started down this path, he needed to see where it led.

In another three minutes, the path disappeared completely. But by now James could see an opening ahead. He shoved his way through a dense layer of bramble, stumbling before he regained his footing.

Swiping sweat out of his eyes, he took in the small pond in front of him, shimmering as the newly risen sun sent a ripple of gold across the surface. At the far end, a mother duck eyed him as she led her babies toward the shore. A light breeze cooled the sweat gathered on the back of his neck and sent a hushing sound through the grasses and leaves.

James let out his breath slowly and clasped his hands together behind his head.

It was beautiful. It was powerful and gentle all at once. It was—

James tilted his head toward the heavens. "What is this?" He shouted the words, leading mama duck to send him a reproving look and veer off with her ducklings. "You can do this? You can make all of this? You can take care of these stupid birds? But you can't keep my sister healthy? You can't keep my daughter—"

James broke off, shaking his head. What was he doing? Yelling at someone who would never listen. Someone who had shown time and again that he didn't care. James had wondered more than once if it was just that God was powerless, if he *couldn't* help. But looking at all of this, this morning, he knew. God wasn't powerless. He was heartless.

He spun away from the pond and plunged back into the brush, ignoring the twigs and branches that slapped at his face and arms, the weeds and bushes that grasped at his feet. He had to get out of here. The moment he reached the path, he drove his feet into a sprint, keeping up the punishing pace all the way back. He only slowed down when his eyes fell on Emma, sitting on the front porch, a blanket around her shoulders and a book—likely her Bible—in her hands.

He ducked into the barn to catch his breath and get his emotions under control. Emma had enough to worry about without adding him to the mix. He needed to be the strong one here.

When he finally felt his heart rate slow, he made his way toward the house. Emma looked up from her book—he'd been right that it was her Bible—as he clomped up the porch steps.

"Have a good run?" She offered him a gentle smile.

"Yeah." Hopefully he'd been far enough away when he'd yelled that she hadn't heard him. "Found a pond."

"That's one of my favorite spots to just sit and pray. It's so peaceful."

James grunted.

"I'm going to go get ready for church." She closed her Bible and stood.

James stepped out of her way, but she didn't move past him.

"I have a favor to ask." She looked tentative, and James's stomach clenched. Whatever she was about to say, he wasn't going to like it.

"Worship with me?" Her voice was upbeat, but her eyes were pleading.

He swallowed. He would do almost anything for his sister, but . . . "I don't exactly feel like worshiping right now."

Emma smiled gently. "You know what Dad always said: 'There are only two times to worship. When you feel like it and . . .'" She looked at him expectantly.

He shook his head but mumbled, "And when you don't."

"Please, James. I know it's a lot to ask. I just need—"

But he had already made up his mind. "I'll go."

He'd go to church. Because Emma needed him.

But it wouldn't change the way he felt about God.

Chapter 26

"Yikes." Bethany looked down as she nearly tripped over Mrs. Whiskers. The cat meowed up at her plaintively. "What's the matter with you?" She glanced toward the cat's dishes in the corner of the kitchen. Empty.

"Poor kitty." Bethany thought she'd taken care of her last night before bed, but she must have forgotten. She quickly filled the food dish, then carefully picked up the water dish and carried it to the sink. "Ruby," she called as she stuck the dish under the faucet. "Are you almost ready? We're going to be late." Not that that was anything new.

Her daughter's bedroom door opened just as Bethany shut off the faucet. She turned to give the dish to the cat. But she stopped so fast at the sight of her daughter's face that a nice big splash of water slopped down the front of her blouse.

"What is that?" She pointed at the pink blush that streaked Ruby's cheeks and the glittery green eye shadow that shimmered from her eyelids.

"Kimberly gave me some of her makeup."

"Some of her . . ." Bethany pointed toward the hallway. "You know you're not old enough for makeup. Go wash it off."

"But, Kimberly's mom lets her—"

"Now." Bethany gestured again, waiting for her daughter to march down the hall with a huff before releasing her own huff and refilling the water dish, wiping at the wet spot on her shirt with her free hand.

Oh well. She didn't have time to change. Hopefully it would dry before they got to church. And anyway, a wet shirt was a minor problem in the scheme of things. Especially when she compared it to what Emma was facing. And James.

She couldn't get his brokenness out of her head. Or the way he'd rejected her hug.

She sighed. The hug hadn't been an impulse control thing. Not really. More like it was the only way she could express what she was feeling.

Ruby reappeared in the kitchen, face sullen but makeup-free.

"Much better." Bethany grabbed her purse. "Let's go."

Ruby made a face but followed her to the car.

Bethany made sure Ruby had her seatbelt on before backing slowly down the driveway.

"Mom?" Ruby's voice was so quiet that at first Bethany thought she was hearing faint sounds from the radio.

"What is it?" she asked when she realized it was her daughter. She checked the time on the dashboard. It was just possible that they'd get to church on time.

"Is Miss Emma going to die?"

Bethany smashed her foot to the brake at the bottom of the driveway. Telling Ruby about Emma's possible diagnosis had been one of the hardest things Bethany had ever done. But she'd been careful to focus on the positive and hadn't once brought up death.

She turned to look at her daughter over her shoulder. "What makes you ask that?"

"Kimberly said people who get cancer die."

Bethany swallowed. "Some do." She didn't want to lie to her daughter. "But many don't. Just like some people who have an aneurysm die. But not everyone, right?"

Ruby nodded slowly but still wore lines of worry too old for her ten-year-old face. "What if she dies though?"

Bethany swallowed. She didn't want to consider that possibility. But she couldn't pretend it didn't exist. "Then she'll go to heaven. That would be pretty awesome for her, right?"

Ruby frowned. "But I want her to stay here."

"I know, Rubes. Me too. You know the best thing we can do for her, right?"

Ruby nodded and folded her hands. "Can we pray right now?"

Bethany glanced at the clock again. The minutes were ticking away. But how could she say no to praying for their friend? "Of course. Do you want to or should I?"

"You drive. I'll pray."

Bethany laughed. Leave it to her practical daughter to come up with a solution. "Sounds like a plan." She pulled the car into the street and headed toward church, Ruby's sweet prayer—for Emma, for James, for all of their friends, even for the horses—filling the vehicle and lifting Bethany's heart.

She might not always be the mother she wanted to be—but in moments like this, she was so very glad God had given her Ruby.

"Amen." Ruby's prayer concluded as Bethany pulled into the church parking lot—only three minutes late.

"Amen," Bethany repeated, parking in the first spot she found. "That was a wonderful prayer, Ruby."

"Thank you." Ruby hopped out of the back seat. Bethany grasped her hand and they speed-walked toward church.

They had just reached the sidewalk, the sounds of the first hymn floating out the open doors, when Ruby stopped abruptly, pulling Bethany to a stop too. "I forgot one."

"One what?" Bethany glanced toward the greeter holding the door open for them.

"Prayer."

"That's okay. You can keep praying in church." Bethany tugged her forward through the doors, mumbling a thank you to the greeter, who nodded with a warm smile. Ruby led them straight for the row where they always sat, with the friends who had become family.

At the front of the church, Dan was beginning his first Scripture reading, and Bethany directed her attention to him.

"Mom." Ruby's whisper was urgent, and she tugged on Bethany's sleeve.

"I told you to go to the bathroom before we left," Bethany murmured.

"No you didn't. But that's not it."

"What?" Bethany directed an impatient glance at her daughter. It was hard enough to concentrate without Ruby's constant whispers. But her gaze caught suddenly on the person sitting next to Ruby. James?

His eyes met hers, and she offered him a smile that he didn't return as he ducked his head.

Eyes wide, Ruby leaned toward Bethany and whispered, "God already answered one of my prayers."

Bethany nodded. One of hers too.

Maybe James had found the same thing she had. That when you were at your lowest, that was when you found out how much you needed the Lord.

Chapter 27

If his neck muscles were any tighter, James's head might pop right off his body. But he couldn't relax.

Not here. Not with his sick sister on one side of him. Not with Ruby, who reminded him way too much of what he'd lost, on the other side. Not with Pastor Dan up front, talking about how good God was.

You're doing this for Emma, he reminded himself, forcing his head toward one shoulder and then the other as the hymn ended and Pastor Dan stood gazing out at the congregation, a small smile on his lips, as if they were all one big, happy family. James crossed his arms over his chest. He wasn't buying it.

"I like to think I'm a relatively calm guy," Pastor Dan began. "Pretty unflappable. But the one thing that can ruffle my feathers more than anything is that little guy over there." He pointed toward a tow-haired boy sitting on a blonde woman's lap, a girl who was probably a little younger than Ruby sitting next to them. His family, James remembered from the Easter dinner. "Hey, buddy." Dan waved at the kid, who giggled and stuffed a piece of cereal in his mouth. "See—" Dan turned back to the congregation. "Matthias is going through his 'why' phase. You know the one—where every question I answer is followed by another: Daddy, why are fire trucks red? So people can see them coming. Why? So they can get out of the way. Why? So the firefighters can get to the fire faster. Why? So they can help people and put the fire out. Why? Because that's their job. Why? Argh."

Dan clutched his head with a chuckle, and the congregation laughed along with him. "And he could happily do it all day long. Don't get me wrong. I know it's good for kids to ask why. I know it helps them learn about the world around them. But sometimes you have to admit that those why questions are a little pointless, right?"

He paused, growing sober. "Let that sink in for a moment. Those why questions are pointless. And yet—" He paced a few steps to the left. "How often do we demand answers to our own why questions? You know the ones: Why did we lose our job? Why were we in a car accident? Why is someone close to us sick? Why did someone die?"

James's neck muscles tightened to the snapping point as he dug his fists into his sides. Next to him, Emma patted his leg once and offered a soft smile. James could only grimace in reply. On his other side, Ruby wiggled, her elbow digging into his ribs. He glanced over at her, and she smiled up at him, whispering, "Sorry."

He was pretty sure his grimace deepened as he lifted his eyes from her to Bethany, who was watching him with lines of worry wrinkled into her brow.

He shook his head and faced the front, using every ounce of self-control to keep himself anchored in his seat. *You're doing this for Emma. You're doing this for Emma.* He tried to focus on the mantra, but Dan's words stabbed through.

"If it makes you feel any better, you aren't the first person to ask those why questions. In fact, we can look all the way back to Moses. God had promised him—*promised* him—that he would lead the people out of slavery in Egypt. And yet, the first time Moses went to pharaoh and asked for permission to leave—and pharaoh not only said no but made the Israelites work harder to produce bricks each day—Moses turned to God and said,

'Is this your plan? Is this why you sent me? Why are you bringing trouble on us? Why is this happening?'"

Dan walked to the small podium and picked up the Bible that rested on it. "Fast forward a little bit, and God brings all these plagues on the Egyptians so that finally pharaoh tells the Israelites, 'Get out of here already. We don't want you here anymore.' So the Israelites go, led by Moses, just as God promised. They get out of Egypt, they evade the soldiers pharaoh sends when he changes his mind again. Not just evade them, but God clears the way for them to walk through the Red Sea on *dry ground*, for heaven's sake. And then there they are, at the door of the Promised Land. And the leaders of the tribes go out to explore and they come back and, even though they know full well that God has promised this land to them, they say, 'There's no way we can take this land. The people in it are much too strong for us.' And the whole community takes up the tantrum."

He looked at the Bible in his hand and read, "'If only we had died in Egypt! Or in this wilderness! Why is the Lord bringing us to this land only to let us fall by the sword?' And then they start making plans to ignore God's promise and go back to Egypt. They're finally talked out of that foolishness, but then they're facing attack by the Amorites, and Gideon says to God, 'Pardon me, my lord—'" Dan looked up with an ironic smile. "At least he showed some humility." He turned back to the Bible. "'But if the Lord is with us, why has all this happened to us? Where are all his wonders that our ancestors told us about?'"

Dan paused. "Of course, those were all big, national things. Things that affected a lot of people. So maybe we can't always understand the politics behind them or the intricacies involved in them. Maybe it would be unreasonable to expect that we would. But what about the more personal suffering we face? Ever ask God why he allows those things to happen?"

James clamped his jaw together tight enough to send a shockwave through his teeth. Of course he'd asked God why. And he'd never once gotten an answer. And from what he was hearing here, neither had anyone else.

"The most famous person to ask why in the Bible is probably Job, right?" Dan set the Bible down and took a few steps closer to the congregation, his voice softening. "And who can blame him? The guy lost everything. His home, his animals, his servants, his children. All gone." Dan shook his head. "Frankly, I don't know what I would do."

James swallowed. Dan was lucky he didn't know what he would do. That he had never had to find out. He felt Bethany's eyes on him again but refused to allow himself to look anywhere but straight ahead. He didn't need to see her worry or compassion or kindness.

"Listen to Job's why questions: 'Why have you made me your target? . . . Why do you hide your face and consider me your enemy?'" Dan winced. "Cuts right to the heart of it, doesn't he? Isn't that what we so often think? That when bad things happen to us, it's because God has turned against us. Because he is evil. Because he's punishing us. Because he doesn't love us enough to keep us from hurting."

"Well." Dan flipped further in his Bible. "I have news for you. It's not because God doesn't love you. It's not because he's punishing you. It's not because he's turned against you. And it's certainly not because he's evil. How do I know that?" He paused. "Because of another why question. This one asked by Jesus—" Dan looked down at his open Bible. "My God, my God, why have you forsaken me?"

Slowly, Dan set the Bible on the podium and looked around the church. "God loves you and me so much that he took the punishment that we deserved for our sins and placed it on his own Son. He loves us so much that he sent Jesus to the cross so that he wouldn't have to turn against us. He loves you so much that he promises that even when bad things happen—things we can't explain, things we don't understand—he will use them for your good and his glory."

There it was. James had been waiting for that line of garbage the whole sermon. That saccharine promise that whatever happened to you, no matter how terrible, it was supposed to be good for you. And yet, somehow, no one ever seemed to be able to explain *how* it was good for you.

"I know what you're thinking." Dan's gaze swept the church, and James looked away. He very much doubted that the pious pastor up there knew what he was thinking.

"You're thinking *how?* How can losing my job be for my good? How can getting into an accident be for my good? How can getting cancer be for my good? How can losing someone I love be for my good?"

James wanted to stand up and scream, "It can't." But he held his seat, digging his fists into his legs, vowing not to listen to another word.

Except Dan's voice wasn't the type of voice that could easily be tuned out.

"You want the hard answer, or the easy one?" Dan asked.

James stared at the floor, watching Ruby's black shoes swing back and forth. *Do you like my new shoes, Daddy? Mama says they can be my church shoes.*

James shifted in his seat, clearing his throat.

"The hard answer is, 'I don't know.' I don't know how any of those things can be for our good." Dan's voice grew louder. "But the easy answer is that God does. He tells us in Isaiah 55:8-9, 'For my thoughts are not your thoughts, neither are your ways my ways,' declares the Lord. 'As the heavens are higher than the earth, so are my ways higher than your ways and my thoughts than your thoughts.'"

Dan closed the Bible and just stood there, as if to let the words sink in. James shifted in his seat again. All that proved was that God was smarter than he was. But it didn't mean God was good—it didn't mean he had James's good, Emma's good, Sadie's good, in his heart.

"You see, even if God told us the why, even if he explained every detail, we wouldn't get it," Dan continued. "We couldn't. We're just too small. Our concept of God's plan is just too puny. We're stuck in the here and now. God sees the big picture, the whole picture, all of time and eternity. And he promises that someday he will bring us to glory with him, and *then* we will see. 1 Corinthians 13:12 says, 'For now we see only a reflection as in a mirror; then we shall see face to face. Now I know in part; then I shall know fully, even as I am fully known.' *Then*," Dan said with a smile. "*Then* we will know how God used all of these things—all of our whys—for his glory. Until then—" Dan held his hands out to his sides. "We walk by faith and not by sight. We trust. We believe. We take him at his Word. I'm not saying it will be easy. I'm not saying we won't ever wonder why again. But I *am* saying that his promises are true. That he has our eternal good in his heart. And nothing can shake that. Amen."

As the sermon came to a close, James's head reeled. There was a part of him—an ever-so-small, ever-so-timid part of him—that wanted to believe what Dan said was true. That wanted to believe that everything he had lost had not been for nothing. But the thing was, he would gladly give up any future joy—any *then*—to have Sadie here with him now. Maybe that was blasphemy or sacrilege or who knew what, but it was how he felt.

Chapter 28

Peace washed over Bethany as Dan finished his sermon. How many times had she asked why over the past couple of years? Why had her aneurysm happened? Why did she have to face this struggle with words and memories? Sometimes her thoughts went back further: Why had God let her get hurt in volleyball, which had led to surgery, which had led to her addiction to painkillers, which had led to her spiral into other drugs? Why hadn't he stopped her from leaving rehab time and again? Why? Why? Why?

And even though she still didn't have the answer to those whys, she felt like she could finally let them go. That she could trust them to God, trust that he had been working through the hard things, even if she didn't know exactly how. The relief was enough to make her grin like a fool as she stood and joined in singing the next hymn.

Until she happened to glance over at James.

His arms were nailed to his sides, his mouth stretched into a stark line, his jaw clenched tight. He looked so much like a statue that she held her breath until she saw a muscle in his neck twitch.

As if he felt her watching him, his eyes came to hers—only for a moment. But it was long enough for Bethany to catch the depth of pain in them.

It wasn't the first time she'd noticed it, but today it pressed closer to the surface than ever.

Before she realized she'd moved, she felt the back of her hand touch the back of his. His eyes darted to hers, and she pulled her hand away with a jerk, resting her palm on Ruby's back instead. Blasted impulse control.

But she couldn't help it. She needed him to know that he wasn't alone. That she was here.

Not that it probably mattered to him.

As the song came to an end and they took their seats again, she was careful to squeeze as far toward the end of the row as she could, even though Ruby made a good barrier between them.

"Please join me in prayer," Dan was saying from the front of the church. "Today we ask God to watch over our sister Emma Wood, who will be having surgery tomorrow for a possible cancerous mass. We also pray for . . ." Bethany lost track of Dan's words as James stumbled to his feet and climbed over Ruby's legs and then her own with a mumbled, "Sorry."

Her eyes followed him as he strode down the aisle and out the sanctuary doors at the back of the church. She lost sight of him as he crossed the lobby and slipped out the exit. She turned around, her eyes meeting Emma's, who gave her a weak, worried smile. Bethany reached a hand out to Emma behind Ruby's back, and her friend took it with a gentle squeeze. Bethany closed her eyes as Dan began to pray. She may not be able to help James, but she could be here for Emma.

As Dan said the prayers and then they ended the service with another hymn, Bethany checked over her shoulder every few seconds to see if James would come back. Something in her said she should go after him, but that was crazy. She didn't know him well enough to go chasing him out of church. Not to mention that even if she did find him, what would she say? No doubt words would fail her, as they always did.

"He'll be okay," Emma murmured as they filed out of church, apparently catching her scanning the crowds for James. "It's just a lot for him."

"It's a lot for you too."

Emma looked at her thoughtfully. "I'm not going to deny that. But I have the peace of God. It makes a big difference."

Give him peace, Lord, Bethany prayed as their group of friends gathered in the lobby. It didn't feel like enough, but she knew from her own experience that prayer was more powerful than anything else she could offer.

"I say we do lunch at the Hidden Cafe," Spencer said to the group. "It's been too long." He turned to Emma. "If you're up to it?"

Emma nodded vigorously. "I'm always up for the Hidden Cafe. You know that. I just need to find my brother."

"I think that's him now." Cam inclined his head toward the exit. James was in the parking lot, striding toward the church doors. "It's hard for a brother to see his sister going through something like this." He shot Bethany a look. "But he'll get through it. We all will."

Emma sighed. "I know that. I just wish he did."

As the group filed toward the door, James looked up, surprise and more than a trace of dismay crossing his face as his eyes roved the crowd of people surrounding Emma.

Cam pulled the door open and gestured Bethany and Ruby through. Bethany hesitated, unsure how to greet James, but Ruby pushed out ahead of her.

"Hey, James. We're going to the Hidden Cafe for lunch. I'm going to get pancakes. Wanna sit by me?"

Bethany followed her daughter, mostly to keep from creating a traffic jam in the doorway.

James shook his head, hands in his pockets, watching the ground. "We can't. Emma should—"

"Eat," Emma interrupted, coming up alongside Bethany. "Emma should eat. She's starving."

James pressed his lips together but walked silently alongside the group as they made their way through the parking lot, breaking off with promises to meet at the cafe as each family reached their own vehicle.

Finally, Bethany and Ruby were the only ones still walking with James and Emma, and Bethany spotted James's truck right next to her car. She'd been in such a hurry when they'd arrived that she hadn't noticed it.

James led Emma to the passenger side of his truck, and Bethany waited, smiling as he opened the door for his sister. That was sweet. As he closed the door on Emma, Bethany moved aside to let him pass, but instead of rounding his truck, he opened her car door.

"Oh. Um, thanks." The gesture shouldn't have meant anything. It was just one person opening a door for another. But for some reason, it touched Bethany. This time when she brushed his hand, it was intentional. "It's going to be okay."

He gave a terse nod, looking away, and she dropped into her seat.

James closed the door behind her, and Bethany started her car, waiting for him to back out of his spot before following.

"I don't think he liked church very much," Ruby said.

Bethany puffed out a breath. Sometimes her daughter was a little too observant. "I think he's worried about Miss Emma."

"Then why wouldn't he pray for her?"

Bethany glanced at her daughter in the rearview mirror. She missed the days when Ruby's questions were simple, like "Why is the sky blue?"

"I'm not sure, Rubes. He probably needed some space or some air or—"

"He needs Jesus," Ruby said definitively. "And us."

"Ruby," Bethany warned. "Don't—"

"I'm going to tell him all the jokes I know until I make him laugh. Even if it takes all day."

Bethany shook her head with a chuckle. She wasn't sure who she should wish luck—her daughter or James.

She followed his truck into the nearly full parking lot at the Hidden Cafe.

Everyone was already gathered in front of the doors, and they all went in as a group. The hostess took one look at the size of their party and led them to the separate dining room at the back of the restaurant, overlooking Lake Michigan. The tips of the waves sparkled like jewels today, and Bethany stood for a moment, captivated. It wasn't that she didn't remember the view of the lake—it was that the view changed every time she looked at it.

"Come on, Mom." Ruby tugged her toward the table James and Emma already stood next to. Bethany's eyes flicked from James's sour grimace to Emma's playful grin—matched by Ruby's. The two maneuvered so that Bethany and James had no choice but to sit next to each other—or make it very obvious they were moving to avoid each other.

They'd just settled into their seats when Cam and Kayla joined them, baby Evelyn sleepily waving a fist in her car seat. Cam set the carrier down and unbuckled the baby, then passed her to Kayla, who nestled the little girl on her lap. Evelyn immediately cooed and sent the biggest smile in James's direction.

"She likes you," Ruby cheered.

James's lips moved into—well, Bethany couldn't place the expression, but it definitely wasn't a smile—and he directed his eyes toward the window.

"Can I hold her?" Ruby asked Kayla.

"Of course." Kayla readjusted her wheelchair so she could help Ruby position the baby on her lap. Cam leaned toward them. "You know what, Evelyn was telling me yesterday that she can't wait for you to teach her how to ride a bike."

Ruby rolled her eyes. "Evelyn can't talk yet, Uncle Cam."

"That's what you think." Cam winked at her, and Kayla laughed—and Bethany was struck again by how good they were, not only with their new baby, but with Ruby too. It seemed to come so much more naturally to them than to her.

Their food arrived, and Kayla took the baby back, holding her with one arm and eating with the other.

"Hey, James."

James looked startled as Ruby called his name. "Yeah?"

"Why did the turtle cross the road?"

James stared at Ruby blankly. Bethany rolled her eyes. He could at least pretend to play along.

"Because he was too slow to catch the bus." Ruby giggled and giggled.

James didn't crack a smile, but Emma laughed and shoved him. "That was a good one, Ruby. Don't mind James. He's never been very good at jokes."

"Well, I bet my mom that I could get him to laugh," Ruby announced.

Bethany winced as James's eyes came to her. "It wasn't a bet," she murmured.

But Emma laughed. "Count me in, Ruby."

For the rest of the meal, Cam, Kayla, Emma, and Ruby took turns telling jokes. Bethany listened and laughed along. She even pulled out her phone to snap some pictures of everyone smiling. But James kept his focus on his food, grimacing occasionally—or maybe that was supposed to be a polite smile.

When they'd all finished eating, Ruby popped up from her seat. "I've got it." She waited until they were all looking at her. Even James lifted his head, Bethany noted with satisfaction.

"What do cows like to do on Friday nights?" Ruby snickered, and Bethany couldn't help but smile. Ruby had told this joke enough times that even *she* remembered the punchline. But her daughter seemed to find it hilarious every time.

"Go to the moooo-vies." Ruby dissolved into giggles, which made everyone else, including baby Evelyn, laugh too.

Bethany accidentally glanced toward James. He wasn't laughing, but his face had relaxed into the smallest smile. Bethany grinned at Ruby. She'd say her daughter could count that as a win.

"Look at this happy group," the waitress said as she brought the check over. "You guys must be celebrating something fun."

James's face went pale, and Bethany felt her own smile wilt as she remembered what had brought them all here. But Emma's smile didn't falter. "We are. We're celebrating life."

"That's a great thing to celebrate." The waitress smiled. "I can take this whenever you're ready."

Cam reached for the bill. "This is on me."

Bethany knew she should argue with her brother. He already did so much for her and Ruby. But she also knew Kayla would take Cam's side and she'd end up losing. It was what happened every time.

But James seemed less inclined to accept Cam's offer. "I'll get it." He plucked the bill from Cam's hand.

Cam looked at him in surprise, then chuckled. "All right. How about we split it?"

James leaned forward, pulling a billfold out of his back pocket. He flipped it open and pulled out a credit card, handing it to Cam, who got up to take the bill and cards to the register.

"I think this little one needs her diaper changed." Kayla patted the still gurgling Evelyn.

"I'll come with you." Emma pushed her chair out.

And then it was just Bethany and Ruby and James at the table.

"Who's that?" Ruby's abrupt question made Bethany swivel her head.

But there was no one in the room that they didn't know. And then she realized that her daughter was pointing at James's billfold, which he still held open in front of him.

James's eyes flicked to Ruby in surprise, then back to the picture. He stared at it so long that Bethany wondered if he'd forgotten the question.

"My daughter." His knuckles stood out white against the billfold, but his voice was soft.

Bethany blinked at him. He'd never said anything about having a daughter, had he? And Emma had never mentioned a niece. At least as far as Bethany could remember . . .

The girl in the picture looked to be four or five. So where was she now? With her mother? Bethany thought James had mentioned he was divorced.

"She's cute." Ruby leaned over Bethany to get a better look. "What's her name?"

James cleared his throat. "Sadie." He touched a finger to the picture, then snapped his billfold closed.

"How old is she?" Ruby was still half draped over Bethany.

"Uh." James rubbed a hand over his chin and looked around, as if seeking an escape hatch. "She would be ten."

Bethany sucked in a breath, and his eyes came to hers. He gave the slightest nod, and her heart cracked clean through the middle. No wonder he looked so broken all the time.

Ruby's forehead wrinkled. "Ten? That's the same as me. You should get a new picture. She probably doesn't—"

"Ruby." Bethany let her hand fall on her daughter's shoulder, though she couldn't look away from James.

His throat rippled as he swallowed.

"What?" Ruby tucked her hair behind her ear. "You should bring her to Hope Springs sometime. We could—"

James shook his head and pushed back from the table. "Tell Emma I'll be in the truck."

"James—" Bethany wrapped her arms around her daughter, watching as James bolted from the building.

"Did I make him mad?" Ruby whispered.

Bethany kissed her daughter's hair. How would she ever live without her? "He's not mad, Rubes. He's sad. I think his little girl died."

Chapter 29

"It's going to be all right, James." Emma gave him a bright smile as she followed the nurse out of the waiting room Monday morning.

"I know." He tried to sound as brave as she did, but the moment she was out of the room, he dropped back into the uncomfortable chair.

A hand fell on top of his and squeezed. He turned, and his mom offered an encouraging smile.

"Aren't you worried?" he asked.

Mom's smile didn't slip. "She's my daughter, James. Of course I'm worried. But I also trust that she's in God's hands. Which are much more capable than mine."

"What if it's cancer?" he asked hoarsely. "What if they don't get it all? What if—"

Mom shook her head, silencing him. "What ifs are only going to drive you crazy. You know that."

Yeah. Better than anyone. But that didn't mean he didn't ask them. All the time. What if he hadn't stopped to help that day? What if Sadie hadn't—

"Excuse me, everyone." Mom stood abruptly and raised her voice over the murmurs of the others who had gathered in the waiting room: Sophie and Spencer, Leah and Austin, Dan, Grace and Levi, and Bethany. And he knew the rest of Emma's friends had promised to stop by throughout the day.

The murmurs stopped, and the gathered friends all gave their attention to Mom.

"I wanted to thank you all for being here for my Emma. For being family to her. She's told me so much about all of you that I feel like I know you already." She paused, and James marveled at her poise. This woman who had already had to say goodbye to her husband and now faced losing her daughter was chatting as if they were at a church potluck rather than in a hospital waiting room. "I asked Pastor Dan if he'd lead us all in a prayer this morning." She looked to Dan, who stood and gave her a warm smile.

James tensed as Mom took her seat next to him and wrapped her hand around his. He wasn't going to be able to run out on this prayer. Not that he could explain why he'd run out of church yesterday. It wasn't like he didn't want people praying for Emma. He might not think God was going to listen, but if there was the slightest chance . . .

But hearing Dan say it like that, in front of the whole church, had made it suddenly move from the realm of surreal to real, and he hadn't been ready for that. And now that they were at the hospital, now that Emma would be going under the knife in minutes—it didn't get any more real than this.

"Heavenly Father," Dan's voice was strong and yet soothing at the same time, and James wondered briefly if that was natural or if he'd had to train to speak like that. "We come before your throne asking for your guiding hand over the surgeons who are operating on Emma today. We ask that you would help them to remove the mass safely, we ask that you would grant her complete healing, we ask that you would bless her with a speedy recovery. Most of all, Lord, help her—and all of us—to know that she is in your hands. Let your will be done. And let us trust that your will is perfect. We ask all these things boldly and confidently, in Jesus' name. Amen."

James remained silent as a collective "Amen" went up around the room. For a moment, no one moved, and then the gentle murmuring started again. James managed to keep his seat next to Mom for another two minutes. But he couldn't take it any longer than that.

"I'm going to get some air. I'll grab you some coffee on my way back up."

Mom looked like she was going to protest but then nodded. "Coffee would be great. Thanks."

James kept a low profile as he slipped out of the room and headed for the end of the hallway. The last thing he needed was to be followed by one of Emma's well-meaning friends. When he reached the bank of elevators, he bypassed them, following the sign down the next hallway toward the stairs. He hated small spaces. And right now he needed to move, to push his body hard enough that his heart had to focus on pumping.

Because otherwise it might stop.

Bethany had never thought of herself as a ninja before.

But she felt like one now, as she slipped out the waiting room door ten seconds after James.

She'd tried to tell herself not to follow him. Tried to convince herself that he might be going to the restroom or something. Tried to tell herself that if he'd left because he wanted some alone time, it meant he wanted to be *alone*. Not with her. But then she'd seen the look on his mother's face and known: even if he wouldn't admit it, James needed someone.

She didn't know why she thought that someone should be her.

She only knew that he'd passed the bank of elevators and slipped around the corner. She scrunched her nose, trying to remember what else was down the hallway. Maybe he really was only making a trip to the restroom.

But she continued to the end of the corridor, glancing down the next hallway, which was dominated by a nurse's station—but no restrooms.

A door at the end of the hallway swung closed with a heavy thud, and Bethany noticed the exit sign above it.

Ah. He was taking the stairs.

Picking up her pace so she wouldn't lose him, she hurried down the hall and through the door, the hammering of footsteps echoing up to her. Fortunately, they were only on the third floor, so if she lost him here, he shouldn't be too hard to find at the bottom. Gripping the railing tightly, she scurried down the staircase and pulled open the door at the ground floor, coming out on a wide corridor. To the left, she could see the bustle of the hospital lobby. To the right, a side exit.

She made a decisive turn toward the exit.

She pushed the door open slowly, in case he was standing near it, but as she stepped outside, she had to second-guess her conclusion. There was no one out here.

She turned to go back inside, but a flicker of movement on the other side of a bush caught her eye. It may have been a bird, but . . .

She stepped outside, easing the door closed behind her, and made her way toward it.

She rounded the bush slowly, ready to discover that she was on a literal goose chase. But instead of a goose, she found James, sitting in the grass, knees bent up in front of him, head tucked down.

She inched forward until she was standing alongside him. When he didn't look up, she lowered herself to the ground next to him, letting her eyes rove across the hospital parking lot toward Lake Michigan across the street. There was a slight chop on the water today, sending frothy foam rolling off the top of the waves.

After a few minutes, James sat up. "What are you doing out here?"

"Enjoying the beautiful day."

James snorted. "Did my mother send you?"

"Nope. I came on my own. I wanted to make sure you were—"

"Okay?" James's laugh was ironic. "I'm not the one under the knife."

"Sometimes it's harder to be the one waiting."

James nodded but didn't say anything.

"It's going to be—"

James turned to her. "Don't say 'all right.' You can't know that."

Bethany glanced at him in surprise. "I was going to say warm out." Already the sun was giving the skin on her arms a toasted feel.

"Oh." James tipped his head skyward. "I guess so."

The silence lasted longer this time, the warmth of the sun and rhythm of the waves lulling Bethany into a sort of awake-sleep.

"I'm sorry about yesterday," James said abruptly, pulling her out of her doze.

"For what?" As far as she remembered, he hadn't done anything to apologize for.

"I didn't mean to upset Ruby. I just didn't expect . . ."

Bethany looked toward him, and he dragged a hand through his hair. "Tell her I'm sorry."

"I will." Bethany had lain awake half the night, thinking about James and his daughter, torn between a desire to forget what she'd learned and a desire to wrap her arms around him and tell him she was here for him. She sat on her hands, just in case. "You know, if you ever want to talk . . ."

But James was already shaking his head. "I don't talk about it."

Bethany nodded. "Okay. We'll just sit then."

Chapter 30

Ask her to leave. Tell her you want to be alone.

Except—did he really want her to leave? Did he really want to be alone?

As much as he shouldn't admit it, sitting here with her—not saying anything, just watching the waves, listening to the gulls, smelling the peachy wafts that floated from her—was more comforting than he would have guessed.

Just a little longer, he promised himself. *Then you have to go back inside. You have to be there for Mom and Emma.*

But another ten minutes had gone by when Bethany turned to him. "Do you think we should go back upstairs?"

Reluctantly, James nodded. He pushed to his feet, then held out a hand to help her up.

Her hand slid into his without hesitation, its warmth sweeping through him. He pulled her up quickly, then let go, but she closed her eyes and swayed, grasping for his arm. He reached for her before she could tip over.

"Sorry." She opened her eyes after a moment. "Happens sometimes when I stand up too fast." She still gripped his arm, and he didn't let go.

"I think I'm good now." She released his arm, but he held on for a moment longer, until he was relatively certain she wasn't going to keel over.

"Want to take the stairs or the elevator?" Bethany asked as he held the exterior door open for her.

As much as he hated elevators, he couldn't see trying to make her climb stairs right now. "Elevator."

Bethany didn't argue, and he led the way. He pressed the up button and it was only a few seconds before it chimed and the elevator door opened. He forced himself to get on but pressed his back to the wall as the door slid closed.

"Your mom seems sweet," Bethany said as the elevator bumped to a start. Her eyes came to him with a smile that fell away. "What's wrong?"

"Nothing. Just not the biggest fan of elevators."

"Really?" Bethany's brow wrinkled. "Why?"

"Claustrophobia. When we were kids, Emma used to trick me into going into her closet and then lock me in there. I haven't been able to handle small spaces since then. Especially ones I can't get out of easily."

Bethany burst out laughing, and the sound made James's muscles relax a little. He didn't mean to let his lips ease upward, but they did.

"Sorry." Bethany coughed, pretending to get her giggles under control, though James could see the mirth in her eyes. "I can't picture Emma doing that."

"You'd be surprised by the things she did to me. She's always been my—" His voice cracked unexpectedly, and he cleared his throat, staring at the numbers on the elevator.

"I know." Bethany moved closer and the elevator seemed to grow smaller—but not in a bad way. "She's become like a sister—"

The car went dark, and Bethany crashed against him. His arms went instinctively around her.

"What was that?" Bethany's voice came from right below his chin, and her peach scent drifted to his nose, temporarily stunning him.

Gently, he unwrapped his arms from around her as the emergency lights came on. "I believe that was the elevator breaking down." He gestured toward the doors, which hadn't opened.

Bethany's eyes widened. "That really happens?"

"Once in a while." He'd responded to a couple of calls to broken elevators over the years. It was never serious—they always got them running again eventually—but he'd shuddered at the thought of being trapped inside one for any amount of time.

He tugged at the collar of his shirt. He was fine. The small space couldn't hurt him. He needed to remain calm for Bethany's sake.

"So now what do we do?" She sounded completely at ease.

"Now we call for help." But he was suddenly reluctant to move away from her. What if the car began to plummet—he needed to be close enough to protect her.

He shook his head at himself. He knew enough about how elevators worked to know that wouldn't happen. So why didn't he want to leave her side?

The truth was—

No, it was too dangerous to examine the truth.

He stepped forward and pressed the emergency call button. It was only a moment before a voice replied, saying they were aware of the problem and had someone on the way to help. "Sit tight," the voice added.

It wasn't as if they had any other choice. There was nowhere they could go. Not up, not down, not forward, not . . . His chest tightened. He didn't like not having an escape.

He could feel Bethany's eyes on him, and he fought to get himself under control. This was not the time to lose it.

"So." Bethany had apparently taken the disembodied voice literally, as she slid to the floor and crossed her legs crisscross applesauce style—he'd learned that term from Sadie. "Might as well get comfy."

James nodded. "I guess."

"So this probably doesn't help your . . ." Bethany blinked up at him.

"Claustrophobia?" He crossed his arms in front of him. "I'm fine."

"You know what they say. The best way to deal with your fears is to face them."

"Maybe *they* should get stuck in an elevator then."

Bethany's laugh was warm and understanding. "Come on. Let's do something to take our minds off it."

"Like what?" he asked cautiously, eyeing her. If she was going to ask him to talk about Sadie again . . .

"How about tic tac toe? I have paper and a pen." She reached into her purse and pulled out a small notebook. She patted the floor next to her. "Come on."

He sighed but crossed the elevator and lowered himself next to her, pressing his back into the wall. Bethany drew a tic tac toe board and put an O in the center square. He took the notebook and added his X in the top left square.

By the time they were three games in, James felt himself start to relax. Sitting here, next to her, he could almost imagine they were still outside rather than trapped in a five-foot by five-foot box.

"This is getting silly," Bethany said after the sixth tied game. "Let's play something else."

"Like what?"

Bethany pressed a finger to her lip, and James found himself watching the way her mouth moved as she answered. "Would you rather?"

James tipped his head to the side. "Would I rather what?"

Bethany's laugh filled the elevator, making him smile a real smile for what felt like the first time in days. "No, silly, that's the name of the game. Would you rather? Ruby and I play it all the time. One person asks a 'Would you rather?' question, and the other person has to answer it. Like, 'Would you rather have to eat only chocolate for the rest of your life or eat only ice cream for the rest of your life?'"

"That's easy. Chocolate ice cream." James gave her a smug look, and Bethany shoved his shoulder lightly.

"No cheating. Okay, your turn."

James tapped his chin, thinking. This was just the kind of game Sadie would have loved. What would she have asked? "Would you rather wear only purple or only red?"

Bethany treated him to a laugh and a surprised look. "I did not see that question coming."

"Why not?" It wasn't a particularly deep one.

"It's just so . . ."

He waited, knowing it sometimes took her a while to find a word.

"Fun," she said finally.

"And I'm not fun?" He raised an eyebrow, though he already knew the answer to that. He used to be fun . . .

Bethany shook her head, but he saw the truth in her eyes. "No, it's not that. It's just . . . What was the question again?"

He snorted. "Nice change of subject. Wear all red or all purple?"

"Right." She rolled her eyes—at herself, he was pretty sure, and he wished she wouldn't do that. It wasn't like she forgot things on purpose or because she didn't care. She couldn't help it.

"Definitely purple," she answered.

"I knew it." He didn't know why that pleased him so much.

"You did? How?" She leaned toward him, and he suddenly noticed how pretty she looked, even in the elevator's emergency lighting.

"I guess I just associate you with the color purple."

"You associate me with a color?" Her eyes widened, and he realized that was probably the most ridiculous thing he'd ever said.

"I mean, it's a cop thing." Nope, *that* was the most ridiculous.

But Bethany grinned as if he'd made her queen. "I associate you with a color too. It's how I remember your name."

"Oh." So that was how she'd remembered at last. "What color?"

"Gray." She cringed as she said it. "Only because you always seemed sort of sad. But now I know why . . ." She drifted into silence.

"Yeah." Sadie had always refused to color with the gray crayon. *Gray is too sad, Daddy,* she'd told him when he'd asked why she'd made her elephant pink.

What would she think if she knew her daddy had become sad and gray?

"My turn to ask a question." Bethany's voice rang with forced cheer. "Would you rather go to the moon or scuba dive in the deepest part of the ocean?"

"Moon. So I could see if it was really made of cheese." It was the kind of answer he would have said to Sadie—the kind that would have lit up her face and brought out that deep belly laugh and made her call him silly.

Bethany's surprised laugh was nearly as rewarding.

"Nice. Your turn."

They each asked a few more goofy questions, and James let himself forget that there was a world outside this elevator. In here, he could tell himself everything was fine. And he could let Bethany's smile convince him whenever he started to doubt again.

"Okay, I've got another one," he said.

"Let's hear it."

Somehow, they'd slid closer together as the minutes had passed, and he kept catching whiffs of her tantalizing scent.

He inhaled. "Would you rather forget everything that ever happened to you or remember everything?"

Bethany's eyes widened, and he realized the question was probably too personal. "I'm sorry. You don't have to answer that. I'll come up with something else."

"No." Bethany shook her head slowly. "It's a good question. I just need to think about it for a minute."

"You do?" James turned toward her. "I would think the answer would be easy for you."

Bethany frowned. "Would it be easy for you?"

James sucked in a breath, considering. If he could forget everything, then this pain that was a constant reminder of all he had lost would finally disappear. But so would his memories of Sadie. On the other hand, remembering everything was no picnic either. "I guess it's an impossible question."

Bethany's smile was gentle. "There are things from my past that I wish I could forget. And things from my present I wish I could remember." Her laugh held a trace of sorrow. "But in the end, I guess it all makes up who we are, right? Even the things we've forgotten. Or the things we'd rather forget."

James swallowed, nodding as her eyes came to his. "I guess you're right."

She slid closer, and he shifted a little as her knee bumped his.

"What was she like?" Bethany's voice was gentle, like a ripple of wind on a spring day. Like Sadie's smile.

"She was..." He dropped his head back against the wall, staring up at the ceiling. A hand slipped into his and squeezed, and he could feel Bethany's compassion all the way to his heart. But that didn't mean he could do this. "I'm sorry, I can't." He worked too hard to push those memories away every single day. And talking about her would only make that more impossible.

"Okay," she whispered. They sat in silence for a few seconds, then she broke in. "I've got one. Would you rather clean horse stalls by yourself for a week or get stuck in this elevator with me for an hour, forced to play Would You Rather?"

James chuckled but considered the question. A month ago, it would have been a no-brainer. He'd preferred to clean the stalls by himself. And he certainly hadn't thought he could enjoy being stuck on an elevator. But now, if he was being honest . . . "I'm going to go with get stuck in the elevator."

"Really?" She wrinkled her nose, but her face lit up. "The horse stalls are bigger. And easier to get out of."

"But you smell better."

Bethany's laugh ricocheted off the elevator walls, taking a bounce and landing smack in the middle of James's heart.

"You'd better be careful," she teased. "Or I might have to change your name from James the Gray to a happier color."

He lifted an eyebrow, feeling much lighter-hearted than he should. "Like what?"

Bethany studied him, and suddenly he couldn't look away—didn't want to. In fact, he wanted to get closer and—

"Orange," Bethany proclaimed.

James blinked. "That was Sadie's favorite color." The words came out of him before he could remind himself that he didn't talk about her.

Bethany's smile was gentle. "Then it's the perfect color for you. James the Orange."

"I guess at least it's not James and the Giant Peach."

She gave him a confused look.

"Like the book. Never mind."

She shrugged and brushed her hair back from her face, exposing a small scar on her forehead he'd never noticed before. He reached for it and ran a finger lightly over it.

Bethany froze a moment before he did. What was he doing?

Would you rather, a voice in his head asked, *kiss her or—*

He pulled his hand back and grasped the railing that ran around the elevator. It was time to get some distance.

He had risen to a crouch when the elevator lurched suddenly, throwing him off balance—and right on top of Bethany.

"Oof." Her arms came to his shoulders as he scrambled to get his legs under him so he could un-crush her.

"Sorry," he grunted as his fingers accidentally got tangled in her hair.

"It's okay." She was laughing, and in the restored lighting, her eyes sparkled. "I guess they got the elevator fixed."

The elevator dinged and the door slid open just as James managed to get his fingers unwrapped from her hair and push himself to his feet.

"Well." Mom stood in front of the open doors, looking amused but not surprised. "I was just coming to see if I could get an update from the maintenance crew, but it looks like you're all right."

"Yep." James tugged his shirt into place, then reached down to help Bethany up. When she was on her feet, he held a hand to the small of her back to make sure she wasn't about to tip over as she almost had outside. He shook his head at Mom's knowing smile and moved his arm away as soon as he was sure Bethany was steady on her feet.

The instant he stepped out of the elevator, the reality he'd managed to pretend didn't exist while he was trapped in there with Bethany came crashing back over him. Forget the elevator—it was this antiseptic, sterile space that made him feel claustrophobic.

"How's Emma?" He managed to squeeze the question out of too-tight lungs.

Mom's expression sobered. "They did a biopsy. And—"

James tensed.

"It is cancer," Mom said gently.

Bethany's hand slid into his, and he held onto it for dear life.

"But they think they can get it all," Mom continued. "They're going ahead with the full hysterectomy. She may have to do some chemo or radiation down the road, just to be safe, but she should be out of surgery in a while."

"James," Bethany whispered.

But he shook his head and pulled his hand out of hers, striding past her and Mom to the waiting room. He wasn't about to give God one more thing to take away from him.

Chapter 31

"So." Mom set a big bowl of her famous potato soup in front of James and took a seat across the table in Emma's kitchen. Emma would be in the hospital another few days to recover, but she had insisted that James and Mom come back here. And since he had to take care of the horses, James couldn't really argue, though he couldn't push away the fear that if he left her there, he'd never see her again.

"So." James played with his spoon and inhaled the savory steam billowing off the bowl but didn't take a bite. The day had left him battered and exhausted.

"Should we give thanks?" Mom folded her hands in front of her.

James let himself nod. For one thing, he knew Mom wouldn't eat until they did. And for another, he didn't have the energy left to argue.

"Would you like to or—" Mom waved a hand over her soup.

"You go ahead." He might be willing to listen to a prayer, but he sure wasn't about to offer one.

Mom closed her eyes, and James followed suit.

"Dear Lord," Mom began. "Thank you for protecting Emma through her surgery and for guiding the doctors' hands. We ask you to be with her in her recovery. And be with James too. Show him that you have hope and a future planned for him—"

"Mom." The word shot out of James as he clenched his fists. This wasn't about him.

Mom didn't miss a beat. "Remind him that he is your child too and that you love him. In Jesus' name we pray. Amen."

"That wasn't necessary," James said as soon as she opened her eyes. "Just stick to praying for Emma."

"I pray for both of you every day, James." Mom stirred her soup. "And to be honest, you're the one I worry about more."

James shook his head, spooning up a bite of soup and shoving it into his mouth, wincing as the hot liquid scalded his tongue. He should have known Emma would tell Mom about the gunshot sooner or later. "It was only a graze. I'm fine."

"What graze?" Mom raised an eyebrow, and James realized too late that his wound wasn't what she'd been talking about.

"Nothing." He downed a gulp of milk to cool his burning mouth. "I'm good," he repeated.

Mom watched him but didn't push the conversation further, and James concentrated on devouring his soup as quickly as possible so she couldn't ask questions about his injury. His bowl was almost empty when Mom set down her spoon.

Uh oh. He knew what that meant: a lecture was coming.

"Seriously, Mom, it was nothing to worry about. Captain overreacted and sent me here. But as soon as Emma's on her feet . . ."

"Don't you think you've run away long enough?" Mom let her penetrating gaze rest on him.

James huffed. "Run away? I've been here for almost two months."

"I know." Mom reached across the table and set her hand on top of his. "And we both appreciate it. But I don't mean that you haven't helped us. I mean you haven't let us—anyone—help *you*."

"Because I don't need help. I already told you. I'm fine." He pulled his hand back and stood to carry his bowl to the sink.

"Emma says you won't talk to her about Sadie. You won't talk to me. What about Bethany?"

James looked at her over his shoulder. "What *about* Bethany?"

"Have you talked to her about Sadie?"

He rinsed his bowl. "She knows." Or well, she knew he'd had a daughter. That was enough.

"So the two of you are close?" Hope blanketed Mom's words. "Are you dating?"

James studied the water flowing into his already-clean bowl. "We're friends, I guess."

"Come on, James. I've been here less than twenty-four hours, and I can tell you see each other as more than friends." He heard Mom's chair slide back and her footsteps come toward the sink.

He turned the water off and set his bowl down, not looking at Mom as he cleared away the rest of the dishes. "I don't know what you think you saw, but—"

"Don't push her away, James. She cares about you, I can tell. And you may not want to admit it, but you care about her too."

James shook his head. That might be true. But it didn't mean he was going to let it go anywhere. "She has a kid, Mom. A little girl. Same age Sadie would be." He didn't mean to sound like a bitter old man, but the truth was, sometimes he felt like one.

"Did you ever think maybe there's a reason for that?"

"A reason?" he spun and stared at his mother. "What, like God hasn't had enough fun with me yet? He had to stick the knife in a little deeper?"

Mom winced. "You don't really believe that."

"Yes. I believe that. Same as I believe I will never date or have a family again, so it doesn't pay to push me."

"I'm not trying to push you. I'm trying to encourage you. Closing yourself off to others isn't the answer."

"And you know this how?" It'd been a long time since James had raised his voice to his mother, and he wasn't proud of it now. "Dad has been gone for over twenty years, and I don't see you moving on."

"Actually—" Mom glanced away. "About that . . ."

James froze.

"I met someone." Color rushed to her cheeks, and she suddenly looked ten years younger. "His name is William. He lives in the same retirement community as me. And he . . . he's really great. I think you'd like him." She fluffed her short curls with a nervous laugh. "Sorry. I wasn't sure how to bring that up, but . . ."

James couldn't quite process what he was hearing. "So you're dating this guy?"

"William." Mom nodded, looking more confident and less nervous. "Yes. We're dating."

"Oh." He swallowed. "Okay."

"That's all? Okay?"

James shrugged. What else was he supposed to say? Mom was a grown woman. She could do what she wanted.

"Why now?" He finally asked. "After all these years?"

Mom gave him a thoughtful look. "For a long time, after your dad died, I wasn't interested in opening myself up to hurt again. And then after a while, I realized that closing myself off from others wasn't the answer. But I never met anyone who could measure up to your dad."

"And William does?" A hard defensiveness rose in him.

"No," Mom said gently. "I learned that I couldn't measure other men against your dad. I had to see them as themselves, completely apart from him. William is a retired accountant who likes to golf."

James laughed in spite of himself—Dad had hated golf with a passion.

"But he's a lot like your father in all the ways that matter," Mom continued. "He loves the Lord, he's funny, he's compassionate. He puts my needs before his own." Mom's face softened. "He loves me, James. And I love him."

James swallowed. It felt strange knowing she was talking about a man other than his father. But at the same time— "I'm happy for you, Mom."

Her face relaxed, and she stepped forward to give him a hug. "Thank you." She pulled back. "And can I give you one piece of advice?"

"Just one?" James raised an eyebrow.

Mom laughed. "For now." Her expression grew serious. "It's worth the risk. Putting your heart back out there. God created us to love and support one another. So don't keep people from doing that for you."

James pressed his lips together and turned toward the stairs. He was glad taking the risk had paid off for Mom. But he was going to stick with his original plan. No risk. No reward. No heartache.

Chapter 32

Bethany shifted the giant bouquet of yellow roses to her left hand as she reached Emma's front door and knocked. She opened the door without waiting for an answer—Emma had just gotten home from the hospital yesterday, and she didn't want her getting up to answer the door.

"Hello, anyone home?" she called as she peeked her head inside, her stomach tightening at the thought that James could be here. She'd hardly seen him since Monday—since they'd been trapped on that elevator and she'd thought he might—

But it didn't matter what she'd thought. Whatever it had been—if it had been anything at all—had clearly passed. On the few occasions she'd seen him this week, he'd done little more than grunt hello and tell her that he'd already cleaned all the stalls so she could go home.

Footsteps—too light to be James's—hurried toward the door, and Bethany prepared to scold her friend for getting out of bed. But instead of Emma, it was her mother who came popping into the room, offering Bethany a bright smile. "Those smell heavenly."

Bethany smiled back—she liked Emma's mom. And it was clear where Emma had gotten her sunny disposition from. James must take after his father. Or a bear.

"Emma is napping. Do you want me to wake her?"

"No. Let her sleep. I'll go help in the barn first. If James didn't finish it all himself already. Again."

Emma's mom regarded her, as if thinking, and Bethany felt suddenly self-conscious. She hadn't meant to grumble against the woman's son. "I mean, it's great that he's—"

"He said he told you about Sadie?"

Bethany blinked at her. Sadie? That name didn't ring any . . .

"His daughter?" Emma's mom prompted.

"Oh." Bethany's heart squeezed. Every time she thought of James and his daughter—whose name she hadn't been able to recall no matter how hard she tried—fresh sorrow rolled over her. "I'm sorry. I'm not very good with names. My memory . . ."

"Emma told me about your aneurysm." Emma's mom pulled out a seat at the table and gestured for Bethany to do the same. "She said you have some short-term memory loss?"

Bethany glanced at the door over her shoulder but took a seat. "Yeah. So I should probably admit that I can't remember your name either." There wasn't much point in pretending otherwise.

Emma's mom smiled. "I'm Anne." She leaned forward. "So he did tell you about Sadie, then?"

Bethany shook her head. "My daughter happened to see her picture and asked about her. I know she died, but . . . he won't talk about it. I think it would probably help if he did."

Anne frowned, worry deepening her eyes. "I think so too." She rubbed a hand over the table. "It's been five years, but to him, I think it was yesterday. He says he's moved on, but what he's doing isn't living."

"Do you mind if I ask what happened?" Bethany asked tentatively. She didn't want to make the woman relive losing her granddaughter.

Anne's forehead wrinkled, but she nodded. "James and Sadie had gone on a daddy-daughter date to the zoo. On the way home, it started to rain, and there was an accident in front of them. James pulled over to help. He told Sadie to stay in the car, but . . ." She pressed her lips together, shaking her head.

"Oh my . . ." Bethany reached forward and clutched the woman's hand.

Anne looked up, offering a gentle smile, though her eyes glistened. "The driver didn't see her through the rain. She made it to the hospital, and James got to say goodbye to her. She told him not to worry, that God would take care of her, but . . ." Anne wiped a finger under her eyes. "I don't think he's been able to forgive God—or himself—since that day." She sniffed and rubbed at her nose.

Bethany could only watch helplessly. Her heart felt like it was being cranked in a vice and the only way to release the pressure was to cry—and yet her eyes remained dry.

"I'm sorry." Anne sniffed again. "That was more than you asked for."

"I'm glad you told me." As much as it hurt, it also helped her understand James better. "I only wish there was something I could do."

Anne patted her hand. "I think you already have, dear. Emma says that you and James are . . ."

"Oh." Bethany's face sucked up all the heat in the room. "Um, no, we're . . ." She searched for the right word. But she wasn't sure if there was one.

Anne patted her hand again, then stood. "I'm going to go check on Emma. I'll let you know when she wakes up."

Bethany didn't know how long she sat staring at the spot where Anne had been sitting before she finally got up and made her way out to the barn.

Her heart hurt and hammered at the same time as she opened the door. What if James was in here? What was she going to say to him? Now that she knew everything he'd gone through, it felt like she should have something profound to say, some sort of comfort to offer him. *Please give me the words I need, Lord.*

But her prayer proved to be unnecessary as she stepped inside and found the stalls all clean, the horses moving quietly, and James nowhere in sight.

Her eyes fell on a stall door that stood open, then tracked to the far end of the barn. James had to be out there with Fancy Lady.

Her heart drummed louder than horses' hooves as she made her way down the aisle, not stopping to greet Ace as he nickered for a sugar cube. It would be easier to leave. Easier to pretend she'd forgotten everything Anne had told her. Easier not to search for words she knew she'd never be able to find.

But she couldn't do that.

Not when James needed her.

Her heart jumped as she spotted him working Fancy Lady at the far end of the training ring. She let herself watch as he turned the horse, trotted her, circled back, and then cantered away. He did it all with grace and precision, holding complete control—the same way he seemed to hold complete control over his life.

A control he didn't need disturbed by someone like her—someone who was nowhere near in control of all the things in her life.

She should leave.

James turned the horse again, setting her on a course directly for the gate next to Bethany. He didn't seem to notice her. But she could tell the moment he realized she was there because his whole face dropped into a frown, and he glanced over his shoulder as if contemplating making a break for the woods. But he continued toward her.

She swallowed and held her ground. He may not want to see her. But she needed to know that he was okay.

"Whoa." He pulled Fancy Lady to a halt in front of the gate. "Hi." His greeting was neither warm nor cold—more indifferent than anything.

Bethany brushed off the hurt and opened the gate for them. "You didn't leave anything for me to do." She gestured toward the barn. "Again."

"I can do it myself."

"I know you *can* do it yourself. But that doesn't mean you have to. Or even that you should." Bethany reached a hand up to stroke Fancy Lady's nose.

James shrugged. "I'd better get her brushed down."

Bethany watched him closely. Now that she knew his stiff, controlled exterior guarded a heart that was aching for his little girl, she longed to wrap her arms around him and tell him it was okay to let go of that control. Okay to hurt.

But she moved out of the way, and he led Fancy Lady toward the barn.

Bethany hesitated. She could walk around the outside of the barn and give him the space he so clearly wanted.

Or—

She followed behind Fancy Lady, waiting until James had dismounted from the horse to step forward.

He startled as he spotted her. "I thought you'd left."

She smiled. "No such luck."

James took off the horse's saddle and bridle, then led her to her stall. Bethany grabbed the curry comb and brush off the pegboard hanging on the wall and followed. She passed the comb to him and watched as he rubbed it in circles over the horse's neck. He studied the movements of his hands as if one slip in concentration would mean disaster.

I still need words, Lord. Bethany waited, too many thoughts swirling in her head to form them into a sentence. Finally, a few worked their way free. "Emma was sleeping when I stopped by the house."

James grunted a reply.

"I talked to your mom."

James glanced up for a second, then back at the comb.

"She told me, James."

"Told you what?" The words were gruff, but at least they represented progress from the grunts.

"She told me about Sadie," Bethany said softly. "About what happened to her."

James's hand jerked to a stop, and he jumped back from the horse as if it'd kicked him.

Fancy Lady pranced and sent him a reproving look that would have been comical if it weren't for the anger in James's eyes. "She shouldn't have—"

"Yes." Bethany said firmly, taking a step closer to him. "She should have. You won't talk about it, and—"

"That's right." James crossed around to the other side of the horse, and she heard the brush start working again. "I don't talk about it. Ever."

"You're so . . . so . . ." What was the word she needed? She balled her hands and closed her eyes, thinking. "Frustrating." She opened her eyes again and moved around Fancy Lady to stand next to James, who kept combing. "Your mom said it's been five years. You can't lock yourself off from the world forever. Sometimes you have to let yourself need other people."

In one fluid movement, he pulled the curry comb off his hand and thrust it at her. It took Bethany's brain a moment to catch up with the fact that he'd disappeared out the stall door.

"Wait! James!" She'd messed it up. Apparently those hadn't been the words she'd prayed for. She sped after him, but he was halfway down the alley, his long strides not slowing. "When are you going to stop being such a coward and running away every time someone asks you to be a little vulnerable?" The words spilled out before she could think them through, and she couldn't help the glimmer of elation at coming up with a word like *vulnerable* on the spot.

James stopped, his back going stiff.

Uh oh.

Maybe those weren't the words she'd prayed for either.

He spun in a slow half-circle. "A coward?" He laughed coldly and held up his arm. "I have the bullet holes to prove I'm not. It's my job to run *toward* danger."

"I know." Bethany took advantage of the fact that he'd stopped moving and hurried toward him. "That's not what I meant. Physically, you're probably the bravest person I know. But emotionally, you're . . ."

James crossed his arms—but she got the feeling he was trying to protect himself more than intimidate her. "I'm what? You have no idea what it's like to lose a child." His voice was hard, controlled, but it stopped Bethany from moving closer.

"You're right," she said softly. "I can't even imagine . . ." She swallowed at the look of anguish that twisted James's features.

"No you can't," he spat. Then he turned and fled for the door again.

Bethany hesitated. Maybe she should let him go. But something sent her feet flying after him. She caught up to him and snatched for his arm, pulling him to a stop. "I may not know what it's like to lose a child, but I know what it's like to need other people. I have to ask for help every day. I have to let other people do things that I used to be able to do myself. I have to make myself vulnerable even when it's hard."

"You want me to be vulnerable?" James's voice rose, and Ace pranced nervously in the stall next to them. "All right. How's this for vulnerable? My daughter is dead. She's dead, and it's my fault. She's dead, and I can't bring her back." He was shouting now. "She's dead, and there are days when I don't know how I can go on." He glared at her, his shoulders rising and falling with his breaths. "There. Are you still glad you asked?"

Bethany could only blink at him. That had been so raw and so open and so vulnerable. She pressed a hand to her heart, praying for words.

When none came, she did the only thing she could think of.

She stepped forward, slid her arms around his shoulders, and rose onto her tiptoes, bringing her lips gently to his.

He stiffened, his hands coming to her shoulders, and she thought he was going to push her away, but then he was pulling her in closer, and his arms were around her.

She concentrated on pouring every ounce of her compassion and her sorrow and her gratitude that he'd finally opened up into the kiss.

Wait.

The *kiss*.

She was *kissing* James.

With a gasp, she pulled back, glancing over her shoulder toward the far door. Would it make *her* the coward if she ran now?

James was watching her, not saying anything, which made the whole situation more confusing.

She touched a hand to her spinning head.

"I'm sorry. I shouldn't have— I just . . ."

James's lips lifted a fraction, and it set something loose in her chest. "Impulse control?"

She seized on that, nodding with a shaky laugh. "I should . . ." She gestured toward the door behind him, and he stepped aside.

Keeping her head down, she scooted past him, then dashed down the alleyway, out of the barn, and into her car. She didn't realize until she was home that she'd never gone back inside to visit with Emma.

Chapter 33

Ah, he was a mess.

Had been for three days.

Ever since that kiss with Bethany. It had been the last thing he'd expected her to do after he'd yelled at her like that. His first instinct had been to push her away, to ask her what in the name of all that was holy she thought she was doing.

But the feel of her lips on his, of her arms around his neck, had undone something inside him that had been coiled tight for years.

He hadn't let himself feel—really feel—anything for so long, and the full impact of his suppressed emotions had been too near the surface ever since.

Sorrow over the memories of Sadie knocked louder than usual, but it was coupled with something undefinable—something close to relief. Relief that Bethany knew about Sadie? Relief that he'd finally admitted that missing his daughter was killing him? Relief that Bethany had kissed him?

He wasn't sure. And he wasn't sure he needed to know.

Because it wasn't like they were ever going to kiss again. She may not be able to control her impulses, but he could.

Not that he'd had to worry about it the last few days, since she'd stayed away from the stables, texting that she had too much to do for Cam and Kayla. He'd wondered more than once if she was avoiding him.

Or if she'd forgotten the whole thing.

Either way, he was thankful. He had no idea what he was supposed to say to her the next time he saw her—which would be any minute now.

"Do you have the snaffle bits?" Emma called from the bench near the barn door that he'd made her promise not to stir from. She should be in bed, but this was the closest he could get to making her rest as he got things ready for today's dressage competition.

"Yep. Single-jointed, double-jointed, and unjointed. And the bridoon bits." He hefted a saddle and loaded it onto the trailer. The sound of tires on the driveway stole his attention, and he glanced over his shoulder—again. It wasn't Bethany—again. But she and Ruby had to be here soon. It was almost time to leave for the competition.

Following Emma's instructions, James helped the other kids load their horses onto the trailers. But still Bethany and Ruby hadn't shown up. Had Bethany forgotten? Had something happened to one of them? His heart roared that he needed to go make sure they were all right.

He took a deep breath.

There was no reason to overreact. And the fact that he *was* overreacting was only proof that he'd let himself get too close to them.

He pulled his truck keys out of his pocket and strode toward his sister. "Aren't Bethany and Ruby supposed to be here?"

Emma gave him a shrewd smile. "Didn't I tell you? You need to pick them up on the way." Her smile grew. "They always ride with me since Bethany doesn't like to drive long distances. And since you won't let me come . . . Unless you want to change your mind." Her eyes sparkled with mischief.

James shook his head. "You're staying here and resting. I'll give them a ride."

"If that's what you want," she lilted.

James growled but got into his truck, following the caravan of horse trailers down the driveway.

The things he did for his sister.

He navigated through the streets to Bethany's house, his thoughts refusing to budge from that kiss. Was it going to be awkward to see her?

Of course it's going to be awkward.

But it might also be . . . really nice.

He shook his head and opened the window. Maybe some fresh air would chase these thoughts away.

But if anything, the fresh air only fueled his need to see her. By the time he reached her house and rang the doorbell, nerves fired through his middle.

"Hi, James." Ruby was chattering the second she opened the door, and for some reason it set him at ease.

"Do you like my new boots? Uncle Cam and Aunt Kayla gave them to me for my birthday."

James dutifully examined the black leather boots. "They're very nice. Are you . . ."

He lost track of his words as Bethany entered the living room behind her daughter. Had she always been so beautiful?

"Hi." Her smile seemed shy, tentative.

"Hi." He cleared his throat and looked away. "Are you ready to go?" He directed the question to Ruby.

"Yep. Oh wait. I forgot my helmet." She charged out of the room.

James's eyes accidentally landed on Bethany's. Was it his imagination, or were her cheeks pinker than usual?

"Um. So." She straightened a precariously stacked pile of books on the coffee table. "How's Emma doing?"

"She's good. Mad that Mom and I insisted she stay home, but she'll get over it. I think she's worried I'll screw everything up. But all I have to do is get there and check everyone in. The kids have to do the hard part."

The kids.

The word felt unnatural coming from his mouth. He'd worked so hard to avoid anything having to do with kids for years. And now look at him. What was he doing here?

Ruby bounced back into the room, helmet dangling from her hand. "I'm ready. Let's go."

Something about the way she said it—as if the three of them went places together all the time—caught him off guard. Not in a bad way. More in an I-could-get-used-to-this way. He held the door open for them, then led the way to the truck. He tried to avoid glancing at Bethany as he fastened his seatbelt, but failed. She had tucked her hair behind her ear and he could see the scar he'd touched in the elevator. As if she sensed his eyes on her, she turned toward him. He swiveled his head quickly and started the vehicle. But when he reached to shift into gear, his hand accidentally bumped hers on the console between them.

"Sorry." Her hand slid away, and he had to resist the urge to grab it and pull it back toward him. Man. He had to forget about that kiss. She probably had. And anyway, it had been a momentary lapse of impulse control on her part. Nothing more.

"I'm so nervous," Ruby said suddenly from the back seat, drawing James's eyes to the rearview mirror. "I've been working on my loops, but I don't know if I'm ready."

James glanced to Bethany, but she seemed to be lost in thought. He supposed he could ignore Ruby's comment and hope the girl would decide to be silent—but that seemed unlikely. Besides, another peek in the mirror told him that she really was nervous.

"If my sister thinks you're ready, then you're ready," he said. "Plus, I've seen you ride. You're very good."

"You really think so?" Ruby sounded earnest and hopeful.

James met her eyes in the mirror. "I really think so."

"Thanks, James." Ruby settled back in her seat, and James nodded, an odd sense of satisfaction rolling over him. Only because Ruby had fallen silent and he could ride in peace.

It lasted all of thirty seconds.

"Can I ask you something?" Ruby sprang forward in her seat again.

"Who? Me? Or your mom?" *Please let it be Bethany.*

"You, silly."

"Um. I guess?" He could always decline to answer. It wasn't like this ten-year-old was the boss of him.

"Do you like Kimberly's mom?"

"Ruby," Bethany gasped.

So she *had* been listening.

"I'm sorry." Bethany's cheeks were definitely pink now.

"I, uh—" James scratched his eyebrow. "She's nice, I guess." Where was this line of questioning going?

"But do you, you know, *like* her like her?"

"Ruby Jane, stop." Bethany turned in her seat, and James caught a glimpse of the warning look she sent her daughter.

"What about my mom?" Ruby asked.

"Ruby Jane Moore!"

James couldn't help it. The horror in Bethany's voice made him laugh out loud. He tried to cover it with a cough.

Unsuccessfully, judging by the death ray Bethany shot him.

"I'm so sorry," Bethany repeated.

"Turn right at Sunset Drive. Your destination will be on the left," an electronic voice cut in.

"Thank goodness," Bethany murmured.

James chuckled. Saved by the GPS. Now he didn't have to answer Ruby's question.

At least not out loud. But that didn't stop his brain from thinking about it the whole time he got the riders checked in and the horses unloaded and everyone to where they needed to be. He got separated from Ruby and Bethany in the shuffle. But as much as he tried to tell himself that was a good thing, he couldn't resist searching them out the moment everything was settled.

He reached them just as Ruby's level was announced as the next event.

"I can't do this." Ruby turned to Bethany, looking panicked.

"Of course you can." Bethany sent James an equally panicked look.

"No, Mom. I'm too scared. I'm going to mess up."

"You know what I used to tell Sadie when she was scared?"

"What?" Ruby looked to him as if he had the answer to the secret of life.

"I'd tell her, the more scared you are to do something, the braver you are when you do it."

Ruby nodded slowly.

"And if that didn't work," he continued. "I'd bribe her with ice cream. That's how I taught her to ride a bike."

"Does that mean we can get ice cream if I do this?"

"That's up to your mom."

They both looked to Bethany. She rolled her eyes. "Like I can say no now."

"Goody." Ruby clapped her hands, and next thing James knew, her arms were around his waist. He lifted his arm to her back. The girl seemed to have her mother's propensity for spontaneous hugs.

"Ruby." Bethany's voice was full of laughter, and it made him accidentally smile too. "Let go of James and get on your horse if you want a chance for some ice cream."

Ruby squeezed him once more, then let go and moved toward her horse.

James helped her into the saddle. "You and your noble steed get out there and show us your stuff."

"Noble steed." Ruby giggled as she rode off.

James and Bethany made their way to the rail so they could watch.

Bethany grasped his hand as Ruby's name was announced over the loudspeaker.

"She's got this," he reassured her.

Ruby put her horse through the required moves, keeping her lines beautifully and guiding her horse through the half-circle loops flawlessly.

"Emma would be proud." James grinned at Bethany as they made their way toward the spot where Ruby was exiting the arena.

"Thank you." Bethany paused and touched his arm.

"Of course." He tilted his head. "For what?"

"For that pep talk before. You didn't have to tell her—us—about Sadie."

James blinked down at her, his gaze getting stuck on her lips. "Someone told me I need to be more vulnerable."

Her face remained neutral, and at first he thought maybe she hadn't heard him. But then she said, "Who?"

He nudged her shoulder. She was kidding, right? "You."

"I did?" She squinted as if trying to peer back in time.

James studied her. "The other day. At the barn. You yelled at me to be more vulnerable and then— You really don't remember?"

Bethany played with a strand of her hair. "I'm sorry. My memory—"

"Did you guys see me?" Ruby barreled into them, nearly knocking Bethany off her feet. James reached out a hand to steady her.

"You were great." Bethany hugged her daughter. "Let me take a picture of you."

Ruby smiled for her mom, then turned to him. "I did it! That means we get ice cream, right?"

"Yep." James looked at Bethany, who was nodding.

So ice cream she remembered. But the kiss that had shaken up his whole life?

Apparently that had been forgettable.

Chapter 34

Bethany's lip felt raw from chewing it all the way to the Chocolate Chicken. Ruby and James had spent the drive analyzing Ruby's performance—which had earned her a third-place finish.

But all Bethany could think about was the fact that for the first time since her aneurysm, she'd lied about not remembering something.

Of course she remembered the conversation she and James had had in the barn—and what had come after it.

She'd been trying for days to forget about the way she'd made a fool of herself, kissing him like that. But it'd been hopeless. The harder she tried to forget, the more she remembered—remembered the caress of his hands and the smell of his cologne and the taste of his lips.

But just because she remembered didn't mean they should talk about it. If she pretended to forget, then they could move on as if it hadn't happened at all.

"Mom!" Ruby's voice blasted through her thoughts, making her jump.

"Sorry. What?"

"We're here. You have to get out of the truck."

"Oh." Bethany startled to find James opening her door. She didn't mean to look into his eyes—they were bluer than usual today, a shade she couldn't think of a word for, and less troubled too.

"Are you okay?" he asked as he helped her down. "You seem quiet today. Quieter than usual, I mean."

She laughed. "And you seem less quiet than usual."

He looked taken aback but then laughed too. "My ex-wife used to say Sadie got her chatterbox tendencies from me. Don't look at me like that. It's true."

Bethany closed her mouth. She hadn't meant to look surprised, but chatterbox? James?

"I guess I haven't felt like talking much in a long time," he said quietly. But even the way he said that didn't feel as heavy as usual.

"I'm going to get bubblegum ice cream," Ruby announced as she hopped out of the truck.

"Ugh." Bethany wrinkled her nose.

But James laughed. "Sadie tried that once. She wasn't a fan."

The three of them strolled toward the ice cream shop together, and Bethany got the oddest sensation suddenly—this was what it would be like if they were a family.

But they weren't.

"What was she like?" Ruby asked. She was walking between them, and it took Bethany a moment to realize she was talking to James—and that she was asking about his daughter.

"Ruby, that's not—"

But James gave Bethany a soft smile. "It's okay." He glanced down at Ruby. "She was funny, silly, always giggling. She had the best laugh—" He cut off, clearing his throat and looking out over the lake.

Bethany's heart ached for him, and she had to clasp Ruby's hand to keep from reaching for his. But then Ruby clasped James's hand with her other hand, making the three of them a chain.

"She sounds special," Ruby said.

Bethany held her breath. This was past the point where James usually shut down or ran away.

But he smiled at Ruby. "She was. She would have loved to ride horses the way you do."

They had reached the door of the Chocolate Chicken, and Bethany was almost disappointed. Something was happening here. She didn't know what, exactly. But it felt like something she wanted to last.

"There you guys are." Tiffany and Kimberly raced toward the Chocolate Chicken from the other direction. "We thought maybe you got lost." Tiffany's smile faltered as her eyes went to the line of their linked hands, but she recovered within half a second. "I'll get a table for all of us over by the window if you'll place our order. I'll have a single scoop of peppermint, and Kimberly likes cookies and cream."

"I— Um. Okay."

Tiffany and Kimberly were already disappearing through the door James held open, and Bethany gave him a panicked look. She'd already forgotten what they wanted.

"Don't worry." James tapped his head. "Sometimes my nearly photographic memory is useful." His hand landed on the small of her back for a second as he ushered her through the door, and a jolt of nerves shot up her spine.

When they got to the counter, he ordered for everyone and insisted on paying, telling the server he'd cover anyone else who came in from Hope Stables too.

It only took a few minutes for their order to be ready. Bethany picked up Ruby's bright pink concoction and held it out to her. But just as Ruby reached for it, James stepped away from the counter with the rest of the order. His elbow hit Bethany's hand, and she lost her grip. The ice cream seemed to fall in slow motion, straight toward Bethany. She gasped as the blob hit her in the stomach, then slid to the floor, leaving a nice pink streak in its wake.

"I'm so sorry." James set his dishes down and pulled a wad of napkins out of the dispenser on the counter.

"It's okay." Bethany blotted at her shirt. What had she been thinking when she'd decided to wear white this morning? Her gaze flicked toward Tiffany, who was also wearing white—her outfit was still pristine.

Bethany gave up on her shirt and shifted to wiping the ice cream off the floor.

"Here. I'll do that. You go take care of your shirt." James squatted next to her, his eyes right in front of hers, his lips . . .

She looked at the floor. There was no reason for her to notice his lips. "I've got it. If you want to bring the others their ice cream, I'll be there as soon as I'm done."

James's hand fell on top of hers, stopping it. Gently, he took away her napkins. "Go. I'll clean this up and then order Ruby a new one."

Bethany stood slowly. She didn't need a dizzy spell on top of everything else. But she wobbled as she straightened and had to reach out a hand to steady herself. It contacted James's shoulder instead of the chair she'd been aiming for. He stilled, his other hand reaching up to grasp her elbow, and she had no choice but to hold on for another second before being certain that she was steady enough to cross the room.

"I'll be right back," she murmured, not quite sure if the fresh wave of dizziness was from standing up or if it was from the care she'd seen in his eyes as she walked away.

***

James's eyes flicked to the back of the Chocolate Chicken as he tried to make small talk with Tiffany. Fortunately, she seemed content to carry the conversation, and all he had to do was nod every few seconds.

Bethany had been in the restroom a while. What if she had fallen and hit her head in there? She'd seemed dizzy when she'd stood from wiping up the ice cream. He should have sent Ruby with her. Should he send her to check on her mom now? Or maybe he should send Tiffany.

But she was still talking. "The field day is the last big thing of the year, and then I can finally relax. Has your mom said how it's coming?" She directed the question to Ruby.

"How what's coming?" Ruby took a bite of the rocky road James had talked her into ordering in place of the spilled bubblegum flavor. He'd been surprised when Ruby had agreed to the suggestion.

"The field day, of course." Every once in a while, James caught a hint of condescension in Tiffany's tone—and he didn't like hearing it directed toward Ruby.

"It's good," James jumped in at Ruby's confused expression.

"Oh." Tiffany raised an eyebrow. "Bethany told you that?"

"Mmm hmm." James concentrated on stuffing a big bite of ice cream into his mouth so he wouldn't be forced to stretch the truth any further. Bethany had said she was planning to start on it weeks ago. Surely she had by now. Just because she hadn't mentioned it again didn't mean she hadn't done anything.

"That's a relief. To be honest with you, I was worried that she might not remem—"

"Nope. It's all under control." James wasn't about to let Tiffany insult Bethany right in front of Ruby. Or right in front of *him*, for that matter. Bethany couldn't help it if she sometimes couldn't remember things—even whole entire kisses.

His pulse kicked up a notch as he spotted her emerging into the seating area. Her forehead wrinkled as she scanned the tables, and he realized she didn't remember where Tiffany had seated them. He waved a hand over his head. Her eyes landed on him and her forehead unwrinkled as her lips lifted. James finished the last large bite of his ice cream so he wouldn't stare.

"Oh no. It didn't come out all the way." Tiffany pouted toward Bethany. "Here. I think I have some . . ." She opened her purse and pulled out a pouch, producing a small wipe that she passed to Bethany. "Stain remover."

"Thanks." Bethany looked embarrassed as she rubbed it over the spot that was now a faded pink. "I keep meaning to put some of these in my purse, but . . ." She shook her head with a rueful smile. "Guess I'd better write it down."

"Here." Tiffany reached into her organizer and passed a handful of the little packets to Bethany. "I have plenty more at home."

James smiled at Tiffany. That was kind. Maybe he'd misjudged her.

"Thanks," Bethany murmured again. The spot was almost completely gone from her shirt now, and she stepped away to throw the wipe out, then returned to the table.

"Hold on." She eyed Ruby's ice cream as she took the seat between James and her daughter. "I know I forget things, but that ice cream does not match the color on my shirt."

"James said rocky road was Sadie's favorite. So I decided to try it. It's good."

"I can't believe you got her to try something new." Bethany smiled at James as she scooped a bite of her own melty Sundae.

"Who's Sadie?" Kimberly asked from the other side of the table.

James froze. Just because he'd been able to talk about his daughter with Bethany and Ruby didn't mean he was ready to talk about her with the whole world. But both Kimberly and Tiffany were watching him with unabashed curiosity.

"Oh look." Bethany pointed toward the window. "There's a new store going in where the barber shop used to be."

"Thank goodness." Tiffany wrinkled her nose. "Every guy in town came out of that place with the same exact haircut."

James laughed at her comment but sent Bethany a grateful smile. He couldn't be sure whether she'd changed the subject to spare him from talking about Sadie or because the flurry of activity across the street had caught her eye, but either way, he was thankful.

"Can we go to the park, Mom?" Kimberly asked after they'd all speculated about what kind of store could be going in.

"Sure. I'll take you girls while Bethany finishes her ice cream. Care to join us, James?"

He glanced at Bethany. She still had most of her ice cream left. "I'll wait here with Bethany. We'll meet you over there."

Tiffany's smile dipped for half a second but then returned. "Of course." As they filed out of the shop, the two young girls seemed to be arguing, both of them looking at him over their shoulders.

"I wonder what that's about."

"No idea," Bethany murmured, sticking her spoon in her mouth. Her cheeks took on a rosy glow.

James felt his own face warming. Now what? Should he make small talk? Maybe about the weather? Or Ruby's ride today? Or the small matter of the kiss she'd forgotten?

"James?" Bethany's voice drew his eyes right to her. She was watching him, looking perplexed.

"Sorry. Did you say something?" He'd been a little lost in thought.

"No. But thanks for telling us about Sadie. It means a lot."

He swallowed and nodded. He wondered if she remembered that she'd already thanked him for that. Right before he'd discovered that she'd forgotten all about their kiss. "Thanks for listening."

"Always."

He looked out the window at all the families bustling by. He used to believe in always. But now he knew it could be ripped away at any moment.

He pushed back from the table to clean up the mess the others had left—and to catch a breath. What was he doing here, acting like Bethany and Ruby were his family—like he *wanted* them to be his family? He'd already had that once and, yes, he missed it with a sting sharper than a hundred bullet wounds. But that was his past. His future was as a single man. What he needed now was for Emma to hurry up and get better so he could get back to Milwaukee—where he'd never once questioned his family-less future.

He took a fortifying breath and made his way back to the table. Maybe he could rush Bethany through the rest of her ice cream. He lowered himself into his seat, sliding a few inches farther from her so he wouldn't be tempted to enjoy her peach scent.

"Oh. Ow." Bethany dropped her spoon into the dish and pushed her palms to her forehead.

"What? What is it?" James sprang toward her. Was it possible for her to have another aneurysm?

"It's okay." Bethany lowered her hands, and one of them fell on top of his. "Brain freeze."

He exhaled. "Don't do that to me. I thought . . ."

"Sorry." She smiled apologetically, and James had to look away so she wouldn't see how much she'd scared him.

But why? He was a cop; he was trained to deal with emergencies. He'd seen some awful things over the years, and he'd never flinched.

Except when it was Sadie.

And now Bethany.

People you love.

No. He didn't love Bethany.

He cared about her—as a friend—yes.

And this was only proof that even that was too risky.

He felt Bethany's eyes on him but resisted the pull as long as he could. When he finally gave in, there was such a depth of understanding in her gaze that he couldn't look away.

But then the bell over the door clanged and snapped him out of it. "I almost forgot to tell you, Tiffany was asking Ruby about the field day. I told her it was going great and you had everything under control."

If he'd wanted her to stop looking at him so sweetly, this had done the trick. Her eyes widened, and she scrambled to pull her phone out of her purse. "The field day! I completely—" Her mouth snapped shut, and then she whispered, "It's in two weeks. I'll never get it done." She dropped her head into her hands and massaged at her temples. "Why did I ever think I could do this? I'm going to have to tell Tiffany. Maybe she can still pull it together. Better than I can."

James's heart tugged. She was a smart, talented woman. She shouldn't feel this way about herself. "Or . . ." He glanced toward the window. Did he really want to make this offer when what he should be doing was putting more distance between them, not less?

But when he looked back to her, her eyes were so full of hope that he had no choice. "I could help you. I bet the two of us—and maybe a few of your friends—can get it done on time."

"Really?"

James shrugged. "Sure."

Instead of impulsively hugging him as he fear-hoped, Bethany narrowed her eyes. "On one condition."

"You're going to put conditions on me helping you? I'm not sure that's the way this is supposed to work."

"Yes it is. My condition is that you have to let me help you too."

"Help me? I don't—"

"With the horses. No more finishing everything before I get there. Deal?"

Oh boy. That would mean even more time together. But he found himself grinning. "Deal."

Chapter 35

"How about this one?" Bethany passed her phone to James to show him the list of field day activities she'd found.

"A water balloon relay race? Sure. I think the kids would like that. But who's going to fill all those water balloons?" He rested his elbows on Emma's desk in her office at the stables, which they'd transformed into a headquarters for field day planning over the last few days. His arm bumped Bethany's, and she jiggled her eyebrows at him. He laughed—it was a sound she heard more and more often lately, and one she never forgot.

"You think *I'm* going to fill them?" He shook his head. "I have no idea how you roped me into this."

"You volunteered," she reminded him.

"Oh, you remember that?"

She nodded, not letting herself mention what else she remembered, though she was suddenly staring at his lips. She tore her eyes away and concentrated on writing water balloons on her list of supplies they needed to pick up. Fortunately, the list wasn't terribly long. They'd already arranged for all the food with the help of Leah and Peyton and Ariana and Sophie and Grace. And James had made a sign-up sheet for volunteers, which Ruby had brought to school and asked her teacher to hand out to parents.

She rummaged through the folder from Tiffany. "Food. Check. Games. Check. Prizes—" She looked up at James. "We need prizes."

"All right. Where do we get those?"

She paged through some sheets in the folder, frowning. "It looks like they usually order them months ahead of time." She sighed. She'd made such a mess of this whole thing. And every time she thought she might pull it off, another obstacle came up.

"Hey." James covered the paper she was reading with his hand. "We've got this. Come on." He stood, turning his hand palm up and holding it out to her.

Okay. As far as she could remember, she'd been the only one to ever initiate contact between them—and that only impulsively. This was . . . unexpected.

But he bounced his hand a little, and she let her palm come to rest in his. His fingers closed around it, warm and secure, making her wish that they always walked around like this.

But then he tugged her to her feet and she came to her senses and pulled her hand back. His hand hovered near her elbow. "No dizziness?"

She shook her head. "Nope. I'm good." Unless you counted the unexplained longing that had taken up permanent residence in her chest as they'd spent more time together. She let him lead her outside. "Where are we going?"

"Downtown. I'm sure there are plenty of places that would love to donate prizes."

"You think so?"

He opened her door. "It's worth a shot."

She climbed into her seat, using the few seconds it took him to reach his own door to calm the nerves that suddenly tingled through her. This wasn't a date. It was a volunteer project. *Her* volunteer project. And yet here he was, pouring his time and energy into it too. Why? For her?

She didn't usually consider herself a quick thinker, but she pushed that thought away as fast as it had entered.

James was just bored. Or he felt sorry for her. Or . . .

He got in the car and smiled at her.

Maybe he was doing it for her. The thought made its way back in. "Um." She tried to refocus her attention. "Maybe we could try the hardware store too? They might have something we could give away."

"Like nails?" James joked.

"No." She shoved his arm lightly, his firm muscles barely moving under her touch. She retracted her hand and folded it in her lap. "Like squirt guns or something."

"That's a great idea."

A glow started in Bethany's middle and worked its way toward her face. "Thanks."

They fell into an easy conversation about Ruby's volcanic science experiment that had made a mess all over the kitchen. Somehow talking with him was never intimidating or hard or tiring. She never worried about forgetting her words or taking her time to find the right one. With him, the words were just there—or he waited patiently until they were. From Ruby, their conversation turned to Emma and her frustration at not being able to work in the barn yet.

"It's a good thing she doesn't know about her surprise party on Saturday, or she'd probably get mad about not being able to help plan that too," James said.

"The party!" Bethany bolted upright so fast her seatbelt tightened. "I think I forgot to get a gift."

"You can always get one at the hardware store," James teased.

But Bethany groaned. "You must think I'm a terrible friend."

James didn't answer for a moment but slowed the truck for a stop sign. Then he looked over at her. "You have to stop thinking that I think you're a terrible anything. Or that anyone does. In case you haven't noticed, people around here really like you. They admire you. *I—*" He turned back to the road and stepped on the accelerator. Bethany's imagination tried to guess the ending to the sentence he'd left unfinished.

"Anyway," James continued, pulling on the collar of his shirt. "Everything worked out fine when you forgot Ruby's present, remember?"

"I forgot Ruby's present?" She gripped the console between them. She was sure she'd given her daughter something . . . though she couldn't remember exactly what it was. Maybe she was a worse mother than she thought.

"No," James said gently. "You gave her that horse necklace, remember? But you had forgotten your purse that day. And then locked yourself out of your car. You don't remember?"

She shook her head. "No. Sorry."

"It was the first day we met," he said softly.

She closed her eyes. It seemed impossible that she wouldn't remember that. And if she'd forgotten that, what else didn't she remember? Had she kissed him more than once?

Her internal debate over whether to ask him lasted all of three seconds. It was better to go on pretending the kiss—or kisses, as the case may be—had never happened.

And to make sure it didn't happen again.

"The lake is pretty today." James had to come up with something to think about other than how much he was enjoying this day with Bethany. They'd made a huge haul—jacks and tops from the toy store, bookmarks and stickers from the book store, squirt guns and Frisbees from the hardware store, and even a few trinkets from Violet's antique shop, where Bethany had also found a Victorian silhouette of a woman and a horse for Emma.

"I think that's one of the things that surprised me most when I moved here." Bethany squinted toward the waves, which slipped gently toward shore today. "I used to think a lake is a lake is a lake. But not this lake. It's like it has its own mood swings."

James laughed—it felt like he'd been laughing all day.

"So what is the lake's mood today? Happy?" James grinned at her. His sure was.

Bethany studied the waves. "I would say more like content."

"Content it is." He fell silent again but only for a moment. He couldn't explain this new desire to talk whenever he was with her—or his desire to draw her out, to learn everything about her. "I don't think I ever asked where you're from."

She frowned as if it was a hard question. "Texas, originally. A bunch of other places in between. But I think this is the first place that has felt like home since I was a kid."

James could see why she would think that. Hope Springs had something about it that said *home*.

But it's not, he reminded himself.

It could be, his thoughts argued.

"So what brought you here?" he asked, mostly to keep his thoughts off his own growing desire to stay.

Bethany looked startled. She didn't say anything for a few minutes, until they reached his truck and he opened her door. "I got pregnant with Ruby." She paused with one foot on the running board. "And I knew I had to get out of the situation I was in."

James's jaw hardened. He'd seen more than one woman who'd had to flee from an abusive "situation," but the thought that it had happened to Bethany made him want to throw up—or punch someone.

"He hurt you?" he managed to growl.

"No." Bethany climbed the rest of the way into the truck and tucked her hands between her knees. "He was . . . into things that I knew I couldn't have around my baby."

"Drugs." He couldn't keep the contempt out of his voice. He'd made too many arrests, been too personally affected by what addicts could do, to remain neutral.

Bethany nodded silently, staring straight ahead out the windshield, and James closed her door. He shoved his hands in his pockets and rounded the truck. He hadn't meant to make her feel bad about it. It wasn't her fault she'd gotten mixed up with the wrong guy.

"You did the right thing," he said the moment he opened his door. "Leaving Ruby's father, I mean. People like that don't change. I've seen it over and over again. The guy who shot my dad had been arrested for possession three times. He was out two weeks before he got high and killed my dad."

"Oh, James. I'm so sorry." Bethany's lip trembled.

Way to go. He'd been trying to reassure her—not leave her in tears.

"Hey. It's okay." He reached for her hand. "It was a long time ago. I just wanted you to know I'm glad you left that situation. I've seen too many beautiful, intelligent women get involved with guys like that and not know when to walk away."

Uh oh. Had he just called her beautiful and intelligent?

Well, she is.

If Bethany had picked up on what he'd said, she didn't show any signs of delight. If anything, she looked closer to tears as she extricated her hand from his and clasped it in her other fist.

He tried to recapture the lighthearted mood he'd managed to single-handedly ruin, but though Bethany offered strained smiles, her replies were short and halting, as if she struggled with every word. When they reached the stables, she silently accepted his offer to unload the donations they'd collected and headed straight for her car.

He watched her leave, trying to figure out what had gone wrong.

And reminding himself that actually it had gone *right*. If she wouldn't speak to him, he wouldn't be so tempted to stay in Hope Springs.

Chapter 36

Bethany tried to focus on Jade's words as she discussed a point Kayla had raised in their Bible study. All these women, living such lives of faith, having everything together all the time. She loved them all dearly—and yet sometimes she had to ask herself if she really belonged here.

"Could someone read the next two verses out loud?" Jade asked.

Bethany's hand sprang into the air.

Jade gave her a surprised smile. And no wonder—Bethany had never volunteered to read out loud before, as far as she could remember. But right now, she felt like she needed to prove she wasn't a waste of space. Like she had a purpose, even if it was just reading a couple of verses.

She directed her eyes to the Bible open in her lap and realized she'd forgotten which verses they were on. She skimmed her finger over the words, hoping something familiar would jump out at her. "Um." She licked her lips. Emma leaned over and pointed at the verse.

"Thanks," Bethany whispered, then read out loud. "For he has rescued us from the dominion of darkness and brought us into the kingdom of the Son he loves, in whom we have redemption, the forgiveness of sins." Her words slowed as she reached the end of the verses, their truth spreading like a warm blanket over her heart. After her conversation with James in the truck yesterday, she'd almost let herself forget this. She'd been dwelling on the sins of her past—the years she'd spent living in the "dominion of darkness"—instead of focusing on Christ's forgiveness. James might think former drug addicts could never change—but she knew the truth: in Christ, she had been set free from those sins.

Of course, that didn't mean James would want anything to do with her if he knew about her past. But that was fine. She didn't need him to have anything to do with her. She had Ruby. And her friends. And her Savior. That was what mattered.

She spent the rest of the Bible study concentrating on the discussion between the other women—and even contributing one or two tentative comments.

When they had closed with prayer, Emma leaned over to Bethany. "Is everything all right? Between you and James?"

Bethany fought unsuccessfully against the flush rising to her face. "There is no me and James, Emma. And I know this isn't the first time I've told you that, so don't give me that innocent look."

Emma laughed. "But seriously. He seemed upset after you left yesterday. I thought maybe he finally got up the nerve to ask you out and you—"

"He didn't ask me out."

"But if he had . . ." Emma prodded.

Bethany's heart jumped, but she shrugged as casually as she could. "I would have said no."

"What? Why?" Emma frowned. "You're as stubborn and hard-headed as he is."

"Thanks," Bethany said dryly. "I think it's best not to complicate things." She patted her friend's leg. "I'll see you tomorrow."

Emma's forehead wrinkled. "Tomorrow?"

"For the—" She caught herself just in time. But how was she going to cover up the slip? "Never mind. I was thinking tomorrow was Wednesday, not Saturday." She tapped the side of her head. "Good thing I have a calendar."

Kayla stopped her on the way out the door. "Nice save."

"Thanks," Bethany murmured dryly. "How's Evelyn?"

"You mean the nocturnal screaming machine who has forgotten how to sleep more than twenty minutes at a time?" Kayla's eyes widened. "Why didn't anyone tell me how hard this would be?"

Bethany could only stare at Kayla. She'd always seen her sister-in-law as a superwoman—and now supermom. Did she really struggle too?

"Oh my goodness. It's just me, isn't it?" Kayla pressed her hands to her cheeks. "I'm not cut out for it." A large tear dropped onto her cheek. She swiped it away. "I'm sorry. I don't know why I'm crying. I love her so much, but I'm so tired."

Bethany squeezed Kayla's shoulder. "Don't apologize. I think I cried every day for Ruby's first month. I had no idea what I was doing."

"I find that tough to believe." Kayla squinted at her. "You seem to find the whole mom thing so easy. And you raised Ruby all by yourself. I can't even imagine how difficult that was."

Bethany swallowed. "It *was* hard. It still is hard. But I have you all. And you have all of us too, you know."

"I know," Kayla sniffled. "But I feel like I should be able to do it all myself."

Bethany laughed. "I know you do—because that's who you are. But I've been learning that it's not so bad to ask for help. How about you drop Evelyn off at my house tomorrow afternoon, and you and Cam can—" When Kayla started to protest, Bethany cut her off. "Just for a little while. Anyway, we have—" She directed a subtle look toward Emma. "The you-know-what tomorrow night, so you won't be able to stay out very long."

Kayla sighed. "You win. Thank you."

As Bethany got into her car, she laughed to herself. Who would have thought she would be the one giving parenting advice? But it felt good to know that for once she'd helped someone else rather than being the one in need of help. Now all she had to do was survive caring for a baby on her own again.

Chapter 37

"Good morning."

James startled as an older man entered the kitchen. Instinctively, he shoved his cereal bowl out of the way and jumped to his feet, his hand going uselessly to his hip.

The man held up his hands. "Whoa! Relax, son. I'm William."

James didn't relax. Was that name supposed to mean something to him?

"Your mom's . . . friend."

"What are you doing here?"

"He came to surprise me." Mom bustled into the room, looking chipper and more youthful than she had in years, and slipped an arm around William's back. "Isn't that sweet? He got in around two o'clock this morning."

James eyed William and then his mom.

"He's staying in the office," Mom clarified.

James nodded. That was a relief, at least.

"Is Bethany coming by today?" Mom asked with a not-at-all subtle grin. "I noticed you two have been spending a lot of time together."

"I'm helping her with the school's field day. I told you that. And no, she's not coming today. We have everything done until we have to set up next week."

"Hmm." Mom nodded thoughtfully. "Then may I make a suggestion?"

"Can I stop you?" James crossed his arms in front of him.

"No." Mom mirrored his crossed arms. "Ask her on a date. Just the two of you. William and I would be happy to watch Ruby."

"Mom, it's not like Bethany and I are dating. We're just friends."

If they were even that anymore. He hadn't heard from her since she'd left Thursday afternoon, and he still hadn't figured out what had upset her.

"Come on." Mom pulled William toward the table. "William has grandkids, so he'll be good at keeping Ruby entertained."

"Yep. Six grandkids." Pride oozed from William's smile. "Oldest is twelve. Littlest one is four. Spunky as all can be. Takes after her mother."

James laughed, letting the dull ache surface but not overpower him. "Sadie was like that too."

Mom's smile was surprised and misty. "She took after you." She moved closer and squeezed his arm. "See, I told you Bethany was good for you. Go on. Call and ask her out."

James studied his mom and then William. He reached for his phone but hesitated with it in his hands. Was he really ready to take this step?

"What's the worst that could happen?" Mom asked. "She says no?"

James swallowed. That wasn't the worst that could happen. The worst that could happen was she'd say yes and they'd have a wonderful time and they'd grow closer and become a family and then God would decide to snatch yet one more thing from him.

"It's worth the risk, James," Mom said quietly. "You can't live your life waiting for the other shoe to drop. God doesn't operate that way. He's not out to get you."

James shook his head. He wished he could believe that. But so far, his life hadn't borne that out. Not with Dad, not with Sadie, not even with Emma—she might still be here, but the doctors wanted her to do a round of chemo, and James knew that God wasn't above taking her too.

He stowed his phone back in his pocket.

Mom's face fell. James ignored it as he took a step backwards. But his phone rang before he could make his escape. He pulled it out of his pocket and gave an ironic laugh as he caught sight of the number.

Bethany.

He pretended not to notice the way Mom's eyes lit up—or the way his own heart did.

"Hey." He didn't mean for his voice to have that little skip in it.

"Hey." Bethany sounded breathless. "I'm sorry to bother you, but Mr. Faber called, and he has the giant Jenga blocks ready, but he needs us to pick them up today because he's going out of town. I'd go get them, but I don't think they'd fit in my car and I'm—"

"No problem. I'll get them." A perfect excuse not to ask her out. Mom couldn't fault him for that.

"Oh thank you. Would you mind bringing them over here after you pick them up? I want to paint them the school colors."

That meant he'd have to see her. He frowned at the kick of adrenaline suddenly surging through him. "Sure, I'll be there in a little while."

He hung up and turned to Mom, who still had an arm around William and was grinning as if she'd orchestrated this whole thing herself.

Honestly, he wouldn't put it past her.

"Have fun," she said. "And stay as long as you want. We'll make sure Emma gets to—" She lowered her voice, though Emma was still in bed. "Her party."

"Would you stop grinning like that?" But James couldn't help smiling himself as he loped out the door. He was only going to see Bethany for a few minutes—but that was enough.

He tried to fight the anticipation, but by the time he picked up the blocks and got to her house, he couldn't wait a moment longer to see her. He knocked, then rocked from foot to foot as he waited for her to answer the door. A loud cry that sounded like a newborn pierced the air, and James glanced around. He *was* at the right house, wasn't he?

When there was no answer, he knocked again. Again he was met with that cry.

Finally, the door opened, and Bethany stood there, her hair askew, dripping spatula in one hand and crying baby in the other.

"Oh hi." She practically had to shout over the baby's cries. "I forgot you were coming."

"I'll try not to take that personally. You look busy."

"I told Cam and Kayla I'd watch Evelyn today, but I forgot how much work a baby is." She bounced a little, but the baby didn't quiet. "Here, will you hold her for a sec? I'm almost done mixing the brownies for tonight and then I can feed her."

"Oh. Uh. No, I don't think—" But Bethany had already shifted so that baby Evelyn was leaning toward him, and he had no choice but to either take her or let her fall to the ground. The baby was lighter than he remembered Sadie being—more delicate feeling—and he instinctively tucked her closer against his chest. She stopped crying for a second but then started in louder than before.

"Don't take that personally either." Bethany gestured him into the house and nudged the door shut with her hip. "According to Kayla, she does this all day and all night. I thought maybe she was exaggerating, but . . ." Her voice trailed off as she crossed the living room and disappeared into the kitchen.

James dropped his gaze to the little bundle in his arms. She looked so much like Sadie had as a baby—same full cheeks, same bright blue eyes. The only difference was the hair—Sadie had been a baldy for almost a year after she was born, but Evelyn had a fuzzy layer of light hair already.

The baby opened her mouth wide in another wail, and James's heart cracked—for this little girl and for the one he missed so much.

"It's okay," he whispered, as much to himself as to the baby. He shifted her to his shoulder and patted her back in a slow rhythm. "Shh." He walked slowly across the room, putting a small extra bounce in each step. When he reached the far wall, he pivoted and paced back the way he'd come. By his third lap, her cries had slowed to occasional snuffles, and he took a deep breath, accidentally inhaling her milky newborn scent.

He closed his eyes against the memories that assailed him. But instead of the familiar stab—or maybe on top of it—the image of Sadie as a baby brought an odd sort of joy.

"Wow."

He opened his eyes to find Bethany staring at him, the unbaked pan of brownies in her hand. "I'm impressed."

James shrugged. "It always worked with Sadie."

"You're going to have to teach me. I sure could have used you around when Ruby was a baby. I mean—" She took a step backwards, her elbow knocking into the door frame and making her bobble the pan of brownies. "I'd better get these in the oven before I drop them."

James couldn't resist following her. "Where's Ruby?"

Bethany closed the oven door. "Riding her bike around the block."

"By herself?" James glanced toward the front window. How long had she been gone? Should she be back by now?

"With a couple of kids from the neighborhood." She frowned. "I miss the days when she screamed all night but stayed right where I put her. It seems so much harder now, especially since—" She broke off, looking stricken. "I'm sorry. You probably don't— You never got to—" She blew a piece of hair out of her face. "I'm making things worse, aren't I?"

But somehow, she wasn't. "No. It's okay. I know what you meant." His eyes met hers, but her gaze skirted immediately away.

She gathered a few dishes and carried them to the sink but then dropped them and turned to him. "Sorry. You probably want to go. I can take her. I'll clean this up later."

Handing the baby over would be the sensible thing to do. Leaving would be the smart choice.

The baby snuggled her head into his shoulder. "I can hold her a little longer if you want."

Evelyn let out a tiny cry, and he patted her back again.

"I think she's hungry." Bethany rummaged through a diaper bag on the counter, pulling out a bottle. She held it out to him. "Do you want to?"

He took the bottle and moved to the kitchen table, settling into a chair and adjusting the baby, whose cries had worked their way up to a full wail again. The moment the bottle touched her lips, she quieted. After a few sucks, a contented sigh slipped from her, and she closed her eyes, still drinking. It was unreal how natural this felt, how familiar, how comforting.

"You look good like that," Bethany said softly.

He let his lips turn up a little bit, but his throat was too full to say anything. The sounds of Bethany cleaning up and the baby sucking lulled him into a weird sort of half-awake state that made him start thinking strange things, like that maybe it was worth the risk to have a family again.

"Mom!" A tearful yell from the front door tore James out of his foolish thoughts. "I fell off my bike."

James jumped to his feet, accidentally pulling the bottle out of Evelyn's mouth. Instantly, her face puckered into a loud cry.

"It's okay. I've got Ruby." Bethany rushed past him into the living room, but James followed, tucking the bottle back into the baby's mouth as he walked.

"Looks like you got a little scraped up." Bethany squatted in front of her daughter, examining her shredded palms and bleeding knees. "But you'll be all right. Let's go get you washed up." She led Ruby down the hall—toward the bathroom, James assumed.

He sat heavily on the nearest seat, making sure not to jostle the baby's bottle. What had he been thinking, imagining that having a family again would be worth the risk?

It's only a few scrapes. She's fine.

This time. But next time it could be worse. It could be—

He had to get out of here.

But it wasn't like he could toss the baby on the floor and disappear.

Fortunately, after a couple more gulps, the baby stopped sucking, her lips going slack as her breaths deepened into little puffs. James lifted her to his shoulder and patted her back until she burped, then carefully laid her in the playpen in the middle of the room.

He was about to make his escape when Ruby bounded in, tears dried, knees bandaged.

"Hi, James."

If he hadn't seen her crying three minutes ago, he wouldn't have believed anything was wrong. "Like my bandages?"

He gave them a cursory glance. "Rapunzel. Nice." And also Sadie's favorite princess. "I have to get going. Tell your mom I'll put the Jenga blocks next to the garage."

"You got them? Cool. Can I see?" Ruby followed him out the door.

James sighed but silently began unloading the truck, taking as many blocks at a time as he could balance. Ruby picked up a block too, adding it to his stack after he set it down.

It only took a few minutes to empty the truck, but by the time they finished, Bethany stood outside, watching.

"Is it lunchtime yet?" Ruby asked. "I'm hungry."

Bethany laughed. "Sure, Rubes. We can have lunch."

"Can James eat with us?"

Bethany looked startled but then smiled toward him. "You're welcome to stay if you'd like. I can't promise a gourmet meal, but . . ."

James backed toward his truck. "Thanks, but I really have to go." He yanked on the handle and dove inside.

"See you tonight," Ruby called before he shut the door.

James glanced at the clock. It was noon. That gave him six hours to forget any notions of family that had been floating around in his head. Plenty of time.

Chapter 38

"Quick. Grab the brownies." Bethany pushed her car door open with a harried check of the time. They were running late, and she didn't want to be the one to spoil Emma's surprise party. Ruby popped out of the back seat, brownies in hand. "This is so exciting. Can I have a surprise party next year?"

Bethany laughed, hurrying her daughter to Sophie and Spencer's door. "It wouldn't be much of a surprise since you asked for it."

"I'll forget I asked. I promise."

"I highly doubt that." Bethany pulled the door to Sophie and Spencer's house open. It was dark inside, although she could hear rustling here and there.

"They're on their way," someone hissed. "Hide."

Ruby giggled, handed Bethany the brownies, and dived into the small space behind the couch.

Bethany glanced around helplessly at the shadowy forms already occupying all the spaces. Did they really have to hide? Surely it would be enough of a surprise that they were all here. But she knew when her friends did something, they went all out.

Her eyes fell on the coat closet as a series of car doors closed outside. She grabbed the closet door, yanked it open, and flew inside, pulling the door closed behind her.

"Ouch." The whisper came from right next to her, and she just barely kept from screaming as she recognized the voice and the warm scent. Of course she had crammed herself into a closet with James.

"Sorry," she whispered. "I can find somewhere else."

"No. There's no time. We can fit." There was a shuffling sound, then his hand fell on her arm and turned her so she had more room.

"How do we know when to jump out?" Hopefully it would be soon. She wasn't sure if it was the small space or his enticing scent or his tangible nearness, but her head was suddenly spinning.

"I guess Sophie has some sort of signal."

She shifted the brownies to her other hand but bumped his side. "Sorry. It's a little cramped in here. Hey. Aren't you claustrophobic?" Or was that someone else?

"Huh. You know, I didn't think about it."

"And?"

"And it's not bothering me right now."

A loud horn blasted from the other side of the door, and suddenly James's hand was on her arm, pulling her out of the closet with him.

"Surprise!" Bethany chimed in a few seconds late as she caught up with what was happening.

Emma stood in the doorway, clutching her heart but laughing.

"You guys." She shook her head. "I can't believe you got me."

"All those years of saying you couldn't be surprised," Spencer called from next to his wife. "We just had to bide our time and wait until you weren't expecting it."

"I should have known something was up when Mom finally decided to let me leave the house." Emma turned to her mom, who stood behind her with an older gentleman. "I really bought your story about William wanting to see the cherry orchard." She made her way around the room, thanking and hugging everyone.

"I'm going to put these in the kitchen," Bethany murmured after Emma had hugged her and James, giving them both a smile that said she thought there was something going on that wasn't.

"I can take them." James reached for the pan before Bethany could protest. He headed toward the kitchen, and she sighed.

She couldn't figure him out. One moment, he was looking at home feeding her niece in her kitchen—and the next he was running out the door as if his life depended on getting away from her.

"Look who's a happy girl tonight after spending the day with her aunt Bethany." Kayla wheeled over with a cooing baby Evelyn in her lap.

Bethany reached down to scoop the baby into her arms. "It's nice to see you happy, little one." She made a face at the baby, who giggled. "You like that?" She made the face again. "See, James isn't the only one who can get you to stop crying."

"James?"

"Yeah. Didn't Cam tell you?" Cam had dropped Kayla off at home to catch a quick nap while he picked Evelyn up from Bethany's house earlier. "James stopped by to drop off a game for the field day. I was in the middle of making brownies and Evelyn was hungry, so he fed her."

"Wow." Kayla raised her eyebrows. "Not every guy would feed a girl's niece to impress her."

Bethany snorted. "He didn't do it to impress me. He did it to help out."

"Even better." Kayla gave her a significant look. "Definitely a keeper."

"Who's a keeper?" Cam sidled up between them. "Evelyn?"

"Of course." Kayla reached for Cam's hand, and Bethany fought not to remember the warmth of James's hand in hers. "But also James."

"James?" Cam directed a perplexed look between his wife and Bethany. "A keeper for what?"

"Nothing," Bethany blurted.

Kayla laughed and rolled her eyes at her husband. "You're adorable when you're clueless."

"Thanks." Cam grinned, then turned to Bethany. "But seriously, do I need to have a talk with this guy?"

"A talk?" Bethany gaped at him. "Oh my goodness, no. There's nothing to talk about. Your wife is . . ."

"Incredible?" Cam filled in. "Amazing? Perfect?"

Bethany and Kayla both slapped his arm at the same time. Before Bethany could come up with the word she'd been looking for, a wolf whistle pierced the room. Everyone's eyes swung to Levi—the only one of the group who could whistle quite like that.

He stepped aside. "Take it away, Emma."

Bethany pulled out her camera and snapped a few pictures of her friend.

"Thanks, Levi." Emma's smile was misty as she looked around at everyone gathered there. "I asked Dan if he'd mind if I led the prayer tonight." There was quiet shuffling as people clasped hands and bowed their heads.

"Lord of glory," Emma began. "What an outpouring of love you have shown me tonight through all these people you have brought into my life. I am thankful for each one of them, Lord, and the ways they have touched my life. I don't know what your plans are for me in this world—whether they are days or weeks or months or years—" Across the room, a throat cleared. It was a sound Bethany instantly recognized, and she looked up to see James grasping the chair in front of him. His eyes met hers for a second, and she sent him a reassuring smile, but he shook his head and looked away.

"But the length of my life isn't what matters, Lord," Emma continued. "What matters is that it belongs to you. Teach me to serve you each day and to trust that whenever it is your will, you will bring me to your side in heaven. And in the meantime, let me never forget that I have the most amazing group of friends and family in the world. Amen."

"Amen." The word resounded from around the room as several people wiped at their eyes.

After a few seconds, the low murmur of voices picked up again, and everyone surged toward the kitchen to fill their plates. Bethany marveled at the selection. Having several friends who cooked or baked for a living meant no one ever went hungry at one of their gatherings. Sometimes she felt bad that her own contributions weren't more elaborate, but—

Wait.

Where were her brownies?

She scanned the dishes more closely. There were cookies and fudge and a big birthday cake. But no brownies.

Her eyes skimmed the room until they fell on James, sitting silently next to his mom and the gentleman she'd come with. She stepped out of line and made her way toward them. "Do you know where my brownies went? I thought you were going to put them out."

James shifted, looking uncomfortable. "Don't be mad. I tasted one earlier. When I took them into the kitchen."

"And what? You ate the whole pan?" Bethany stuck a hand on her hip.

But James shook his head, grimacing. "Not exactly."

And then she realized. "Oh my goodness. They're terrible, aren't they?"

"Not terrible," James hedged. "Just— I think it's possible you missed an ingredient. Maybe the sugar?"

Oh. Oh. Oh. How could she have done that? She rubbed at her forehead. "So where are they?"

"In a cupboard," James admitted sheepishly. "I was going to throw them away later when no one was looking, and then you'd think they'd been a big hit."

Bethany stared at him. "You were going to . . ."

"I know. I'm sorry." James half-stood. "I can get them out now if you want."

"No. That's . . ." Possibly the sweetest thing anyone had ever done for her. "I can't believe I did that."

"You were a little busy," James said. "And I interrupted you right in the middle of making them."

"Don't worry, dear," James's mother piped in. "I've had more baking fails than you could count. I forgot to add the eggs to James's birthday cake one year." She turned to him. "Remember that?"

"Yeah. I spit it out."

"Hey." His mother hit his arm, then smiled at Bethany. "At least now you know he likes you better than he likes me."

Bethany had no idea how to respond to that—and she didn't need James's mom to see the way her face was warming. She waved toward the kitchen. "I guess I should go get some food."

"Of course." James's mom smiled warmly. "And then come sit by us. We'd love to get to know you better."

"I— Um—" Bethany looked helplessly around the room. Maybe she could use Ruby as an excuse. But her daughter had already filled a plate and was sitting with a group of the other kids.

"Sure." Bethany finally murmured. "I'll be right back."

Chapter 39

James sucked in a deep gulp of the damp night air. As much as he was coming to understand why Emma loved this group of people, he couldn't handle another moment inside with everyone. Especially with the way Mom had spent the past hour chatting with Bethany—and he'd spent it not letting his heart get caught up in how much he was going to miss hearing her voice when he left. Unless he didn't . . .

"Mind if I join you?"

James winced at the sound of a male voice behind him. All he wanted was a few minutes of peace. A few minutes to get his head back on straight and remind himself of all the reasons he couldn't stay in Hope Springs.

He glanced over his shoulder, but Cam hadn't waited for an invitation and was already carrying a chair over to the edge of the deck, next to James.

"Nice night." Cam sat with a long sigh—the happy kind, James was pretty sure.

James didn't bother to reply. He had a feeling Cam hadn't sought him out to discuss the weather.

They sat silently for a few minutes, and James began to think that maybe Cam had simply needed to escape the chaos in the house too.

"So . . ." Cam sat forward. "Bethany said you were a big help with Evelyn today. Thanks for that. Kayla and I appreciated the break."

James shrugged. "No problem."

"Bethany told me about your daughter," Cam said quietly. "I'm so sorry."

James stiffened instinctively, but then found he didn't mind so much that Cam knew. Not that it meant he wanted to talk about it. "Thanks."

"So, you're great with babies, an old hand in the stables, and you even solve crimes. You ever considered that Hope Springs might be the place for you?"

James eyed him. "Emma put you up to this?"

Cam laughed. "She mentioned that the Hope Springs police department offered you a job, but I promise I'm out here of my own free will. I just thought you should know that we all appreciate having you around. My sister and Ruby seem rather attached to you."

There it was. James leaned forward and ran a hand over the smooth wood of the deck railing. "I don't know what you think but—"

"Bethany's sort of . . ." Cam interrupted. "I think she's vulnerable. I mean, she's smart. But she's been through a lot. With the drugs. And then she got cleaned up and had Ruby and was getting back on track. But the aneurysm . . . I wouldn't want her to go through more heartbreak, if she thinks there's, you know, more between you two than there is." Cam shifted, looking uncomfortable, but James had gotten stuck on one word.

"Drugs?"

Cam let out a breath. "She didn't tell you?"

"She said Ruby's father was an addict, but . . ." But she hadn't trusted him enough to tell him she had been one too. Of course, with the way he'd been spouting off about how addicts never changed, it was no wonder.

"It was a long time ago," Cam said. "The moment she got pregnant with Ruby, she left that all behind."

James nodded silently. So she'd not only left a bad situation, but she'd gotten herself cleaned up as well. She was so much stronger than he'd imagined.

"I'm sorry." Cam ran a hand over his head. "I shouldn't have—"

"I'm glad you did."

"Well, I'm going to go inside before I wreak any more destruction." Cam stood. "Do me a favor and don't hurt them. They've been through enough already."

James nodded. So had he.

He sat outside for a while longer, watching the stars appear one by one until he could make out the Little Dipper, which Sadie had called the Little Digger.

By the time he went inside, the house had cleared out considerably.

He didn't mean to seek her out, but his eyes went instantly to Bethany, and when she looked up and smiled, something funny twanged right in the middle of his heart, puncturing straight through his Kevlar. Was Cam right—did she think there was more between them than there was? Or—better question—did he?

"Hey, James." Sophie looked up from her conversation with Emma. "The guys were talking about going out fishing on Tyler's boat tomorrow if you're interested. Bethany said you helped Ruby catch a bunch. Maybe you can bring these guys some luck. They sure could use it."

"Hey." Spencer nudged her but then looked to James. "She's not wrong. You're more than welcome to come."

"Oh. Uh." He wasn't sure he was up to more socializing. "I was planning to run up to the Ploughman farm tomorrow to pick up some hay."

"I almost forgot!" Emma pulled out her phone. "Irene Ploughman texted me the other day. Their new calf was just born. She sent pictures of bottle feeding it."

"Really?" Though Ruby had been sitting on the floor looking sleepy, she bounced upright. "Can I see?"

"Sure." Emma passed the phone to Ruby.

"It's so cute. I wish I could do that."

"I'm sure Mrs. Ploughman would let you. You and your mom should go along with James tomorrow." Emma's triumphant smile shot to James.

Wait. How had his plan for some alone time backfired?

His sister, that was how.

"Can we?" Ruby pleaded—though James couldn't tell whether she was asking him or Bethany.

Neither of them answered at first, but then Bethany came to the rescue. "We have church tomorrow."

James relaxed. That made things easier.

Ruby frowned, but then her eyes brightened. "James can come to church with us first and then we can go to the farm after."

James's mom chuckled. "I like the way you think, Ruby. That's a great idea. Isn't it, James?"

"Uh." James looked helplessly from his mom, who nodded with certainty, to his sister, who grinned gleefully, to Ruby, who folded her hands in a pleading gesture, to Bethany, who wore a smile that bore a hint of . . . hope?

"All right. I'll take you to the farm."

"And you'll come to church with us?" Ruby persisted.

"We'll see," was the only answer he could give to that.

But Ruby seemed satisfied. "Good." She yawned.

"Time to get you home to bed." Bethany stood and laid a hand on her daughter's head. "Looks like we're going to have a big day tomorrow. Goodnight, everyone. Happy birthday." She leaned down to hug Emma, her eyes coming to James as she stood. "See you tomorrow."

Maybe he shouldn't, but he really liked the sound of that.

Chapter 40

"Hey, Mom?" Ruby asked from the back seat.

"Yeah, Rubes?" Bethany glanced at the clock with satisfaction. They were going to be on time for church today. If the person in front of her ever decided to drive faster than ten miles per hour. She tried to peer around the car to see what the holdup might be.

"If you and James get married, will Emma be my aunt too, since she's James's sister? Like how Kayla is my aunt because you're Uncle Cam's sister?"

"Um, yeah— What are you doing here, buddy?" she muttered to the driver ahead of her. Her thoughts caught up with her daughter's words as the car turned into a driveway, giving her room to accelerate. "Wait. What did you say?"

"I said if you and James get—"

"Ruby!" Bethany didn't need to hear the rest of the sentence again. "We've talked about this. James and I are not getting married. We aren't even dating. We don't even like each other."

Ruby started to protest, and Bethany amended her statement. "Not like that, I mean. We're just friends."

"Isn't that how relationships start?" Ruby sounded smug.

"I— What?" How old was her daughter anyway? When had she started thinking about things like relationships? "No. I mean, yes. I mean, not every friendship is the start of a relationship."

Ruby didn't say anything else, and Bethany let out a slow breath. With any luck, that would be the end of that. But then she heard Ruby's low song drifting from the back seat: "Mom and James sitting in a tree, k-i-s-s-i-n-g."

Oh goodness. It was a good thing Ruby couldn't see her face—it had to be glowing like a furnace. But there was no way her daughter knew about their k-i-s-s. She was just being silly.

But that didn't stop Bethany's thoughts from wandering back to the feel of James's lips on hers.

She tried to banish the memory, but it lingered as she pulled into the church parking lot and her eyes fell on the man himself, getting out of his truck. Her heart danced. "I didn't think he was going to come," she mumbled to herself, pulling into a spot a few spaces away.

Before she had turned off the engine, Ruby bounced out of the car. "Ruby, wait!" Bethany scrambled to grab her purse and follow her daughter.

"James," Ruby called.

Though he was already halfway to the church building, he stopped and waved. Bethany fully expected him to turn around and keep walking toward the church, but he waited for them. She fell into step next to Ruby, trying to ignore the flighty swirls in her stomach. Though James wasn't wearing a tie, he tugged at the collar of his white button down, then tucked his hands into the pockets of his jeans.

Bethany pulled her eyes off him.

"Mom didn't think you would come," Ruby announced the moment they reached him.

"Ruby—" Bethany was going to have to talk to her daughter about knowing when things weren't meant to be repeated. "Sorry, I—"

"That's okay." James's smile seemed to hold an edge of nerves. "I didn't think I would either."

"I'm glad you did." Ruby stuck her hand into his and marched him toward the church doors.

Bethany followed them. "Where's Emma?"

"She came with my mom and William. They're already inside." James glanced over his shoulder at her. "You look nice."

"Oh." She suddenly couldn't remember any words at all.

Ruby turned around with an I-told-you-so smile, and Bethany found her voice. "No, Ruby."

James looked at her, forehead wrinkled in confusion. "Did you say something?"

"Uh. Nothing. I mean, thanks."

※

You look nice? What had he been thinking?

Cam had already warned him that Bethany might think things between them were more than they actually were. Telling her she looked nice sure wasn't going to help with that.

But that didn't change the truth. She *did* look nice. More than nice. She looked tear-your-breath-out-of-you gorgeous.

"Hey, James, nice to have you join us." Dan held out a hand, and James shook it, surprised to find that he didn't resent being here today.

He let Ruby lead them to the row where Mom and William and Emma had joined Emma's whole posse of friends. James laughed to himself at his own description, but he had to admit that she was lucky to have this group around her. Every one of them had been there for her through this hard time.

People were there for you too, but you pushed them away. You're still pushing them away.

Ruby slid into the row, and James stood aside so Bethany could go next. But the moment he sat down, he realized he should have gone first and let Ruby sit between them. Because now he'd be smelling Bethany's tantalizing peach scent the entire service. He tried to put some space between them, but he was squeezed against the very end of the row.

A giggle came from next to him, and James looked over, assuming it was from Ruby. But Bethany had a hand over her mouth, her eyes sparkling. She leaned closer and pointed to something in the worship folder. "Sermon theme: Amnesia About God's Goodness," James read.

He chuckled along with her, just barely resisting the urge to wrap an arm around her shoulder and tuck her in close to him. As much as he appreciated the irony, he also felt an overwhelming need to protect her from all the struggles she'd faced.

As the service began, James found himself listening to the hymns and prayers and Bible readings as if he were hearing them for the first time. The sharp edge of anger that usually pulsed behind his heart when he thought about God was a little duller today.

As the final strains of the hymn "It Is Well with My Soul" faded, Dan walked toward the small podium at the front of the church, still humming the melody. Instead of standing behind the podium, he slid it aside and stepped in front of it, moving closer to the rows of gathered people. "I love that hymn, don't you?"

All around James, heads nodded, Bethany's more vigorously than any. Not that he was surprised. He'd seen her wear a shirt with those very words on it.

"So," Dan continued. "How is it with your soul today?"

A heaviness settled on James's shoulders at the question. It hadn't been well with his soul for a long time. And he couldn't see how it ever could be again.

"Before you answer that." Dan lifted a finger. "Let's talk about what it means for it to be well with our soul. It's maybe not something we think about all that often. It's not like we go around asking people how their soul is doing today. Like, 'Hey Joe, It is well with my soul today. How about yours?'" Around the church, a few people laughed.

James shifted, accidentally bumping Bethany's arm. "Sorry."

"It is well with my soul," she whispered back.

James smiled at her quick response, though at the same time a strange pang took hold of his middle. What would it be like if it were well with his soul?

"This hymn is so uplifting," Dan was saying now, "that you'd be forgiven for thinking it was written at the high point in the writer's life. But its author, Horatio Spafford, penned these words at the lowest point in his life. Lower than probably most of us could imagine. Not only had he lost all his property in the Great Chicago Fire of 1871, but two years later, his wife and four daughters were sailing for Europe when their ship sank, taking the lives of all four of his girls. Changing his life in a single moment."

Dan paused, and James clenched his jaw against the sharp jab to his solar plexus.

"On his way to Europe to get his wife, who had survived, Horatio passed right over the spot where his daughters had drowned."

James closed his eyes, but he couldn't block out the image of the side of the road, where Sadie . . .

A hand slipped into his, and he clutched at it, even as he considered getting up and walking out of church. But something made him feel like he wanted to hear the rest of the story. Like he *had* to hear it.

"And *that's* when he wrote these words, 'It is well with my soul,'" Dan said.

James let out a breath. *How?* How was it possible for anyone to say it was well with their soul after something like that? He sure couldn't.

"Is that how we respond to trouble and hardships and sorrow?" Dan asked. "Is our first reaction, 'You know what, even though this terrible thing has happened, it is well with my soul'? Or do we get angry? Or hurt? Or resentful? Or defiant? Or . . . the range of our reactions could go on and on. But most of them aren't positive. So what made Horatio Spafford different? Why could he say that? Was he just putting on a brave face, pretending everything was okay, living in denial? Or was he somehow better than all of us?"

Dan shook his head. "Horatio Spafford could write these words because he knew God's goodness. And he didn't forget it in the middle of his troubles. He knew that in his goodness, God had willingly given up his own Son to save Spafford's girls from their sins. He knew what Paul tells us in 1 Corinthians 15:19: 'If only for this life we have hope in Christ, we are of all people most to be pitied.' His hope for his girls wasn't only for this life. He knew that God had prepared a home for them in heaven. And he knew that whatever hardships he faced in this world, he would be with them in heaven one day too."

Dan paused, looking thoughtful. "Just like Job, who even after troubles maybe worse than Spafford's, could still say, 'I know that my redeemer lives, and that in the end he will stand on the earth. And after my skin has been destroyed, yet in my flesh I will see God; I myself will see him with my own eyes—I, and not another. How my heart yearns within me!' You can hear it there, can't you? The truth of what Solomon says in Ecclesiastes: 'He has also set eternity in the human heart.' Our hearts long for something that lasts forever. He is that something."

James had to swallow against the painful rock that had lodged itself in his throat. Bethany set a hand on his forearm, and he realized he was probably crushing her other hand. He loosened his grip but didn't let go.

"It's easy to get amnesia about God's goodness, though, isn't it?" Dan paced to the far side of the church, but James's eyes followed him. "The Israelites sure did. Over and over again. God would bless them with all kinds of good things, but soon they'd forget that all those things came from him, and they'd turn to false gods or their own ideas, and they'd experience all kinds of hardships. And then, after a while—sometimes a long while—they'd snap out of their amnesia and remember God's goodness. It was a long list. He'd brought them out of Egypt, provided manna for them in the desert, defeated their enemies, and on and on. And when they finally remembered that, they'd turn back to God and it would be well with their souls. Until the next time they forgot about his goodness."

Dan laughed sadly. "It's a lesson they had to learn over and over again. It's a lesson *we* have to learn over and over again. And like I told my daughter Hope when I was teaching her to ride a bike, the best way to learn something is to practice." He took a breath, surveying the room. "You might feel silly doing this, but humor me. Close your eyes and think of five ways God has shown his goodness in your life. I'll wait."

He fell silent, and James glanced around. Next to him, Bethany had closed her eyes and seemed to be concentrating, one hand still in his, the other still on his arm. Next to her, Ruby wiggled but smiled over at him. Beyond her, several members of their group had either closed their eyes or were looking at their hands folded in their laps.

James sighed. He wasn't willing to play this game. All the goodness in the world could never make up for what God had taken from him. But in spite of himself, images came at him one after another: Sadie wrapping her sticky arms around his neck, his family at his side for her funeral, Emma smiling at him after her surgery, Ruby and Bethany sitting next to him right now—

"I'm sure you could continue to think of things all day," Dan interrupted James's thoughts. "But it might eventually get awkward for me to stand up here silently. Plus, here's one you maybe didn't put on your list: He remembers you. Even when you forget his goodness. Listen to his words—" Dan reached behind him and picked up a Bible off the podium. "'Can a mother forget the baby at her breast and have no compassion on the child she has borne? Though she may forget, I will not forget you! See, I have engraved you on the palms of my hands.'"

Dan set the Bible down and looked at the palms of his hands. He held them up. "That's pretty extreme. It'd be difficult to forget anything engraved on the palms of your hands. And someday we're going to see that love engraved on Jesus' hands in the shape of nail marks. We're going to be at his side—and he's going to remember us. He's going to call us by name. He's going to wipe every tear from our eyes and 'there will be no more death or mourning or crying or pain.' *Then* we won't be able to forget his goodness. Because we'll be living with him in it. Forever. *That's* why Horatio Spafford could say it was well with his soul. And that's why we can say it is well with our souls too. Amen."

As the sermon ended, Dan invited the congregation to join in singing "What a Friend We Have in Jesus."

"And in case you're interested in more hymn history," Dan said, "this one also came out of tragedy. Joseph Scriven's fiancée died the day before they were to be married. As you sing this hymn, notice that Scriven points to another aspect of God's goodness: He hears our prayers and carries our burdens."

Dan sat down and the music began, and James couldn't block out the words. It was a hymn he'd learned as a child. But the words seemed to hold new meaning now, as the congregation sang, "O what peace we often forfeit, O what needless pain we bear, All because we do not carry everything to God in prayer."

As the hymn continued, James ducked his head. He wasn't sure he remembered how to pray anymore. *I need* something, *Lord*. They were the only words he could find. Now he would have to wait and see if God remembered him.

By the time the service ended, James felt as if he'd been shaken and stirred and sifted. Not bodily, but in his heart. Maybe in his soul.

He was still trying to sort it all out as Bethany pulled her hand out of his. "If you don't want us to come along to the farm, I understand." She kept her voice low. "I can tell Ruby I have a headache or something."

James frowned, glancing at Ruby over Bethany's shoulder. "You don't want to come?"

Bethany shook her head. "No, I mean . . . Ruby forced the invite. And if you'd rather not . . . I know it's . . . After everything . . . And then . . ." She blew out a breath that stirred her hair. "I'm not explaining this very well."

James touched her arm. "I know what you're saying. And I think we should go."

Chapter 41

"Look how cute he is," Ruby squealed as they entered the barn at Ploughman Farms. "Isn't he cute, Mom?"

"He's the cutest." Bethany smiled at her daughter, trying to ignore the slight twinge at the base of her skull that signaled an oncoming headache. She was *not* going to ruin this day. Not when Ruby was so excited. Not when James seemed like a different man—lighthearted and hopeful. Not when her stomach sent itself into a spiral every time he looked at her like he was right now. Something was different today. She wasn't sure what it was, but she sure wasn't about to wreck it.

Mrs. Ploughman popped out of a door behind the calf's pen.

"What's that?" Ruby's eyes widened, and she pointed to the large bottle in the woman's hand.

"This is his bottle." Mrs. Ploughman held it out toward Ruby. "Do you want to feed him?"

"Yes." Ruby sprang forward and took the bottle. "How?"

Mrs. Ploughman laughed. "Just hold it out and he'll do the rest. He's a messy eater though. Here, Dad, it might help if you hold his head."

Bethany froze. Had she just called James "dad"? As in, she thought he was Ruby's dad?

James opened his mouth and Bethany assumed he was going to correct Mrs. Ploughman. But then he closed it and stepped forward, wrapping an arm over the calf's head and scratching its ears with his other hand.

"Thanks, Dad." Ruby grinned at James.

For heaven's sake. She had not just said that.

"Ruby Jane." Bethany used her most dire warning tone, but Ruby gave her an innocent look. Bethany rubbed her temple.

Poor James was probably ready to run out of here screaming.

But he said, "You're welcome."

Ruby brought the bottle to the calf's mouth, and the animal wrapped its tongue around it, sending milk splashing everywhere. Both Ruby and James laughed, readjusting as Mrs. Ploughman coached them through it. After a few minutes, they seemed to get the hang of it, and the calf guzzled down his milk, making a mess but seeming content.

As Bethany watched, an unexpected ache formed deep in her middle. Or maybe it wasn't an ache. More like a . . . what was the word Dan had used in church? Yearning. *For what?*

But she already knew the answer. She just couldn't let herself think it. Because it would never happen.

"Do you want to try?" James's question cut into her thoughts.

"Huh?" Bethany jumped. She hadn't voiced her thoughts out loud, had she?

He pointed to the calf.

"Oh. No. I'm good. You two make a good team."

She pulled out her phone to take a few pictures, then leaned against a post and closed her eyes. The twinge in her head had grown to a dull throb.

"Are you okay? You look pale."

Bethany opened her eyes to find James peering at her, his forehead creased into sweet wrinkles of concern. She blinked and looked around. Ruby was petting the calf's neck, and Mrs. Ploughman was gone. How long had she closed her eyes?

"Just a little headache." Her pulse throbbed against her forehead as she pushed herself upright.

"You should have said something. Come on, Ruby," James called over his shoulder. "Let's go tuck your mom in the truck and then you can help me load the hay. I need a supervisor to help me figure out how to stack it."

Ruby kissed the calf between the eyes, then skipped over to them. "That was so fun. Can we come along again next time?"

"I don't see why not." James gently turned Bethany toward the door and wrapped an arm around her lower back, as if afraid she would tip over.

"I'm okay. Really," she murmured.

But he didn't move his arm away, instead pulling her in closer. Bethany shut her eyes for a moment, letting the overwhelming feeling of safety overcome her common sense.

"Come back anytime," Mrs. Ploughman called from the far side of the barn. "You have such a nice family."

Bethany couldn't find the energy to correct the woman. James waved to her, and Ruby called, "Thanks. We will."

When they got to the truck, James opened her door and held her arm to help her in. "Close your eyes," he whispered as he shut the door quietly.

Her head was pounding too hard now to argue. She was vaguely aware of James's and Ruby's voices—first outside the truck and then in it, vaguely aware of movement, vaguely aware when they stopped and the engine cut out.

"Bethany." James's whisper cut through her fog. "We're home."

She dragged her eyes open and pain exploded in her forehead. She couldn't hold back a quiet moan.

"That bad, huh?" James brushed a hand over her forehead. "Should I take you to the emergency room?"

Bethany started to shake her head, but the throbbing was too intense. "No," she whispered. "Just need to lie down."

"Stay right there." He opened his door and jumped out and next thing she knew, he was on her side of the truck, reaching across her to unbuckle her seatbelt and then sliding an arm under her to lift her out of the truck.

"I can walk," she protested weakly.

"I've got you," James murmured, grunting a little as he started toward the house.

She should protest more, but she didn't have the energy, and his arms felt so strong against her back and his shirt smelled so good against her face.

"I'll open the door." Ruby ran ahead of them.

"My purse," Bethany mumbled. They'd need the keys.

"Ruby has it." James's chest moved as he spoke, and it was strangely comforting. He carried her inside and straight to her room, where he laid her on the bed.

"Oh," Bethany sighed as her head sank into the soft pillow. That was better already. She vaguely registered someone lifting her foot and easing her shoe off. "You don't have to—"

But he already had the second shoe off as well. "Can I get you anything?" James spoke softly, his voice drawing nearer her head. "Some medicine?"

"No thanks. I'll be fine in a minute."

"You're sure? I really think you should take some—"

"No." The protest came out louder than she intended and she winced at the extra jab to her forehead. But she refused to take any medications that weren't necessary for her survival.

James pulled the blankets up to her chin. "Just rest then. I'll take care of Ruby."

"Thank you." She wasn't sure if she spoke the words out loud or only in her head before everything else faded.

Chapter 42

"I won!" Ruby threw her hands in the air with a triumphant yell.

"Shh." James glanced down the hall toward Bethany's bedroom but then gave Ruby a fist bump. "Good job. I'm impressed. Not many people can beat me at checkers. Another game?" They'd already played six, not to mention the hour-long game of Monopoly they'd played before that. But James wasn't tired of it yet. Maybe he never would be.

Somehow, spending time with Ruby was like a balm for his heart, sliding into cracks he hadn't known were there, filling them with her laughter and her earnest expressions and her sheer joy.

"I'm hungry," Ruby announced. "When do you think Mom is going to wake up?"

"I'm not sure." He'd poked his head into Bethany's room a few times, just to make sure she was okay. She'd seemed to be sleeping peacefully. He hoped that meant her headache had gone away. It had cut at his heart to see her in so much pain. "Tell you what." James folded the checkerboard and stuck it into the box. "How about I make you something?"

Ruby squinted at him. "Can you cook?"

"Can I cook?" James chuckled. "Of course I can. Does making toast count as cooking?" He laughed at her wrinkled nose. "Just kidding. Let's go see what you have."

He followed Ruby into the kitchen, where Mrs. Whiskers was perched on top of the refrigerator.

"Mrs. Whiskers." Ruby giggled.

"At least she's not in the tree this time." James rummaged through the cupboards, refrigerator, and freezer, feeling oddly at home. After a quick inventory, he announced, "I can make eggs, spaghetti, hamburgers, or peanut butter and jelly."

Ruby made a face. "Not peanut butter and jelly."

"What kid doesn't like PBJ?"

"I like it." Ruby climbed onto a stool next to the counter. "But Mom gives it to me every day for school."

"So why don't you tell her you don't want it?"

Ruby gave him a look.

"You do tell her. She forgets?"

Ruby nodded.

James exhaled. "This is hard on you too, isn't it?"

Ruby lifted a shoulder. "It's not that bad. I just wish . . ."

James waited.

But Ruby hopped off the stool. "Let's have hamburgers."

"Hamburgers it is." He studied her as she washed her hands. It wasn't at all like her not to blurt out exactly what she was thinking. Should he press?

He passed her a towel. "What were you going to say before? What do you wish?"

She bit her lip, looking older than her ten years. "I wish my mom could stay like this."

"Sleeping?"

But Ruby didn't giggle like he'd expected. "No. Happy. Kind of . . . sparkly. Like she used to be."

"And why wouldn't she?"

"Because you're leaving," Ruby said simply.

"Because I'm— Oh." He opened the refrigerator and stuck his face in it. The ground beef was right in front of him, but he rummaged around to give himself a moment to figure out how to respond.

But finally, he had no choice but to come out. Mrs. Whiskers meowed indignantly as the door closed harder than he intended.

"Sorry," he muttered to the cat, who blinked at him with haughty eyes, then stood, stretched, and jumped elegantly to the floor. He set the meat on the counter and turned to Ruby. "I'm glad you think your mom is happy, but I'm sure it has nothing to do with me." Just like the fact that he felt happy for entire days at a time lately had nothing to do with Bethany. Or very little to do with her. Or— He swallowed as the realization hit him—almost everything to do with her.

"It does. But I know you can't stay."

"Yeah, my job is in Milwaukee, and—" And right now, going back to it held almost no appeal. Not when it meant he had to leave all this behind.

But he had to. Because otherwise he'd only risk losing it all in some much more painful way.

"I'm going to go start the grill." He didn't wait for a response but tore out the back door. The patio was small but tranquil, and James took a moment to breathe the fresh air, which still held a trace of warmth, though the sun was setting, staining the sky in shades of pink and red. A longing strong enough to steal back the breath he'd just taken crashed against his ribs.

What if this was what he wanted? Quiet nights at home. Surrounded by family.

Except Bethany and Ruby weren't family.

Yet.

The word refused to leave him alone, and he moved to start the grill so he'd have something else to think about. When he returned to the kitchen to get the meat, he found Ruby peeling carrots.

"Mom makes me have vegetables every night," she explained when James said he was impressed.

He laughed. "Your mom's a smart lady." He started forming the hamburger into patties.

"Yep." Ruby kept peeling. "Can I ask you something?"

Oh boy. This could be dangerous. But he couldn't refuse. "Go for it."

"Do you think God answers prayers?"

Wow. She couldn't have started with something easy? He was *so* not qualified to answer this question.

"Because I do," Ruby cut in. "When my mom was in her coma so long, I was afraid that maybe he didn't. But Pastor Dan told me God always answers our prayers. Just not always in the way we want him to."

"Hmm." James picked up the plate of meat, hoping the conversation was over.

"Did you pray for Sadie?" Ruby asked.

"Uh." James cleared his throat. "I did."

Ruby nodded, as if she'd already known the answer. "I'm sorry God didn't answer the way you wanted. But she's with Jesus now."

James turned to the door. "I have to get these on the grill."

Ruby set down her carrot and followed him out the door. "Would it be okay if I prayed for you?"

James opened the grill. "That depends. What are you going to pray for?"

"That you'll be happy when you think of Sadie being with Jesus."

James pressed his lips together. He didn't see how that could ever happen, but he wasn't sure there was a way to tell her that.

"And," Ruby continued. "That you make good hamburgers."

James laughed and ruffled her hair, the same way he'd always done to Sadie. "Now *that* you can pray for."

Bethany blinked at the dim room around her. Where was she?

When was she?

She brought a hand to her head, which felt heavy and groggy.

Had she been napping?

She felt for her phone on the nightstand, but it wasn't there. Sitting up gingerly, she searched the bed for it.

There. Next to her pillow.

She flicked it on to check the time. Seven o'clock.

She groaned. Ruby must be starving by now. She'd better get some dinner going.

She pushed her feet to the floor and stood slowly, testing her head. When there was no throbbing, she made her way to the bedroom door, calling that she'd have supper ready in half an hour. There was no answer, and when she inhaled to call again, she smelled something. Smoke.

"Ruby!" *Oh Lord, where is she?*

She raced to Ruby's bedroom, but it was empty. "Ruby!" Where was the smoke smell coming from?

She flew down the dark hallway toward the kitchen, where a light glowed. Had Ruby tried to cook something herself and started a fire?

"Ruby!" Bethany didn't know how she'd hear her daughter if she answered, the way her blood thumped in her ears.

There was no one in the kitchen either. And no fire.

Bethany stopped as she spotted two forms out on the dark patio. She made out faint wisps of smoke drifting up from the grill.

Her knees turned wobbly, and she leaned against the counter, forcing herself to take a few slow, deep breaths. Her heart had finally returned to near normal speed when the back door opened. Ruby walked through, followed by James carrying a plate of hamburgers. Her heart sped right back up at the way he smiled at her. "Feeling better?"

"Much. Thank you. You didn't have to do that." She gestured to the burgers.

"Yes I did. Ruby here questioned my cooking abilities, so I had to prove myself. You're sure you're feeling better? You still look pale." He stopped next to her, touching the back of his hand to her forehead.

She closed her eyes, letting herself lean into his hand. "I'm okay." She realized he probably wanted his hand back and stepped away. "I just woke up and smelled smoke, and I was afraid . . ."

"Oh wow. I'm sorry. I didn't even think of that."

She shook her head. "I should have realized it was the grill. It smells delicious."

"I think that's our cue." He gestured Bethany toward the table. "Dinner is served. Don't forget to bring your pièce de résistance, Ruby."

Ruby carried a bowl of haphazardly peeled and uncut carrots to the table. Bethany considered taking them and finishing the job, but Ruby looked so proud that Bethany couldn't bring herself to do it. A little carrot peel wouldn't hurt them.

Bethany pulled out a chair and sat. Ruby chose a chair on one side of her, James on the other. Her heart ballooned with contentment. This was what a family meal should be like. *Cooked by someone else?*

She giggled, and James gave her a funny look. "Something amusing?"

"No. Sorry. I just— It was really sweet of you to do this."

Was it her imagination, or was that a little flush under the scruff on his cheeks?

NOT UNTIL THEN

"It was Ruby's idea to make hamburgers. I was just the grill man." James passed the plate around and Ruby passed her carrots. Bethany made sure to take several.

Once they all had food, Ruby folded her hands in front of her. "I'll pray."

Bethany glanced at James. What if he didn't want—

But he already had his head bowed and eyes closed, a faint smile dusting his lips.

That was new. But welcome.

Bethany closed her own eyes as Ruby began to pray.

"Dear Jesus. Thank you for a fun day with James and Mom. Please help James when he misses his little girl."

Bethany sucked in a breath, her eyes popping open. "Ruby."

James kept his head bowed. His lips turned down, but he shook his head. "It's okay." Gravel roughed his voice, but he nodded for Ruby to go on.

Ruby looked to Bethany, who hesitated, but then reached to take James's hand and nodded too.

Ruby got up onto her knees on her chair so she could reach across to take James's other hand, then continued. "Help him be happy that she's with you, Jesus. And help him be happy that he's here with us right now and he'll see her again someday."

Ruby stopped, and Bethany slowly opened her eyes, not sure she was ready to meet James's gaze after that. How had her daughter so perfectly put her own heart into words?

"Oh," Ruby added, "and please let his hamburgers be good too. Amen."

James laughed, and it was the most wonderful sound Bethany had ever heard. "Thank you," he said to Ruby. "That was . . ." He cleared his throat and stared at his hamburger.

"That was lovely, Ruby," Bethany finished for him, and he sent her a grateful look. She smiled and let go of his hand. It felt good to help someone else find the words for once.

They were mostly silent as they ate, although every few minutes Ruby would start chattering about one topic or another. Bethany listened and responded as appropriate—but her eyes refused to leave James for long. And if she wasn't mistaken, he kept looking at her too.

"I have to get ready for bed," Ruby announced when her plate was clear.

Bethany raised an eyebrow. Ruby wasn't wrong. It was almost past her eight o'clock bedtime. But since when did she volunteer to go to bed? But Bethany would take the easy win. "I'll be there to tuck you in as soon as I get this cleaned up."

"You're going to tuck me in too, right James?" Ruby bounced out of the room, flinging the question over her shoulder.

"Ruby, I'm sure James—"

"Wouldn't miss it," James cut in.

"You don't have to," Bethany murmured as Ruby disappeared. She turned to grab a dishrag, but he was right there.

"It's all right." His smile was warm and gentle and only a little bit haunted. "It's been a long time since I've tucked anyone in, but I think I remember how."

"James, if it's too hard . . ." Her eyes caught on his, and she couldn't remember what she'd been about to say.

"Bethany." His whisper was hoarse, and his palm slid softly against her cheek.

Next thing she knew, she was on her tiptoes, and his lips were catching hers, and she was inhaling his scent of spice mixed with the burgers he'd grilled, and her hands were gripping his shoulders, and her head was spinning in the best way, and—

"Mom, James, I'm ready!"

Bethany broke away with a gasp. "Ruby." But she spun to find that she and James were still alone. Ruby must have called from her bedroom. *Thank you, Lord.*

"I— Um." She touched her lips, which were still tingling. "Sorry, I should—" She tipped her head toward the hallway. "I can tell Ruby you had to leave."

James reached for her, as if he was going to tuck her hair behind her ear, but then shoved his hands in his pockets instead. "Do you want me to leave?"

No. But *yes.* But *no.*

His smile wrapped her in tenderness, and she pressed a hand to her stomach. Why was this so confusing?

"Mom! James!" Ruby called again, poking her head into the kitchen this time. "Come on."

James gave Bethany a questioning look, but she couldn't move. He turned to Ruby. "Lead the way."

Chapter 43

James watched as Bethany hugged Ruby, then pulled the blankets up to her daughter's forehead.

"Mom," Ruby protested.

"What? Oh." Bethany pulled the blankets down and hugged Ruby, her movements flustered. "Sorry."

James would laugh at her, except he felt the same disconnected, dazed feeling after that kiss. He wasn't quite sure if he'd started it or Bethany had—all he knew was that he'd been more than disappointed when it had ended.

"Your turn, James." Ruby held out her arms to him.

James moved toward her bed, bending easily for her hug. She smelled of mint toothpaste and the same strawberry shampoo they'd used on Sadie's hair. Instead of tightening like it usually did, his chest eased at the memory. "Goodnight, Ruby."

"Goodnight, James."

He'd half-expected to hear the word "dad" from her lips, and he had to take a quick step back after he released her. He wasn't her dad.

But maybe—

He crashed into Bethany as he turned to leave the room, nearly sending her sailing onto the bed. He caught her at the last second.

Ruby giggled. "You guys look like you're dancing."

"Go to sleep, Ruby," Bethany said, not looking at him as she led the way out of the room.

James turned off the light, pulling the door closed behind him but leaving it open a crack out of habit. Sadie could never fall asleep with her door closed tight.

"That's perfect," Ruby called. "Goodnight."

James followed Bethany down the hall, the word *perfect* hanging on the edge of his thoughts.

When they reached the living room, Bethany stopped, glancing from him to the front door. "So. Um. Thanks for a great day. And thanks again for making supper."

Ah. That was his cue to leave, then. He should probably thank her for having enough sense to send him on his way. Because he wasn't certain he had that kind of sense right now.

"You're welcome." He couldn't think straight as his eyes fell on her kissable lips.

"Do you have to get going or . . . ?" Bethany tucked a strand of hair behind her ear. "I could make some coffee or lemonade or something."

"Yeah, okay." He didn't care that he sounded way too eager. He couldn't leave her right now. "How about lemonade?" His senses were still buzzing from that kiss, so adding caffeine to the mix would probably be a bad idea.

He followed her into the kitchen and got out two glasses while she mixed the lemonade. Neither of them said anything, and James needed to know if her mind was still on their kiss too.

Unless—

What if she had forgotten it, the way she'd forgotten kissing him in the stables?

But it wasn't like there was a good way to ask her.

"Should we sit outside?" Bethany smiled lightly and passed him a glass.

"Sure." He watched her movements, but she seemed calm and collected. Maybe he'd only imagined she was flustered when they'd tucked Ruby in. Or maybe she'd forgotten the kiss between then and now.

He followed her out to the small wicker love seat. It was the only piece of furniture out here, which left him no choice but to sit right next to her—or remain on his feet.

He chose to sit. And then wished he'd remained standing. Being this near her, with that peach scent floating to him on the breeze, he could barely keep himself from leaning closer.

He lifted his glass to his mouth and took a long drink. The tart lemonade burned slightly on its way down—but it was the best way to resist the urge to kiss her.

When he lowered his glass, she was staring at him. "Wow. You must have been thirsty."

He glanced down to find that his glass was nearly empty. Hers was still full.

"Would you like me to get you some more?" She set her glass on the deck and held out a hand for his.

"I'm good, thanks."

She tucked her hands into her lap and tilted her head back, exposing the long, delicate line of her neck.

James let out a breath.

"Is everything okay?" Bethany sat up. "If you don't want to stay . . ."

"I'm sorry about before," he blurted.

"Before?" Bethany's forehead wrinkled. "I don't . . ."

"For kissing you." There. Now it was in the open and he could see if she'd forgotten.

"Oh." It was impossible to read her expression in the dark. "I— It was— You don't need to apologize for that."

Okay. So did that mean she remembered it? If he wanted to know, he was going to have to come out and ask. "So you remember . . . ?"

She chuckled. "Of course I remember. But I thought I was the one who kissed you."

James's heart rocketed around his chest cavity as he laughed. "It's just . . . Last time you forgot. Not that I blame you. But—"

"James." Bethany's hand fell softly on his arm. "I didn't forget."

"Yes, you did. You forgot the whole conversation we had—"

"No, I didn't. We were in the stables and I yelled at you for not talking about Sadie and you yelled back at me and then I kissed you."

James stared at her. He very clearly remembered each of those details. But she hadn't seemed to. "Then why . . ."

She ducked her head. "I was embarrassed. You hadn't shown any sign you wanted me to kiss you and I just threw my lips on yours."

He laughed but then leaned closer. "If you're looking for a sign that I want you to kiss me . . ." He lifted both hands to her cheeks and brought his face toward hers.

Her laugh was low, and it only lasted a second before she closed the gap between them and brought her lips to his. He closed his eyes, letting his hands slide into her hair as her hands came to the back of his neck, tugging him closer. His mind searched for the perfect word for this, but the only thing it could land on was *something*.

He slowly pulled away and opened his eyes. Bethany looked at him quizzically, and he stroked his thumb over her cheek. He'd prayed in church this morning for *something*. Was this it? Bethany and Ruby?

"James?" Bethany asked tentatively.

"Sorry. I was just thinking."

"Me too." But instead of smiling as he was, she frowned. "I have to tell you something."

Chapter 44

Bethany forced herself to swallow. To breathe. But she couldn't make herself speak.

Once she told him this, she wouldn't be able to take it back—and she knew he would never forget it.

"Hey." His hand brushed over hers. "Whatever it is, you can tell me. Or you don't have to. It's up to you."

Oh, the compassion in his eyes. Bethany wanted to bury her face in his chest. It would be so much easier.

But he had to know this. Had to know who she really was.

Even if it destroyed *this*—whatever this was. She couldn't live in a lie. She had left that all behind.

"I'm a drug addict. I mean, I was. I've been sober for ten years, but . . ."

James's expression changed almost imperceptibly—a slight downturn in his lips, a slighter crease in his forehead. But he kept his hand on hers and squeezed her fingers. "I know."

"What? You . . . Have I told you this already?"

James laughed softly. "No. Cam mentioned it. I don't think he meant to," he rushed to add. "I think he was trying to protect you. Making sure I wouldn't hurt you after everything you've been through."

Bethany watched his thumb trace circles on the back of her hand. This wasn't the reaction she'd expected. She'd been prepared for him to get up and walk away.

But he didn't know all of it.

"Did he tell you that he was the one who first found me shooting up? On Thanksgiving?"

There it was. The flinch. "No." James's thumb stilled, but he kept his hand wrapped firmly around hers. "Bethany, you don't have to do this. It doesn't matter."

But she did have to. "I was in high school. I had surgery on my shoulder for a volleyball injury. The pain pills . . ." She hadn't realized how quickly she'd started to rely on them, to need them, to crave them. But when her prescription had run out, she'd easily found new ways to get her hands on more. And when she couldn't get pills, she'd found people who could get her what she needed easily enough.

"My parents got me into the best rehab program they could, even though it cost them a fortune. I did okay for a while. But I kept going back to the drugs. It was like they . . . owned me."

"That's what addiction does," James said. "You couldn't help—"

She shook her head. She hadn't gotten to the worst part yet. "I stole from them, James," she whispered. "I was out of rehab and they wanted to help me, so they gave me a job at my dad's landscaping business. And I . . . took it all. They had no idea until it was too late." She pulled her hand out of James's and wrapped her arms around her middle. Why couldn't she forget these memories, instead of all the new things she wanted to hold onto?

"They lost the business. And then my dad had a heart attack. He didn't make it."

James reached for her, tried to pull her close, but she pushed him away. She still wasn't done. "I promised myself I'd get cleaned up after that. But it was so . . . hard." It sounded lame. A lot of things were hard, but people did them anyway. "It was like . . ." She groped for words. "Like they consumed me. When I didn't have them, they were all I could think about. It was like I would die if I didn't get some." She swallowed, clearing her throat.

"My mom tried to help, let me live with her, but I pushed her away. She—" Bethany pressed her fingers to her burning eyes. Water pooled on her fingertips, and she pulled them away in surprise. Was she crying? She sniffled, but she had to see this through. "She had a stroke a few years after my dad died. I'd come home a few weeks before that because I needed some money. She talked me into staying. But I was strung out when she needed me." The tears built into a full-out sob. She had never talked about this before, never told anyone—not even Cam—where she'd been while Mom was lying helpless on the floor of their house, dying. While a repairman had discovered her body. "I didn't mean for them to—" She choked as a pair of strong arms circled her shoulders. She clutched at him. It had been so long since she'd cried, and the tears came so hard that she wasn't sure how she would ever breathe again.

James stroked her hair silently, his arm wrapped tightly around her back. She should pull away, let him flee, as he no doubt wanted to, but she couldn't let go. Finally her tears abated, and she lifted her head off his chest. His arms loosened, but he didn't let go completely. Still, Bethany knew he couldn't want to stay. He was just too nice to say so. "You can go if you want. I'm fine." She eased his arms off of her.

"What if I don't want to go?" he whispered.

"You don't?"

He shook his head, wiping the tears off her cheeks. "I don't think you understand how strong you are. You left that life."

"Because I got pregnant," she said. It wasn't like she'd had the strength to quit on her own. If it hadn't been for Ruby, she'd likely still be living like that today.

"Exactly." James leaned forward and pressed a kiss to her forehead. "You gave up something you thought you were going to die without for the sake of your daughter. That takes an incredible amount of strength. And courage. And selflessness."

"Stop." Those words didn't apply to her.

"And determination." He grinned. "And perseverance. And—"

She had to stop him somehow. So she launched herself forward and pressed her lips to his.

He chuckled as his arms came around her and he pulled her closer.

Satisfied that she'd silenced him, she pulled away after a moment.

"And bravery. And resil—"

She had no choice but to kiss him again.

Chapter 45

James hummed as he grabbed a protein bar out of the cupboard.

"Look how happy you are." Emma's eyes danced as she strolled into the room. "I wonder why. Or should I say I wonder who?"

James eyed her jeans and boots. "You'd better not be planning to work in the barn today."

"Relax. I'm just meeting a potential new rider. I promise I won't lift a thing." She held up three fingers.

"What's that supposed to be?"

She shrugged. "Some kind of scout signal or something?"

He laughed. How had his sister made it through all of this—with the prospect of starting chemo still looming—with her humor intact? Was it because she was like that Horatio guy Dan had talked about in his sermon yesterday—she didn't forget God's goodness?

"Anyway." Emma poked his side in the way that had made him jump since they were kids. "You got home late last night."

He snorted. "If you call eleven o'clock late." Though it had taken an extreme act of willpower to get up and leave rather than sit outside holding Bethany all night. He hoped his grin didn't look as goofy as it felt.

"So you and Bethany kissed, huh?"

"I— What? She told you?" When had they even spoken? It was only seven in the morning.

Emma laughed, clasping her hands together and pointing at him. "No. But you just did."

He made a face at her. "That's really mature."

"Seriously though." She laid a palm on his forearm. "I'm happy for you. It's good to see you smiling again. Does this mean you're staying?"

"Staying?" He'd be lying if he said he hadn't sat up all night thinking about it. But staying meant saying his future was here. With Bethany and Ruby. And what if that future was ripped away from him?

"You're staying?" Mom flew into the room, her face wreathed in a huge smile. "That's wonderful news."

"No." James held up a hand. "I'm not— I mean, I can't— I mean—" He couldn't make sense of his thoughts. "I don't know," he finally relented.

"What's not to know?" Emma asked. "You're in love with Bethany, right? And you love Ruby too. I can tell." She squinted at him, as if challenging him to deny it.

He shook his head. "I have to go." They'd realized as he was leaving Bethany's last night that her car was still in the church parking lot. He'd promised to come by to take Ruby to school and then drive Bethany to get her car. "I'll be back to take care of the horses shortly."

All the way to Bethany's house, he tried to get the *l-word* out of his head.

But the moment he pulled into the driveway and Ruby came bounding outside with her enthusiastic wave, Bethany trailing behind with a shy but joyous smile, the word hit him powerfully in the chest.

Still, that didn't mean he loved them. He *couldn't* love them. He wouldn't let himself love them.

He got slowly out of the truck.

"Good morning, James." Ruby skipped right to his side. "I like seeing you every day."

He ruffled her hair, unable to talk against the sudden well of emotion.

"Good morning." Bethany's voice was soft, and she only brushed her hand over his, as if she could sense his turmoil. He nodded, hoping his smile would speak for him since he couldn't get the words out.

Ruby chattered all the way to school, and James listened gratefully.

But the moment they dropped her off, a charged silence fell over the truck.

"The lake looks happy today," Bethany said as he turned onto Hope Street.

He glanced toward the waves, which seemed to be dancing in the sunlight. "Yeah. It does."

"Are you?"

"Am I what?"

"Happy?" The question in her voice made him reach for her hand and squeeze.

"Yeah. I am. Really happy. For the first time in a very long time."

She exhaled. "Oh good."

He pulled into the church parking lot and parked next to her car. She didn't reach for the door handle but instead turned toward him, looking troubled.

He slid her hair behind her ear. "What's wrong?"

"Hmm? Nothing." She leaned forward and brushed her lips lightly over his, but he caught her and pulled her close, deepening the kiss. The tightness in his lungs eased, like she was his oxygen.

But after a minute, she pulled back.

"What is it?" He took both of her hands in his.

But she pulled them away and ran a finger over her lips. "I'm sorry. I just— What is this? Between us?"

He thought of that l-word again. But it was so much more complicated than that. "I don't know," he finally whispered. "I'm not sure if I'm ready for . . . whatever comes next."

She nodded, as if that was the answer she'd expected. "Then I think," she said quietly, "that we probably shouldn't do this anymore." She touched her lips. "Until you know. I have to think about Ruby. She's so attached to you already, and if . . ." She trailed off and looked out the window, toward the church.

"Bethany." This was torture. He couldn't do this to her. Or to himself. "I'm . . ." He swallowed. "Sorry," he whispered.

She smiled gently. "It's all right."

Chapter 46

"How many more are there?" Ruby peered into the kiddie pool Bethany had spent the past hour filling with water balloons. Bethany squinted at the bags of uninflated balloons at her feet and sighed. "Lots." She was soaked through already by the dozens of balloons that had popped in the process.

"Cool." Ruby picked up a balloon and juggled it from hand to hand.

"Please put that down." Bethany cringed as Ruby missed and the balloon hit the ground, dousing her legs.

"Oops. Sorry." Ruby ducked her head.

Bethany sighed again. It felt like all she'd been doing for the past two days was sighing. "Why don't you go see if Uncle Cam needs help setting up the picnic tent?"

"Where's James? I thought he was going to help."

Bethany swallowed. "I'm sure something came up. But we have plenty of other helpers." Nearly all of her friends had shown up, along with lots of other parents from the school. A group of dads was diligently setting up the giant Jenga game. And Tiffany had looked more than a little impressed at all of Bethany's plans.

"But I miss James." Ruby pouted. "I haven't seen him since Monday."

"I know." Bethany missed him too. She kept hoping he'd suddenly appear, take her into his arms, and tell her he was ready for whatever came next. But that didn't seem likely to happen, and she needed to prepare her daughter for the probability that he wouldn't be in Hope Springs much longer. But not right now. "Go help Cam."

"Fine." Ruby sulked over toward Cam's tent.

The deepest sigh yet worked its way up from Bethany's core. She paused, stretching out a kink in her neck, letting the afternoon sun warm her face. She could be content like this. Just her and Ruby forever. She really could.

She only wished she hadn't let herself indulge those fantasies of family life. And that she hadn't let Ruby get caught up in them too.

She didn't blame James. After all he'd been through, she understood why he wanted to protect his heart. Too bad knowing that didn't make her own ache any less.

James didn't know how he'd ended up at the marina. He was supposed to be at the school, helping set up for tomorrow's field day. But he couldn't seem to get his truck to drive in that direction. So he'd been driving around aimlessly for the past hour. Until he'd arrived here. He pulled into a parking spot and shut off the vehicle.

Now what?

He gazed at the waves, choppy today, though the sun shone brightly on their frothy tips. What mood would Bethany say the lake was in?

Conflicted.

With a hard breath intended to beat back the questions that had been assaulting him for the past two days, he got out of the truck and strode toward the breakwater. He didn't expect that he'd find any answers here, but maybe, with the wide expanse of the lake stretching in front of him, he'd be able to breathe at last.

He didn't know what to say to Bethany. He understood why she wanted to know what *this* was before . . . whatever came next. But he didn't know what it was—what he wanted it to be. Sometimes—most of the time—he wanted it to be everything. He wanted to be with her and Ruby forever. But other times—when he was thinking rationally—he wanted to run screaming from all of this and wrap his heart back up in its Kevlar vest.

He reached the end of the breakwater and stared out over the expanse of the lake. But the longer he looked, the less empty it seemed. Gulls swooped low over the water, then wheeled toward the sky. Sailboats rode the waves, their masts pointing toward the heavens. James tipped his head skyward. "As the heavens are higher than the earth . . ." The verse Dan had shared in his sermon a few weeks ago surfaced in his mind. Was this part of God's plan? Bringing him here, to Hope Springs? And had God brought James here to heal him from something deeper than a bullet wound?

He closed his eyes. *I want to trust your ways, Lord. But I don't know how.*

Water doused his shoes, and he opened his eyes, taking a step backwards. Was that God's way of saying he was in control? Or was it just a wave?

He watched the water for another minute, but when no clarity came, he turned toward the parking lot. Standing here wasn't getting him anywhere.

Halfway there, two teenage boys stood perched on the rocks, fishing poles in hand. James slowed as he recognized them. "Catch anything?"

"Hey, man." Pete waved at him. "I thought that was you who barreled past us before, but you seemed like you were on a mission."

James laughed. "You could say that."

Chris eyed him but didn't speak. Nor did he tense like he was getting ready for a fight, which James took as an improvement.

"You want to join us?" Pete asked, gesturing toward an extra pole dangling between two rocks.

Chris watched him out of the corner of his eye, as if sizing up his answer.

NOT UNTIL THEN

"Nah, I should—"

Chris turned away, a defeated sneer on his lips, and James wondered how many people had said they didn't have time for this kid.

"Maybe a couple of casts." It wasn't like he'd figured out what to say to Bethany. Maybe a few minutes of fishing would help. He worked his way over the rocks and picked up the pole, casting the line easily out over the water.

"How are Bethany and Ruby?" Pete asked.

"They're—uh—good." He reeled the line back in slowly.

"Uh oh. Trouble in paradise?" Pete joked.

James shook his head. "Speaking of trouble, you guys staying out of it?"

When neither answered, James stared them down.

"Mostly," Pete muttered.

James stopped reeling. "What does that mean?"

"Shut up, Pete," Chris called. "It was nothing. It's all taken care of now."

"Yeah, with more community service," Pete muttered. "We still got thirty hours to do."

"You'd better do them, and then some." James sounded like his dad. "And then clean up your act. How many second chances do you think you're going to get?"

The crashing waves swept the words away, but James heard them echo in his head.

How many second chances was he going to get to have a family?

He finished pulling the line in and set the pole down. "I have to go."

"Chill, man. You don't gotta leave. We learned our lesson and all that." Chris seemed genuinely regretful.

"No. Sorry. I just realized—there's somewhere I have to be."

"Let me guess." Pete grinned at him. "It has to do with Bethany and Ruby."

"Actually." James scrambled up the rocks. "It does."

Chapter 47

Bethany sank into the couch, too tired to lift her aching feet onto the footstool.

The doorbell rang, and Bethany's heart catapulted right from her stomach to her throat. She forgot about her fatigue as she vaulted for the door.

It had to be James.

He'd never shown up to help with getting the field day ready, and her multiple calls to him had gone unanswered. Her brain insisted on sticking by what she'd said to Ruby—something must have come up. And now he must be here to apologize.

She yanked the door open. "Oh." Exhaustion submerged her. "Hi, April."

"Hi," the neighbor girl said cheerfully. "Can Ruby come bike with me?"

Bethany eyed the sky. The sun was sinking but hadn't set yet. "Sure. For a little while." Maybe that would give Bethany some time alone to figure out how to answer Ruby's constant questions about when they were going to see James again.

"Ruby," Bethany called toward the hallway. "Do you want to bike with April?"

Ruby popped out of her room, as energetic as ever even though she'd bounced from station to station, helping whoever needed it as they'd set up the field day. "If James comes over, tell him to wait for me. I want to talk to him."

Ah. Now Bethany remembered why her first thought when the doorbell rang had been of James. Ruby had been talking all the way home about how he'd probably come over to explain why he hadn't been able to help.

She considered telling her daughter not to get her hopes up, but she didn't have the energy to have that conversation right now. "Be home in half an hour. And watch for cars."

"Yes, Mom," Ruby said dutifully. Then she took off for the garage to get her bike. Bethany watched until Ruby and April pedaled down the street, making sure they used proper hand signals as they turned at the end of the block.

The little pit of worry that always opened in her stomach when Ruby was out of sight tried to grow, but she pushed it back. *I trust that she's in your hands, Lord.*

She plopped onto the couch and closed her eyes. But James hovered behind her eyelids, and the feel of his kisses floated over her lips.

The doorbell rang again, and her eyes sprang open. Had she fallen asleep? She glanced at the clock. No, she'd only sat down three minutes ago.

Limbs heavy, she pushed herself up from the couch. Was it really only 7:30? She could happily go to bed right now.

But her whole body sprang awake as she opened the door. "James."

"Bethany, I'm sorry. I should have been there. I was at the marina and I saw Pete and Chris and I realized I was being stupid and I do want a second chance and—" He cut off. "Am I making any sense?"

She laughed. "Not one bit. But that's okay. Do you want—"

"I want—" He stepped forward, his hands coming to her face. He leaned closer and she closed her eyes, letting herself anticipate the moment his lips would contact hers. Something soft brushed past her leg, and before she could register what it was, James had let go of her and dashed into the yard.

"Mrs. Whiskers," he shouted as the cat bolted for the street.

"Oh no." Bethany pressed her hands to her cheeks.

At the last second, the cat veered right, toward the tree. But James was in her path and managed to scoop her up. The cat fought for a second but then settled into James's arms.

"Well." James reached the door. "That didn't go quite like I expected."

"It seems like kids and cats have a way of changing our plans."

James tilted his head, cat still in his arms, a soft smile on his lips.

A flutter went through Bethany.

"They're not the only ones." James stepped closer and brought his lips to hers. Even with the cat between them, the kiss was everything Bethany had ever longed for. It went beyond the physical sensations, as if she could feel his heart and soul right through his lips.

When James pulled back, he was smiling a full-out, glorious smile. "Sorry. I just had to do that. Now maybe I can slow down and make some sense. If you don't mind if I come in?"

Bethany stepped back from the door, her mind too full of that kiss to find any words.

She swung the door shut behind him, but at the last second before it closed, James called, "Wait."

"Huh?" She turned to look at him over her shoulder, but he was already reaching past her to yank the door open wide.

Bethany followed his gaze to the girl on the bike. "That's April," she told James.

It took her a moment to realize that the girl was alone. "Where's Ruby?"

"There was a car," April gasped, swinging her leg off her bike. "Ruby's hurt."

Chapter 48

James burst out the door. "Where?" The word barked out of him.

The girl on the bike pointed. "Around the corner. She's—"

But he didn't have time to listen to the rest of her sentence. He turned around long enough to shove the cat at Bethany, then took off down the street. His hard footfalls drummed in his head, marking the rhythm of his prayers. *Not her, Lord. Not her.*

Sadie's image floated in front of him, merging with Ruby's.

Not her, Lord.

Why were his limbs encased in concrete? Why couldn't he run faster?

He wasn't going to get there in time. He wasn't going to be able to save her.

Finally, he rounded the corner. His eyes fell on a small form halfway down the block, sitting along the curb.

Sitting. Moving.

That meant . . .

Thank you, Lord. Thank you. His knees turned to melted butter but still he ran.

"Ruby," he called.

She looked up, tipping her head back so she could see him past her helmet. Tears shone on her cheeks, but she smiled as she spotted him. "I knew you'd come," she called.

He commanded his legs to slow as he drew closer, then crouched at her side, his momentum nearly toppling him into her. "What happened? What hurts?" He inspected her for abrasions. She had a pretty good scrape on her knee, but other than that, she looked okay.

"My arm." Ruby sniffled as tears speckled her cheeks again. "Where's my mom?"

"She's coming. She had to put Mrs. Whiskers inside." He should have taken care of the cat. Let Bethany run for Ruby. But he hadn't been able to wait. Not when he'd thought she might be . . .

James couldn't breathe normally, the adrenaline from the run, from finding her okay, still pumping through him. He took Ruby's arm, grimacing at the purple swelling already marring her wrist. "Looks like you might have broken it. Your friend said there was a car?" James scanned the street. If this was a hit and run . . .

"On the other side of the road. I got nervous and crashed into the curb and fell off. Is my bike okay?"

James unclasped her helmet and pulled it off. "I'll check in a minute. Did you hit your head?"

"I don't think so. My arm really hurts." Her tears fell faster, and James pulled her in for a hug, smoothing her hair. "I know, sweetie. It's going to be all right." The sound of footsteps drew his attention.

"She's okay," he called to Bethany, who kept running until she reached them and dropped to the ground, throwing her arms around them both. She didn't say a word, just held them until James eased back and let her hug her daughter.

He went to inspect the bike. The front wheel appeared a little off kilter, but it was nothing that couldn't be replaced.

Unlike Ruby.

A wave of nausea rolled over him, and he bent over, bracing his hands on his knees. What would he have done if . . .

"James?" Bethany called. "Do you think you could help me get her home?"

"Yeah. Of course." He straightened and drew in a painful breath. He moved toward them and scooped Ruby carefully into his arms.

Bethany righted the bike and walked it next to them.

When they reached the house, James waited for Bethany to grab her car keys, then tucked Ruby into the back seat for the ride to the emergency room.

"Call me and let me know how she is, okay?" he said over the seat to Bethany as he helped Ruby fasten her seatbelt.

"But you're coming along, aren't you?" Ruby asked.

James swallowed, his eyes going from Ruby to Bethany. Both wore the same hopeful, needful expression.

He let out a breath. "Of course I'm coming."

*

Bethany couldn't stop looking from Ruby—seated next to her in the doctor's exam room—to James, seated on the far side of the room.

Never had she been as scared as she had when April had said Ruby was hurt. Scared and frozen.

By the time her mind had caught up with what was happening, James had already been almost to the end of the block. He'd run toward Ruby as if . . . as if she were his own daughter.

There was a knock on the exam room door, and a second later, it squeaked open.

"I'm Dr. Kramer." A youngish looking woman stepped through the door. "Which one of you is Ruby?" She stopped in front of James. "I understand you hurt your arm."

"*I'm* Ruby." Ruby giggled, and Bethany smiled, but James's face didn't move. He hadn't cracked the hint of a smile since he'd carried Ruby home, and he'd barely said a word since then either. It was like Bethany could physically feel him transforming back into James the Gray. Her heart longed to hold him and tell him it was okay—Ruby was okay—because of him.

"That makes more sense," the doctor was saying to Ruby. "Just between you and me, he doesn't look much like a Ruby."

Ruby giggled again but then winced. "It really hurts."

Across the room, James's face tightened.

"I know, honey." The doctor moved closer to examine the wrist, and Bethany gripped her daughter's other hand. "Did you hurt your head at all?"

"Nope." Ruby sounded proud. "I was wearing a helmet."

"Good job." The doctor smiled at Ruby, then made some notes on her computer. "And good job teaching her to wear one, Mom and Dad."

Bethany's head jerked up in time to see James's jaw jump.

"Oh, we're— I mean, I'm—" The words twisted themselves into knots in her head.

"They're the best," Ruby cut in.

Bethany huffed out a breath. Her daughter knew very well that wasn't what she'd been trying to say.

The doctor turned from the computer. "I have a hunch we're looking at a broken bone, but we won't know for sure until we take some X-rays. Do you want Mom and Dad to come with you or wait here? It's just down the hall."

"I'll come." Bethany stood, but Ruby shook her head.

"I can do it myself."

"But—" For one thing, Ruby was Bethany's baby. And for another, Bethany wasn't sure she wanted to be left alone with James right now.

"Really, Mom," Ruby insisted. "I'll be fine."

"Don't worry." Dr. Kramer smiled. "I'll have her back to you in a jiffy."

"Okay," Bethany said feebly, retaking her seat.

The door closed behind Ruby and the doctor. Bethany glanced across the room to James, who seemed to be concentrating on the floor.

She sat silently, trying to organize her words before she spoke them out loud. But every time she thought she had them in order, she lost them. So she simply said, "Thank you."

James met her eyes, the torture in his own evident. "For what?" His voice was hoarse.

"For being there." Emotion thickened her voice and brought tears to her eyes. "I know it had to be . . . hard." So much more than hard, but it was the only word she could think of.

He nodded once, his teeth clenched as if he was determined not to say anything else.

She let him sit in silence for what felt like forever, but finally she couldn't take it anymore. "I think you were going to say something? At the house. Before . . ." She waved a hand around, as if that could take them all back in time. She tried to remember what he'd been talking about, but all she could remember was that it involved a kiss. A wonderful, amazing, heart-stirring kiss.

James shook his head without looking up. "I don't remember."

"Oh." She played with a broken fingernail.

Fortunately, Ruby and the doctor burst back into the room a few minutes later. And then the doctor was showing them the X-ray results—it was broken—and setting Ruby's arm and giving Bethany care instructions.

And then they were on their way home. Ruby made a few half-hearted attempts at conversation, but Bethany could tell she was exhausted and in pain and finally told her to just rest.

James didn't say a word the entire ride, and when Bethany turned the car off, he just sat, even after Bethany and Ruby had gotten out. Bethany was debating whether she should go around and open his door when he climbed out slowly, moving straight for his own truck.

"See you tomorrow, James," Ruby called, and he startled as if he'd forgotten they were there.

"Tomorrow?"

"The field day." Ruby grinned. "You're still going to be my partner in the three-legged race, right?"

James swiveled his head, as if judging how long it would take to make a getaway in his truck. "I'm not sure—"

"Ruby, you know the doctor said you have to be careful so you don't hurt your arm," Bethany jumped in.

"It's a three-*legged* race, Mom, not a three-armed race. And James will keep me safe, right James?"

"Uh. Safe." James gripped the door of his truck.

"See, Mom." Ruby sounded victorious, but Bethany saw the look on James's face as he climbed into his vehicle.

"We'll see," she mumbled, gently turning Ruby toward the house.

Chapter 49

James did one final scan of the room he'd lived in for the past two months. He'd gotten everything . . . except the blue plastic Easter egg from Ruby. He'd left it on purpose, intending to make a clean break from this place and all it held—all he'd almost lost. But something made him go back and grab it now. He stuffed it into a pouch in his duffel bag, then swept the bag over his shoulder and pounded down the stairs.

Emma, Mom, and William stood in a line across the kitchen—a human barricade of sorts. James grimaced. He'd told them an hour ago that he planned to leave, and though they'd tried to talk him out of it, he'd thought they understood.

Apparently not.

They advanced toward him as one, and he tensed. Couldn't they make this easier on him?

"I'm sorry." His voice cracked. "I know you don't—"

But then Mom was hugging him on one side and Emma on the other, and William was patting his shoulder. He let out a ragged breath and dropped a kiss on Mom's head, then Emma's. When they pulled back, he held out a hand to shake William's.

"You'll be all right?" He looked to Emma. He hated to leave when she was just starting her chemo, but he didn't see any other way. And Mom was going to stay until Emma's treatments were done. Plus he knew now that Emma's friends would be at her side even when he couldn't be.

"I'll be fine." Emma nudged him. "And I'll be here. You know you're welcome anytime."

James nodded, though he knew it would be a long time before his heart would be able to handle coming back. "Tell them I'm sorry," he whispered, then rushed out the door.

At the end of the driveway, he hesitated. It wasn't too late to change his mind. He could turn right, head into Hope Springs, and go to the field day with Bethany and Ruby, and then . . .

And then what?

Going would only make it harder to say goodbye.

So don't say it. Stay.

A car whizzed past the driveway, headed toward town. James gripped the wheel, easing his foot off the brake.

Everything you love is here.

The *l-word* hit him, sharper than a bullet. He punched at his chest, as if that could dislodge the feeling. Then he wrenched the wheel in the opposite direction, pressing his foot to the accelerator as he aimed his truck away from town.

Chapter 50

Bethany scanned the living room, wrinkling her nose in concentration.

She'd come in here for a reason—but what was it?

Her eyes fell on the trophy she and Ruby had won in the three-legged race at the field day, and she moved toward it, picking it up with a sigh. Ruby had been so crushed when James hadn't shown up—and so had Bethany, though she'd half-expected it.

He'd called the next day to explain, to apologize, and as much as she'd wanted to ask him to come back, not to give up, she couldn't. She'd seen the fear in his eyes when Ruby had gotten hurt—and she couldn't ask him to go through that again. That was why every time her fingers were tempted to tap on his name on her phone, she put it away.

With another sigh, she set the trophy down. It wouldn't do any good to dwell on what could have been—the family they could have become.

Keep busy. The words had served as her mantra over the past three weeks. She'd worked for Cam and Kayla. She'd helped out at the stables. She'd taken Ruby for ice cream. But all of it reminded her of James until it felt like she had started to get her short-term memory back—but all the memories were of him.

What she and Ruby needed to do was make some new memories. And she'd take plenty of pictures to make sure she didn't forget them.

"Ruby," she called, rushing down the hall toward her daughter's room. "Let's go to the beach."

Ruby looked up from her desk. "No thanks."

"Ruby." Bethany tried not to sound impatient. "I know you miss James, but we can't just sit here being sad. We need to do something fun, just the two of us."

"Okay. Then I know what I want to do."

Bethany smiled. She'd expected a harder fight. "And what's that?"

"I want to go see James."

"Oh." The syllable was barely a breath. How was she supposed to tell her daughter no? But there was no way she could say yes. "Ruby, sweetie, I don't think James wants to see us."

But Ruby shook her head, a stubborn glint in her eyes. "That doesn't mean he doesn't need us, Mom. Plus, we never got to tell him that we love him."

"What?" Bethany's eyes snapped to her daughter. "Who said—"

Ruby rolled her eyes. "It's obvious, Mom. Don't worry, I love him too. He's like . . . the dad I always wanted."

Oh no. How was Bethany supposed to hold it together, when her heart was being pulled in so many directions at once?

Protect Ruby. That was what she had to do. Protect Ruby.

No matter if her own heart was screaming that Ruby was right and she did love James.

"Ruby, I don't think James wants a family," she said gently. "Losing his daughter was very hard for him. He's too afraid of what would happen if he lost someone else."

"But Miss Emma says when you fall off the horse, you have to get back up and try again. Otherwise, you'll be afraid for the rest of your life, and no one can live like that."

Bethany blew out a frustrated breath. How did you tell a ten-year-old that life wasn't that easy?

"We have to at least ask him to come back," Ruby added before Bethany could respond. "I know he might say no." Ruby bounced past Bethany and out her bedroom door. "But maybe he'll say yes."

Bethany chewed her lip. She had to be the responsible one here. She had to keep Ruby from getting hurt. She had to . . .

What if Ruby was right?

"All right." Her heart took control of her tongue. "But before we go, I need two things from you."

Ruby nodded.

"First, you have to promise not to get your hopes up."

Ruby nodded again.

"And second, please use the bathroom before we go."

Ruby threw her arms around Bethany. "It's going to be good, Mom, you'll see."

"What'd I say about getting your hopes up?" But Bethany couldn't keep her own hopes from soaring right out the door, leading the way to James.

Chapter 51

James's feet dragged across the grass of the cemetery, the flowers in his hand weighing him down almost as much as his heart. Clouds had begun to roll in a few hours ago, building to an ominous gray mass that seemed to press him harder to the earth with every step.

He hadn't been to Sadie's grave since the funeral. But today was the six-year anniversary of her death, and as much as he'd told himself not to come, he'd felt something pulling him to it. He'd worked all day to ignore it, to push it to the background as he'd always done before. But it was too insistent, and he'd stopped to pick up the flowers, shooting the poor florist a death glare when she had asked the occasion for the bouquet.

He reached the row Sadie's grave was down, and his feet drew to a stop. He stared toward the end of the row, to the third headstone from the edge. The flowers fell from his hand.

He couldn't do this. He couldn't go down there and think about the fact that his little girl was buried under it. A sharp sob threatened to work its way up, but James stuffed it down, the force of the grief folding him in half.

He didn't know how long he stood there, hands braced on his knees, fighting against the waves and waves of memories that surfaced, mingled memories of Sadie and Melissa, of Ruby and Bethany, of laughing and crying, before a hand on his shoulder made him ratchet upright.

"James?" The woman's voice was tentative but familiar, and a fresh rush of pain washed over him.

"Melissa." He should have realized his ex-wife would be here today. His gaze snagged on Melissa's stomach. It bulged the same way it had when . . . "You're expecting?" Gravel filled his words.

She nodded, glancing over her shoulder toward a man who hovered a few rows away. Her new husband, James presumed. Or maybe not so new. They must have been married for two years now, he realized with a start. It still seemed wrong that time kept moving without Sadie.

"Emma didn't tell you?" she asked.

He shook his head dumbly.

"I called her a few weeks ago, but . . ." Melissa looked over her shoulder again, then back at him. "She said you met someone. She has a daughter?"

James sighed, running his hand over his head. He'd been trying so hard not to think about Bethany and Ruby. About the way he'd left them. About how much he missed them. About how badly he wanted to go back. "How do you do it?"

"Do what?" Melissa tipped her head to the side, the way she always had when she wanted to understand someone better. How had he never appreciated that about her?

He searched for words. What was it, exactly, that he didn't know how to do? "Keep going, I guess," he said. "Build a new family? Aren't you terrified something could happen to them too? I couldn't handle it if—" His voice cracked, and he stopped before he broke down.

Melissa smiled gently, rubbing a hand over her belly. "If I knew today that I was only going to get five years with this baby—or one year, or one month, or one day—I'd still want to have that time. I'd cherish it. Isn't that how you feel about . . ." She tilted her head, and he realized she was waiting for him to fill in a name.

"Bethany," he said reluctantly. "And her daughter Ruby." Saying their names made his heart heavy and light all at once. He sighed. He wouldn't have willingly given up a day with Sadie, even if he'd known how short her time would be.

But . . . "I can't just replace her, Melissa. I miss her so much." He pinched the bridge of his nose and blinked up toward the clouds.

"You're not replacing her." Melissa shuffled closer to him. "You'll see her again one day in heaven. But until then, while you're still here, you have to live. Loving Bethany and Ruby doesn't mean you love Sadie any less."

"It's my fault she's gone, Mel. You said it yourself. I don't deserve to love again. Or to be a father again."

A beat of silence followed the awful truth—and then a pair of arms wrapped tightly around him.

He stiffened. It had been a very long time since his ex-wife had hugged him.

"It's not your fault, James." Melissa's voice was thick. "I should have told you that a long time ago. I'm sorry I ever blamed you."

All the resolve, all the determination not to fall apart, seeped out of James, and a sob burst out of his chest, its echo ricocheting off the headstones around them. He gulped, trying to hold back the rest of his grief, but it was useless.

Melissa's arms tightened around him. "You were helping people, James. That's who you are. That doesn't make it your fault. You couldn't have known. You couldn't have done anything differently. You were there with her at the end, and I'm so glad you were." She kept whispering, kept holding him, until his grief was spent.

When he finally pulled away, he swiped at his face and cleared his throat. "I'm sorry. I didn't mean to fall apart like that."

Melissa wiped at his cheek. "I wish you would have fallen apart back when it happened."

Shaking his head, James worked to pull himself together. "I was being strong for you."

Melissa's head shake was adamant. "Maybe that's what you told yourself. But you were doing it for *you*. So you wouldn't have to feel it. And now you're running away from your feelings again."

"I—" James started to argue. But then he let Melissa's words sink in. She was right. He'd directed every ounce of his energy for the past six years to not feeling. To not letting anything hurt him. Until he'd met Bethany and Ruby, and the feeling had started to come back. "I'm sorry," he said instead.

"I know." Melissa bent to pick up his flowers, then wrapped her hand around his elbow. "Come on. Let's go put these on her grave. And then I think you have a call to make."

James sniffed and swallowed. Maybe. He was going to have to take this one step at a time.

Chapter 52

Bethany pulled her phone away from her ear and hung up. Again.

They shouldn't have come. It was her job to protect Ruby, and sitting on the porch of James's house for two hours wasn't the way to do it. She should have insisted they go to the beach instead of letting Ruby talk her into coming here. Stupid impulse control.

Except she knew she couldn't blame her impulse control issues this time. She'd thought it through. And she'd made a deliberate decision to come. She'd wanted so badly to believe that Ruby was right, that James just needed to see them, to hear that they loved him, and then everything would be perfect again.

But given the fact that she'd called him a dozen times since they'd gotten here and he hadn't once picked up, she had to admit that wasn't going to happen.

She turned her phone on again and searched for something nearby that she and Ruby could do. Maybe they could salvage the day before they headed home.

"You want to go to the zoo?"

Ruby shook her head, looking sullen.

"How about this? They have a botanical garden inside domes." She angled her phone so Ruby could see the pictures.

But Ruby barely looked at it.

"Oh, Rubes. I'm sorry. I shouldn't have brought you here."

Ruby's lip trembled, and a tear slid down her cheek. "I'm sorry."

"Oh, sweetie." Bethany wrapped her arms around her daughter. "You don't have anything to be sorry for. I shouldn't have let you think that James could maybe one day be your . . ."

Ruby sniffled and pulled away. "No. That's not it. Do you remember when my school had bring your mom to school day and you didn't come?"

Bethany tightened her arms around her daughter, closing her eyes. How was it that she didn't even remember letting her daughter down yet again?

"I'm sorry, I—"

But Ruby shook her head. "You couldn't have come because I didn't tell you about it on purpose. I didn't want you to come."

"Oh." Bethany kept her grip on her daughter as tears filled her own eyes. She couldn't blame Ruby. But that didn't make it hurt any less.

"I was worried," Ruby said. "Because you always forget things and what if you forgot something and then the kids made fun of you and—"

"Oh, Ruby." Bethany closed her eyes against the ache. She so wanted to be a normal mother for her daughter. To give her a normal life and a normal family. "It's not your job to protect me. It's my job to protect you."

Ruby sniffled. "You do, Mom. And next time I want you to come."

"All right then." Bethany wiped the tears off her daughter's cheeks. "Next time I'll be there. But you might have to do me a favor."

Ruby waited.

"Remind me." Bethany tapped her daughter's nose, and they both giggled.

"Look!" Ruby jumped to her feet and pointed to the street, where a pickup made its way slowly toward the house. "That's James's truck!"

Bethany stood too, grasping at the porch railing as a wave of dizziness she was pretty sure had nothing to do with vertigo almost knocked her off her feet. Her heart thundered so hard that she couldn't hear what Ruby said next, and her mouth dried, gluing her tongue to the back of her teeth. All the things she'd been thinking she'd say when she saw him leaked from her brain, leaving her with only one thought: she loved this man.

He eased the pickup into the driveway, his eyes not coming to them until he'd turned the truck off, and then Bethany saw the surprise on his face. Surprise and— Was that dismay?

Bethany's heart thudded harder as Ruby bolted toward the truck. She wanted to call out to stop her daughter, to keep her from getting hurt if James didn't want to see them.

But her words were trapped under a layer of hope. And Ruby was already to the truck, already throwing her arms around James.

James's arms immediately went around Ruby, but his eyes came to Bethany. They were red-rimmed and his face was drawn.

"I'm sorry." Bethany managed to find her voice as she stepped off the porch. She had to get over there and pull Ruby away from him. He clearly didn't want this. "Ruby, come here."

But James shook his head and lifted one arm from Ruby's back, holding it out to Bethany. She looked to it, then to his face, and he nodded, gesturing her forward.

With a sharp gasp, she let her feet rush for him and threw herself into his arms behind her daughter.

James didn't say a word, just wrapped his arm around her and inhaled, holding them both close.

Ruby was the first to wriggle away. Unwilling to lose the contact with James, Bethany snuggled into her daughter's spot.

"Where were you?" Ruby asked. "We were waiting *forever*."

"I'm sorry." James's voice sounded raw. "I went to the cemetery and then I just . . . drove around."

Bethany pulled back a fraction to study his face. "Are you okay?"

He nodded, but his body shook. "It's been six years. Today."

"Oh, James. I'm sorry. I didn't know. We shouldn't have come." But she held him as tightly as she could, rubbing her hand up and down his back.

He squeezed her so hard that her ribs hurt, but she didn't complain. After a few minutes, he loosened his grip but didn't pull away. "I'm glad you came."

"Me too," Ruby piped up. "When you guys are done hugging, Mom and I have to tell you something."

James's chuckle was quiet but so good to hear. He kept one arm wrapped around Bethany but turned to look at Ruby.

"Well," Ruby said boldly, and Bethany smiled, overwhelmed by how fortunate she was to parent this little creature. "We came here because—" Ruby broke off. "Um. Because we—"

She gave Bethany a helpless look.

And for once, Bethany didn't have to search for words. They were right there. "We came here to tell you we love you," she said to James.

"Yeah," Ruby jumped in. "And we know you're scared. And we know you might not come back to Hope Springs. But we thought you should know. And also we hope you do. Come back."

Bethany laughed at her daughter's boisterous return to speaking but grew serious as James cleared his throat.

"You came here to tell me that?" He looked from Ruby to Bethany and then back to Ruby, who nodded vigorously.

James tipped his head back, blinking up at the sky, and Bethany's heart nearly gave out. He was going to say it didn't matter. That he couldn't come back with them. And she was going to have to pick up the pieces for her daughter. And for herself.

Finally, James brought his eyes to hers. "I'm glad you came." He turned to Ruby. "Because I love you too." And then his eyes were on Bethany's, and he was pulling her tight to him. "Ruby," he called. "Close your eyes a second." He brought his face toward Bethany's. "I love you," he whispered, before his lips closed over hers.

"I'm not closing my eyes," Ruby called. They both laughed but didn't pull apart, until Ruby was there too, throwing her arms around them both.

Chapter 53

"Mom says she'll be ready in a second." Ruby bent to scoop up Mrs. Whiskers as the cat tried to make an escape out the door. "Want to see the bracelets I made with the kit you gave me for Christmas? They're so cool."

"Absolutely." James danced from foot to foot. "But first come outside for a second."

Ruby eyed him doubtfully, readjusting her hold on the cat, who was struggling to jump out of her arms. "It's cold out."

"I know." James's breath floated in front of his face. Though they'd only had a dusting of snow so far this winter—just in time for Christmas—the days had grown frigid as the New Year approached. "Just for a second. I have to ask you something." He was going to burst if he didn't ask her right now. But he couldn't risk Bethany overhearing.

"What?" Ruby seemed totally oblivious to the fact that he was trying to be sneaky.

"It's a secret."

Bingo.

Ruby's eyes lit up and she tossed the cat to the ground behind her, stepping out the door in her socks. "What secret?"

James reached behind her to pull the door closed. "Here." He took off his jacket and wrapped it around her, pulling the hood over her head. Ruby giggled as her whole face disappeared.

That was no good. James needed to see her reaction to his question. He slid the hood back enough that he could see her face. The sun was just setting, but there was still enough light that he could read her expression.

"What's the secret?" Ruby whispered, leaning toward him and looking around furtively, as if they were spies.

"I—" James swallowed. Was he really ready to do this? But he knew he was. His certainty had grown day by day for the past six months.

Ruby tilted her head at him. "Did you forget?"

James laughed. "No. I have to ask you something."

Ruby watched him expectantly.

"Remember when you said I'd make a good dad?" James rubbed his hands together against the cold. He hadn't expected a second chance to be a father.

Ruby nodded.

"Now that you know me better, do you still think that?" He held his breath as Ruby stared at him.

"No," she said slowly, and his heart flopped. "You wouldn't make a good dad. You would make the best dad." She giggled as if she'd told a great joke.

He let out a rough breath.

Ruby tilted her head at him. "Why?" Her eyes widened. "Wait. Do you mean . . ."

"I want to ask your mom to marry me. But that would mean—"

"You would be my dad!" Ruby threw her arms, clad in the puffy sleeves of his jacket, around him. "Are you going to ask her tonight? On New Year's Eve? That's so romantic."

James mock frowned. "If I'm going to be your dad, I don't want to hear any more from you about romance. You're too young." But he couldn't keep the huge smile from overtaking the frown.

"Do you have a ring?" she asked.

James pointed to the jacket she wore. "In the pocket."

"Can I see it?"

He glanced at the door. No sign of Bethany. "Sure."

Ruby reached her hand into the jacket pocket, withdrawing a velvety ring box. She eased it open to reveal the simple marquise cut diamond.

"Wow!" Ruby gaped at it. "It's so pretty. You have good taste for a guy."

James laughed. "Thanks. I think. Now put it away before your mom—"

The door opened behind them, and Ruby snapped the box closed and slid her hand into the pocket with a conspiratorial giggle.

"What are you two doing out here?"

"Nothing, Mom." Ruby squeaked past her and back into the house.

"Hmm." Bethany gave him a questioning look, and James pulled her in for a kiss.

"Happy New Year's Eve." He ran a hand down the sleeve of her soft blue sweater, incredibly grateful once again that he'd come back. That he hadn't let his fear keep him from experiencing this joy. "You look beautiful. As always."

"Thank you." Bethany dropped her eyes for a moment, then looked up at him with a smile. "So where are we going?"

"You'll see. Grab your coat. And a hat. And gloves."

Behind them, Ruby giggled, and Bethany glanced over her shoulder at her as she pulled on a thick white jacket. "What's going on with you?"

Ruby peered past her mom toward James, and he winked and held a finger to his lips.

"Nothing." Ruby giggled again. "I'm just excited to play with baby Evelyn. Plus Uncle Cam said I can stay up until ten." She passed Bethany her purse and nudged her toward the door.

"Ruby?" James looked at the jacket she was still wearing. "I think you're going to need to change into your own coat."

Ruby clapped a hand over her mouth. "Oh yeah. I almost forgot about the—"

James shot her a warning look, and she clapped a second hand over her mouth.

He rolled his eyes.

If he wasn't careful, Ruby was going to ask Bethany before he had a chance. Ruby wriggled out of the coat and passed it to him.

"You two are up to something." Bethany gave them each a mock suspicious look.

"I'm sure we don't know what you're talking about." James held the door open for Bethany, reaching behind to give her daughter—maybe soon his daughter—a fist bump.

Chapter 54

You have to tell him. The thought pounded against Bethany's brain again and again. First, she'd told herself that she'd wait until after they'd dropped Ruby off at Cam and Kayla's. But they'd dropped Ruby off twenty minutes ago, and still she hadn't found the courage. James hadn't said much either, but he'd probably had a long day at work.

Work. That was what they could talk about.

"How was work today?"

"There was a break-in at Mrs. Marzetti's."

Bethany gasped. "Is she all right?"

"Yep. Caught the burglar with his hand in the cookie jar. Literally."

"Someone broke in to steal her cookies?"

"A raccoon. I had to call the DNR. Took us an hour, but we got the little guy. I thought about giving him to Ruby as a pet but . . ."

"Don't you dare." But Bethany laughed with him.

This was so good. So right.

But she had to tell him—

"I think I've convinced Pete to be a mentor for the new fishing program too." He glanced toward her. "The one we're starting for at-risk kids."

"I remember." But she smiled. She appreciated his thoughtful way of reminding her of things she may have forgotten without making her feel foolish.

"I'm still working on Chris, but he's harder to get through to. Got into a fight at school last week."

Bethany nodded. She knew too well how hard it was to leave a lifestyle you'd grown accustomed to. But she trusted that James would get through to the kid eventually.

Silence fell for a moment, and Bethany knew she couldn't put it off any longer.

"We're here." He slowed the truck and turned into a driveway, smiling at her with such a look of anticipation that she swallowed her comment and directed her eyes out the window.

James eased the vehicle past an old farmhouse and parked in front of a large red barn with Christmas lights twinkling along its roofline.

"Is this the same place you took Ruby and me to?" It looked similar but not quite right—unless that was her memory playing tricks on her.

"Nope." James grinned at her. "Austin and Leah told me about this place. They have sleigh rides, and I thought since you can't ride a horse, it would be the next best—" He faltered. "You don't like it?"

"It's not that. It's—" No. She couldn't do this to him now. "It's just that there's not much snow."

James smiled mysteriously. "Don't worry about that." He opened his door, pulling a stocking cap over his ears as his breath curled around his face.

Bethany exhaled slowly as she watched him round the truck to open her door. She had to tell him. It wasn't fair not to. But what if it was too much for him? What if he ran again and didn't come back this time?

He reached her door and pulled it open, taking her hand to help her out. The moment her feet touched the ground, he pulled her to him in a crushing hug. "I love you," he murmured into her hat. "Do you know that?"

She bobbed her head against his jacket, tears pricking at her eyes. She did know that. And it only made this so much harder. James kissed her forehead and wrapped his hand around her mittened one. "Come on." He tugged her toward the barn.

As they stepped inside, Bethany gasped. It was a winter wonderland. A path of Christmas trees and fake snow and lights wound through the building, ending at large doors on the far side.

James opened them, and Bethany could only stare.

"It's . . ." She took a careful step outside and bent to touch the fluffy white powder that extended in a wide ribbon from the door into the woods in front of them. Sure enough, it was cold and powdery and melted in her hands. She looked at the ground on either side of the trail, where brown grass showed through the sparse dusting of snow they'd gotten before Christmas. "How in the world . . ."

An older woman chuckled as she came up next to them, pointing to a gray pipe that stood in the shadows at the side of the trail. "We make it. Because everyone needs a little Christmas magic." The sound of jingle bells floated on the wind, and the woman smiled. "And speaking of magic. Here comes your ride."

Bethany couldn't ignore the wave of excitement that rolled over her as she spotted the beautiful draft horses pulling the sleigh, and she wrapped her arm around James's.

He smiled and kissed the top of her hat. "So this was a good idea?"

"The best." She let herself forget everything else as she climbed into the sleigh and snuggled into the seat next to him. The warmth of his arm around her enveloped her in a cocoon where it felt like nothing could ever hurt her. Nothing from outside. And nothing from inside.

The driver urged the horses forward, and Bethany let herself marvel at the lantern-lined path that stretched in front of them, the stars that twinkled above them, the sleigh bells that jingled around them. If only this moment could last forever. If only she never had to tell him.

James shifted, unwrapping his arm from around her and sliding his hand into his coat pocket. "I have something for you."

"James. You just gave me a Christmas present. You can't give me another—" Her eyes fell on the hand he'd pulled out of his pocket. It held a small velvet jewelry box. She swallowed, telling herself it wasn't what she thought it was. It was probably a necklace. Or maybe a pair of earrings.

With his other hand, James reached for hers and pulled her mitten off.

She swallowed. It wasn't a necklace or earrings in that box.

"James. Wait." She gulped at the cold night air. *Lord, give me strength.* It wasn't fair to let him do this without telling him the truth.

"I— Wait?" Confusion wrinkled the part of his brow that peeked out from under his hat.

"There's something I have to tell you."

James wrapped his hand around hers but didn't put her mitten back on. "What is it?"

"I—" Oh, why did she have to do this?

"Bethany?" A quaver of fear shook his voice, and he slid closer to her. "What is it?"

"I had a doctor appointment yesterday." The steam from her words hung between them, blurring her view of him.

"And?" His grip on her hand tightened.

"And—" Bethany rocked forward as the sleigh drew to a halt, and James threw out his arm to steady her.

"Here we are." The driver hopped down from the sleigh and held out a hand to help Bethany down. "You two are in this gazebo." Bethany's eyes swept over the glass-enclosed gazebos that dotted the woods, soft lighting glowing from inside each, but then went right back to James. He had climbed out of the sleigh and stood a few feet from her. But he may as well have been miles away for the gulf she felt between them. His jaw was tight, his hands fisted at his sides—she wondered briefly where the ring had gone.

"Your server will be by with your food shortly." The driver climbed into the sleigh. "Enjoy your meal. I'll be back for your return ride." The bells jingled cheerfully as the horses trotted off.

Bethany stared after the sleigh, then gazed at the gazebos. Couples were already dining and laughing in a few of them, and one pair was dancing.

"Let's go inside." James's voice was hollow. He gestured her forward but didn't hold her hand.

The rush of warm air that surrounded them as they entered wasn't enough to chase away her chill.

James led her to the table and held out a chair for her, then sat down across from her.

Bethany fiddled with the zipper on her jacket but didn't take it off. As soon as he heard what she had to say, he might want to hop the next sleigh out of here.

"The doctor," he prompted.

She let out a breath. She could tell him everything was fine. That she had a clean bill of health. But he'd find out eventually. "It was a checkup. But she wanted to do a scan, just to make sure there weren't any new aneurysms."

James sucked in a breath so loud it made her jump, but he nodded for her to continue.

"She found something," Bethany whispered. "It's small and not an immediate danger, but she wants to do surgery to clip it. Just to be safe." She choked on her swallow as James's face crumpled. He shoved his chair back, pacing to the other side of the small space, his hand gripping the back of his neck.

When he didn't move, she took a breath, slid her chair back, and stood. "Do you want to leave?"

Chapter 55

James blinked, unseeing, at the blurred forest out the gazebo window.

How could this be happening? Again? Every time he loved someone.

"James?" Bethany's tentative voice cut through the fog of his thoughts, piercing him right to the heart.

He wanted to be with Bethany more than anything.

For however long they might have together.

The realization hit him so hard that he staggered backward, then spun and strode to her, sweeping her hands in his as he dropped to one knee.

"James." Bethany's eyes widened as she shook her head. "You don't have to—"

But he gently pulled her down so that she was sitting in the chair in front of him. "I want to." He nearly choked on his emotion but he wasn't going to let that stop him. "I want to marry you, Bethany. For better or worse. For richer or poorer. In sickness and health. I want to be with you through all of it."

"But what if . . ." She looked away.

James dropped his head to her knees, unable to breathe. What if . . .

He straightened and reached a hand up to her cheek. "I've spent the past six years regretting all the days I didn't have, when I should have been thanking God for the ones I did. I won't make that mistake again."

Bethany bit her lip, and he could see the uncertainty in her eyes.

"Do you remember the day we met?" he asked.

Bethany shook her head, her eyes falling.

"That's okay. I'll remember it for both of us. I had just gotten to Hope Springs, and I was feeling bitter and resentful and angry. And you were in line, looking all beautiful and flustered at the same time because you forgot your purse and you were trying to buy Ruby a birthday present."

Bethany winced, and he slid his hand into hers. "I know you hate when things like that happen. But look how God used it. You told me once that God puts people in our lives for a reason. I didn't understand that then. But I do now. He put you in my life for a reason. You showed me that it was possible to love again. And that he hadn't abandoned me. I love you, Bethany. And Ruby."

Bethany gasped. "Ruby! She—"

"Sends her blessing." James chuckled. "I asked her when I came to pick you up. That's what we were doing outside."

Bethany laughed, the sound filling James with hope.

He swallowed and gripped both of her hands tightly in one of his as he pulled the ring box back out of his pocket. "Bethany, I don't know how many days we have in this world. Only God knows when he'll call us home. But until then—" He had to stop to clear his throat. "Until then, I want to spend every day at your side. As your husband." He let go of her hands to open the ring box. "Will you marry me?"

Bethany looked from the ring to his eyes, biting her lip and giving him a thoughtful look. James's heart sank. "What is it? What are you unsure about?"

"Nothing." Her lips slid slowly into a smile. "I just wanted to make sure that I had my impulses under control before I answered."

"Okay." He nodded slowly. "I can wait."

"I think that's long enough." Her smile grew into a full-out laugh. "Yes, James. I will marry you." She bent and lowered her face to his, her lips catching his on a breath as his arms went around her.

"Oh wait." She drew back suddenly.

"What? What's wrong?" He grabbed her hands, but she pulled one away and reached into her jacket pocket for her phone.

"Nothing." She grinned. "I just don't want to forget this moment." She snapped a picture of him still on one knee.

He slid the ring onto her finger. "Trust me, I won't let you forget."

Epilogue

"It's snowing!" Ruby's gleeful cry rang through the house.

Bethany shot upright in bed, reaching for her notebook. She already knew what was written on today's date, but she wanted to verify it anyway.

There was only one item on her list: "Get married!"

With a silly laugh at herself, she sprang out of bed, then immediately clutched the dresser so she wouldn't tip over. Passing out wasn't the way she wanted to start her wedding day. She felt for the stitches on the back of her head where they'd cut a small incision for the successful surgery to clip her aneurysm last week. Fortunately, Kayla had offered to let Bethany borrow the veil from her wedding, so it would be hidden. And she was going to wear Leah's dress. And Grace's shoes.

Warmth went through Bethany as she thought of the friends who had surrounded her since she'd moved to Hope Springs. Who had made it possible for her to plan this wedding in only three weeks when Ruby had insisted that she couldn't wait until summer to be a family and James had heartily agreed. Who would be here with her on this new adventure.

She followed the sound of Ruby's voice to the living room window, gasping at the thick layer of white that covered everything. Windswept flakes whipped past the house, blowing into large drifts that blocked the driveway. It wasn't just snowing. It was a blizzard.

And from the looks of it, the plows hadn't made it through yet. Bethany glanced at the clock. They were supposed to be at the church in two hours.

Hopefully the roads would be cleared by then. They'd planned a small wedding since it was such short notice, but at this rate, they'd be lucky if even she and James made it.

"We may have to sled to church," she muttered to Ruby.

"Really?" Her daughter's eyes widened, as if she was totally up for that.

But Bethany shook her head. "No, silly goose. I'm not going to sled in a wedding dress. Should we—"

She broke off as the lights flickered, the thrum of the furnace suddenly cutting out. With a groan, she reached for the light switch. Nothing.

"Now what, Mom?" Ruby asked, as if Bethany would have an answer.

Bethany ruffled her daughter's hair. "I have no idea. But we'll figure it out together. First things first, let's get some breakfast. How does cold cereal sound?"

Once she had Ruby settled, she picked up her phone to call James. But there was no answer.

She supposed she'd have to get ready as planned and pray the roads cleared by the time she had to leave.

She was just pouring Ruby a second bowl of cereal when the doorbell rang.

She blinked at Ruby. "Who on earth could have made it through that snow?"

As she pulled the front door open, a joyous laugh burst from her. "James." She stepped into his arms, looking over his shoulder at the crew he'd brought with him: his mom and William—who had gotten married a few months ago and moved back to Hope Springs—along with Emma and Cam and Kayla and baby Evelyn.

"Spencer and Tyler are picking up everyone else. They said they'd take trips if they need to." He brushed a kiss on her forehead, then stepped aside so the others could enter the house.

"I don't— What are—" Bethany tried to make sense of what was happening here. Other than the fact that her little house was soon going to be bursting at the seams.

"Did you think I was going to let a snowstorm keep me from marrying you today? Dan called me last night to say the heat was out in the church."

"Last night?" She blinked at him. "Why didn't you call me?"

James took her hand. "I didn't want you to worry. Everything's under control. We have a contingency plan."

"We do?" She didn't remember making one.

"We're getting married here." James grinned at her.

"Here?" Bethany looked around her small house. "But the power just went out."

"Nothing a little firewood and candles can't fix. We'll be nice and cozy." He kissed her lips gently, then gave her a nudge toward the hallway. "And besides, you're here. That's the most important part. Now go get ready. Unless you want to get married in that." He grinned at her flannel pajamas. "Which I'm totally fine with, by the way."

"Give me an hour."

"I'm not sure I can wait that long." He smiled at her, then turned toward the door.

"Wait. Where are you going?"

"To grab my tuxedo out of the truck. Can't get married in this thing." He patted the puffy sleeves of his ski jacket.

"Come on. Let's go get you ready." Emma pointed down the hall, pulling off her stocking cap to reveal the short layer of hair that had grown back since she'd finished her chemo and been declared cancer-free. "You too, Ruby."

"This is going to be the best day ever, Mom." Ruby skipped ahead of them.

Bethany swallowed, too overcome for a moment to answer. "Yes," she finally managed. "I think it will."

As she got ready, Bethany heard the sound of the door opening and more people filling the house with laughter. Her stomach looped in anticipation, and her hand shook so much that Kayla had to help with her makeup.

But an hour later, as promised, she emerged from her bedroom in her wedding dress and veil—she'd decided to forgo the shoes, since she was at home.

"Wait here," Kayla said as she wheeled down the hallway. "I'll tell them you're ready."

"You look pretty, Mom," Ruby whispered as they waited.

"Thank you, sweetheart. So do you."

Ruby beamed at her. "I'm glad you're my mom." She slipped her hand into Bethany's, and there was no way to hold it in anymore. Tears burst from Bethany in a gasp, and she bent to pull her daughter into a hug.

"I'm glad you're my daughter." She sniffled, trying to pull herself together as Kayla returned and gestured for them to come forward.

The voices drifting toward them quieted as she and Ruby followed Kayla toward the living room.

But the moment she reached the end of the hallway, Bethany burst into tears all over again, even as her lips stretched into what might have been the world's biggest smile. She beamed at the room through her blurry vision. Candles glowed on the mantle and the shabby little TV stand she'd picked up at a garage sale years ago, a fire roared in the fireplace, her friends were seated and standing on every available surface, and at the front of them all stood James, blinking and wiping at his own eyes as he waited for her.

This, she thought suddenly. This was the purpose she'd been searching for. The way she could be a woman God used. She'd been so convinced it had to be something big, something that would prove her worth. When really, she could see it in the faces of all the people gathered here. God had created her to be part of this family of believers. To serve him together with them.

From somewhere, strains of Canon in D filled the room, and Bethany's feet moved as if the music were pulling her forward. Ruby's hand was still in hers, and she tugged her daughter with her. She and James had already agreed that they wanted Ruby to be standing next to them as they said their vows.

As they reached James's side, he pulled each of them into a hug, then they all turned to Dan as the music stopped.

"I know this isn't what you had planned for this day," Dan started, and everyone chuckled. "But in a way, I think it's fitting. You both have been through a lot of things you didn't plan for. Hard things and good things. And God has been with you through them all. Even when you didn't realize it."

James reached for Bethany's hand as Dan invited them to recite the vows they'd written.

"Bethany—" James's voice cracked, and he cleared his throat with a rueful smile. "Sorry. I didn't expect— Well, you. I didn't expect you to come into my life. Or you." He turned to smile at Ruby, and Bethany's heart hummed. He was going to be a wonderful father to her daughter. "But I'm so glad you did. You helped show me the way back to faith. And that I could love again. I don't know what this life is going to hold for any of us. But I promise that whatever it holds, we will face it together. Because I will be with you through it all: sickness, health, lost cats, and crazy homework projects, good days and bad days. I want to live it all with you."

Bethany took a shaky breath and wiped her cheeks as James's eyes reflected the sincerity of his words.

"Bethany?" Dan looked to her expectantly.

"What?" She couldn't peel her gaze away from James.

"Your vows?" Dan prompted.

"My . . ." Her mind went completely blank as she turned to him. Had she written vows? She was pretty sure she had. But what had she done with them? "I'm sorry, I . . ."

"Here, Mom," Ruby whispered, passing Bethany a crumpled sheet of paper.

Bethany gave her a quizzical look, but Ruby nodded toward the paper. "Read it," she whispered.

Bethany unfolded the paper, staring down at her daughter's handwriting. *Sometimes my mom forgets things,* it began, and Bethany blinked again at her daughter.

"Out loud," Ruby whispered.

"Ruby—"

But Ruby looked so earnest that she couldn't refuse.

"Sometimes my mom forgets things," she began, licking her too-dry lips. "But there are three things I know she'll never forget. 1) Me." Bethany chuckled along with the rest of the group, reaching to give her daughter a hug before directing her eyes back to the paper. "2) God. And 3) You, James."

Bethany's hand shook as she looked up at James, whose face glowed with a tender smile in the candlelight.

She let the paper fall to her side. She would read the rest later. But right now, she had some words of her own she needed to say. "James." It came out as a whisper, and she tried again. She wanted everyone to hear this. "James, my life has been . . . a mess at times. And I don't even remember all of it. But I do remember that when I was a little girl, I used to dream about the kind of man I would marry. Someone who was patient and loving, who made me laugh, who would do anything for me. As I got older, I realized that kind of man didn't exist." She offered him a wobbly smile. "But then I met you. I might not remember the exact date we met or where or even what happened. But I do remember that it changed my life. And I know that sounds corny and maybe exaggerated, but it's true. Because until then, having someone at my side, someone to go through this crazy life with, to be a family with us, was only a dream. And now—" She smiled from him to Ruby. "Now it's real."

The rest of the service, as they exchanged rings and prayed and Dan said a blessing, passed in a blur, until the next thing Bethany knew, Dan was introducing them as Mr. and Mrs. James Wood and their friends were clapping and Ruby was throwing her arms around both of them.

"I was right. This is the best day ever!" Ruby declared.

Bethany nodded, her head pressed against James's chest.

"Okay, I brought food," Leah called. "I left it out in the car so it would stay cold. Who wants to help me get it?"

As their friends volunteered to help Leah get things set up, James grabbed his ski jacket and wrapped it around Bethany, then tugged her out the back door into the still-falling snow. The wind had calmed, leaving a peaceful hush over the backyard.

"James, what—"

But he pulled her into a kiss that stole her words, stole her thoughts, stole everything but the overwhelming joy that filled her from the inside out.

"Sorry." James pulled back, keeping his arms wrapped around her waist. "I just needed a minute alone with my wife."

Bethany giggled at her new title. "Thank you for this." She snuggled closer to his warmth. "It was perfect." But a slight shadow hovered in the back of her mind. "What if I forget it?"

James shook his head. "You won't. We made a video. You can watch it every day if you want."

"But—"

James silenced her with a kiss. "It doesn't matter if you remember this day. It's only a moment. We have forever ahead of us. I'll help you when you can't remember. You'll help me when I get scared about the future. And we'll figure it all out together. Deal?"

Bethany nodded, bringing her lips to his again. "You've got yourself a deal."

"Good." James's lips played over hers. "We should probably go back inside and get some food."

"I know. But first, there's something I have to do." She dug in the pocket of the jacket he'd wrapped around her, coming out with his phone.

He raised an eyebrow. "Who could you possibly need to call? Everyone we know is here."

She laughed, swiped at the screen, leaned back into him, and held the phone out at arm's length. "Say 'just married.'"

James wrapped an arm around her and pulled her in close as they recited the phrase together. Bethany snapped the picture, then studied their smiling image. "There." She tucked the phone back into the coat pocket. "The first memory of our life together."

"With many more to come." James nuzzled his face into her hair, then led her into the house.

Thanks for reading NOT UNTIL THEN! I hope you loved James and Bethany's story! Up next, it's Emma's turn to finally get her happily ever after in Not Until The End.

And be sure to sign up for my newsletter to get Ethan and Ariana's story, Not Until Christmas, as a free gift.

Visit https://www.valeriembodden.com/gift or use the QR code below to join.

A preview of NOT UNTIL THE END (Hope Springs book 10)

Chapter 1

This was hard—harder than Owen had expected.

He pressed three fingers to his lips, then brushed them across the heart he'd carved into the closet door frame the day he and Katie had moved into this house. He'd done it secretly, before she could tell him not to, and when he'd shown her, she'd swatted at him, just as he'd known she would, and he'd pulled her into his arms, her pregnant belly a warm buffer between them.

He sighed and closed the closet door, wondering if the new owners would even noticed the heart. Maybe they'd cover it with wood filler.

"I hope I'm doing the right thing here," he muttered to the empty room.

A horn sounded from the driveway below, and Owen jumped, then shook his head. Apparently, the kids were getting impatient. Whether this was the right thing or not, there was no turning back now.

He hurried down the stairs, resisting the urge to allow himself one last tour of the house and the countless memories it held.

They would make new memories in their new house. And the memories of Katie—those would be with them wherever they went. Always.

He stepped out the front door and pulled it closed behind him before he could change his mind. With a quick turn of the key, he locked it, then jogged down the front steps. His three youngest had already piled into the crowded minivan he would drive, while the older two girls sat in the car they shared. He'd prefer not to have them drive so far on their own—but with no other adults in the family, he really had no choice.

Besides, he reminded himself with a glance at Catelyn, who looked strikingly like her mother, with her dark hair and emerald eyes, his oldest was an adult. If you considered twenty an adult. Which he supposed he had to.

He made his way to the driver's side of their car, and Catelyn rolled down the window.

"You have your map open, in case we get separated?"

"Sure do." Catelyn gave him a patient smile—the one that said he was being overprotective but she wouldn't call him on it.

"We'll try to make it two hours and then stop for a break, but if you need to stop sooner, have Claire call me, and—"

"I've driven more than two hours at a time, Dad. We'll be fine."

"I know you will." Owen nodded, wishing he could feel the same easy assurance of his children's safety as they seemed to. "But Carter will need a bathroom break by then anyway. Drive carefully."

He looked past Catelyn to Claire. The sixteen-year-old was the polar opposite of Catelyn in appearance, the only one in the family with blonde hair and blue eyes. She sat with her arms crossed, staring out the window toward the house. Of all the kids, she'd been the only one strongly opposed to the idea of moving, and Owen still felt bad dragging her away from her friends for her junior year of high school. But an opportunity like this wasn't likely to come around again anytime soon.

"Make sure you get some rest," he said to Claire, "so you two can switch off when we stop."

Claire didn't indicate she'd heard him—not even a blink—but Catelyn patted his arm. "We'll be good, Dad," she reassured him again.

Owen nodded, grateful that Catelyn had been willing to change her original plan of staying on campus for the summer to instead come home and help them move. He patted the top of her car and forced himself to back away and turn toward the van.

Lexi, their golden retriever, had taken up residence in his seat and sat grinning at him, her tongue lolling to the side. He laughed, grateful for the slight easing of tension in his shoulders.

He pulled the van door open and poked his head in past the dog. "Should we let Lexi drive today?" he asked eleven-year-old Kenzie and nine-year-old Carter, who both sat in the back.

Kenzie gave him a weak smile and a shake of the head, pressing a hand to her stomach. Owen frowned. She hadn't said much about the move, but he could tell she was nervous. Carter didn't look his way at all but had his eyes fixed on something in the sky. His fingers flicked against his thighs, but Owen didn't try to stop him. It was one of his stimming behaviors, and the doctor had assured them after his diagnosis of level 1 autism that he wasn't hurting himself.

Owen swiveled his head to follow the boy's gaze. "Stratus today?" he asked.

Carter sighed and shook his head, not taking his eyes off the wispy clouds above. "Cirrus."

"Oh. Right." Owen nodded. He'd seen clouds from pretty much every angle conceivable, and yet he still couldn't get it through his head which were which.

He gave the dog a shove to dislodge her from his spot and got in, glancing at Cody in the passenger seat. The fourteen-year-old was usually loud and outgoing, but he was watching the house the same way Claire had been—as if working to soak in every last detail. A lump tried to form in Owen's throat, but he cleared it away.

"Hey," he said to Cody. "This is going to be good." He paused, half-expecting one of the kids to fill in Katie's customary response: "It's going to be *really* good." When no one did, he added, "I already talked to the baseball coach in Hope Springs, and he said you can join the team right away when we get there. They have a league that runs all summer."

Cody nodded, and Owen started the van. He supposed that was as much as he was going to get. *Please don't let me be making a big mistake,* he prayed as he backed the vehicle down the driveway, careful to avoid the moving pods they'd spent the past week filling with all of their memories.

When he and Katie had moved into this house, they'd had next to nothing. But twenty years and five kids later, it had taken three of those things to fit all of their furniture and boxes. He'd done the best he could to donate things ahead of the move—but, though he'd never really thought of himself as sentimental, all of this stuff held too many memories to part with.

He pulled onto the road, then waited, watching in his rearview mirror as Catelyn pulled out of the driveway too. Then, with one last glance over his shoulder at the house, he turned and pressed his foot to the gas. "Hope Springs, here we come."

Chapter 2

Glory in his holy name; let the hearts of those who seek the Lord rejoice. Emma reread the words from Psalm 105, then signed the card she'd written out for one of the shut-ins from church she was planning to visit tomorrow.

She knew from experience that it was harder to rejoice some days than others. But if God had taught her anything over the past year, it was that every day was a gift from him.

The sound of tires crunched on the gravel driveway outside, and Emma tucked the card into an envelope and tossed it on top of the plate of cookies she'd made, then rushed out the kitchen door onto the farmhouse's large porch. The gusty early June breeze caught at the short, spiky curls that had finally grown long enough to brush her forehead, and she zipped her sweatshirt, then waved to her brother James, his wife, and their daughter as they pulled up to the house.

The car engine was still running when eleven-year-old Ruby sprang out of the back seat. "Are they here yet?" She lunged toward Emma, tripping over her own feet. The girl must have grown a good six inches in the last few months, and sometimes she ran like a newborn foal still trying to figure out how to use its long limbs. She was nearly to the porch before she got her legs under control and came to a halt. "Did I miss them?"

Emma laughed, jogging down the steps to hug her niece. "You didn't miss anything." She greeted James and Bethany, who were both grinning oddly from one another to her.

"What's going on with you two?" She eyed them. "You're not going to try to talk me out of this again, are you? Because I told you, I've made up my mind." She crossed her arms defiantly.

But even James, who had been the most opposed to her latest plan, insisting that adding one more thing to her to-do list wouldn't be good for her recovery, shook his head. "Look at Ruby."

"Why? Does she have an extra head today?" She made a face at Ruby, who laughed but stood stark still—Emma was pretty sure it was the first time she had ever seen the girl not wiggling. "She's as beautiful as al—" Her eyes fell on Ruby's shirt, and she clapped a hand over her mouth.

James, Bethany, and Ruby all burst into laughter, but it took a moment before Emma could speak.

"Ruby," she finally gasped. "Why does your shirt say *big sister*?"

Ruby bounced up and down, the words bouncing with her. "Mom's pregnant."

Emma's eyes shot to James and Bethany, who were holding hands and grinning like newlyweds. Which, Emma supposed, they still were. "You're having a baby?" She ran and threw her arms around both of them.

"Wait. We are?" Bethany asked as Emma let go, but her laugh gave her away. Apparently this was one thing she remembered in spite of her short-term memory struggles.

Inadvertently, Emma's hand strayed to the spot where her own shirt covered the six-inch reminder on her abdomen that children were not in her future. Of course, her dreams of having a large family had already dissipated well before the radical hysterectomy. At forty-two and single, it hadn't been likely she would ever have children anyway. The hysterectomy just solidified it.

And it was fine. She may not ever have children. But she did have a family. And it was growing.

"I'm so happy for you." Emma gave her brother a quick glance, trying to tell if the news brought lingering sadness over the daughter he had lost years ago, before meeting Bethany and Ruby. But he looked absolutely radiant, and Emma's heart rejoiced for them. After all they'd both been through, she couldn't have imagined a happier ending for them.

"When are you due?" she asked, turning to lead them toward the chicken coop.

"In January," Bethany announced proudly. "On our one-year anniversary. Which means I won't have to remember another date."

"And also that we'll never be able to go out on our anniversary," James grumbled. But he wasn't fooling anyone with that gruff act. Emma had never seen him happier.

"I see a truck! I see a truck!" Ruby pointed to the end of the driveway. "Is that them?"

"I think so." Emma grinned at her niece.

"I've never seen anyone get so excited about chickens," James muttered.

"It's on Aunt Emma's life list," Ruby informed her father importantly. "Right, Aunt Emma?"

Emma nodded and wrapped an arm around her niece's shoulder. "That it is."

She'd made the list after she completed chemo last year, as a reminder to make the most of each day the Lord gave her. Actually, it was two lists: one that included "everyday" items—the things she strived to do every day, like spend time in the Word, serve others, pray for someone new. And the other list she liked to think of as her "possibilities" list—things she would love to do if God gave her the opportunity. Including today's item: raise chickens.

"I think Aunt Emma needs less lists, more rest," James retorted.

"That's why I'm here," Ruby explained patiently. "To help her with the chickens."

"Exactly." Emma smiled gratefully at her niece—one of the few people who didn't seem to think she was suddenly more fragile just because she'd survived cancer. "You two get going. You're going to miss the movie." She shooed James and Bethany away as the pickup truck from Ploughman Farms pulled to a stop.

She and Ruby jogged toward the truck, stopping at the open passenger window. "You can bring them right over there." Emma pointed across the yard toward the deluxe chicken coop she'd asked her friend Cam to build. Though it was a bit outside the scope of his usual landscaping work, he had

NOT UNTIL THEN

outdone himself with a mini-replica of the stables that stood just beyond it.

By the time she and Ruby reached the coop, Mrs. Ploughman had already backed the pickup truck to it and was unloading large wire crates from the back.

"Oh, they're so pretty," Ruby gushed as Emma opened the mesh door on the large chicken run Cam had built surrounding the coop. She hefted one of the carriers and brought it inside, grateful she'd asked Cam to build the run and coop tall enough for her to stand up in.

She opened the carrier, and the big red and black chicken with a bright red comb stalked out as if she owned the place. She went straight for Ruby, who instantly dropped to the ground to pet her.

"She's soft," she called in delight.

"That's a Sussex," Mrs. Ploughman said. "And this beautiful gal is a blue Australorp." She opened a cage holding a striking bird with shimmery blue-green-black feathers.

They unloaded a large gray Orpington, a golden Friesian, and another Sussex. Emma chatted with Mrs. Ploughman a bit about their care, and then it was just her and Ruby and the birds.

"What do you think, ladies?" Emma asked. "Do you like your new home?"

Ruby giggled. "I think they *love* it. Can I help you name them?"

"You'd better." Emma adjusted the chickens' water dispenser. "I haven't been able to come up with a single good—"

She broke off as the chickens burst into a flurry of squawks and flapping. Reflexively, she raised an arm and ducked as one flew straight toward her face.

"Aunt Emma," Ruby cried, and Emma reached out a hand to pull her niece to her feet, hugging Ruby's face to her chest to protect her from the crazed chickens.

An involuntary shriek escaped as Emma felt a hen's weight settle onto her back, its thin toes stabbing into her skin as it fought for purchase.

"What is happening?" she cried, half hunched over, trying to shield Ruby and dislodge the bird at the same time. But the chicken's toes gripped harder as a large dog bounded right up to the chicken wire, its barks wild and frenzied.

"Shoo," Emma cried. "Go home."

The dog kept barking, and the chickens kept squawking and flapping, and Emma tried to figure out how to get the one off her back without injuring it—or herself.

"Let me see the dog." Ruby wiggled out of Emma's grip just as a voice shouted, "Lexi, come."

Emma scanned the yard for the source of the command, but the dog's only response was to perk its ears and keep barking.

"Lexi? Is that your name?" Emma spoke to the dog the same way she spoke to her horses, in a low, soothing voice, even though pain sliced through her back from the chicken's claws. "Your owner is looking for you. Go home now."

The dog tilted its head to the side, then crouched low and pounced at the chicken wire, sending the hens into a fresh frenzy. Fortunately, in the chaos, the one on Emma's back apparently decided there were safer places to be and dismounted. Emma straightened gratefully, waving her hands over Ruby's head so none would land on the girl.

"Lexi, come!" This time the voice was closer, and Emma followed the sound to a teenage boy, who was sprinting toward them. A girl who looked about Ruby's age chased behind him. Two more figures—one adult-size and one child-size—followed another hundred yards or so back.

"Hi, there!" Emma called to the boy in the lead. "This your dog?"

"Yeah. Sorry." The boy jogged closer and grabbed the dog's collar, then looked from her to Ruby to the chickens. "Are your chickens always this crazy?"

Emma laughed. "I don't know. I just got them today. But I sure hope not. They don't seem to be big fans of dogs though."

"Oh." The boy ducked his head. "Sorry about that."

"It's okay." Emma ushered Ruby toward the door, cracking it open just enough for the two of them to slip through, then latching it behind her. "But maybe we should bring Lexi away from the coop to let them calm down." The girl who had been running behind the boy reached them and drew to a stop.

"Hi," Emma greeted her. "Are you here for Lexi too?"

The girl nodded, her dark hair bobbing, but didn't say anything.

"What's your name?" Ruby asked. The girl didn't answer, but Ruby continued, undaunted. "I'm Ruby. How old are you?"

The girl stepped a little closer to the boy, who Emma guessed was her brother.

"I'm Cody, and this is Kenzie," he said, and Emma caught the protective note in his voice. "She's eleven."

"Me too," Ruby bounced on her toes. "Can she talk?"

At that, Kenzie smiled a little and nodded but still didn't say anything.

"She's shy," Cody explained.

"Where do you guys live?" Emma asked. She knew pretty much every neighbor who lived within five miles in every direction, not to mention most of the people who lived in town, but she didn't remember ever seeing these two.

Cody pointed across the field that bumped up against Emma's yard. "There, I guess. As of today."

"Oh, I saw that the house sold. I was hoping I'd be getting new neighbors soon." Emma waved to the adult and child who had almost reached them now, and Emma could see that one was a man—the kids' dad, she supposed—and the other was another, younger boy.

"I'm so sorry," the man called as he closed the last of the space between them. "Lexi doesn't usually run like that, but I guess she got excited to be out of the car and—"

"Please, don't worry about it." Emma waved off his apology, then held out a hand. "Welcome to Hope Springs. I was just telling the kids I'm glad to know I'll have new neighbors. I'm Emma, and this is Ruby."

"Owen." The man shook her outstretched hand. Up close, he looked to be about her age. A few grays shone from his dark hair and in the light layer of stubble on his cheeks.

"And this is Carter." Owen gestured to the young boy next to him, who was squinting up at the sky as he flicked two fingers against his leg.

"You have good clouds here," the boy announced.

Emma laughed, crouching down so she was at his level, though he didn't look at her. "Thank you. I think so too."

"Where are you guys from?" Ruby asked, bouncing as she always did when she was excited—and nothing excited her more than meeting new people.

"Tennessee." Owen gazed around him as if taking in the scenery for the first time.

Before Emma could ask what brought them to Hope Springs, Ruby jumped in. "Our friend Grace is from Tennessee. Hey, do you want to see our chickens?" The question was addressed to Kenzie, who sent a timid glance toward her dad.

He nodded and gave her what appeared to be a tired smile. "Go ahead. I'll keep Lexi over here."

Kenzie stuck a hand in his. "I want you to come with me."

"I'll take Lexi back to the house," Cody offered. "I already saw the chickens anyway."

"They weren't exactly at their best when you saw them." Emma raised a hand to her hair, suddenly realizing what a fright it must be after that whole debacle. She wondered vaguely if there were feathers in it.

"Come, Lexi." Cody pulled the dog across the yard toward the field.

Owen's face creased into lines of worry as he watched the boy go, but he didn't stop him.

"Don't worry," Emma reassured him. "You'll be able to see him all the way across the field." It wasn't until after the words were out that she realized they might make it sound like she regularly watched their house. She scrambled for a way to fix it, but Owen nodded, looking slightly relieved.

"Come on," Emma urged Kenzie. "Let's go meet the ladies."

Kenzie giggled. "The ladies?"

Owen glanced at his daughter, his mouth opening as if in surprise.

"Well, yes," Emma said, feigning seriousness. "These are no ordinary chickens. They're fancy chickens. So I call them my ladies."

"I know!" Ruby turned and walked backwards so she could talk to them all. "You guys should help us name them."

"That's a great idea." Emma smiled at her niece, always so eager to include everyone.

"It's perfect," Ruby crowed. "There are five of us and five chickens, so we can each name one."

Owen shook his head. "I'm sure you don't want complete strangers to name your chickens."

"You're not strangers, you're neighbors," Emma reassured him.

"You and I should name the matching ones," Ruby said to Kenzie. "Since we're friends."

Kenzie gripped her dad's hand but nodded, her eyes bright.

"I'm going to name mine Corazón," Ruby declared. "That's Spanish for heart, and her comb looks like a heart in the middle. What do you want to name yours?" She blinked eagerly at Kenzie.

"Um." Kenzie half hid behind Owen. "Maybe, um, Unicorn?"

"I love unicorns," Ruby cheered so loudly that Kenzie took another step closer to Owen, but she was grinning.

"That's perfect." Emma smiled at the girl, then turned to Carter. "Which one do you want to name?"

"The gray one," Carter announced, flicking his leg. "Its name is Stratus."

"Like the clouds?"

Carter turned and met her eyes, only for a fraction of a second but long enough for Emma's heart to melt. "Yes," he said. "Stratus clouds are low and gray, just like Stratus the chicken."

"Perfect." Emma smiled. "We'll call her Strat for short, if that's okay."

"Strat." Carter said the word a few times, as if testing it out, then nodded. "Strat for short is good."

"All right then." Emma looked to Owen, who had turned toward the field. She followed his gaze to where Cody was almost to their house, Lexi bounding ahead of him. "Which one do you want to name?" she asked him.

"Hmm." Owen turned to study the two chickens that were left. "I'll take the blue one."

"She's so shimmery." Kenzie stepped out from behind her father, apparently forgetting her shyness as she peered at the chicken. "What do you want to call her, Dad?"

"How about Sapphire?"

"Like Mom's ring," Kenzie said quietly. She slipped her hand back into her dad's, and Emma couldn't help but admire the picture they made together.

Owen nodded.

"Very elegant." Emma watched the blue chicken ruffle her wings proudly, as if she knew they were talking about her.

"What are you going to name yours?" Ruby asked, pointing to the golden chicken that had landed on Emma's back earlier. "Goldie?"

Emma shook her head. "That's a good name. But I think I'm going to call her Trixie. I have a feeling she's going to be a bit of a mischief-maker."

"Oh, I like that." Ruby clapped her hands. "Hey, do you ride?" She spun to Kenzie.

Kenzie blinked at her, moving closer to Owen again. "Ride?"

"Horses." Ruby gestured toward the pasture, where several of Emma's horses were currently grazing.

Kenzie shook her head, though her eyes lit up. "I don't know how."

"Oh, you should take lessons here," Ruby announced. "You'll love it."

Kenzie gave her dad a pleading look but didn't say anything.

Owen shook his head. "We should get going. The rest of our crew was picking up dinner, and they're probably getting impatient to eat. Or, knowing Cody, he's already polishing it all off without us." He smiled wryly and glanced over his shoulder. Emma followed his gaze. Sure enough, there was another car in the driveway now, and she imagined his wife—and possibly more children, the way it sounded—waiting at the house for them.

"Of course. It was nice meeting you." Emma tucked her hands into her pockets. "If you need anything, please don't hesitate to ask."

Owen gave a polite nod, then squatted to allow Carter to climb onto his back. He stood and took Kenzie's hand, and they started toward the field, the perfect picture of a family.

Emma brushed off a stab of longing. She had her own version of a family. It may not be what she'd once envisioned, but she was blessed, nonetheless.

"I like them," Ruby announced.

Emma nodded. "Me too." She watched them for another moment, then pulled her phone out of her pocket and checked raise chickens off her life list. Ruby grinned at her, then reached up and plucked something from her hair. She held it out.

It was a feather.

Emma took it from her with a laugh. "And I suppose this was in my hair the whole time?"

"Yep," Ruby answered cheerfully. "I didn't want to embarrass you by pulling it out in front of them."

"Gee, thanks." Emma fuzzed her hand over her niece's hair. "Oh well, now they know their new neighbor is a crazy chicken lady."

Ruby folded her arms into wings and let out a joyful bawk.

KEEP READING NOT UNTIL THE END

More Books by Valerie M. Bodden

Hope Springs

While the books in the Hope Springs series are linked, each is a complete romance featuring a different couple.

Not Until Forever (Sophie & Spencer)
Not Until This Moment (Jared & Peyton)
Not Until You (Nate & Violet)
Not Until Us (Dan & Jade)
Not Until Christmas Morning (Leah & Austin)
Not Until This Day (Tyler & Isabel)
Not Until Someday (Grace & Levi)
Not Until Now (Cam & Kayla)
Not Until Then (Bethany & James)
Not Until The End (Emma & Owen)

VALERIE M. BODDEN

River Falls

While the books in the River Falls series are linked, each is a complete romance featuring a different couple.

Pieces of Forever (Joseph & Ava)
Songs of Home (Lydia & Liam)
Memories of the Heart (Simeon & Abigail)
Whispers of Truth (Benjamin & Summer)
Promises of Mercy (Judah & Faith)

River Falls Christmas Romances

Wondering about some of the side characters in River Falls who aren't members of the Calvano family? Join them as they get their own happily-ever-afters in the River Falls Christmas Romances.

Christmas of Joy (Madison & Luke)

Want to know when my next book releases?

You can follow me on Amazon to be the first to know when my next book releases! Just visit amazon.com/author/valeriembodden and click the follow button.

Acknowledgements

I'm going to be honest: for a long time, I resisted the idea of writing about a character who had lost a child. As a mother, I just didn't think I could go there. I didn't think I could put myself in the shoes of someone who was living out one of my worst fears. But a funny thing happened as I wrote: God worked on my own heart. He reminded me that he loves each one of my children (who are, ultimately, his children) and that he holds each one of them in his arms. And although sometimes I feel, like Bethany, that my children are taking big steps into independence that they may be ready for but I'm not, I also know that no matter how far they may move from me, they are never outside of God's reach. So I thank him for this book, for seeing me through the hard and dark parts to the hope that James found—to the promise that our hope in him is not only for this world, but for eternity. To the promise that though we know only in part right now, *then* we shall know fully, just as we are fully known.

And I thank him also for the family he has given me to walk through this life with: my husband and four children. I see so much of them on these pages. For example, Kayla's description of baby Evelyn as a "nocturnal screaming machine who has forgotten how to sleep more than twenty minutes at a time." Ha. But seriously, I also see my children in Ruby's care for her mother and her desire to make sure James is happy. And in Bethany and James's "Would You Rather" game. And in Ruby's silly jokes. And I see my husband in James's protectiveness. And his patience. And his claustrophobia (thank you to my sister-in-law for locking him in a closet when they were kids to inspire that scene). I guess what I'm saying is, I'm thankful for the inspiration you all are to me, both in what you do and in who you are.

I'm thankful also to my parents, who parented me through all those hard, exciting, scary, uncertain years that I'm now going through with my own kids. And to my sister, in-laws, nieces and nephews, extended family, and friends. We may be spread wider than the people of Hope Springs, but I am so grateful for the support and encouragement you offer me.

And thank you to my amazing advance reader team. I feel like Hope Springs lives in your hearts as much as it does in mine, and I am so thankful that you have embraced these characters as friends and family. A special thank you to: Vickie, Patty Bohuslav, SLG Virginia Beach VA, Margaret N., Terri Camp, Patti Stephenson, Rhondia, Lincoln Clark, Mary S., Diana A., Barbara J. Miller, Connie Gandy, Chris Green, Teresa Malouf, Michelle M., Vickie Escalante, Jeanne Olynick, Chinye Ukwu, Kathy Ann Meadows, Ilona, Bonny Rambarran, Trudy Cordle, Becky Collins, Sherene, Jan Gilmour, Trista, Seyi Aderinola, Deb Galloway, Jaime Fipp, Kelly Wickham, Korin Thomas, Evelyn Foreman, Jenny M., Jennifer Ellenson, Becky Carrell, Ellie McClure, Pam Williams, Shelia Garrison, Carol Witzenburger, Sandy H., Karen Jernigan, Lisa Gallup, Tonya C., Ann Diener, Brittany McEuen, and Ann F.

And finally, thank you to *you* for spending your time in Hope Springs. As ever, my prayer is that your visit has left you with a happy sigh and an uplifted spirit. Whatever you have walked through or are walking through, may it be well with your soul. Because God remembers you. He has engraved you on the palm of his hand. And he has set eternity in your heart.

About the Author

Valerie M. Bodden has three great loves: Jesus, her family, and books. And chocolate (okay, four great loves). She is living out her happily ever after with her high-school-sweetheart-turned-husband and their four children. Her life wouldn't make a terribly exciting book, as it has a happy beginning and middle, and someday when she goes to her heavenly home, it will have a happy end.

She was born and raised in Wisconsin but recently moved with her family to Texas, where they're all getting used to the warm weather (she doesn't miss the snow even a little bit, though the rest of the family does) and saying y'all instead of you guys.

Valerie writes emotion-filled Christian fiction that weaves real-life problems, real-life people, and real-life faith. Her characters may (okay, will) experience some heartache along the way, but she will always give them a happy ending.

Feel free to stop by www.valeriembodden.com to say hi. She loves visitors! And while you're there, you can sign up for your free story.

Printed in Great Britain
by Amazon